A Train to Nowhere

Marilyn Campbell

Camitzke Press
NAPA, CA

Camitzke Press
1436 2nd Street #323
Napa, California 94559

This is a work of fiction. Names, characters, and incidents (other than those based on historical events) are the product of the author's imagination. Real places and locales are used to enhance the fiction and lend historical significance only. Any mistakes in the representation of same are those of the author and are not meant to be regarded as fact. Any resemblance to persons living or dead is entirely coincidental.

Cover Design by Amber Lea Starfire
Book Layout ©2017 BookDesignTemplates.com

A Train to Nowhere/ Marilyn Campbell — 1st ed.
ISBN-978-0-9964748-4-9

Dedicated to Sam and Sydney
for whom all things are possible

CHAPTER ONE

Charley

June 1900

When the freight train began slowing down, Charley O'Brien inched open the boxcar door and ventured a look. He saw that they were laboring up a steep grade— so steep that he couldn't see the mountain's summit.

"Where do you think we are Charley?" Christina yawned and stretched as she awoke from her nap on a stack of feed bags in the corner.

"Don't know, but it's like nothing I've ever seen before." He tried to remember when they came to Kansas by orphan train whether they had crossed mountains this grand. There were some, but once they had passed through them, they had pretty much emptied out on to an endless expanse into what they now called The Great Plains.

He and Christina Batachi had been riding for days across terrain that looked like the countryside surrounding the town of Concordia, Kansas—flat land with waving grasses and low rolling hills with views of more hills in the distance.

1

As if he had read Charley's mind, Clayton piped up. He had been traveling with Charley and Christina almost from the start of their journey.

"We had mountains this big where I came from," he said from his spot on the opposite side of the car. He uncurled his lanky body and stood up. "My ancestors traveled through the Black Hills of South Dakota before the white man tried to tame the mountains." He joined Charley by the door and, gazing out, cleared his throat. He prepared to spit into the wind, but thought better of it. "This fool mountain ain't nothin'."

"Well, it sure looks big to me." Charley joined Christina on the feed sacks. He hoped they would be stopping soon so he could get off the train and stretch proper. He hadn't slept well last night. He'd had that dream again. The one where he bends down to loosen a shoestring stuck under the railroad track with the sound of a train bearing down on him—just like it had with Pap.

He is one with the hot metal rail that vibrates when he hears Mum crying out to him. But before he can answer her, he finds himself on the roof of the building in which his family lives. Charley is a boy again looking down on the Monongahela River as Pinkerton guards fight men like his Pap, who is on strike. The steel company stands vigil, looming over the rail yard like a sentry over the river. There is smoke and the choked cries of men. He is sure that one of them is Pap.

Charley leaned into Christina and watched Clayton

pull out his bag of tobacco.

"I'm a quarter Lakota as it turns out," he said.

It seemed that every time he rolled a new cigarette and lit his smoke, the Indian launched into another long story about his people from the South Dakota Lakota tribe.

"What did you say your name means?" Christina asked.

"Clayton means Hawk or Falcon. You can call me Clay, for short, if you've a mind to."

Charley was surprised at how talkative Clay was. He had heard that Indians were mostly quiet and stoic. But this Indian was different. He had turned out to be a big help guiding him and Christina through some rough spots at various train stops. He knew how to sneak into a car when the switchman wasn't looking. He showed them how to board without having to run alongside a fast-moving train, and on one hot afternoon, the three of them were suspended on the underside of framework that supported the wooden boxcars. The ledge was just big enough to lie down on. Once the train stopped at a water tower, the three of them climbed the metal ladder to a gondola car carrying coal. They rode in the belly of the open car, getting covered with black soot. There was nothing to do about it except lean back, point at each other, and laugh.

Clay, although friendly to Charley and Christina, appeared to have a sixth sense regarding other riders who crossed their path. Clay seemed to know the good ones from those looking for trouble, like the burly man called Gus, who had boarded outside of Osborne, Utah.

The man had looked all three of them over, but especially concentrated on Christina, who had quickly shoved her hair back under her cap to hide wild black curls. For the purpose of disguise, she had tried to make herself inconspicuous, wearing men's clothing and speaking little. She stayed in the background around strangers and avoided eye contact. Charley had insisted—for safety reasons.

"What kind of cap you wearing?" Gus asked. "Looks too small for your head. Ain't gonna keep the sun off your nose." He reached over to pull the cap off, but not before Charley grabbed the man's hand.

"You don't want to do that, mister. No one here is bothering you."

"What's it to you? I'm just trying to make friendly conversation."

Christina had pulled the cap lower around her ears, but the man wrestled free of Charley's arm-hold and yanked it off. Christina's curls tumbled out around her shoulders.

"Well, well. What have we here?" I knew you was too pretty for a man." Gus touched Christina's hair, leering. His smile revealed a mouth full of bad teeth.

"You need to step back, mister," Charley said. "Think we'll all get along fine if we keep to ourselves." Charley stepped between the man and Christina. Gus stood solid, a dark, heavy presence. He was like a dense wall that would injure a body foolish enough to take a run at it.

"Don't much like your attitude," Gus growled. "Ain't you heard that men of the rails share and share alike."

Christina retreated to her corner just as the man punched Charley, sending him reeling across the floor. He slammed against the side of the boxcar. As he scrambled to his feet, Clay stepped in and, yielding a knife, lunged for Gus, tackling him. Once floored, Clay grabbed the man's hair and pulled his head back. He poised the knife across his greasy neck.

"It don't do to show bad manners. Think this is your stop, mister. Time to get off."

"Are you crazy! We must be moving forty, fifty miles an hour."

"That's your problem." Clay pulled Gus up easily and pushed him toward the door.

"Now git."

Charley righted himself and stood up. "Wait, Clay. He might kill himself jumping off here." All he could think of were the jagged rocks that comprised this range of mountains, devoid of any foliage that might cushion a fall.

"Like I said, that's his problem now, ain't it?" Clay wore a vicious expression that invited no discussion.

Charley had seen Clay in a new light. He hadn't thought of him as a threat until that moment, but only as a colorful harmless character. After all, he had taken Charley and Christina in tow and taught them all kinds of things to survive in the wilderness they were traveling through. He killed a rattler on one of their stops. Saved their lives! But, what if that knife were to be directed at him—or at Christina?

Although he was grateful that Clay had come to their aid, Charley didn't want to be responsible for killing a man, even a man like Gus. Forcing a man to jump from a fast-moving train would be like giving him a push. It would be committing murder.

"Listen, mister, I didn't mean nothin' by it," Gus said. "You know how it is riding the rails. Sometimes you get a little crazy. And I ain't seen a woman—a pretty one, leastways—for a spell."

"That right?" Clay had jerked Gus's head back harder.

"Yeah. I'm telling the truth. I promise I'll jump soon as we're through these mountains or when the train slows some."

"Let him go, Clay. There are two of us to watch him. He won't try anything else."

"That's right. Listen to your friend!"

Clay let go of Gus and stepped back, sheathing his knife. "Hope you're right, Charley. Where I come from, garbage gets thrown out. Makes good food for the coyotes."

Gus rubbed his neck and stumbled a step before

heading for cover away from the doors. It didn't take long, however, for him to jump once the train had reached level ground. Charley watched him leap wide and roll, and finally get up on wobbly legs to flash an obscene sign their way.

"I knew you wasn't a man right off," Clay said to Christina, crushing the cigarette butt in his palm.

"How? I kept covered up."

"A cap and britches can't fool everyone. I could tell by the way you walk and move."

"Why didn't you say something?"

Clay shrugged. "I reckoned you didn't want anyone to know. Folks have a right to their secrets."

CHAPTER TWO

Charley

Charley was still upset long after the train slowed and Gus had jumped from the boxcar. He wondered how safe they were if the Indian and the degenerate Gus could make out Christina's disguise. In fact, once that he knew that Clay had a sharp weapon and a temperament to match, he wondered if they knew him at all. He *had* protected them. They owed him that. But Charley wasn't sure when his temper might turn against them or someone else—another Gus—and then they might be involved in something not of their making.

He thought he knew what men were capable of when he witnessed violence during the Homestead Steel Strike. Charley had been only twelve years old at the time. His pap survived the gunshot wound he received—but at a terrible cost—for his role in the strike. An injured leg that never healed properly resulted in a limp and eventually led to his demise when he was run down by a train. It seemed that the brand of justice out West was different. Men were tough because they had to be, their character rough and chiseled like the rocks they passed. An underlying meanness emerged from them whenever they felt the least bit threatened. With one false move, a man was likely to be wounded.

For all of Charley's uneasiness about Clay, Christina acted like the Indian's words had liberated her. In spite of the limited space in the boxcar, she was sashaying around like it was her own personal parlor.

"Well, since you know I'm a woman, guess I'll let my hair down for a while," she said. She shook her head and laughed, prancing like some horses Charley had seen after they had been led out of their stalls for the open field; they shook their heads and flicked their tails, claiming dominance over the paddock, just as Christina had over this rough domain.

Clay nodded. "That's much better." He smiled while retreating to his corner.

Charley wondered, not for the first time, the wisdom of bringing Christina along on this journey. "I'll go ahead and search out the best land," he had said. "And as soon as I'm settled, I'll send for you."

Many people who had gone west were lucky enough to have obtained homestead rights. Those were harder to come by now that it was 1900. The last big land rush he had heard about was the Oklahoma Land Rush of 1893. His plan involved searching for acreage in California or cheap land adjacent to the rail lines, whichever came first.

Time had slipped away. Charley had promised Christina three years ago that they would marry. She had been preparing to leave Concordia on her own and he felt desperate. She had been almost nineteen and he was nearing his eighteenth birthday. At eighteen he would no longer be obligated to his foster father, Enoch Neamott, who had taken him in when he arrived on the orphan train.

"Give me a year and we'll get married," he had told Christina. "I'll demand wages from Enoch or go elsewhere where they'll pay for an experienced worker like me. We'll buy our own ranch," he had bragged. He knew that Christina wanted a horse to replace Gabriel, the stallion she had cared for and fallen in love with while working at Carl Schmitz's stable. Having their own place would enable them both to fulfill their dreams. Or, so Charley had thought.

A year passed and then another. Enoch claimed he didn't have the cash to pay him outright, but offered to make him a partner in the profits his farm made. Problem was—there had *been* no profits. Everything that was earned was poured back into the land until another disaster affected his crops. Finally, Charley found work as an extra hand on several neighboring farms. But he never earned enough to support a wife. The promise to marry Christina went unfulfilled, wasted like a dead fish drawing flies.

The idea to head west was embraced by Christina as

long as she could come along. Charley had tried to convince her that riding the rails was too dangerous for a woman, but she was adamant.

"Charley, you know nothing scares me," she had said. He knew perfectly well that nothing scared Christina. *Nothing but sameness and boredom.* She was a woman of action and liked nothing better than a challenge—especially if it had to do with horses. She had been searching for Gabriel, who had been sold by Carl and then sold again by the new owner. If she couldn't locate *him*, she would seek out a likeness. The idea of becoming a horse breeder had become an obsession with her.

In the end, he reluctantly agreed that they should travel west together. Being separated for six months to a year was the deciding factor. Charley couldn't imagine being alone without Christina after he had finally won her over.

Charley sighed and listened to Christina and Clay exchange stories about their exploits with horses. He resigned himself to accepting Christina expressing herself in the free and easy manner she had adopted. All she had done was let her hair down in front of Clay, not shucked her shapeless, baggy clothes. He still was the only one to know what loveliness was concealed underneath.

CHAPTER THREE

Christina

After the excitement earlier in the day with the nasty rider named Gus, Christina felt exhausted.

Hoping to catch a bit of breeze from the open boxcar, she lifted her hair away from her neck. In the last few hours the weather had turned hot as the train rumbled across the desert. Sagebrush and cactus had replaced the wildflowers of The Great Plains and the Rocky Mountains. They passed mountains here too, but these were flatter on top. Clay called them "mesas."

"You know, my people used bluffs something like these to scout out Custer's soldiers at the Battle of the Little Big Horn. We had them surrounded in the canyon below." Clay pulled out his tobacco pouch. Christina wondered if she and Charley were in for another long story.

"The government called it a massacre. But, what we did was nothing like what the blue coats did to my ancestors." He spat in the corner and squinted at Charley and Christina before continuing.

"We read about it in school," Christina said listlessly.

She had not been much interested in Indian lore, but Miss Maggie, the teacher in Concordia's only school, felt it important for her students to learn both sides of recent history. "Remember, class," she had said, "when white men moved west, they took over lands belonging to Indian tribes long established here." Hers was not the most popular view among the townspeople. But when Maggie Schmitz had been unmarried and went by Maggie Cooper, she had lived in different regions of the country. Christina thought that this may have given her a broader view of life.

She felt akin to her for that reason, because Christina, too, had been exposed to a variety of people after she took to living on the streets of Pittsburgh, Pennsylvania. Eventually she was placed in the Pittsburgh Children's Home where she first met Charley and his sister, Jennie. The only variety she found inside the Home was in the sad details of how children ended up there."What happened to your people, Clay?" she asked, knowing that the question was likely to release a torrent of complaints. But she wasn't much concerned. Certainly, the Indian knew she and Charley were his friends by now and meant him and his people no harm.

"Well, Missy, I ain't got much family left. I come from the Lakota band of the Sioux tribe. Army pretty much ended the Sioux War about 1877. First they stopped us from hunting buffalo and then they herded us onto reservations. I took off. Said goodbye to my mother and sister. The men were kilt or..." He took one last puff of his cigarette that was spilling hot ash on his shirt. "Anyways, here I am, still moving. Still looking for a place to roost, a way to get by."

Christina fidgeted, unable to think of something to say. What happened to Clay was not so very long ago and clearly it was still fresh in his mind. She guessed there was trouble and unfairness everywhere whether you were looking for it or not. She figured if she and Charley could get their own place, they would be beholden to no one. To do this, however, she needed to be as strong and determined as he, working alongside him. She would not settle for just being a wife and mother confined to a dark, musty house. She required fresh air and sunshine and needed to be Charley's equal so that no man or institution could ever again determine their fates.

The train had slowed by another water tower. It looked as if the deserted area adjacent to the tower had been a fair-sized community at one time. Unpainted buildings were boarded up and appeared to be falling in on themselves. Christina wondered what it was named and why it was abandoned. It did confirm what Charley had told her about towns cropping up near railroad lines. "Railroad companies encouraged people to form settlements, which needed plenty of goods, *and* railroads moved goods across the country faster than wagons could," he had said. "You see, railroads were good for everyone."

A sudden burst of steam and the sound of steel couplings rubbing against each other confirmed that the train had come to a full stop.

"Guess this is as good a place to get off as any," Clay said as he grabbed his bedroll.

"You're leaving us?" Christina said.

"Thought you were going farther west," Charley added.

"Well, I thought on it, but there's something about these wide open spaces that remind me of home. I'm not sure I want to cross more mountains. Those Sierras are fierce. 'Course, the Atchison, Topeka, and Santa Fe might not cross the Sierras. Heard it don't go anywhere near Sacramento like you two were talking 'bout." He scratched his head and dropped down on the gravel bed next to the tracks.

"What?" Charley cried. "Where *does* it go?"

"Heard it might veer south."

"Where south?" Christina shouted.

"Mebbe into Arizona. Don't know for sure. Now, if you want a guaranteed ride to California, you'll have to find a way to sneak onto the Central Pacific at Promontory, Utah. 'Course, I hear their bulls have clubs they're not afraid to use." He slapped his cap against his thigh, dislodging a plume of dust. "It's downright discouraging. But, good luck to you two."

With that, the Indian took off in big, certain strides like he knew where he was headed.

"What should we do, Charley?"

"I'm not sure. We can't stay out here in the middle of nowhere. Let's keep riding until we come to a place where there's a real settlement and maybe get some answers. I thought this train went all the way to California."

"Don't worry, Charley. It will be all right. As long as we're together we'll figure something out."

CHAPTER FOUR

Charley

Christina might not worry, but Charley did. His plan depended on them getting free transportation. They needed to save their money for basics such as food, not train tickets. Christina had convinced Charley that they should sell her mother's ring and use the proceeds for this venture. It was the last thing Christina had of her mother's to remember her by; therefore, Charley did not accept it lightly.

"It was always meant for an emergency," she had said. But Charley knew what Christina's mother sacrificed for that ring. She had received it from one of her gentlemen callers. Christina admitted that the ring had probably been for services rendered. Though she was worldly about such matters, Christina said she no longer wanted to discuss the matter. "Just take it, Charley. Get what you can for it." The cash from the sale of the ring would be spent carefully.

The train had started again. Charley slid open the boxcar door for air. He scanned the landscape and felt hopeful that when they reached their final destination he would find work on a farm or ranch, earn money, and eventually buy land of his own. The weather was with them. There should be months more of good weather they could count on—not like the sudden extremes of a Midwestern climate. He had been told that California was so garden-like that blizzards were unheard of and that dust storms were little more than gentle breezes stirring up the rich dirt to air it out.

They heard the thunderous hooves before they saw the herd of horses running in the distance. The sound drowned out the screeching of metal wheels on iron tracks.

"Charley, look at all of them running free," Christina shouted into the wind as she stood gazing out at the sight. "Aren't they magnificent?" Horses of all descriptions, their manes flying behind them, raced across the Plains following the lead of a palomino mare. The horses seemed to know intuitively in which direction to turn and, from a distance, appeared as undulating waves as they first moved one way and then another.

"They're beautiful all right," he said pulling Christina close. They were alone at last and Charley savored the feel of her body leaning against his side. After the Indian left, it was their good luck that no one else boarded the train. This privacy was a gift—a gift that would surely only last a short time because of the many men riding the rails.

"Do you think we could get off here and find out

about those horses?" she asked.

"Too late now. There probably won't be another place to stop until we reach the town Clay called Promontory.

"We could jump."

"Jump! Are you mad, Christina. We're going way too fast!"

"I know that," she said with a mischievous smile. "Don't get so excited." She sighed and looked at the disappearing cloud of dust that followed the herd. "But those are the kind of spirited horses I like. I'll bet that Gabriel came from a herd like this."

"Maybe. I heard the army captures wild horses for soldiers assigned to the forts. Taming them must take a special man."

"Or a special woman," she said. "A very special woman could do it, I'll bet."

"Meaning yourself?"

"Why not? I helped Carl train Gabriel. Bet I could do it with one of those mustangs."

"Aren't you overlooking something, Christina? You need a horse to capture a horse."

"Oh, Charley, what do you know about horses? You're a farmer, remember?"

Charley felt stung by Christina's remark. It was true that he wasn't experienced at training or caring for horses like she was. After all, she learned from the best. Carl, the blacksmith, had taken her under his wing when she first arrived in Concordia. While she'd worked in his stable, he had taught her all about horses. Charley knew that Christina's biggest disappointment had come when Carl sold Gabriel. It was as if her heart had been snatched right out of her chest.

Charley's strengths lay in a different direction. After working on Enoch's farm for four years—and then spending two more as hired help around the county—he knew most aspects of farming. Charley and his partner, Peter Stuyvesant, had a well-conceived plan to use the newest invention—a gas-powered tractor—to cultivate the land of Concordia farmers. They were able to buy the tractor cheap since it wasn't selling to the locals who were suspicious of new-fangled inventions. But they convinced these same obstinate men to hire *them* to plow the fields with the noisy machine. Charley promised to double, even triple, their land's yield in a season. The concept was a good one, but Charley's financial plan was naive. Extending credit to farmers instead of collecting cash was no way to run a business. It hadn't helped that Peter cheated him out of what little profits they earned.

Charley tried to get past the disappointment and anger. He worked twice as hard—hired on as a ranch hand by the same men he had tried to impress with his business. It was humiliating. But Charley was encouraged by the fact that men not much older than him had crossed the Plains and homesteaded. He guessed that he had been born too late to get in on the land rushes, but he still hoped to find opportunities to buy cheap land once they reached California.

"Guess you're right," Christina said as she let out another big sigh. She left her perch by the door to sit in the corner by the feed bags. "We might as well finish up what's left of our food," she said. She opened a handkerchief containing hard biscuits, a handful of nuts, and a container of molasses they bought in the last small town in which the train had stopped. She licked the molasses before taking a bite of the hard biscuit.

Charley still couldn't stand the sight or smell of the dark, viscous syrup that was a mainstay of the diet at the Children's Home. He would always associate it with the orphanage no matter how hungry he was.

"You know, Charley, when I agreed to come west with you it was with the idea that I would find a way to get a horse again."

Charley almost laughed. She made it sound like she was doing him a favor when in fact he had tried discouraging her from the trip.

"I know, Christina, but you'll have to go about it the way most people do. Work for the money to buy a horse. Those wild ones in the middle of nowhere have probably been free since they were born. They aren't going to simply prance in place while you throw a rope over their necks."

"Like you know so much," she said. A smile was creeping up on her face. "You know a lot Charley, but you don't know everything!"

Charley's mood took a turn for the better as he joined Christina on the floor where he pulled her into his arms.

"Watch out, Charley, you're going to crumble the last of our biscuits," she cried.

"To hell with the biscuits," he said as he unbuttoned her shirt and kissed her throat. "Let's not waste time. We won't be alone for long."

"Whatever you say, Charley." Christina was already wriggling out of her trousers.

CHAPTER FIVE

Charley

It was a good thing that Charley and Christina had scrambled back into their clothes because the train had stopped and someone was banging on the side of the boxcar.

"Open up in there. This is the end of the line," a deep voice announced.

Charley slid open the door to be faced with a beefy-looking man carrying a night stick.

"Anyone else in there with you?"

"Just my friend. We were getting ready to get off."

"Good thing, 'cuz you'd be going back the same way you came. This is the final stop for the Atchison, Topeka, and Santa Fe before it changes course." The man studied Charley. "And if I was you I'd forget about hopping on the Central Pacific."

"Why's that?" Charley asked.

"Because you'd have to get past me." The man laughed and waved his stick in the air for emphasis. Charley and Christina gathered their bedrolls and back-packs and reluctantly jumped down off the train. It was later than Charley thought. The sun was already dropping behind the distant mountains to the west. The man slid the boxcar door shut with a final slam and walked to the next car.

"Hey, mister. Where are we?" Charley called after him.

"You're in Promontory, Utah, son. This here is the site where the two railroads met in 1869. Ever hear of the First Transcontinental Railroad?"

Charley shrugged.

"We learned about it in Miss Maggie's class," Christina piped up. "Promontory Summit is where the two railroads met to celebrate completion of the transcontinental railroad. Made it possible to ride trains clear across the country for the first time."

"Oh, yeah," Charley nodded. This wasn't the only time that Christina had shown him up with her knowledge. He was glad she was so smart, but he couldn't help but feel ashamed for not having as much book learning as her. Of course, mismatched couples weren't so unusual. *Look at Maggie and Carl.* Maggie Cooper was the school teacher and Carl Schmitz, a blacksmith. When they married, they were the talk of the town. People said things like, "What's a pretty young thing like Maggie doing marrying a middle-aged bachelor like Carl?" Charley thought they were doing just fine.

They looked around and found little of interest in Promontory. Besides the train station the only other building in town that looked occupied was a hotel with a café on its first floor. Other businesses that may have thrived at one time were now boarded up. It was near dusk and they were surrounded by an orange and purple sky.

"Look at that, will you," Charley said. "I see why people say that there's nothing like a desert sunset." Across the way, lanterns were being lit in the café, a welcome sign. They automatically headed in its direction. As they dragged themselves up to the boardwalk fronting the café, they heard raucous laughter coming from inside. Charley considered this a good sign. His stomach rumbled for real food. The dry biscuits and molasses had long lost their charm.

Inside the café plain furnishings filled the space; the counter was made of one long rough-hewn plank while the rest of the room was crammed with trestle tables and benches. Customers were mostly men—hardworking men from the looks of them—dressed in overalls and dungarees and striped engineer caps. Charley and Christina headed for the only table that still had available seating. Their tablemates seemed oblivious to their presence. They were hunched over their steaming food and never looked up. Finally, as Charley dropped their belongings by the side of the coarse wooden bench, a man with a long, scraggly beard that reached his chest raised his head. He nodded a greeting and then began attacking his food again.

"You two looking for a meal?" A large, big-boned woman wearing an apron with food stains greeted them. "Got a little beef stew left. Lots of beans. What'll it be?"

"What will two bits get us, ma'am?" Charley asked as he fingered the precious coins in his pocket.

"Not much, son. But I tell you what, I'll bring you some beans and all the bread you can eat."

"Fine, ma'am. That'll be just fine."

"Name's Myrna."

"Myrna, is there anything to drink?" Christina asked.

"Not for two bits, but I'll bring you a pitcher of water."

As she left, the man poked Charley in the ribs. "If you was hoping for something stronger to drink, forget it. These Mormons don't believe in anything stronger than water. Not hard cider, not even a decent cup of coffee, except one watered down cup in the morning."

Mormons? Wasn't that some kind of religion?" Charley laughed to himself. He hadn't been thinking of alcoholic beverages. Ever since that first time Enoch introduced him to whiskey in the barn, he rarely imbibed. And when he did with his partner, Peter Stuyvesant, spirits got the best of him.

Christina was unusually quiet. "You okay?" he asked. She nodded and then leaned over to whisper in his ear. "I have to go to the bathroom in the worst way."

Charley looked around, wondering if the café had indoor plumbing. They had to make do with an old tin can in the boxcar and quick trips behind bushes at train stops for their relief, but Charley heard some places had modern plumbing—indoors!

"Excuse me," he said when Myrna brought their food. "Where are your accommodations?"

"Our what?" she said, looking puzzled. "Oh, you mean the privy. It's out back about twenty yards from the hotel. Can't miss it."

Christina wrinkled her nose, but got up from the bench.

"I'll go with you," Charley said. "Hey mister, we'll be right back. You mind saving our seats and keeping an eye on our gear?" he asked the bearded man, indicating their backpacks sitting under the table.

"Don't mind a bit." The man wiped breadcrumbs from his beard.

It was not easy finding their way toward the outhouse in the dark. It was like trying to maneuver an obstacle course; in places the ground was dry, but uneven, and in others there were mud puddles. It must have rained earlier in the day. They knew they were near when the stench of the outhouse greeted them.

A few minutes later, after Christina emerged from the privy, she almost stumbled. Charley caught her. "You okay?"

"Ooh, Charley. It was the worst in there. I think I've lost my appetite."

"Not me. Come on, let's get back before someone eats

our food."

Their beans and bread were waiting for them.

"Much obliged," Charley said to their tablemate who was busy picking his teeth. Their food looked untouched and Charley dove right in. He didn't say a word until he had consumed a full plate of beans and two hunks of homemade bread slathered with butter. He drank half the water in the pitcher in thirsty gulps before turning to Christina. She was still poking at her uneaten food and had turned pale.

"You gonna finish that?" he said, studying her beans.

"No, guess not." She pushed her plate toward Charley. "I feel awful tired, Charley. Wish there was someplace I could lay down and rest a bit."

"Mmph," he murmured while finishing Christina's food.

"Where will we sleep now that we were kicked off the train?"

"I don't rightly know. Maybe we'll have to sit it out at the station until another train comes through. I didn't catch when that would be."

"About four tomorrow afternoon," their companion said.

"Not until then?" Christina cried. Her voice came out an octave higher than normal. She had forgotten to lower her voice in an effort to pass for a man.

"Yes—ma'am?" the man replied, lifting his eyebrows. Several men nearby turned to stare at them.

This changes things. They were in a room full of men who probably didn't see that many women. Now it would be harder to just blend in.

"This *is* a hotel," Charley said. "Maybe Myrna will let us stay for a few hours." He approached the counter where Myrna was clearing away dirty tin plates from her last customers.

"My friend is pretty tired. Been traveling a long time. Any chance of a spare room?"

She looked him over before answering. "I think I have one left. Cost you fifty cents a night.

"Oh, I was hoping it didn't cost that much."

"How much you got to spare?"

He pulled out the coins and counted them. "After I pay for our supper, it looks like there's about a buck left." Charley was hedging a bit. He had squirreled away coins in other pockets of his clothing. And, sewed into the lining of his jacket were two-one-hundred dollar bills that he hoped were enough of a stake to get them started in California.

"You should never show what you got, boy. Lucky for you, I'm not greedy," Myrna said. "I'm a fair business-woman, if not a rich one. Tell you what, supper is on me and you can have the room for the two bits." In spite of her slight mustache, Myrna's soft features were feminine and friendly like a maiden aunt's.

Charley beamed and forked over the coins. Myrna handed him a key from her apron pocket. "First room at the top of the stairs," she indicated. The narrow staircase was in the back of the cavernous room to one side. He returned to the table, picked up their gear, and led Christina up the stairs.

"I'm sorry, Charley. I just don't feel well." The room was small with an iron-framed bed, a chair, and a wash-stand holding a basin and pitcher. Its only window looked out on the main street at the end of which the railroad depot stood.

After getting Christina settled, Charley lay next to her, but didn't fall asleep. He heard loud men below, laughing, and later, men hacking and coughing through the thin bedroom walls.

He couldn't help replay in his mind their leave-taking from Concordia. Was it just ten days ago? Seemed like forever, with getting on and jumping off at various stops. A couple of times, they even missed connections and had to wait for the next scheduled train heading west before continuing their journey. Charley hoped that their plans would not stall out in this small burg. *Heck, it's not even a burg.* One of the men at the table had been talking about how Promontory used to be thriving before it was almost reduced to a ghost town. "Course, now that the Central Pacific is here, things could look up," he had said.

Charley certainly hadn't thought or planned on either of them coming down sick—especially Christina, who always seemed as strong as the horses she tended. Maybe it was her woman's time. He was aware of such things having lived on a farm. And, after all, he was present for Emma Neamott's two births—Rose's and Willie's—and sadly for her death while giving birth to Willie.

He still regretted not marrying Christina in Concordia before the trip. He was willing, but Christina convinced him that they should wait until they got settled. He thought it unusual for a woman not to insist on being properly wed before becoming lovers. But Christina was different. He thought it part of her independent nature to resist convention and follow her free spirit ways. If she had agreed, they could have used her mother's emerald ring for a wedding ring. He couldn't afford to buy her one. He declared that they wouldn't touch the two hundred dollars for anything but land, and he intended to keep that promise.

Charley turned on his side and curled up against Christina's warm hip, trying not to waken her. He felt the heavy mantle of sleep creep over him and gladly gave in to the feeling.

CHAPTER SIX

Christina

Christina awoke confused. She looked around the room. *Where am I?* Added to her bewilderment were stomach cramps and a terrible headache. *Must be from not eating much last night.* Apparently Charley got a good night's sleep; he lay on his back snoring. She decided not to wake him just yet. It was still early from the looks of the scant light peeking around the torn window shade. She got up and, looking out, saw that men were already working at the railroad depot. She dressed in a hurry and made her way downstairs. Myrna stood behind the counter, alert and as cheerful as the night before.

"Morning. Feeling any better?"

"Some." Christina, no longer pretending to be a man, pulled her wild hair away from her face and pushed it behind her ears.

Myrna poured a cup of coffee and shoved it toward her. "Here, looks like you could use this."

Christina grabbed the steaming cup with both hands and inhaled the strong nutty aroma before taking a first swallow.

"I thought Mormons didn't drink coffee," she said.

"They don't. I'm a lapsed Mormon, so I do what I want. I choose to serve coffee only in the morning to get the men going, but I still draw the line at alcohol. Don't need the trouble that comes with a bunch of drunken men." Myrna poured herself a cup and went on. "With the coffee, you see, they're breaking rules, but that's not as bad as drinking alcohol. Men have to do something sinful or there wouldn't be anything to forgive."

Christina smiled. She liked the way Myrna expressed herself.

"Mind if I ask you a question?" Myrna said. "You and your young man. Got any definite plans on where you're going?"

"We're trying to get to California."

"Ah, California," Myrna said, nodding her head. "Met lots of men heading for California over the years. Some of them came back when they didn't strike it rich. And when you get there, what then?" she pursued.

"Hope to get some land. Our own place to set down roots."

"Roots, huh? Sounds like a man all right." She began wiping down the counter with ferocity. "Gonna have lots of children, I 'spose."

Christina jerked her head up, her eyes filled with alarm.

"Takes a big family to run a farm," Myrna pointed out.

"I'd like to raise horses," Christina interjected without answering Myrna's question.

"That's an ambitious plan. Here, let me get you fed before any stragglers drag themselves in. Most rail workers have come and gone by now. They're pretty hungry by dawn."

While Christina picked at her food, Myrna began frying up bacon and cracking eggs, all the while bombarding Christina with questions, and offering her own opinions.

"Got to excuse me, but I don't get many women to talk to around here. 'Cept for the Eilers. When John Eiler comes to town he brings his whole brood—women *and* children." She turned to Christina. "You know, if you and your mister want to earn a bit more of a grubstake before heading to California, John might have some work for your young man. He has a ranch just outside of Promontory. Raises various crops, mainly alfalfa, I think. Has some livestock and horses."

At the sound of horses, Christina perked up. But then she remembered that Charley's desire was to keep moving west.

"I don't know, Myrna. Charley might not want to delay our journey."

"Just thought you looked like you could use a breather. Talk to him. Let me know and I'll introduce you when Eiler comes to town. Come to think of it, he's just about due." Her face brightened. "Comes once a week when the trains bring the mail and delivers supplies from the east. That's about the only way people get their goods since all the other businesses and shops in Promontory shut down."

"I'll see what he thinks," Christina said. But she already knew what he thought—that they were growing short on time *and* money. If she could convince Charley that taking a break would solve their money worries, maybe she could even figure out a way to go after one of those wild horses she saw from the train. It thrilled her to see their manes flying and their fine muscles quiver. There were even a few colts running along side of the mares. Yes, she definitely would talk to Charley about staying.

Charley soon joined Christina, looking embarrassed to be so late for breakfast. Most of the working men had already come and gone.

"Guess I was pretty tired," he said. He peered at her from under his cap. "How you feeling this morning? Sleep okay?"

"I'm okay, Charley. Just don't have much of an appetite."

"Well, I'm sure hungry. You got any of those flapjacks left, Myrna?" he said. He was eyeing Christina's cold untouched food.

"Here, take it," she said, pushing the plate toward him.

He wolfed down what was left of the cold flapjack, a

little soggy from syrup that had soaked in.

Myrna joined them with a slightly burned flapjack and a large pot of black coffee, which smelled bitter. "Last of the batter. It's on the house," she said as she placed it on Christina's plate that Charley was now hunkered over. She came around the counter and dropped down on a stool to join the couple.

"Gets harder being on your feet so much," she said. "Expect they're going to be as flat as these pancakes some day." Myrna laughed at her own joke. "Your lady tell you about the Eiler family?" She leaned in toward Charley, gazing hard at him.

"I haven't had the chance yet, Myrna." Turning to Charley and lowering her eyes, she said, "Charley, do you think we might lay over a while before getting back on that train?"

"What? We're only about halfway there according to my calculations."

"I know, Charley, but I'm ailing some and could sure use some rest on something other than those old gunny sacks and that hard boxcar floor."

Charley scowled. Christina saw that he didn't like this turn of events. Not one little bit. He had warned her about the hardships the trip would entail, but she had insisted she could handle it. She hated admitting that in this aspect she might be like other women after all.

"Your lady does look a little peaked," Myrna remarked.

He ignored Myrna.

"How we gonna get by?" Charley asked. Christina knew Charley would say little with a stranger listening in.

"I was telling your missus that the Eilers are expected any day now. John Eiler is the biggest rancher out here and he can always use extra help on his place. If you're so inclined," Myrna added, pulling herself away from the counter. "I'll leave you two to talk. I gotta get things cleaned up before the next meal. There's always the next meal," she laughed and lumbered off.

"How is that she knows so much about our business, Christina?"

"She kind of guessed at most of it. She could see that I'm kind of sick, Charley."

Christina hated to admit weakness. Sickness seemed to pass her by. She liked to think that she had the strength and stamina of a man.

Charley took her hand in his and moved his head toward hers. He spoke barely above a whisper. "Okay, Christina. Sure we'll stay here a bit until you're well enough to travel again."

She pulled back to look at him. He was smiling at her, but a little less light shone in his eyes.

CHAPTER SEVEN

Charley

John Eiler rode into Promontory the next morning, his wagon filled with bonneted women and young children. A stout man of middle years, his face was framed by a wiry graying beard. After tying up his horse team and loading the wagon with goods he obtained from the incoming 11:00 a.m. train, he and his family walked from the railroad station to the café. Charley had been watching the Eilers from a distance. He and Christina sat in matching rockers on the hotel porch as Charley sized up John Eiler unfavorably, comparing him to Enoch Neamott; both were large men who moved and walked as if they were in charge.

The three women who padded along behind him had their heads bowed. *Too much like cowing.* The ladies reminded him of Emma Neamott, who had also been subservient to her husband much of the time, too afraid to cross him.

Like most children, the Eiler offspring trailed behind in an unruly line.

"Come on, Charley. We might as well meet the Eilers

and see if they have anything they can offer us," Christina said, interrupting his thoughts. "Just on a temporary basis, of course." Charley got up and reluctantly followed Christina into the hotel dining room. John Eiler was sitting down with a fistful of mail he had just been handed by Myrna, the unofficial post-mistress of Promontory. The family bowed their heads in prayer before beginning their meal.

After a few minutes, Myrna motioned for Charley and Christina to approach the Eilers. They had been hovering near the counter, unsure of how to proceed. Even though they were infrequent churchgoers, they had enough manners not to interrupt a man in prayer.

As they made their way to the table, Mr. Eiler stood up and broke into a big smile. He offered his hand for Charley to shake and then motioned for them to join him and his family.

"Hear you all are strangers looking for work?" he began. "Name's John Eiler and these are my wives, Ruth, Agatha, and Brynn."

Wives? Three of them? From what Charley had heard, having one wife could be trouble enough, let alone three. Although in the next second he wished he had secured the hand of just one wife—the one he had been pursuing for years—Christina.

The eight children Charley counted wriggled on the hard benches. They varied in age and size. The smallest was a boy who reminded Charley of Willie, the youngest of the Neamott children. He had been his favorite.

"We might be interested in some field work for a short time," he said. "Until we can catch the Central Pacific over the Sierras. Aiming for California before winter." As an afterthought, he added, "Of course, it depends on the pay."

"Well, son," Eiler laughed, "You come right to the point, dontcha? With it being hay season, I could use someone for a few weeks. With room and board, I could pay..." John Eiler looked up at the ceiling as if in great thought. "About seventy-five cents a day. How would that suit you and the missus?"

"Don't know, Mr. Eiler. I know how hard haying is and back in Concordia, Kansas, we paid a man more for his labor." This wasn't entirely true, but he no longer was going to work for slave wages after having been taken advantage of enough times by cheap farmers. "That's room and board for *both* of you and over five dollars a week."

"I don't know." Charley hesitated.

John Eiler sucked on his bottom lip for a moment and pulled himself up straighter.

"Okay, young man. I'll pay you eighty-five cents a day—which is almost six dollars a week—if you'll also help my man Bert take care of the livestock. Got some cows and horses need tending."

"Horses?" That sounds great," Christina blurted out. "When can we start?"

Charley gave her a look. He didn't like her taking over like this without discussing it with him first. But he gathered he had little choice. "Okay, Mr. Eiler. For an even six dollars a week and room and board for both of us, you've got a deal."

"Good. If you a mind to, you can go back with us this afternoon. Might be a tight squeeze in the wagon, but if you don't mind sitting on the sacks of corn meal and beans in the back, we should do okay."

"Heck. We've been sleeping on bags in boxcars ever since we left Kansas, haven't we Charley!" Christina said. All of a sudden, she looked like she might be feeling better. There was a new rosiness to her cheeks and her eyes lit up as if on fire.

The ride from Promontory reminded Charley of another buckboard ride when he and Jennie were chosen by the Neamotts and they were headed back to the farm. It was the hardest seat he had ever sat on, and the constant ruts in the road made for an uncomfortable ride. The road from Promontory ran parallel to the railroad line. It was bare, wind-whipped land with an open vista facing the Promontory Mountains that jutted south in the direction of the Great Salt Lake. From time to time, John Eiler shouted out, pointing to a sight he wanted Christina and Charley to notice. The wives were quiet. Never said a word. The children were obedient, but fidgety in the buckboard; their heads shifted from their father to Charley.

After what seemed like an endless ride, they pulled into a narrow lane that led to a house in the distance sitting on a slight knoll. It looked like an oasis, surrounded by fields of grasses in various shades of green and yellow. Scraggly cottonwood trees surrounding the property had dropped their seed pods. Bits of white fuzzy fluff spewing from them looked like snow floating through the air. Charley spotted a large barn and stable downwind of the house and a large fenced-in paddock in which about a dozen horses were held. Little clouds of dirt rose around their stamping hooves. Christina perked up considerably when she saw them.

"Oh, Charley, will you look at that. I think they have more horses than Carl did at any one time. Charley muttered something agreeable under his breath. It was good to see her happy again.

When the wagon came to a halt, the children all piled out and scattered, except for the oldest. Charley tried to remember his name. *Chester, wasn't it?* Introductions had been made back at the café, but he couldn't remember all eight names. Chester looked about eleven or twelve, and although scrawny, he surprised Charley by carrying hundred-pound sacks of beans and cornmeal. They were awkward to get unloaded from the wagon with their pliable contents constantly shifting inside. But the boy managed without complaint.

The house was large, with a warren of rooms. It appeared that as the family grew, rooms were added on, one next to the other with no specific plan. However, the large main room served as the kitchen and parlor all in one. A cast iron cook stove stood at one end of the room with a stone fireplace situated at the other end. A huge trestle table, occupying the center of the room, looked like it was used for more than meals. Primers were stacked at one end as well as two large tomes of a religious nature. Charley guessed that this was a devout family who also took the education of their children seriously.

The women hung up their bonnets and shawls and donned aprons. They stored the purchases in a huge pantry they called a "larder."

"You certainly have a lot of food in here," Charley remarked as he brought in the last big bag of staples and plopped it down on the floor.

Ruth, the oldest of the three women, said "It's our way. The Descendents follow the Mormon practice of storing extra provisions in case of emergencies." Charley was impressed with their preparations. After years of being hungry, first as an orphan in the Pittsburgh Children's Home and during periods of drought and deprivation on the Neamott farm, he could see the wisdom of planning ahead. Whatever this group called The Descendents was all about, the Eiler family appeared to plan *everything* carefully. He wondered just how well the family got along with multiple wives and all. *Guess I'll find out.*

He went outside in search of Mr. Eiler. He wanted to know what kind of work he was going to be asked to do, come morning. He found him tinkering with the mowing rake outside the barn.

"Let me show you around, so you know what we're all about," Eiler said. Charley could see that this man was proud of his holdings as he conducted a tour of the barn and stables, and then walked to the edge of one of the alfalfa fields. The waves of alfalfa were just about ready to be mown and cut for hay. Charley noted that the farm didn't appear to have any equipment that was different or more modern than that used by Kansas farmers. Boy, would he like to run that gas-powered tractor he had used in Concordia through this lush Utah alfalfa. With a cutter attached to the tractor, harvest time would be cut in half.

However, Charley was impressed with the farming operation and said so.

"Thank you, young man. Glad to have you on board." Charley wanted to remind Mr. Eiler that he was not actually on board as much as passing through, but he bit his tongue. Finally, he was introduced to Bert, the only other farm hand, who also was good at tending the livestock.

"Bert had some training as a horse doctor before he came to work for me," Eiler explained. "Couldn't do without him."

Uh oh. It didn't sound like Christina would get to do

any hands-on work with the horses if Bert was so capable. She knew a lot, but not as much as someone with actual veterinary skills.

CHAPTER EIGHT

Christina

Christina entered the kitchen with their belongings. "Where would you like me to put our things, Ruth?"

"Was going to split you up and have you sleep with the girls and Charley with the boys. But since you're a couple—"

"Oh, we're not married," Christina blurted out. "At least not yet, but we're going to be as soon as we get settled."

"Oh," Ruth said. If she was surprised or shocked, she didn't indicate it. She promptly picked up Christina's backpack and ushered her through a series of rooms to one with bunk beds. A row of pegs held jumpers and dresses, and a large window looked out on the barn and horse paddock. "Alice can bunk with Piper in this bottom bunk if you don't mind climbing to the upper one with Cecelia," she explained. "The youngest girl, Willow, still sleeps with her mother."

"And Charley?"

"He'll have to bunk with the boys. Follow me."

They walked deeper into the cavernous house and entered a compact room with a similar arrangement. A row of bunk beds were flanked against one wall, and only a single window, smaller than the one in the girls' room, partially relieved the gloominess of the crowded space. Christina was glad she'd have access to the larger one, which would admit more light. She was tired of the dark, limited view they'd had from the boxcars. She dropped Charley's belongings on one of the beds.

She knew Charley wasn't going to like this arrangement at all after the two of them had finally had some privacy. She didn't like it either, but after being ill the last few days, she figured it was just as well that she get some extra rest for that time when they boarded another train.

Christina meandered away from the house soon after Ruth had pointed out where she and Charley would be sleeping. She eagerly looked over the barn and stable and found them in excellent condition, and the horse stalls clean with fresh hay in each. Outside, she leaned against the fence and studied each horse in the paddock. Most were mares with one new foal. A couple of geldings paced along the corral fence, but the stallions were in a separate stable farther away—to keep them away from the mares.

"Heard you liked horses," Bert said by way of introduction. "Had much experience caring for them?"

"Yes, I was taught by the best: Carl Schmitz, a farrier and blacksmith back in Concordia, Kansas."

"Good to hear. Name's Bert, by the way." He offered a rough, calloused hand.

"Christina Batachi," she answered, looking into coal black eyes pocketed in deep sun-burned flesh. She accepted his hand and shook it.

"I could use a little help with the animals while I lend a hand during the harvest. Old man Eiler needs all the workers he can get."

"Just tell me what you need."

After he showed her where all the equipment was stowed, they returned to their spots by the corral fence. Bert pointed out the different horses and described their personalities and histories.

"Lightning Rod is temperamental. Got to give him wide berth. Mariah is the fastest horse, but a little skittish at times. Buttercup is—well, she's just like her name," he said." Good disposition and easy to ride."

What Christina really wanted to ask Bert was how to go about capturing one of those wild mustangs she had seen running across the prairie. But that would have to wait. She needed to prove that she was good at handling horses before asking him any favors—like helping her lasso a wild one.

CHAPTER NINE

Charley

The wives waited on the men and children before actually sitting down and eating dinner with them. Again, prayers were delivered before eating. Even the youngest child folded chubby hands and bowed his head and murmured "Amen." The large table practically groaned with food and Charley ate eagerly. Except for the beans at the café, this was the first hot meal he had eaten in almost two weeks.

Charley conducted a new head count. Besides the head of the family, his three wives, and eight children, there was Bert, Christina, and himself. That was fifteen people at the table. It was like sitting at one of the large tables at the orphanage, except this one had decent food. Charley didn't know if he could keep all the Eiler names straight, but he would try. There was the oldest boy, Chester, who helped unload the wagon. Then there were: Jasper, Noah, and Titus. The girls were named Alice, Piper, Cecelia, and Willow.

After the women cleaned up, the men retired to the parlor end of the great room.

"Desert nights get a little chilly, even in the summer," John said as he lit a fire in the fireplace.

Bert excused himself to go outside and have a cigarette. "You want to have a smoke with me?" he asked Charley.

"Thanks, but I don't use tobacco."

"That's good," John said when Bert took his leave. "Mormons don't believe in tobacco or strong drink," he added. "Neither do we."

"Excuse me, Mr. Eiler, but I thought you *were* Mormon."

"We were until the Mormons outlawed multiple marriages—which is a God-given right!" he said, his face turning red. "We broke away and became The Descendents. Anyway, glad to see you haven't developed bad habits, Charley. We overlook it in Bert because he's not a true Mormon or a member of our group—yet."

Charley wondered what that was supposed to mean. Although he didn't smoke or imbibe very often himself, it was only because he didn't like the taste. He didn't begrudge any man comfort where he could find it unless it interfered with his responsibilities or resulted in harsh behaviors. He wondered if John was trying to convert Bert. He hoped he wouldn't try that with him and Christina.

CHAPTER TEN

Jennie

Concordia, Kansas
Summer 1900

Jennie Hunsinger trailed behind Violet, her adoptive mother. They were at the Atchison, Topeka, and Santa Fe train depot to pick up Violet's cousin, Mary Belle, arriving from New Orleans. Normally, Jennie looked forward to a houseguest because that gave Violet someone else to focus on instead of her, but another fussy woman in the house was not at all what Jennie hoped for. All of Violet's kin were old, or formal and aloof. There wasn't a young cousin among the whole lot and Jennie longed for the company of someone her own age.

Although she had had many advantages since Violet took her in from the Neamotts when she was eleven, relieving her from the hardships of farm life, it also deprived her of the company of other children. She was even home schooled instead of being allowed to attend the country school.

It was bad enough that she had been torn away from her brother, Charley, but having no other children to grow up with made her feel impaired—like a person with one leg shorter than the other. Jennie had limped through her days of privilege with few surprises and little joy.

Now, at sixteen, she wished to meet other young adults: make a best friend, meet boys—a boy who was sophisticated, not gawky like some she had seen. She instantly thought of Charley's business partner, Peter Stuyvesant. She had met him when Charley and Peter came by to show off the bad-smelling gas tractor they dragged all over the county to cultivate the fields of other farmers. She wasn't certain how the tractor worked exactly, except it was supposed to take the place of a horse and plow.

Peter was fair haired like Charley, but he was taller and leaner. His features were ordinary and, yet, she would describe him as handsome. He also had a special way about him; he made her laugh and seemed an awful tease. She had not seen him in person since he and Charley had some kind of falling out when their business failed, although she did see Peter in town occasionally; she saw him go in and out of saloons or pass the time of day in the general store where he'd tip his hat to the ladies and engage in long conversations with men in business suits.

She sighed. There was no sense in wanting something out of her reach. Peter was at least as old as Charley—twenty-one—or older. She knew that, even if he passed inspection in all other respects, Violet would forbid her to keep company with a man five years older. Jennie would be better off to set her sights on someone else—even though she would love to go dancing with Peter or even share a quiet buggy ride with him. However, Violet had informed Jennie that when she was ready to "come out and meet society like the debutantes in the civilized south," a suitable young man would be found to be her escort.

Before Violet and Jennie left for the train station this morning, Violet had said, "You know, Mary Belle is different from us, Jennie. She is very delicate and used to fine food and a kind of society we don't enjoy here in Concordia." She scowled over her breakfast of poached eggs with capers and ham. "So we must do everything we can to make her feel at ease and comfortable."

"Of course," Jennie agreed. She had learned that it was best to agree with her mother and not ask too many questions. She became prickly if challenged. Jennie didn't have anyone to compare her to, but she thought that sometimes Violet's ideas were a little strange. Even the practice of asking Jennie to call her by her first name seemed at odds with her otherwise more formal manners. Jennie had been encouraged to call Violet by her first name from the beginning of their relationship and, after adopting Jennie, Violet had said, "You needn't call me Mother. I think Violet sounds so much more modern."

It suited Jennie just fine because Violet was nothing

like her real mother anyway, whom she always called "Mum."

Thinking of Mum made Jennie think of Charley. Since he and Christina had left Concordia, Jennie missed Charley more than ever. While he remained in town there was always a chance that they would become close again, but now she felt truly alone, almost abandoned. The old feelings of being a lost orphan had returned.

There was a time when Charley was very upset with her because she didn't want to return to the Neamott farm. She hated almost everything about the dirt farm, except for Emma, who was like a second mother to her, and the children: Sarah, Ruthie, and later, baby Rose. Violet had arranged with Mr. Neamott to pay him for Jennie's keep all the months before taking custody of her. Charley was angry at Enoch *and* at Violet, and later, angry with Jennie as if she had been privy to the plan from the outset. He couldn't seem to appreciate Jennie's good fortune and the opportunities available to her with this move. Of course, she suspected the real reason Violet chose her was because of her uncanny resemblance to her lost daughter, Lotta, who had died the year before Jennie arrived in Concordia.

"Jennie, where is your head this morning?" Violet said as she stopped and waited for Jennie to catch up with her. They were on the train platform searching faces among the riders disembarking from the train. "Help search for Mary Belle. She has to be here somewhere."

"Yes, Violet," Jennie said, dreamily. She must have forgotten that I've never met Mary Belle. I don't even know what she looks like.

She couldn't help but think back to the last time she saw Charley a few weeks ago. He had come to say good-bye before leaving Concordia. He stood on the front porch of the Hunsinger mansion with cap in hand as if he were a beggar.

"Goodbye? Where are you going, Charley?"

"Christina and I are going west to see if we can find land of our own—a place to settle, get married, and start a family. We may go as far as California."

"But that's so far. I'll never see you," she complained, even as she remembered all the times she was too busy to see Charley when he came calling.

"We can write and we'll come back some day. Or you can come and visit us."

"Oh, I don't know, Charley. Violet only likes to travel to big eastern cities or to foreign places."

Charley looked crestfallen. "Well, in case I don't see you again for a long time, I have something to give you." He reached into his pocket and pulled out a worn leather booklet that fit snugly into the palm of his hand.

"What is it?"

"They say it belonged to Mum. I don't recognize it. Can't say I ever saw it before, but the Children's Home wrote that some personal things were sent to them from our flat in Homestead. They were put into storage in the home's basement for safe keeping. They just now sent it on to me."

"After all this time? What's in it, Charley?" She thumbed the book open to reveal a tightly compressed scrawl. Jennie peered more closely at the faded ink. The letters looked different from the ones in the English language. "I can't make out what it says."

"I think it's Gaelic, from the old country." Charley looked over Jennie's shoulder. "See the names listed on this page? There's Mum's name, there's her sisters and brothers, and finally our Grandmum—Katherine. They're all our kin, Jennie." He craned his neck to one side, following Jennie's study of the booklet. "Doesn't look like Mum ever wrote our names in though. I wonder why?"

"Oh, Charley, do you think we'll ever get to see any of our kin?" The thought of going to Ireland someday to look up their lost relatives crossed her mind. But then she remembered that Mum said most of the family had left Ireland due to the potato famine. Those who did stay were probably dead by now or had scattered who knew where. She would have to be satisfied with this book as proof of their ancestry. She turned another page and a lock of golden hair fell out.

"Oh," she said. "Is this what I think it is?"

"Looks like your hair, Jennie. Mum must have clipped it when you were just a babe."

"There should be two locks." Jennie stroked the fine

hairs that felt like silk. "Where's yours?"

"Don't know. Think it's a miracle that yours is still there."

"I'll treasure it always." She sighed and gave Charley a big smile. "I'm going to write our names in this book under Mum's name, our ages, today's date, and where we live." Jennie stopped, her smile fading. "Since you're leaving Concordia, what can I put down as the place where *you* live?"

Charley shrugged his shoulders. "Guess I'll have to let you know as soon as we're settled." He leaned down and gave Jennie a hug. She hugged him back—hard. It would have to last them both for a long time.

CHAPTER ELEVEN

Jennie

They had only been waiting a few minutes when the steam engine chugged into the station. Before they could spot Cousin Mary Belle, a slew of children streamed from the train, swamping the small platform. To Jennie's surprise, she recognized Mr. Buckminster, the head of the Pittsburgh Children's Home—the orphanage where she lived before being transported cross-country by orphan train. He had changed little except for a balding pate and extra pounds spread evenly across his middle. Jennie had been aware that the train continued to bring orphans and abandoned children to towns along the Atchison, Topeka, and Santa Fe line in hopes of placing them. But this was the first time she was actually in the station when they arrived.

One child—a girl who looked about the same age Jennie had been when she first came to town—stood out. She was thin and her pale skin was spattered with freckles. The freckles didn't disguise her somewhat sunken cheeks. Unruly red hair was piled on top of her head in a bun, but stray hairs had slipped out of the knot and down

her neck, giving her an untidy appearance. Jennie remembered how hard it was to keep clean and neat when
she was young—especially when all she really wanted to
do was join in the games other girls played. *I wonder
what her interests are?* Just then, the girl's eyes darted
around the platform until they locked with Jennie's. Her
shy smile took Jennie by surprise. She smiled back.

Mr. Buckminster moved slowly as he herded the children inside the depot waiting room. Jennie could hear
him wheezing as he passed by.

"I'll be back in a minute," she said as she left Violet's
side to follow the group. She approached the old headmaster.

"Hello, Mr. Buckminster," she said.

"Miss?" He looked puzzled. "Are you interested in
fostering one of the children? You appear a little young,
but..."

"No." She laughed. "I'm hardly in a position to take
care of a child, Mr. Buckminster. I'm barely past being a
child myself." When he didn't respond, Jennie went on.
"I was one of your charges about five years ago. You
placed me and my brother, Charley, with a farm family.
Jennie and Charley O'Brien. Do you remember us?" Jennie was surprised at how unintimidating the man before
her looked. At one time the power he held over their lives
had felt frightening.

"Let me think." He brought a hand to his chin, trying
to puzzle out this new information. "There have been so

many children over the years, you see. Please forgive me my fading memory."

"I understand." She started to move away, but turned back. "I didn't remain with the Neamott family. Instead, I went to live with Mrs. Hunsinger in town."

His eyes opened wide at the name. "Violet Hunsinger?" he asked.

"Yes. She adopted me."

Jennie pointed to the glass doors through which Violet could be seen pacing back and forth on the train platform searching for Cousin Mary Belle. "There she is."

"Why yes, now I remember. She wanted to take you when the man of the family was reluctant to care for another girl. But your brother refused to have the two of you separated, didn't he? A very loyal young man. And what happened to Charley, if I may ask?"

"He stayed with the Neamotts until he turned eighteen. Actually, he stayed a little longer to help out. He and Christina Batachi just left Concordia heading west."

"Christina Batachi? I'll never forget her."

"No one will, sir."

The red-headed girl had edged closer. "And who might this be?" Jennie asked.

"My name is Lucy McCleery," the girl said, curtsying. Her voice was raspy and especially loud for such a small person.

"Glad to meet you, Lucy McCleery. How old are you?"

"I'm nine years old—almost ten. I'm good at taking

care of babies and sweeping up and such."

"Yes," Mr. Buckminster agreed. "Lucy worked in the foundling part of the orphanage and was most helpful to the matron. Jennie, do you think Mrs. Hunsinger would be interested in helping us out again? Make a home for Lucy?"

"I don't know. I don't think so. We don't have any young ones in our home."

"If I remember, she was eager to take you in at the time. Besides working with babies, Lucy is good in the kitchen too, aren't you, girl?"

Jennie grew uncomfortable with Mr. Buckminster's pushy manner. She didn't remember him being like this.

"Yes, I am." Lucy's voice sounded like two saws being rubbed together. "I can help the cook and wash up and scrub floors."

Jennie glanced at the girl's hands and saw how red and rough the skin appeared. Her hands were those of an old scrubwoman, not a young girl. Thanks to Charley, who had protected Jennie while they lived in the orphanage, Jennie had never been subjected to hard labor. *Had no one protected Lucy?*

"I don't know, Mr. Buckminster. You'll have to talk to Violet. She's here to pick up her cousin." Jennie scanned the room. "Oh, there she is." Violet had returned inside the depot and was fanning herself furiously.

Mr. Buckminster approached her with Jennie and Lucy in tow.

"Mrs. Hunsinger, so nice to see you again," he said. "As you can see, another orphan train has arrived and is placing youngsters with families."

"What's this to do with me?" Violet asked.

Jennie was surprised at how rude Violet sounded. She felt embarrassed.

"You were so sensitive at one time to the plight of our orphans. Therefore, I wonder if you could help out by fostering this lovely young girl in your home." Lucy hid behind Mr. Buckminster.

"Well, if nothing less, you're certainly direct." Violet appeared flustered. "Mr. Buckminster, I don't wish to take someone in. I've already done that, as you can see. Don't you remember Jennie?"

"I do indeed. And I'm delighted to see how well she's done with your protection and under your tutelage." He turned and motioned for Lucy to step forward. "With your wisdom and Jennie's guidance, little Lucy here would benefit greatly from your charity."

Lucy curtsied again and kept her eyes trained on Mrs. Hunsinger.

Violet turned to Jennie, looking at her sharply.

"Whose idea was this?"

"Does it matter?" Jennie boldly pressed forward. "Violet, she's in just as much need as I was when you took *me* in."

"I'm much too distressed to discuss this or consider such a proposition right now."

Violet's cheeks had turned a splotchy red. "My cousin is missing. I need to talk with the station master and get to the bottom of this. I just know she was supposed to be on this train." She turned and headed for the ticket window. "Come along, Jennie."

Jennie regretted having to leave Lucy's side. Impulsively, she removed her hat with the lilac flowers attached and placed it on the girl's red crown. "I'm sorry," she said. "Please enjoy wearing this. It will protect your sweet face from the sun and keep away the freckles."

"But I like my freckles," Lucy declared as she raised her arms. She patted and stroked the flower-laden hat and pulled it down close to her ears, making sure it was secure. "Thank you, Miss."

Jennie reluctantly followed Violet. *It would have been so nice to bring Lucy home.* The house was too big and empty for just the two of them. It would be fun to have someone there who made a little noise—yelling at times, giggling, and running up and down the stairs with her. In the meantime, Jennie wished she could help Lucy. Something in the child's demeanor touched her. She saw herself in the young girl, and detected a spirit that couldn't be snuffed out. She liked that. Jennie sighed and rushed to catch up to Violet.

CHAPTER TWELVE

Jennie

Violet was walking too fast, a sign she was agitated. Jennie ran to keep up with her.

"Oh, look, there she is after all," Violet said, grabbing Jennie by the arm. "Yoo-hoo, Mary Belle. Over here!" She waved her handkerchief in the air.

A short, plump woman waved back. Jennie thought that she dressed like a much younger woman—a girl actually. The full-skirted, floral-design of the dress made her appear even pudgier. A nosegay of artificial roses hung askew on the bodice, accenting her ample bosom, which only added to her frumpy image. The porter who followed Mary Belle struggled with a luggage cart bearing a steamer trunk and a stack of carpetbags that threatened to fall. Jennie wondered if she had brought her entire wardrobe.

"Where were you, Mary Belle? We had almost given up on you." Violet reached out and circled her cousin in a gentle hug. "Thought you missed the train. Never mind. You're here now."

"We had to track down all my bags," Mary Belle tittered, fanning herself. She turned to Jennie. "You must be little Jennie I've heard so much about. Except, you're not so little anymore, are you?"

"No ma'am, I guess not."

"There will be no ma'ams while I'm here. I get enough of that down home. 'Yes ma'am. No ma'am.' Call me Mary Belle."

"Welcome to Concordia, Mary Belle." Jennie made a slight bow.

"I see you've taught Jennie well, Violet."

While Violet gave the porter directions on where to take the luggage, Jennie's eyes returned to Lucy across the room, still standing alone. A man had stepped forward from the crowd to speak to her. She shook her head and looked about frantically. When she began sobbing, Mr. Buckminster interceded and said a few words that Jennie couldn't hear. The man who had been speaking to Lucy threw his hands up in exasperation and left.

"Excuse me a minute," Jennie said. Without waiting for a response, she started across the room, easing toward the children and Mr. Buckminster. "What did that man say to Lucy to make her cry?" she asked the headmaster.

"Lucy tends to be shy. Placing her out with a stranger can be difficult."

Jennie nodded politely, recalling her own tears when Enoch Neamott wanted to take Charley into his home, but excluded her. "Just want the boy. Don't have need for a girl," he had said.

"It will be okay," she said, offering Lucy a handker-chief.

"Couldn't I go with you?" Lucy wailed.

"I'm sorry, Lucy." Jennie bent to the child's level and looked her straight in the eye.

"I would take you if I could." She looked to Mr. Buckminster for help in explaining the unexplainable.

"Lucy, Jennie is not of age. I can only release you to a responsible adult," he said.

"I'm sorry," Jennie said as she stood up and backed away. She lowered her eyes.

She couldn't look at Lucy in distress. There was something about her that was heartwrenching.

She rushed across the room, catching up with Violet and Mary Belle.

"Excuse me, but I must talk to you, Violet. Privately, if you don't mind, Mary Belle."

"Well..." Mary Belle looked startled.

"Where are your manners, Jennie?" Violet did not look pleased.

Jennie took a deep breath and went on. "Violet, I feel so strongly that that young girl standing across the room with Mr. Buckminster will be neglected or abused if not placed with the right person like—someone like you. Look how well you did in caring for and shaping me."

Mary Belle looked astonished at this outburst, but remained silent.

"Jennie, this is not an appropriate time or place for this conversation," Violet reprimanded.

"But if we don't do something, Lucy will end up with someone as coarse as Mr. Neamott or worse. You didn't want that for me. How could you let it happen to someone just as needy?"

"Your behavior is bordering on the boorish. I ask you to stop this kind of talk immediately."

Jennie hesitated. She lowered her voice and moved closer to Violet. "Can't you open up your heart to help Lucy the same way you did for me?" When this got no response, Jennie stammered. "In fact, you could probably use some extra help right now with Cousin Mary Belle visiting and all."

"Oh, I don't want to be too much trouble," Mary Belle began.

"Nonsense! I have adequate household help."

"But your cousin shouldn't have to be dependent on kitchen maids to help with the care of her clothes, drawing her bath, and..." She turned to Mary Belle. "I'll bet you had a personal maid in New Orleans, didn't you?"

"Well, I do have a young lady to help with my daily toilette," Mary Belle chimed in.

"See, Violet. We should make our guest as comfortable as possible."

Violet's cheeks had taken on color, but she managed to maintain control.

"I was going to hire someone extra from town," she

said. "But perhaps I can take this opportunity to help both Mary Belle feel at home and assist this homeless youngster." She stiffened her shoulders and pulled herself up straighter. "Although, she looks too young to be a maid."

"In the South, ladies' maids are trained from a young age," Mary Belle offered.

"See, Violet. And I'll help show her what to do," Jennie said.

"Hmm." Violet hesitated. "Very well, Jennie. But I expect you to be *totally* responsible for her behavior and training. Is that understood?"

"Yes, oh yes, Violet. Thank you." Jennie hugged Violet and took her by the arm, gently guiding her across the room before she changed her mind.

"Well, Mr. Buckminster. I've reconsidered your request and have decided to accept Lucy into my home—on a trial basis, mind you."

Lucy bowed again in front of Violet. This time it was a deep curtsy that almost caused her to trip over her skirt. She caught herself just in time and rasped in her loud, croaking voice, "Thank you, missus."

"Oh my, what an unpleasant voice," Violet said, taken aback. Lucy straightened up and ran to Jennie, her hat flying off. When she threw her arms around Jennie's middle, her hoarse-sounding "thank you" was muffled in layers of fabric.

CHAPTER THIRTEEN

Charley

The routine on John Eiler's ranch was exhausting. The man sure expected a lot from his hired help, Charley thought. Of course, he was no worse than Enoch had been and a lot better at conversation. In fact, sometimes Charley wished Eiler were a little less talkative so that he could hear himself think.

"When I first bought this land from the railroad, there was nothing here," he told Charley that morning. "Nothing but thistle and sagebrush. Tried planting corn at first, but couldn't count on enough rain to produce a decent crop. A shame, when you think about it. Folks always have to have food." He removed his hat and wiped his forehead with a red bandana. Leaning on his idle pitchfork while Bert and Charley continued to work, Ei-ler went on. "'Course animals have to be fed too. That's why I planted alfalfa."

They spent hours in the hot sun, cutting the hay, and then letting it dry in loosely raked rows, only to return and pitch it into bigger piles several days later. When it was judged to be dry enough for storage, the men came back with a team of horses pulling a long wagon on which the hay was pitched a final time. It would later be hoisted into the barn loft until needed by Eiler's livestock; the rest was put through the Mormon Beater Hay Press to be shaped into bales and shipped by train to other farmers. Charley had heard that the same folks who invented the gas tractor were working on a hay baler that automatically bundled and bound hay with wire in the fields. All that was left for the farmer to do was gather the bales, stack, and store them. Just as he promised himself a gas-run tractor some day, he vowed that he would save up for a baler. The fact that it hadn't been invented yet didn't discourage him.

John, Charley, and Bert put in long days from sunup to sunset with only time enough for supper, after which John gathered his family in the parlor to conduct a bible study. They read from something called The Book of Mormon and at times from the King James Holy Bible.

"We like to cover all bases," John explained. Although invited to join them, Charley and Bert and Christina would excuse themselves to play a hand of cards called Pinochle in the kitchen or poker out in the barn, using oil lamps for light. Bert and Christina won a few hands, but Charley usually won the pot. They played with wooden match sticks, not money, as gambling—just like coffee and alcoholic spirits—was prohibited by the Eiler's religion. Charley missed the coffee most. That, and sleeping with Christina at his side.

One evening when Bert went to town and everyone had bedded down for the night, Charley and Christina snuck into the barn as planned. They scrambled up the ladder to the loft where they fell on each other almost immediately.

"Oh woman, how I've missed you," Charley murmured into her hair. "Seeing you every day without touching you drives me crazy."

"You're not the only one," she said, helping him out of his shirt. The hay rustled under them as they tumbled into a thick pile of straw. Charley noticed that Christina was a little thicker through the waist. Her breasts were fuller too. She finally had gotten her appetite back and had filled out to his surprise and delight. He reveled in the sweet smell of her and the way their legs and arms intertwined. He rolled over on top of her and their bodies joined together effortlessly like two perfectly paired puzzle pieces.

One of the horses below them nickered.

"Shh, Charley. You're too noisy."

He made a slurping noise into Christina's ear and nipped one of her lobes with his teeth a little too roughly.

"Charley!"

"You're right." He would try to curb his enthusiasm, but after so long, it was almost impossible. They resumed their lovemaking, only more quietly in order to not disturb the horses. They didn't need them giving away the fact that someone or something else was in the barn. To do so might cause old man Eiler to come out with a loaded shotgun aiming to shoot a wolf or coyote, both of which were plentiful.

After they had their fill of loving, they lay on their sides in the warm afterglow studying one another. There was just enough light from the moon for Charley to make out Christina's silhouette.

"You grow more beautiful every day," he said. "How lucky I am to have found you."

"Oh Charley, we're lucky we found each other, even though we were right under each other's noses for so long."

He laughed and sat up. "Yeah, I was a little slow about showing my feelings when we first met. I can't wait until we're together again like this, not separated like a couple of green kids."

"As long as we're here, I guess we have no choice."

"Well, that's about to change," Charley said. "I think haying season is almost over. I figure Eiler owes me about eighteen dollars by now and I intend to ask him for it. So we can leave here and continue on to California."

"Oh, so soon?"

"I thought you'd be more excited to hear this."

"Well, I am Charley, but I was hoping while we were here that I'd get a chance at one of those wild horses. Bert said as soon as the chores let up a little, he'd take me out to an arroyo where horses run. He says we need to do it before the winter rains come and cause the river to swell."

"Bert says this, does he?" Charley slipped back into his shirt and struggled into his denims. "First of all, we're not going to be anywhere near this place when winter comes. We should be long gone. And second, we can't get a horse if we're going to travel by train."

"Don't be upset, Charley. We talked about this before."

"I know, Christina. But I thought we agreed to get settled first. What good is it going to do to capture a wild horse *here*. We can't very well take one with us in a boxcar."

"Why not? Cattle and horses are shipped on freight trains, aren't they?"

"Yeah, but they're in special stock cars which is different than riding in a regular boxcar where they can get injured or sick. They're not on a vacation, you know," he added as he stood up. "Usually the poor animals are on their way to slaughter."

"But, Charley..."

"Christina, listen to what you're saying. It's hard enough for two people to sneak on board. How do you expect to cover up the fact that a horse is in one of the cars? Be practical."

"But, Charley, you promised."

Charley saw a side of Christina he hadn't noticed before. She was acting like a spoiled child.

"We best get back to bed before someone discovers we're missing," he said.

This was not the way Charley had planned things. There had already been too many delays and surprises. He was determined to talk to John about the money owed him and how soon he could expect to receive it. He wouldn't just leave the man high and dry, but there was no point in hanging around indefinitely. He knew from experience that there was always more work to do on a ranch. If he and Christina lingered, if they agreed to stay any longer, the weather might change dramatically. You never knew when it might turn into an early winter, making travel more difficult. And then there was the spring planting season and—*It would never end!*

No, it was best that they move on as soon as possible.

CHAPTER FOURTEEN

Christina

"Found a piece of hay on your pillow this morning," Ruth said the next morning. "You visiting the livestock at midnight?"

Christina blushed and fumbled for an explanation.

"Well, missy, if you and your man want to be right with God, we could wed you right here."

"Marry us?" Christina exclaimed. "How could you do that?"

"John could do it. As founder of The Descendents he has authority to unite couples in marriage."

"Is it a legal marriage then?"

"It's legal in the eyes of God."

"Oh, I don't know," Christina said. This was becoming too complicated. She turned to attend to some kitchen task so that Ruth could not read her face. If she finally married Charley, he might want to start a family right away. *God knows I love the man, but I like things the way they are.* Besides, she didn't quite trust the authority of John Eiler and this offshoot religious sect.

"Well, you had better do something soon by the looks of you."

"What do you mean?"

"I know you've been getting sick of a morning. It's the first sign."

"Ruth, forgive my manners, but I don't think this should be of any concern to you." Christina slammed the plates down a little too hard as she set the table for breakfast. Before any more was said, the other wives and children began wandering in, followed by the men, who had been up at dawn to care for the animals. Eggs and hotcakes were cooking on the huge cook stove, and mush was being ladled into bowls for the younger children. It was much too busy and loud for personal talk. Christina was relieved. She didn't want to think about what Ruth had said. *I couldn't be pregnant, could I?*

After the meal, Agatha gathered the children together for their day's school lessons. She had explained to Christina that first day, that because of her ease with reading and writing, it became her job to homeschool the children. Christina studied the brood and noticed their physical resemblance to one another; three of the eight children were borne by Agatha and five by Ruth. Brynn, the third wife, the quietest of the three, was also the youngest—barely sixteen according to Agatha. She was pregnant with what would be John's ninth child. Christina was shocked at Brynn's young age, although it wasn't unusual for women to be married by sixteen in these frontier towns. She was more surprised that this pretty young thing agreed to bed down with John. He was an unattractive older man who seemed way too smug for her taste.

They had been on the ranch a month already and although not part of the family, they had been welcomed into this community. Except for the sleeping arrangements and somewhat demanding expectations of Ruth for Christina to be a house servant, Christina was content to stay for a while. Charley, however, was becoming insistent on their leaving. So, if she was going to get a chance at those wild horses it had better be soon.

Christina found Bert in the stable going through riding gear, intent on his work.

"Good day for riding?" Christina said, startling him.

"Good as any, I guess."

"I was wondering when I could get a look at those wild horses we talked about?"

"You were serious, then?"

"Of course I was serious."

"Well, I guess we could give it a try. Check out the arroyo near Jackass Gulch. You really think you could train one of those creatures?"

"I know I could. You've seen me working with these fellows," she said, stroking the velvety muzzle of an Appaloosa. He snorted his pleasure at her touch.

"Yep, you're pretty good for a woman."

His eyes rested on hers a beat longer than necessary, Christina thought.

"But it's about an hour's hard ride to the arroyo and if we're lucky enough to find horses, it could be another couple hours catching them—roping and hobbling them—to get them tired enough to lead back. You up to all that?"

Christina nodded, eagerly. "I can do it. Trust me."

"Well, we'll see. I'll talk to John to see if he can spare us. If he agrees, we could light out early tomorrow morning." Bert cleared his throat before continuing. "Better bring that young man of yours along too. It takes more than one cowpoke to handle wild horses. How is he with riding and roping?"

"Charley knows the basics, but I know more," she boasted.

All day Christina was restless. She paced and everything she did in the kitchen or in the stables was done by rote. Her mind was far away thinking about the wild horses she might encounter the following day. If they were anything like the ones she and Charley had seen from the train's boxcar, it would be a challenging round-up.

"Christina, what have you gotten yourself committed to?" Charley said as he came sauntering toward her across the paddock.

"What do you mean?" she asked innocently.

"The horse roundup. Tomorrow morning. Bert said

you were going out with him."

"Well, yes. We talked about this, Charley. You're going along too, aren't you?"

"Guess I'll have to if you're determined to do this," he said.

"I am. I have to at least get a closer look at those mustangs. You don't have to come along if you don't want to."

"Well I'm sure as hell not letting you go alone—with Bert."

"What does that mean?" she demanded.

"You're my woman. My responsibility. I'm not turning that over to another man."

"If that's the only reason, then don't go. You'll take all the fun out of it."

"Fun!" he yelled. "I'm thinking it will be hard work and dangerous, not fun."

"Anything worthwhile is work and maybe—too dangerous for some," she challenged.

Charley's face turned red and his eyes narrowed. She had seen him like this only one other time, when he told her about how Peter Stuyvesant had cheated him in their business deal.

"Guess it's settled then," he said, backing away. "I'll see you in the morning." He took off his hat and slapped it against his thigh.

That night, lying in the bunk she shared with Cecelia, Christina thought over the fight she'd had with

Charley. Was she being stubborn and inconsiderate? She didn't think so. Charley had never been much of a horseman. In fact, that first year he was on the Neamott farm, he was afraid of horses. And still, he learned enough to work with them like most farmers. He had never broken a horse or helped train one like she had, but she didn't fault him for that.

It unnerved her to argue with him. She liked it when they made up though. She tossed and turned and barely had fallen asleep when it was time to get up. She put her feet on the floor. "*Oh no!*" She had the stomach flip flops again. "*Not now. Not when I finally get the chance to chase down a horse.*

She dressed and entered the kitchen. Ruth was already at the cook stove making the morning beverage they drank instead of coffee—a chicorybean concoction that was free of caffeine. Christina didn't like the taste, but at least it was hot and she had grown accustomed to it.

"You don't look so good," Ruth commented.

"It'll pass. It always does," Christina answered. "Could I have some bread and butter?

"If you'll wait a minute, I'll dish up some of these grits and bacon before the others get to the table."

"Oh no!" she gasped. "Just bread please." Christina's stomach lurched at the thought of eating the greasy meat.

Ruth gave her a searching look. "Fresh bread is in the

oven, but there's some leftover from yesterday if you're in a hurry."

"Yes, please." Christina hugged the cup of hot chicory to her face, letting the steam envelope her.

When the hunk of bread was placed before her, Christina felt a wave of nausea overtake her. She ran from the kitchen to the outhouse where she threw up. Sweat glistened on her face and she felt wobble-kneed afterward, but was determined to not miss out on the morning's trip to Jackass Gulch.

Without a word, she reentered the kitchen where Bert and Charley sat hunkered over their food. Ruth and the men looked up when she sat down and watched her choke down the bread.

"You look a little pale, Christina. You feeling okay?" Charley asked her.

"Fine. I'm just fine."

"Gotta be better than fine if you're going out on this ride," Bert said.

"I'm going," she said. Her insides still felt raw, but she was damned if she would back out of the roundup.

Christina made her way to the stable, where Bert was leading out two horses for the trip—his Appaloosa, Lightning Rod, and Buttercup, the gentle mare who followed him around like a puppy. She had become fond of the mare for her gentle ways and the rich tawny color of her hide. But she did question whether Buttercup would withstand hard riding and the rough business of chasing down wild mustangs. Since Christina was still a little queasy, she decided not to argue. At least riding the mare would be easier than trying to handle one of the larger, more spirited horses.

"You ready, Christina?" Bert said. "Not too late to back out and go another day."

"I'm ready." She checked the cinch and tightened it a bit. With reins held loosely in her left hand, she placed her left foot in the stirrup and swung her right leg over, coming to rest in the saddle. From the seat of a saddle she always felt better, stronger—prepared for anything.

"I'm ready too," Charley said as he appeared from around the corner.

"Glad to have you. Was hoping to have another hand," Bert said.

Christina didn't respond, and Charley held his tongue as well. The black cloud of silence was almost visible between them. He entered the stable and returned with a black gelding in tow. By the time he had the horse saddled, Bert and Christina were outside the paddock trying to control their restless mounts. Christina was finally feeling better; the excitement and expectation surrounding them had made her come alive.

CHAPTER FIFTEEN

Christina

They had been riding for over an hour, putting a fair distance between them and the ranch. The sun was warm, but not yet hot, and the smell of sage filled the air. The terrain was changing as they climbed gradually to a mesa that overlooked a canyon with a stream running through it.

"Looks peaceful, now, don't it?" Bert said. "But there's a lot more water running through here during the rainy season. Have to be watchful for flash floods."

A herd of about thirty mustangs were taking turns drinking from the river. They playfully pawed at the water, splashing and lounging. Some rolled on their backs on the wet, gravely shore.

"Oh, there they are, Charley," she cried. "Aren't they beautiful?"

"Got to admit, they are quite a sight." He smiled at her.

"This is a smaller-than-usual herd," Bert said. "If you notice there are quite a few young horses—yearlings I'd say—and a few foals. They don't look like they're ready to travel anywhere yet. With water nearby, other horses will probably join them." He turned away from the canyon rim. "Follow me," he said. "The arroyo I'm taking you to is just a ways farther."

They rode a short distance and began descending into an arroyo that fanned out at the bottom and then narrowed again. They dismounted and drank water from canteens that Bert had brought with him. It wasn't long before they saw a dust cloud dancing across the horizon.

"Saddle up!" Bert yelled over the sound of thundering hoofs. Horses were winding toward them at a terrific speed. "They're coming through here. They'll have to slow some because it narrows further on. That's when we'll try for one!" he shouted, pointing to a spot just south of them. "Pull up your bandanas. They kick up a shitload of dust!"

As the horses neared, Charley's horse turned in tight circles, rotating back and forth restlessly.

"Get control of your horse, Charley," Bert yelled "or he'll spook the others."

Charley reined in harder, but his horse only became more agitated, crow hopping and finally rearing up. By comparison, Butternut was relatively calm, although she shivered with excitement—just like Christina.

The herd became a dark blur of motion obscured partially by the dust they created. Leading the pack was a sorrel-shaded stallion whose muscular trunk and neck supported a wider head than the others. There were stripes of a darker color on its lower legs. These leg bars gave him an exotic look. As he navigated toward the water, the others followed.

"What kind of horse is that?" Christina shouted to Bert.

"Looks like he's got some Spanish blood in him," he shouted back. "With those leg bars, I'd make him out to be a Kiger Mustang, a Spaniard. They're a little smaller in stature, but well suited for this terrain."

As the horses settled down, nickering, and nudging one another in a getting acquainted ritual, most took to the water—except for a gray mottled stallion on the fringe of the group . When the gray caught sight of the Spaniard, he rushed forward; the two stallion bodies reared up, bumping chests. The momentum of their bodies slamming tossed them back on their haunches. Neither horse appeared ready to back down. The Kiger struck the gray in the shoulder and the gray spun to aim the double barrel of his hind end at the golden Spanish stallion. His hind hooves landed against the smaller horse's flank with a solid thud. Furious screams echoed through the arroyo.

"Can't you do something!" Christina appealed to Bert.

"Move if you don't want to get hurt!" he ordered.

Christina sat horrified as the gray horse continued the attack. Finally, when pushed back as far as he could go against the bluff, the Spaniard retaliated. He used the hard-packed earth behind him for leverage and reared back, his front legs spinning like a windmill. He struck his front hooves across the massive chest of the taller, bulkier horse. The gray retreated with a large gash across his chest and a cut above his muzzle. Both wounds were bleeding profusely.

"Oh my God," Christina cried. "They're going to kill each other!"

"It just looks that way," Bert said. "They're fighting for dominance. I'd say we may be interrupting their plans to mate. Maybe today's not the best time to try and capture a horse."

"Couldn't we at least try?" Christina worried that this trip might be her only chance. "I'd sure love to have that Spaniard." She knew in her gut that the Spanish mustang was the horse for her. He had the perfect spirit, size, and conformation to make her a good partner. He was magnificent.

"Better listen to Bert!" Charley yelled. "He knows what he's doing."

As if Bert hadn't heard Charley, he reversed his opinion. "Course, this might be the closest the herd will be in this area for some time. Let's see if they settle down a bit and then try for the Spaniard."

"But I thought you said—" Charley began, but gave up when he saw the expression on Christina's determined face.

Not thirty minutes later, Bert ordered, "Get your

ropes ready. We'll approach him from three sides. I'll take a run at him first. When you two get your ropes on him, stay in your saddles and hold on tight. I'll jump down and hobble him."

As they rode toward the herd, most of the horses fled, frightened. This was okay with Christina since they were only there for one horse. A few stood their ground out of curiosity, blowing and snorting their greetings. As planned, Bert was the first to lasso the Spaniard; he gave him just enough rope to struggle against, not pulling it taut. Christina rushed in and threw her rope, but missed. She circled again for a second try and thrilled to see her rope arc in the sky and make a solid landing around the stallion's neck. She pulled hard on the rope, dallying it around the saddle horn, which sent the mustang into a spasm of motion.

Charley advanced a bit too close as he threw his rope. He, too, missed and circled around for a better angle. His horse was bucking and Charley's limited experience with roping showed. He had enough to do just getting his horse calmed down for another try.

The Spaniard continued to rear back, straining against the ropes, his eyes wildly scanning his would-be captors as he attempted to escape. Foaming spittle flew from his mouth and his blood-curdling screams only grew stronger the more desperate he became. Bert jumped off his horse and pulled the rope tighter, digging his heels into the ground. But the stallion was too strong for him. Bert fell face first into the stone-covered soil.

Christina was losing strength; her arms and thighs quivered with exhaustion. She didn't know how long she could hold out. Buttercup was no match for the stallion, and it felt like she was faltering just as Charley's horse had.

The stallion dragged Bert through punishing sage-brush until he finally released his rope. When he did, the Spaniard reared up and loomed over him.

"No!" Christina screamed.

At the last minute, Bert rolled away from hooves that struck just inches from his head.

Christina backed up to keep the rope taut. Hers was now the lone rope securing the stallion who appeared to have lost interest in the prone cowboy and had concentrated on wrenching away. At the last minute, Christina released the rope from her horn to avoid injury. The glistening stallion bolted and ran with ropes trailing after him to the top of the bluff. He stamped the ground and violently tossed his head from side to side while releasing horrible, screaming sounds like something a banshee might make.

"You okay?" Charley dismounted and went to Bert's side.

"Yeah, I'm okay." He stood up and retrieved his dusty hat. "That bastard Spaniard is a demon. Don't think anyone is going to capture him."

Want to bet, Christina thought. She was shaken, but

thrilled. A second later, she felt ashamed of herself. Her first thought had been about losing the horse, not about Bert's close call.

She stroked Buttercup's neck, noticing the lather the mare had worked up. She needed to be rubbed down and cooled off. Christina led the horse to water and, after grabbing a towel from her saddle bag, she wiped down the mare's wet hide.

Charley came up behind Christina. She felt his presence but refused to acknowledge him until he touched her on the shoulder.

"Sorry I couldn't have been more help, Christina."

"Yeah, sure you are," she said. "You didn't want me to get a horse in the first place."

He dropped his hand. "That one could have killed Bert. Is that what you want? A horse at any cost!"

"No, of course not. It's just that—I'll probably never find another horse like him."

"Sometimes I just don't understand you, Christina." Charley turned and headed back to his own horse, tending to it as Christina had done with Buttercup.

Bert joined Christina by the stream, dunking his head in the water. When he pulled himself upright, he shook the water off like a spaniel.

"Ah, that's better," he said. He unbuttoned his shirt pocket and pulled out a metal flask he put to his lips. He took a long pull on it and thrust it toward Christina. She shook her head.

"I thought you didn't drink alcohol," she said. "The Eilers discourage it, don't they?"

"Well, old man Eiler wasn't almost trampled by a horse now, was he? They have their beliefs and I have mine." He patted his shirt pocket where he had returned the flask. "I believe in the church of moonshine." He flashed a quick smile. "We'd better head back. That's enough excitement for one day."

"Of course," she agreed, but didn't feel like giving up and heading back to the ranch. When she pulled herself up on Buttercup, Christina suddenly felt dizzy. *No sense in saying anything. It'll pass like the other times.*

The three riders slowly worked their way out of the arroyo to higher ground and headed north toward the ranch. Bert led, Charley followed, but Christina lagged behind. No one said a word. Christina didn't want to talk anyway. She just wanted to savor the memory of those moments when sheer animal power, greater than any she had experienced—even from Gabriel—charged through her from that magnificent Spanish beast. She wondered if they *had* successfully captured him, would he have been more horse than she could have managed.

In addition to the exhaustion that had slowly overcome her, Christina felt a stab of pain low down in her abdomen, radiating to her back. With every rhythmic sway and four-beat step that Buttercup took, Christina grew more uncomfortable. The sun was hot and they were still miles from the ranch. *What's happening to me?*

She felt herself wavering in the saddle and the next thing she knew she was on the ground, her head cradled in Charley's lap, he gently slapping her cheeks.

"Christina, wake up, honey."

She opened her eyes to find Charley's face close to hers, worry lines creasing his forehead.

"Thank God you came to!" he said.

"What happened?" She tried to sit up and then plunked back down, succumbing to vertigo.

"You fell from the saddle and—" His eyes moistened and shifted to the long trousers she was wearing.

"Am I okay, Charley?" Something in his expression alarmed her. She forced herself to sit up and then she saw her trousers covered in blood.

"Did I scrape my leg?" She reached down to touch the spot and then felt a stickiness between her legs. "What happened to me?"

"I checked where the blood was coming from and—"

"What? What is it, Charley?"

Bert was sitting on a rock a short distance away looking in the opposite direction, but apparently was within earshot.

"Boy, are you two green," he said from his perch. "Your woman was pregnant, Charley. Didn't you know?"

"What? Is that right Christina?"

"Charley, I..."

"Why didn't you say something? Why would you risk coming out here if you knew?"

"Charley, I can explain."

"I wouldn't have brought her if *I'd* have known," Bert said. He pulled out his tobacco pouch and began rolling a cigarette.

"Christina, I don't understand." Charley looked perplexed. Soon, anger replaced confusion and finally his face collapsed into sorrow. He bent his head to touch her forehead. "We lost our baby?"

"I'm sorry, Charley." Christina threw her arms around his neck and began to cry. "I've made such a mess of things."

He held her tight. "As long as you're okay..." He failed to finish his thought.

Later that evening after she had been bathed and was put to bed, Christina couldn't get the image out of her head: lying on the ground with Charley holding her, his eyes looking so sad. How could she explain that she didn't know her own body? Or did she choose not to know it since she wasn't ready to have a child.

"Why didn't you say something before?" he had asked her.

"I don't know, Charley. I was kind of hoping it wasn't true. You know, I told you before that I wasn't keen on having a bunch of babies—at least not yet."

It was the wrong thing to say. Charley pulled back from her as if she were a hot stove he had just touched.

CHAPTER SIXTEEN

Jennie

As they left the train depot, Lucy inspected the features of Violet's lavishly appointed carriage and gawked out the window at the sights. Jennie smiled at Lucy's reaction to the bustling activity on the streets. It was market day in Concordia, when farmers traveled to town to buy or barter for goods.

Jennie remembered her first ride in Violet's carriage when she went to live with her. She was so excited to be leaving the shabbiness of the Neamott farm that she had waved and smiled at her brother through the rear window, even as his image receded. It wasn't until they reached the end of the rural lane that Jennie saw Charley running after them and realized their separation might be permanent. She began to cry.

"What's this? What's that?" Lucy asked as they passed the tea room, the post office, and the general store.

Violet looked sternly toward the duo as Lucy's raspy voice was loud and excitable, drowning out the conversation between her and Mary Belle.

"Speak a little more softly, Lucy," Jennie said into the child's ear.

"You mean like this?" Lucy whispered. Her whisper was almost as loud as her normal voice. Jennie couldn't help but laugh.

"Please, Jennie. Don't encourage her."

Violet's being her prim self this afternoon, Jennie thought, annoyed. Lucy was just expressing a child's natural curiosity. If Violet wasn't as welcoming to Lucy as she had been toward her when she first joined the household, Jennie definitely would have to take Lucy under her wing.

When they arrived at the mansion, Violet busied herself with seeing to her cousin's needs. She had given her the large guest room down the hall from her boudoir.

"I'm not sure where we'll put Lucy," she said to her housekeeper. "Perhaps the servant's quarters."

"Or she could stay in my room with me," Jennie suggested.

"I'm not sure you know what you're letting yourself in for," Violet said. "You'll have little privacy."

Lucy looked uncertain as her eyes shifted between Violet and Jennie.

"I think it would be a comfort to Lucy on her first night."

Violet's hand fluttered in the air helplessly.

"Do as you wish. For now, I need to get Mary Belle settled." She turned and headed down the hall.

Lucy hugged Jennie and padded after her.

"First thing we need to do is find room for your belongings," Jennie said as they entered her bedroom. Lucy
ran from window to bed to chifferobe, spinning to take in
her new surroundings.

"Oh," she cried. "It smells so good in here."

Jennie laughed to think that the way a room smelled
was the first thing the child noticed. Of course, having
lived in an orphanage herself, she remembered the variety of unpleasant smells of too many bodies crowded into
too small a space. She especially remembered the odors
of bad food, often on the edge of spoilage.

"Let's see what you have in here," Jennie said as she
opened up the small cloth bag that held Lucy's things.
She pulled out a plain cotton dress and one pair of dingy
looking bloomers as well as worn tights with a run in
them. A rag-thin coat with a missing button was rolled
up at the bottom. There were no extras or frills like ribbons for her hair. These were Lucy's sole possessions.

"Do I get to sleep in this bed with you, Jennie?"

"You certainly do." She smiled as she recalled how
the feather bed seemed too big for her at first and how
she fancied sharing it with Ruthie and Sarah Neamott—
just as they had shared their bed in the loft with her. But
of course, the Neamott sisters were never invited. Violet
always found an excuse when Jennie brought up the subject.

"Let's make room for your things in the chifferobe

next to mine," Jennie said, getting back to the business of helping Lucy settle in. She opened the mirrored door of the closet and Lucy's mouth dropped open.

"Look at all the beautiful dresses!" Lucy reached out to touch a turquoise blue gown.

"Yes, they are nice," Jennie scolded herself; she should have thought better of exposing her large wardrobe to a child who had nothing. It was insensitive. She gently closed the doors. "Better yet, we'll launder your things and first thing tomorrow we'll go to town and get you a few new frocks to hang next to mine. Would you like that?"

"May I pick them out myself?"

"Of course you may—or maybe with Violet's help. She has such good taste." She should have thought better of making a promise she might not be able to keep.

While Lucy was busy exploring the big house, Jennie sought out Violet.

"Violet, the child has nothing," Jennie explained. "Did you notice that Lucy doesn't even own a decent pair of shoes? Maybe we could take her shopping tomorrow."

"I never promised to outfit her, Jennie. Isn't it enough that I've taken her in?"

"Violet, it's not like you to deny a child what she needs. I'm not asking for anything more than the basics. You wouldn't want people to judge you for not providing for a helpless child." Jennie let this remark sink in for a minute. "She will be accompanying us from time to time, and I know you and Mary Belle want her to look proper, don't you?"

"Well, when you put it that way, I guess I don't have a choice. But I'm much too busy to attend to it. You'll just have to use your best judgment and accompany her." Violet fanned her face with her hand, a sure sign that she was frazzled. "I'll have the carriage brought around in the morning. But," she added in a firm voice, "you must be back for the afternoon tea I'm hosting to introduce Mary Belle to the ladies of Concordia."

"The Ladies of Concordia," as they were referred to, were an older group of women like Violet—rich and demanding—with lots of idle time on their hands. Jennie was bored and restless in their company.

As an afterthought, Violet said, "When did you plan on training Lucy to help serve Mary Belle? Wasn't that the reason we took her in?"

"Can we talk about her duties later, Violet? She's just getting adjusted to her new surroundings."

"Of course. I'm not sure how much help such a young girl can be anyway. Since this is only temporary, we won't worry ourselves about it just now."

Uh oh. Maybe, I should worry. Somehow, she would have to make Lucy look indispensable.

That evening, while Violet, Mary Belle, and Jennie dined in the dining room on roast pheasant, Lucy was assigned to eat with the servants in the kitchen. Violet was firm that Lucy not be included in their formal sharing of meals. Although it bothered Jennie that Violet was being insensitive, she knew she must pick her battles carefully. Lucy was oblivious to the slight and seemed delighted with the steamy, warm ambience of the kitchen while Lily, the maid, chattered in her Irish brogue. Lily had taken a liking to Lucy as they exchanged stories about Boston. Cook was not quite so friendly. Jennie overheard her comment to Lily: "Isn't it enough that I have to prepare all of Mary Belle's favorite dishes? Now I have to cater to a street urchin as well."

"She's no street urchin!" Lily retorted. "She comes from a proper orphanage I'll have you know."

That evening after dinner, Jennie asked Lily to make sure that Lucy had a bath in the copper tub. "And add a few drops of my jasmine water, will you."

"But, Miss Jennie, it's going to take a good long while for the water to be heated for the bath and Miss Violet wants me to help Miss Mary Belle prepare for her evening toilette." Lily wrung her hands.

"Oh, of course. If you just ask cook to heat the water and fill a pitcher, I'll assist Lucy in at least getting a good sponge bath."

"Bless you for looking out for her, Miss Jennie."

Over the years, Jennie developed a fondness for Lily, even though as a child she disliked her for a time. At Violet's insistence, Lily gave Jennie a severely short haircut. She had cut off all of her long curls, marking her as different from other Concordia girls, just when she desperately desired to fit in. And when Jennie dropped and broke the hand mirror, the superstitious Lily had predicted bad luck. Thereafter, every time something went wrong or was an unpleasant surprise, Lily would exclaim: "See, there's the bad luck from breaking the mirror, Miss Violet."

"Nonsense, Lily," Violet scolded.

When Lucy was down to her bloomers, Jennie helped her with a sponge bath. She noticed that the child's arms were especially thin and her ribs visible. She gently sponged Lucy's back with a soft cloth. It almost made her cry to see Lucy's spine jutting out. She was all skin and bones. Jennie remembered orphanage meals, where the portions served were meager. She felt a pang, not unlike the hunger pangs she had experienced in the Children's Home. She didn't think she would ever forget.

"I heard you talking to Lily," Jennie said. "She enjoys meeting someone else from Boston. Where in Boston were your people from?"

"They say the North End, but I don't really know. I was too little to remember much about the old neighborhood." Jennie turned Lucy around to face her.

"How old were you when you went to the Children's Home?"

"They say I was only three years old."

"Did you have any brothers or sisters?" Lucy hesitated as her eyes shifted away from Jennie.

"I don't know. They said I was the only child, but I

remember a baby in our flat being nursed—right before I was taken to the Home." She looked up and blinked. "Some things they told me I don't believe."

"Like what, Lucy?"

Jennie helped Lucy into one of her old shifts. It hung on her, but would have to serve as a nightgown until one in Lucy's size could be purchased tomorrow.

"I don't know." Lucy looked embarrassed at not being able to answer a simple question. "I don't remember." She shook her head as if to shake her memories loose. "They told me Mama and Papa brought me there because they couldn't take care of me anymore. I don't believe they would give me up. But that's what they said!" Lucy's words sounded desperate, the harsh rasp more prominent in her distress.

"Your folks didn't die, then?"

"I—don't—know!" Lucy began to cry.

"Oh, Lucy. I'm so sorry. We don't have to talk about it if you don't want to. I'm sorry I asked."

Lucy leaned into Jennie and snuffled. Jennie pulled her into an embrace, being careful not to hug her too hard for fear of breaking something in the fragile girl. She fought back tears of her own. It was one thing to have your parents die, but quite another to have them abandon you. She was determined to make up for what Lucy lost by convincing Violet to become the girl's new permanent guardian.

CHAPTER SEVENTEEN

Jennie

Lucy was a little subdued after last night's talk about her family. However, she had slept deeply, and during the night cuddled up against Jennie. Unused to sleeping with anyone, Jennie found Lucy's warm little body was like a heater. The child gravitated to a spot lying against her hip. Jennie didn't have the heart to push her away. It reminded her of the times she, Sarah, and Ruthie all cuddled in their loft bed.

Jennie lay awake for a long time, thinking about the time she and Charley spent in the orphanage. She barely remembered Mum and Pap from her days in Homestead, Pennsylvania. But she knew in her heart that they never would have given up on caring for their children.

Once they reached town and entered the general store, Lucy's spirits lifted.

"Oh, Jennie. Look at all the pretty dresses," she exclaimed, barely touching the fabric. "Do you think I could have one of these?"

"You may choose more than one, Lucy. And let's not

forget bloomers and socks and a nightgown that fits."

The inventory of dresses in the general store was limited. They were mainly made of gingham cotton in floral patterns. Nice enough for everyday, but certainly nothing special for more formal occasions when Lucy might be invited to sit at the dining table or be present at one of Violet's teas that she was fond of hosting.

As they made their way down the aisle with Lucy oohing and aahing, Jennie spied Peter Stuyvesant up front talking to the store owner. He turned and saw that Jennie was watching him. He nodded and approached her. Jennie felt embarrassed to have been caught staring at the man. She couldn't help herself—he seemed to fill up a room with his presence. She hadn't seen him since her last visit with Charley when Peter tagged along.

He had been very attentive that day, complimenting her appearance and asking questions about her plans for the future—something no one else did. She guessed most people expected that she would do whatever Violet had planned for her. Even Charley never asked what she wanted to do with her life or what her views were about a bigger world outside Concordia.

There was something about Peter that attracted Jennie. His manner was sophisticated and he appeared more stylish, even in the work pants called Levis that he and Charley wore. They were something new named after Levi Strauss, the man who invented denim jeans. Peter's straw colored hair had natural waves and complimented his tan complexion. She felt drawn in by his deep-set blue eyes and strong, broad chin when he smiled. She couldn't help picturing herself at his side.

Jennie hadn't been exposed to many young men in Concordia. Even if she had been, she doubted that any who passed Violet's inspection and gained her approval would be a match for the dashing Peter.

"Good morning, Miss Hunsinger," he said, approaching her. *Why the formality?* He had called her Jennie in Charley's presence.

"Good morning, Mr. Stuyvesant."

"If I may ask, what brings you out so early in the morning?"

"You may ask, but I doubt that it will be of any interest to you. I'm here to outfit Lucy—a new member of our household." As if on cue, Lucy peeked around a display of dresses at Peter.

"I heard your guest was a lady from the South, not a young girl."

"Yes, Violet's cousin Mary Belle from New Orleans is staying with us too. Lucy came in on the orphan train yesterday." Jennie motioned for Lucy to join them. "Actually, she has agreed to make her home with us."

Peter's eyebrows lifted in surprise. "Well, she chose very wisely. I must add that you are looking especially lovely this morning. I'm sure Charley would be pleased that you are getting on so well."

At the mention of Charley's name, Jennie started. It

saddened her that her brother was so far away—heaven only knew where. She remembered that Violet would not be persuaded to give Charley a loan to help keep their business afloat. If she had, Charley would still be in Concordia. She didn't know the details of the falling out between her brother and Peter, but it must have had some bearing on why Violet refused to back their business venture. She overheard Violet tell a friend: "Why should I invest money in their enterprise? Any business that Peter Stuyvesant is involved in is sure to fail."

"May I call on you sometime, Miss Hunsinger?" Peter asked, surprising Jennie.

"You'll need to ask my mother." The minute the words left her mouth, Jennie turned crimson. "I...I...mean—" she stammered.

"She checks out your suitors? That's a good thing. I'm sure that many young men in Concordia desire time with you." He smiled.

"Not so many that I wouldn't have time for you," Jennie said without thinking.

"I'm flattered to hear it."

What's gotten into me to act so forward? She looked down at Lucy as an excuse to end the conversation and escape further embarrassment. "If you'll excuse us," she said. "We need to see to our purchases. Come along Lucy."

"Of course. Until I see you again." Peter bowed his head, but Jennie acted as if she hadn't noticed.

By the time they left the general store, she had outfitted Lucy in the basics, including an extra pair of shoes and bright ribbons for her red hair. But they left with more than baubles. For Lucy, it was clothing and necessities she had done without for so long. For Jennie, it was male attention that she had missed altogether. She no longer wanted to forego it, finding it a very pleasant diversion. However, the idea that Peter could convince Violet to let him call on her was out of the question. Surely, Violet would not consider him a worthy suitor after what she had said to her friend. If Jennie ever hoped to see him again, it would have to be in town like today—by accident. A chance meeting was all she could hope for.

CHAPTER EIGHTEEN

Christina

As exhausted as she was from the day's sad ending, Christina lay awake and turned over in her mind the events that had occurred in the last twenty-four hours: she had lost a baby and she had lost a horse. And if she wasn't careful she would lose Charley.

To be honest, Christina was relieved to not have the responsibility of an unwanted pregnancy. Her attitude was a terrible disappointment to Charley, but she hoped he would eventually get past it. Neither of them was in a position to be parents at present, knocking about the country in a boxcar. There would be another time—a better time—after they married and were settled and when they were *both* ready to start a family.

However, the lost opportunity to capture a wild horse still rankled. What if there wasn't another time when she could take part in a roundup? Someday she might find a horse with the same qualities Gabriel had, but she may never see another Spaniard with wild blood coursing through its veins and a free spirit she had come to love in the huge beasts.

Where had this obsession with horses come from? It couldn't have been from birth. She had no exposure to the world of horses in the big city of Pittsburgh. It wasn't until she came to Concordia and worked in the livery stable with Carl that she had been taken with the animals. Ever since she bonded with Gabriel, she felt the need for a horse in her life to be content. She remembered how upset she was when Carl sold Gabriel. Helpless to prevent the sale, Christina allowed her desire for another horse to overshadow other parts of her life. Later, when a stranger came by the stables one day, she thought they had a chance to reclaim Gabriel. She overheard the man talking to Carl.

"Say, didn't you have a quarter horse a while back, fiery as all hell?"

"Yep. He turned out to be a good mount. Sorry I had to sell him."

"That's what I'm getting at. Saw a horse looked just like him at a stud farm over Garberville way."

"Could be," Carl replied. "I sold him for stud. Glad to hear he's still being used for breeding."

"I don't know how useful he is. I learn't he was up for bid. Stud farm is going under is what I heard."

Christina cornered Carl as soon as the man left.

"Carl, did you hear what he said? You interested in getting Gabriel back?"

"Sorry, girl. That's all in the past. I don't have need for a big stallion. Boarding horses and shoeing them is all

I'm into these days."

Christina screwed up her face before responding. "Well, then *I'd* like to bid on him. We know his training. He's family!"

"What! Even if you had enough money squirreled away to buy him, do you know the expense involved in keeping a horse?"

"I've saved a little money and if you let me board him here for free, I'll pay you back. I promise." Carl looked uncomfortable and scratched his head vigorously as if digging for answers. "I told myself that if I ever found him again," Christina said in her most convincing tone, "I'd try to get Gabriel back. Isn't Garberville only a half-day's ride from here?"

"It is, but you can't make that hard ride by yourself."

"I wouldn't have to if you'd go with me," she said, batting her eyelashes.

"Now Christina, I'm too busy this time of year to take off."

"If you would lend me one of the livery horses to go and get him, I'd be grateful."

Carl paced a bit before taking a firm stand: "I'll loan you a *couple* of horses for the ride over, only if you find someone to go with you."

Christina imagined riding the big-boned quarter horse again and ponying the livery horses back. "Thanks, Carl." She threw her arms around him, and raced off to find Charley.

"I don't know, Christina," Charley said when she proposed the idea. "That's a long way and I've got farms lined up for plowing. I can't take the time off right now."

Christina's shoulders dropped as she tried to think of a persuasive argument to convince him. With Gabriel so close by, she couldn't let the opportunity to buy him disappear. She could almost smell his scent and feel his quivering flesh when he was excited. She searched her mind for anyone else who could come with her. But there was no one, really.

Christina returned to the stable and told Carl that she and Charley would make the trip the following day. "I'm meeting Charley at the Neamott farm where he's been working. We'll take off from there." Carl looked doubtful but released two horses with the promise that she and Charley give them proper breaks.

"Don't ride 'em too hard," he said. "They're my best horses."

Christina hated lying to Carl, and to Charley too. But she wasn't going to let anything stand in her way. She had hidden her savings in her saddlebag, along with food and canteens of water for the journey. But first, she took enough time to drop the second horse off at the Neamott's with no other explanation than she would pick him up on the way back the following day. Old man Neamott had never been her favorite person because of his history with Charley. But he would never neglect or mistreat an animal. He had a good relationship with Carl too. Knowing that the horse Christina left in his care belonged to Carl guaranteed he would be mindful of its needs.

All she could think of during the long hours of riding was that if she had known Gabriel was this close to Concordia she would have tried to buy him sooner.

Just outside of Garberville, Christina saw a cloud of dust and knew she was close to a place where horses gathered. The stud farm, nestled in a valley near a freshwater creek lined with poplars, appeared on the horizon. Green grass flourished by the stream, but farther away, the wind and spring warmth had turned the grass dry. A small herd of horses grazed among the trees.

She soon entered a compound consisting of a large ranch house and barn with multiple stables and outbuildings. A small group had gathered around a man with a clipboard who was auctioning off livestock. She sidled up to a ranch hand who stood apart from the bidders. "Excuse me, where are all the horses for sale?"

"They're in the stable." He jerked his head toward the nearest outbuilding. "Most have already been sold."

When Christina entered the stable it was to the sound of hooves stamping and snorting.

"Gabriel?" she called out and made the clucking sound he had liked. Some horses responded, but she didn't recognize Gabriel's distinctive greeting—two snorts followed by nickering. She could tell by the increased activity that the horses were anxious. She walked down the wooden aisle looking in at each stall to see if she could find him. When she completed the search, she doubled back, certain that she had missed him.

"Ma'am, the time for inspecting the animals is over and the auction is underway," said the ranch hand Christina had spoken to just minutes before. "Seems you're upsetting the horses."

"I'm sorry. I was just trying to find Gabriel, a quarter horse stallion who was bought a few years ago in Concordia. He was chestnut colored," she added.

"We had a horse of that description, but I don't know where he came from."

"Had?" Christina cried. "What happened to him?"

"You just missed him, ma'am. He was sold earlier today and should be on his way to a Kentucky stud farm."

"Oh no!" Christina felt her stomach sink. "I missed him? But I was going to bid on him. I have money and everything."

"Sorry, ma'am, but you're too late. He's already gone."

Christina dropped onto a nearby stool and lowered her head into her hands. She hated to show weakness in front of strangers.

"You okay? Can I get you some water or something?"

"No, I'll be fine." She sat up straight and rubbed a hot, dirty fist across moist eyes. Clenching her jaw to keep from crying, she mumbled, "I'll just be leaving."

She remounted Carl's horse and headed for the creek.

After resting the mare and drinking freely from the cold water, Christina mopped her forehead, neck, and face. She barely registered her surroundings, as the heaviness of loss hung over her.

Finally, she decided that instead of camping out for the night, she would begin the long trip back to Concordia where she could nurse her disappointment. *How could I have lost Gabriel a second time?* Her burning desire for ownership of the stallion could not be quenched even though she knew she would no longer attempt to locate him. Kentucky was too far away to even contemplate.

When she returned to the Neamott's place, Charley was there waiting for her. It was past sundown, but there was still enough light to see that his face was sunburned. And by the slouch in his shoulders she knew he was upset. *Well, I'm upset too.* Defeat tasted bitter in her mouth. Christina was ashamed of her deceit, especially when it failed to get her what she wanted. Charley helped her dismount without saying a word and then led her horse to the water trough and busied himself with wiping down the reddish coat.

Sarah Neamott emerged from the house and unable to mask her curiosity said, "We heard you went to Garberville on your own." Now that Sarah was growing up, she resembled her mother, Emma. Christina recalled that Sarah was especially close to Emma before she died giving birth to Willie, who was now an energetic four year old. "Was it scary on the range all by yourself?"

"Not too much." Christina looked anxiously toward Charley, who was just out of earshot and busy ignoring her.

"Papa says Charley got upset when you promised Carl that he was going with you."

"I can see that, Sarah," Christina whispered. "What did he say?"

"Said he didn't take you for a liar and—" Sarah stopped herself. She was very fond of Charley, who had been like a big brother to her all the years he lived with the family. She would never say a bad word about him. Christina wouldn't be surprised if Sarah was developing a little crush on Charley. But, at thirteen years old, she was way too young for him to notice her.

Enoch emerged from the barn and glared at Christina. It seemed that she was surrounded by frowns and silence. It might have been worth it if she had bought Gabriel. But as it stood, she returned empty handed and was shown to be a liar once again.

What was the use of bringing up all her misgivings in the middle of the night when she needed to sleep? What was done was done. Christina would just have to be patient while she waited her chance to go after another mustang. In the meantime, she would have to make things up to Charley and try to get him to see things from her point of view.

Sometimes she wished Charley expected less from her. Before meeting him, there was no one in her life who thought she would accomplish much. So, when she failed, there was no one standing by who was disappointed. There was a freedom to this.

She glanced out the window and saw the full moon sliding behind the mountains. It was heading for morning. She punched her pillow and turned over, determined to clear her mind and get a few hours of sleep before facing Charley again.

CHAPTER NINETEEN

Christina

The next morning, Christina purposely stayed in bed until the others had eaten and left the kitchen to do their chores. She didn't want to deal with Charley and Bert so soon after yesterday's drama, and she certainly didn't want to face the questioning faces of the Eiler clan. She was tired and still a little weak, but at least she wasn't nauseous.

When she finally dressed and entered the kitchen, Ruth was busy cleaning up after a large breakfast. She was up to her elbows in water, washing dishes, and had the cast iron frying pan sprinkled with coarse salt for scrubbing later.

Christina grabbed a cup from a shelf and picked up the coffee pot simmering with the chicory brew the Eilers favored. She poured a stout cup of the black steaming liquid. Sure enough, it was bitter and tasted stronger for having set awhile. But it jolted her awake and that's what she needed.

"Good morning," Ruth said without turning around. "How are you feeling this morning?"

"Okay, I guess."

"Heard about your sorrow. But you're young. You'll have other babies."

As if this was meant to be comforting, Christina accepted it for what it was—an effort to make her feel better. However, it *didn't* make her feel better. Instead, it only served to leave her anxious about another pregnancy. What could she do to prevent it? The women she knew didn't usually talk about such things. Maggie, the school teacher who took her in when she no longer could remain with Carl at the stable, was the closest thing Christina had to a big sister. Like a sister, she had taught her many things about being ladylike and respecting herself as a woman. But Maggie's most important contribution had been to encourage Christina to get as much education as she could to prepare for a world beyond the kitchen. It was her doing that sparked Christina's interest in reading.

"That's just it, Ruth," Christina began. Her voice quavered. "I don't want to have a baby." This got Ruth's attention; she turned from her task and looked queerly at Christina.

"I mean, it's not the right time for Charley and me to begin a family."

"I see," Ruth said and grabbed a towel to dry her hands. "God determines the time."

She poured a cup of chicory coffee for herself and poured a generous amount of fresh cream into it. "I never could get used to this strong a brew," she confided. "Cream helps. Want some?"

"Thank you, but I don't want to get used to having cream in my coffee," Christina said, smiling. "Where we go, we never know if we'll get cream in our coffee—or even coffee for that matter."

Ruth sat down across from Christina. "It's clear you're troubled," she said. "And from the looks of him, so is Charley. He barely spoke a word this morning at breakfast."

"I figured he would be upset. But you see, Ruth, I'm not ready to settle for just having babies. There's so much more I want to do before that happens. If only there was some way that I could—"

"Prevent it?" Ruth said, sharply. "Well, you can stop bedding down with Charley. That should do it."

Christina blushed and took a shallow breath. "No, I mean, isn't there some other way?"

"Women have been asking that forever," Ruth said, clearing her throat. "That's why Mormons figured it all out. If one of the wives is—indisposed—or feels her fertile time is upon her, she abstains. The man can be satisfied with one of his other wives."

"I thought the reason there were more wives was that Mormons wanted to multiply more quickly than would be possible with just one wife."

"That's true too. There are many reasons as laid down in The Book of Mormon. Too bad Mormons decided to ban polygamy," Ruth said with displeasure. "That's why we broke away and formed our own religious group. So we could continue the practice. But you're asking about how to prevent having babies. Abstinence is the only way I know, even though I've heard about potions and other primitive methods." She shook her head and stood up. "Those who do things to prevent a baby or try to get rid of it are—evil." The blazing look Ruth gave Christina left her with goose bumps. "You best get used to being a woman," she said.

Before Christina could respond, Agatha and the children streamed into the room.

"Time for lessons," Agatha said. "Okay if I clear the table, Ruth?"

"Go ahead. I think we're finished here."

"Yes. Of course," Christina agreed. She scooted her chair back and felt a little wobbly as she moved away from the table.

"Will you be helping us today?" Chester asked Christina, his sharp, clear gaze trained on her.

"Not today." She felt tearful and didn't want anyone to see how upset she had become.

Christina was overcome by confusion. It was as if sexuality was a trap. It could bring pleasure. But it could also place a woman in danger. Besides the risks of childbirth, there were other circumstances in which a woman was at a disadvantage. She thought about the time she was twelve years old and living alone on the streets of

Pittsburgh. She had been sleeping in one of the alleys when she awoke to see two men standing over her, unbuttoning their trousers. She screamed as she tried to scramble up and escape. If it hadn't been for Sean and his gang, who heard her cry for help, Christina knew what would have been in store for her.

She turned back to Chester. "Maybe later we can read together, okay?" He flashed a big smile her way. It was too much. She ran for her room before she broke down and cried in front of him.

CHAPTER TWENTY

Charley

Charley braced himself for the conversation he was about to initiate with John Eiler over his back wages. He wanted his pay and wouldn't take no for an answer. Christina and he needed to leave the Eiler ranch without further delay. At the beginning of their journey, Christina had convinced him that there were no obstacles to them hopping a freight together and making their way west. But after her accident, he saw that Christina was as physically vulnerable as other women and shouldn't be riding roughshod through life like it was a Sunday trotting horse she had tamed. He mourned their unborn baby. But even more, he missed the carefree, trusting relationship he and Christina had enjoyed.

"John, I need to collect my wages so that Christina and I can move on," he began.

Mr. Eiler scrunched up his eyes and removed his hat. "Well, Charley, I'd sure like to pay up, but I don't have the extra money just yet."

Charley felt his neck muscles tense as he tried to keep the anger from his voice.

"When *will* you get the money?"

"As soon as I can get some more bales sold and shipped out. Shouldn't be more than a couple of weeks."

"A couple of weeks! That's no good. We really need to leave *now* if we're going to get to California by fall. I want to get settled before winter sets in."

"You don't need to worry much about a California winter, Charley. They don't get harsh weather like in the Midwest. That is, unless you settle in those Sierras. I hear they caught some folks trying to get through in, or about, 1846. The Donner-Reed party, I think. Terrible business," Eiler said, shaking his head. "They turned to cannibalism, you know."

"Wasn't thinking of settling in the mountains. We're heading for the flatlands. Hear the Sacramento Valley is fertile and easy to farm."

"Sacramento? Isn't that where they found gold?"

"Thereabouts, I hear. About our wages, Mr. Eiler..."

"When there's fertile soil to be tilled, only a man bent on folly would waste his time with a gold pan," Eiler interrupted. Before Charley could respond, the old man rambled on. "Say, I'm right sorry about Christina losing your baby. She should stick around a little and rest up."

"She'll be okay." Charley turned and looked off into the distance. He didn't want to discuss Christina's condition with John—or anyone—for that matter. The subject was too raw.

"I might be able to advance you half your wages if

you're in a hurry to leave," Eiler said. "It would probably see to *your* needs, but not both of you."

Charley abruptly turned back to face John Eiler.

"What are you saying?"

"Just that if you're in such a hurry, you might go on ahead and get settled. Let Christina stay with us for a while. She could join you later."

"And just how would she join me then? I'm not letting her ride the rails alone," Charley sputtered.

"I agree. That would be unsafe." Eiler smiled. "In due time, when you're settled, Christina could buy a passenger ticket with the other half of your wages and train west to meet you. How does that sound?"

Even though he didn't want to go on without Christina, Eiler's suggestion made sense. Charley wouldn't have to worry about her and could move about more quickly. That is if he could count on John Eiler to pay the balance of his wages to Christina. And if Christina agreed to the plan and could be trusted not to pursue another wild mustang once he was absent.

"Let me think about it, John."

His thinking about it was only half the solution. Convincing Christina might be the hardest part. Charley walked the perimeter of the ranch, kicking at rocks and dirt clods and anything else that crossed his path. His anger and frustration finally spent, he took in the smell of sagebrush and the sound of the wind blowing through his hair. It calmed him some.

Charley looked west to the faded outline of mountains surrounding the valley and made his decision.

"Let's go for a walk, Christina," Charley suggested several evenings later. It was after supper—a meal he barely touched. He was too preoccupied about the proposal he was about to make. Christina readily agreed to a stroll and, though they were silent for the first few minutes, it wasn't unusual. Most times he chose his words carefully before he spoke.

"A couple of days ago I talked to John about my wages," he began.

Christina perked up. "What did he say?"

Charley looked off into the distance. "Said he couldn't give me what's owed. Offered half for now and the other half when the crop gets hauled for shipping."

"How long will that take?"

"Weeks." He stopped and looked at her. "Weeks we don't have."

"Well, Charley, what else can we do?" She turned to look at him and stepped into a gopher hole. Charley grabbed her by the arm before she tripped and fell. "Guess I'm still a little weak," she admitted. "Do you mind if we find a place to sit down for a minute?"

They were near one of the hay wagons ready for hauling. Charley lifted Christina onto the wagon seat and climbed in beside her. He took her hand in his.

"That's what I was thinking, Christina—that you're

still weak and need a little time to rest up after..." He cleared his throat before continuing. "You're not in any shape to continue our trip just yet."

"What do you mean?"

"I'm going to accept John's offer of the wages he has to give me now. When the hay goes to market, he'll give you the other half owed me. You can use it for a train ticket to California." He smiled. "You'll be able to ride in style instead of bouncing around in the back of an old boxcar."

"I don't understand."

"I'm leaving in the morning to continue on and find a place for us to settle. I'll write and keep you informed and when you're ready, you can join me."

"You're leaving without me!" she cried as she stood up. It was too sudden. Christina's knees gave out and she plopped back down hard on the bench seat. "Why are you in such a wildfire hurry to leave? You don't even know where you're going," she sputtered. "Or what you're going to find when you get there!"

"I'll know it when I see it, Christina. A man has to have direction. Without plans he might as well be riding a train to nowhere."

"I don't understand," she repeated, covering her face with her hands. "Are you so upset with me over the baby that you don't want to be with me anymore?"

"Oh no, not at all, Christina." He slipped an arm around her and pulled her close. "What's happened just proved to me that a trip like this was not meant for a woman. I don't want to risk your health and—"

"I'm just too much trouble—that's really it!" Christina stood and stumbled out of the wagon. "You didn't want to take me in the first place and now when the least little thing looks like a problem to you, you're giving up on me. If that's the way you feel, Charley, then go on. I won't try to stop you." She stormed off toward the house.

"Wait, Christina," he called after her, but she refused to answer as she stomped over the dirt clods with surprising vigor.

Charley saw some truth in what she said. But there was no time to argue with her or stick around and debate the matter further. He intended to be on that first train leaving in the morning.

He reasoned that she would see the wisdom in this plan when she cooled down. And he felt that she was in safe hands with the Eilers. The women and children would keep Christina occupied and perhaps some of their ways would rub off on her. She needed to have some of the rough edges smoothed if she was going to be a good wife. He still smarted over the way she kept the baby a secret from him. Had he known, he would have watched out for her better and insisted that she not go on a wild goose chase—or, in this instance, a wild horse chase—in her condition.

The next morning came early. Charley had his few belongings stowed in a rucksack and was saddling up one of the stable horses to ride into Promontory. It had been arranged for him to leave it tied up at the café for Bert to pick up later.

"You got to have something to eat for the long ride over the Sierras," Ruth said as she followed him outside and handed him a parcel tied with string. "There's a loaf of fresh bread inside, a block of cheese I wrapped in cloth to keep it moist, and some wild crab apples. They're kind of tart, but you'll get used to them."

"Thank you, Ruth. I appreciate it."

Ruth brushed off his thanks with a wave of her hand. "And don't worry," she said. "We'll take good care of Christina."

"I don't doubt it." Charley tried to give Ruth a hug, but she shrugged away.

"No need for that," she said.

She's not much for showing her feelings. But then Charley figured she reserved her hugs for those closest to her—family members of The Descendents.

He was about to mount the horse when he glanced back at the house and saw Christina looking at him through her window. He had tried to say his goodbyes earlier this morning. But when his gentle tapping on her door went unanswered, he figured there wasn't much sense in waking everyone up. There was also another reason he didn't knock louder: he feared her reaction to last night's parting. She had definitely been mad at him—and by the looks of it she had not forgiven him yet.

He hoped that she would come to understand his decision when she felt better. He waved at Christina, but she withdrew behind the curtain, disappearing from sight. There was nothing for Charley to do but leave with a heavy heart, vowing to make it up to her.

CHAPTER TWENTY-ONE

Jennie

It didn't take long for Jennie to figure out that if she were to see Peter again, it would only happen if she went to town without Violet. On several occasions she used Lucy as a ruse: "Lucy needs a cooler summer night-gown," she said, or "I forgot to pick up a petticoat for Lucy's new dress." Apparently, Violet didn't question why Lucy's needs increased with the length of time she was in the household instead of diminishing. She agreed to the extra shopping trips.

On those afternoons when she and Lucy ventured out, unaccompanied, Jennie pointed out Concordia's landmarks and ended their day at the soda shop. Peter must have followed them the last time, as he conveniently joined the two at the entrance.

"You ladies seem to enjoy your sweets," he said, open-ing the door for them. "Allow me to treat you to the best ice cream sundae in town." Lucy's eyes lit up as she rushed through the door. He seated them at a small, round, marble-topped table supported by wrought iron while he placed an order at the counter.

The weather had turned hot, and the paddle fan overhead whirred lazily. Jennie wished she had worn something lighter than the dress with multi-layered ruffles. Lucy, who was dressed in a similar manner, made no effort to hide her discomfort. She scratched where the fabric bunched up and she lifted her skirts above her knees for air.

"Lucy, lower your skirts. You don't look ladylike." To her own ears, Jennie sounded just like Violet, who had reprimanded her frequently when she first came to live with her. *Don't be so hard on Lucy. She's been through enough.* Teaching her the rules of the house was okay when they were *in* the house. Jennie decided the girl deserved a little freedom when they were away from Violet's scrutiny.

"That's okay, Lucy. You can lift them a little bit, but please keep your legs together," she whispered. Lucy smiled a toothy grin.

"Here we go. Sweets for the sweetest ladies in town." Peter lowered a tray loaded down with ice cream sundaes covered in chocolate and whipped cream with cherries on top. A vanilla wafer set into the ice cream at a jaunty angle completed the picture. Lucy's eyes widened at the sight and, without another word, she grabbed a spoon and began to dig in.

"This is very kind of you, Mr. Stuyvesant." Jennie lifted the red cherry to her lips and skimmed it from its stem with her teeth.

Peter smiled and nodded, but did not pick up his spoon. "I wonder if I may speak candidly, Miss Hunsinger?" His penetrating blue eyes rested on hers. "I mean, is it okay to speak freely in front of..." He looked at Lucy, who appeared oblivious to her surroundings as she worked in earnest on the sundae. She had already dug past the whipped cream. A fair amount of chocolate sauce had smeared on her upper lip.

"I think it's okay to speak in front of Lucy."

"Well, it's just that I look forward to seeing you when you come to town. But I wish we could meet openly with your mother's knowledge and approval."

"I'm afraid that might not be forthcoming."

"Then how can I show her *and* you that I'm a serious young man and feel privileged to be in your company? I would like to pay her a visit—so that I might ask permission to court you."

Jennie's eyebrows shot up with surprise. She didn't see Peter as a man who followed social convention. How would Violet respond if she heard him speak in this manner?

"I don't think Violet would welcome someone into her home who has a—reputation."

"I'm sorry to hear that, Miss Hunsinger." He looked uncomfortable and shifted in his chair. "Would she judge a man without hearing his side first? Would you?"

"I can't answer for Violet, but *I'm* willing to listen."

Looking relieved, Peter smiled. "Then, that's all I can

ask for, Jennie. I mean Miss Hunsinger."

"You may call me Jennie."

"Jennie." Peter smiled. "And I'd like you to call me Peter." He glanced at Lucy before going on. "I'm afraid that Charley's ill feelings when our business failed may have colored my reputation in Concordia. But the failure of our plan was unavoidable." Peter moved closer to Jennie and lowered his voice. "Pardon me for saying this, but your brother was not a very good businessman. Probably because he didn't get the proper education. No fault of his, of course." Peter reached across the table and put his hand on Jennie's arm. "I just want you to know that I liked Charley and am sorry things didn't work out." He sat up straight and resumed speaking in a normal voice. "I can offer my credentials for your mother to check out if you think that would make a difference."

"I don't know," Jennie said, feeling uneasy. She wanted to keep Peter a secret for the time being. No sense in risking Violet's outright rejection of him as a beau. She would rather continue meeting him in this clandestine manner. "Violet is especially busy these days with entertaining her cousin Mary Belle. I wouldn't want to trouble her just yet."

"You know best." Peter looked disappointed.

"But of course, Lucy and I do go out each week—and encountering you like this is so pleasant. We could *accidentally* meet here each Wednesday afternoon if you like." Jennie couldn't believe how bold she had become.

"I'll look forward to it," Peter said, smiling broadly. He had not removed his hand from her arm. He gave it a little squeeze now and then picked up his ice cream spoon.

On the buggy ride home, Jennie said. "Lucy, we must not speak of our meetings with Mr. Stuyvesant. That will be our little secret, okay?"

"Okay, Jennie. Will we get ice cream when we see the nice man?"

"Yes. I'm sure Peter will see to it that you receive ice cream or some other treat." Being the object of Peter's attention would be Jennie's special treat.

CHAPTER TWENTY-TWO

Lucy

Nothing much was lost on nine-year-old Lucy. She had learned to be quiet and observe those around her for clues. Sometimes the adults at the orphanage smiled, but there was no warmth in their eyes and she found their smiles often were a cover for something bad to follow. The matron was especially cruel. At the very least, she was indifferent to the pain and loneliness of the younger children like Lucy. She never comforted a child by taking one in her arms or even patting one on the back. She avoided the nursery filled with babies altogether. Her strident voice bore no softness. And more often than not, the matron raised her voice at those who cried. "Quit going on like that!" she yelled, covering her ears with both hands. That made the upset children cry even harder.

Lucy feared that underneath her fine manners, Violet Hunsinger might be cold like the matron. Although she dressed in beautiful gowns, she carried herself stiffly and followed you with her eyes without moving her head. She noticed that Violet showed affection for Jennie, but she was not one for a lot of touching. Where were the hugs and kisses she heard mothers and their children shared? All she had observed were dry pecks on the cheek and careful half-hugs. Violet was like a porch with a leaky roof. She wasn't protective and shouldn't be trusted.

Lucy barely remembered her own mother, but hoarded a dim image of a beautiful lady with hair as red as her own who appeared in her dreams. She recalled how her soft voice caressed Lucy as she sang songs before bedtime. Lucy hoped that when she grew up her own voice would change into one with a breathless quality like her mother's.

She had been puzzled by the gradual croaking noises that emerged from her that refused to go away. It happened after a bad winter of sickness that included wheezing and gasping for breath. Some nights she had to sit up in bed instead of lying down. At those times, she was so hot and feverish that she ripped off the bed covers. The bouts of coughing exhausted her and made her throw up. The whooping sounds she made were like the high-pitched noises cranes made while flying over a lake.

The doctor who visited the Home finally placed her in isolation away from other children. "Sounds like she has the hundred-day cough," he declared at last. "Just has to run its course," he told the matron. Lucy remembered the bitter taste of the elixir that calmed the cough some, but not completely. Months later she was told that she was lucky to have recovered from her illness. She didn't feel lucky because she was thin and weak and tired all the time. Worst of all, she still retained her raspy voice. "You got a frog in there?" the boys at the orphanage teased.

"Lucy, it's Wednesday." Jennie's velvety voice pulled her back to the present. "I think we should dress for our afternoon in town," Jennie suggested. They had just finished a simple breakfast in the kitchen, where they both ate now. Lucy had overheard Jennie argue days earlier with Violet about meal arrangements.

"I understand you wanting dinner in the dining room without a child, but banning her from breakfast, too, is hurtful, Violet," she had said. "Either Lucy joins us for breakfast or I'll eat with her in the kitchen."

"You're impudence is surprising, Jennie. Since when do you neglect your hostess duties to family over a stranger."

"She wouldn't be a stranger if you included her in more activities."

"I doubt that she would even be interested in the adult pastimes that cousin Mary Belle and I share—and in which you should be more involved. Instead, you seem to be wasting your time on this child."

"I don't consider it time wasted, Violet. I'm only trying to do for her what you did for me when you took me in. I believe that Lucy has great potential if given an opportunity. In fact, I'd like to see to her schooling. I would like permission to take her to meet Maggie Schmitz and see if we can get her in school for the fall term."

"*If* she's still with us, Jennie. Remember, this was to
be a temporary situation."

"The girl needs help, Violet."

There was a long silence before Violet's voice softened. "Very well. Help her if you must. I can't find fault
with your reasons. For the time being, you're excused
from breakfast with Cousin Mary Belle and me if you
insist on having breakfast with Lucy. You have permission to dine in the kitchen with Lucy and the staff."

Jennie touched Violet's shoulder and then turned toward the kitchen, smiling. Lucy was peeking around the
corner and had heard the last part of the conversation.

"What will we do in town today?" Lucy asked. "Will
we meet that Mr. Stuy—Stuy—" *Why does he have such
a dumb name?* "—Stuy-ves-ant at the soda shop?"

"Shh, Lucy. That's a secret, remember?"

Lucy was willing to keep the secret if it meant getting
more ice cream.

"We may stop at the soda shop, but first I'm taking
you to meet Maggie Schmitz. She's the town's school
teacher. Let's see if we can get you enrolled for the next
school term."

Lucy wasn't sure about that. She didn't want to disappoint Jennie when she found out she didn't know her
numbers and letters very well. She had missed what little
instruction was provided at the Home because she had
been sick so much.

"Can't I just stay here, Jennie? Do I need to go to school?"

"Yes, you must."

"Did you?"

"Not for long. Violet arranged for me to be schooled at home with a tutor."

"Couldn't I do that?"

"It's not the same as going to school and meeting other children, who could become your friends. Wouldn't you like that?"

Lucy shook her head and felt tears starting to form. "I'd rather be with you."

"I can help you, Lucy. I can teach you things not covered in school, but you need to know the basics: reading, writing, and your numbers." Jennie knelt down on her knees in order to be at Lucy's eye level. "Come, you'll see. It will be an adventure."

I've had enough adventures, Lucy thought. But she smiled and threw her arms around Jennie's neck.

"Okay, Jennie. *Then* can we go for ice cream?"

CHAPTER TWENTY-THREE

Lucy

Lucy followed Jennie up the hill to reach the one-room schoolhouse. She saw that the whitewashed building had windows all across its front, like curious eyes. A huge tree with a swing hanging from one thick, gnarly branch dominated the playground. It looked lonely with no children clustering around it waiting to take turns.

"Oh good, you made it." A pretty lady came toward them when they stepped through the classroom's double doors.

"You got my message, then," Jennie replied.

"Yes, I received your note and am happy to meet a new student before the term officially begins."

At the Boston Home for Children there was no official school term. They had lessons at odd times, whenever they got a new teacher. The teachers smelled bad and often were nervous creatures whose eyes darted about as if looking for an escape route. They didn't stay long. So, there were times when no learning took place at all.

"You must be Lucy," the lady said, coming closer. She smelled real good.

"Lucy, this is Maggie Schmitz," Jennie said. "She will be your new teacher."

"You may call me Miss Maggie. Everyone does."

"My name is Lucy McCleery. You may call me Lucy," she rasped. "Everyone does."

Miss Maggie's eyebrows lifted in surprise and then she laughed. "Thank you. I'll just do that."

The long room, filled with desks, smelled of chalk. A girl older than Lucy stood at the front of the room by the teacher's desk stacking primers. She was watching the interchange between the adults with great interest.

"Sarah, come and meet Lucy McCleery and Jennie Hunsinger," Miss Maggie said.

"Sarah?" Jennie yelled in surprise. A small smile washed over Sarah's face.

"Jennie!" The two moved toward one another, uncertainly for a moment, and then ran into each other's arms.

"It's been so long," Jennie squealed. She sounded like a little girl to Lucy instead of an almost grown woman.

"Oh, I forgot that you two lived together for a time," Miss Maggie said.

"You're almost—grown up," Jennie observed.

"I'm fourteen."

"You look like your mother. I can see Emma's eyes in yours."

"Thank you." Sarah beamed.

"She was so kind to me while I was on the farm."

"Yes, she was." Sarah dropped her head. "She missed

you when you left."

Who was Emma? Lucy wondered.

"Sarah is going to be my teacher's helper this term," Miss Maggie said. "Just as Christina was when she was in Concordia." At the mention of Christina's name, Jennie and Sarah sobered.

Who was Christina? Lucy thought. She felt forgotten for a moment.

"This is my last year in school," Sarah said. "Papa said I could stay until I completed the eighth grade. Then I'll have to stay home and help out."

"Come Lucy. Let me show you around while Sarah and Jennie visit." Miss Maggie steered Lucy away from the two and began pointing out things in the room. There were hooks on one wall for jackets and a shelf below for winter snow boots. A pot-bellied stove in the front corner near the blackboard looked promising. It reminded Lucy of how cold it was in Boston during the winter. There was never enough heat in the drafty old building that housed the orphanage. She hoped she would have a desk near this stove. But she was soon disappointed to learn that children were seated alphabetically. The name McCleery was smack dab in the middle. She might be seated a long way from the stove.

The teacher smiled and changed the subject. "Tell me, Lucy. Do you like to read?"

"I—don't know, Miss Maggie. We didn't have many books at the Home to read."

"But you can read some, can't you?"

Lucy stared ahead toward Jennie at the front of the room. She wished she wouldn't have to answer this embarrassing question.

Jennie must have heard the teacher's question because she returned to Lucy's side in time to answer for her. "She may need help to catch up, Maggie. Lucy told me she was ill a lot and that put her behind in her studies."

"I did notice your voice is a little raspy, Lucy. Does it hurt when you talk or eat?"

"No, ma'am. Not much anyway. And ice cream makes it feel better."

Jennie and Miss Maggie exchanged glances.

"Will we be meeting Mr. Stuy-ves-ant today?" Lucy asked Jennie. "You said he'd buy me more ice cream."

Jennie blushed. "We'll see, Lucy. But, let's not talk about that here."

"Are you talking about Peter Stuyvesant?" Sarah asked. "Charley's old partner?"

"Why, yes. They were in business together," Jennie replied. "How do you know him?"

"He was at our farm trying to talk Papa into buying one of those new-fangled tractors."

"Yes, well."

"Papa said he was a crook. And later, Charley didn't have anything nice to say about him either."

"They just had a misunderstanding, Sarah." Jennie

turned to Miss Maggie. "Are we all set then? Do we have any papers to fill out?"

The teacher took Jennie aside and lowered her voice, but Lucy heard what she said anyway. "The records you sent me weren't very complete. But if that's all that Mr. Buckminster provided they'll have to do. I *am* curious about Lucy's health, though. Her voice sounds very strained. A number of students over the years sounded just like her and it turned out that there was a problem with their tonsils." Lucy flinched at the word tonsils.

"Infected tonsils were the cause of frequent sickness," Miss Maggie went on. "Jennie, it might do to have Dr. Martin check Lucy. See if there is anything that can be done for her."

"I hadn't thought of that, but it's a good idea."

Lucy wandered back to Sarah's side where she had resumed sorting books.

"It sounds like Jennie and Peter Stuyvesant are sweethearts, Lucy. What do you think?" Sarah asked.

"I don't know anything about that, but he's awfully nice to Jennie."

"Uh huh," Sarah replied. She rolled her eyes.

Jennie motioned for Lucy to join her. "It's time to go, Lucy. Nice seeing you again, Sarah," she added, smiling. "We should try to meet again, soon."

Sarah shifted her attention to Jennie and met her eyes. "Yes, I'm sure we would have lots to talk about," she agreed without enthusiasm. Lucy noticed that

Sarah's manner was no longer warm toward Jennie.

"Lucy, here are a couple of books for you to look over before school starts the end of August." Miss Maggie handed her a small bundle of books tied together. "Jennie will help you if you need it."

Lucy accepted them, but wasn't very excited about actually opening up the books to see what was inside. Reading had been her worst subject. She didn't want to disappoint Jennie and Miss Maggie. And she sure didn't want the other children to make fun of her. But since it was important to Jennie for her to be in school, she would make the best of it.

On the way back to town, Jennie directed the driver to stop by Dr. Martin's office.

"I think Miss Maggie's suggestion to have your throat checked is a good one, Lucy. We might have him schedule a full physical while we're at it."

Lucy didn't agree, but she didn't want to make a fuss either, so she just nodded.

"What were you and Sarah talking so earnestly about back there?" Jennie asked.

"Nothing much," Lucy fibbed. She sensed that the change in Sarah's disposition when Mr. Stuyvesant was discussed might also be a mood changer for Jennie. Besides, she didn't want to do or say anything which might affect plans for the remainder of the afternoon.

"Are we still going for ice cream after we see the doctor? You promised."

CHAPTER TWENTY-FOUR

Christina

Christina couldn't believe her eyes. Charley was leaving without her. She dropped the curtain and turned from the bedroom window. *How could he betray me like this?* She saw now that the events of the last couple days—especially after she lost their baby—had changed him. He was determined to move on whether or not she begged him to stay. Well, she hadn't begged him. She was too proud for that. If he let a little thing like her keeping a secret turn him against her, their relationship was destined to be a rocky one.

Before they began their journey, he had been so trusting—like a boy. And as recently as a few days ago he was still easy to influence. But now, there was a new toughness about him, an almost steely quality woven into the fabric of his easygoing nature. She wasn't sure what to make of it. Christina dropped back into bed. It was too early to get up.

What in the world was she going to do staying behind with the Eilers? On the one hand, she could rest up and get her strength back. And when she was back to normal, she would continue working with horses. She might even get another opportunity to chase after that stallion if she could convince Bert to give it a go. She imagined what it would feel like to be atop the Spaniard, clamping her knees tight against its flanks, sensing his power for her to command. In the next second, she feared that Bert would be reluctant to ever take her out again after what happened. She tossed and turned, and finally got up and dressed. When she opened her door, she could smell the strong aroma of chicory brewing. She entered the kitchen and found Ruth stationed at the stove, as usual.

"Oh, you're up then?" Ruth looked surprised to see Christina. "You missed Charley. He already left."

"I know. I saw him through the window." Christina dropped down heavily on the nearest chair. "We said our goodbyes last evening." She wasn't going to give Ruth the satisfaction of knowing that she had been abandoned.

"Well, I suspect this is for the best."

Best for whom? Christina bristled at Ruth's self-righteous opinion. But, before she could reply, Agatha rounded the corner.

"Christina, you're up?" She glanced at Ruth.

"Yes. I couldn't sleep."

"I don't wonder, with people getting up at all times of the early morning and—" She caught a look from Ruth and stopped. "Uh, how are you feeling, Christina?"

"I'm still very tired."

"I think you should be taking a tonic to get you feeling better. Don't you think so too, Ruth? I remember after I had my first child how tired I was. Remember, Ruth?"

"I remember that you talk too much," Ruth said.

"I just thought we could take a ride up to see the goat woman and get Christina one of her special tonics."

"Goat woman?" Christina screwed up her face.

"They call her that because she raises goats. But she also collects herbs and makes special tonics for almost everything, doesn't she Ruth? They say that's because she's part Indian and knows all kinds of things about healing," Agatha prattled on. "She's the next best thing to a doctor out here and since we don't have a doctor—"

"Agatha, get over here and help me get breakfast going," Ruth said. "You're talking like a jabbering blue jay this morning."

Agatha *was* talkative this morning, Christina thought. It appeared that much could be learned from her on subjects about which Ruth was not forthcoming. Although she doubted she would need a tonic since she had never been ill in her life, this information might be helpful in the future. *Future?* She did not plan to spend her future on this ranch. As soon as Mr. Eiler shipped his hay, she expected to be paid Charley's remaining wages. And if Charley had not written her a letter by then asking her to join him in California, she would take matters into her own hands. She could hop a train just as easily as he could and would strike out on her own. She would not be beholden to a man who had spurned her. Love him or not, Christina Batachi was her own woman and would determine her own future.

"I'll set the table and cook the oatmeal," Christina offered. She hoisted herself up and away from the table.

Several days later, Agatha and Christina were hanging laundry on the clothesline.

"You still look a little tired—and pale." Agatha spoke carefully around the wooden pins clamped between her lips.

"I'm okay." Christina pulled a pair of wet overalls from the willow basket and struggled to lift them to the line. "Doing outdoor chores instead of wasting away in the kitchen makes me feel better. I used to brown up pretty good every summer when I was taking care of horses and riding them every day."

"Did you do a lot of man's work back where you came from?"

Christina brightened at Agatha's line of questioning. She loved talking about the times she spent with Carl at the livery stable. While Carl Schmitz saw to his blacksmith jobs, forging and repairing farm implements, she took care of the horses in the stable.

"Guess I did, but I never considered it strictly man's work," she bragged. "Although I met my match in Gabriel."

"Gabriel? Who was he?"

"A chestnut stallion that Carl bought and trained. I rode him almost every day. The hardest thing to learn was roping. I used to practice on fence posts and such. But there's no challenge unless you're trying to rope a moving animal." Christina laughed. "After he got to know me better, Gabriel tolerated me roping him as he ran around the paddock."

Agatha nodded as she pinned girls' bloomers all in a row. A sudden breeze moved between the white cotton undergarments, setting them to sway in unison like petticoats in a can-can dance.

"You like horses more than I do. One of the mares bit me a while back."

"Can't let them scare you, Agatha. Have to show them who's boss."

"That's what Bert says, but I don't know."

"You seem to have good control of the children. You're a good teacher," Christina said, giving Agatha a smile. "That's important work too."

Agatha acknowledged the compliment.

"It takes a lot of patience," Christina added. "I know because Concordia's school mistress, Miss Maggie, helped me catch up on my reading and writing."

"Tell me more." Agatha squinted into the sun.

"I lived with Maggie during the school year and helped her with the younger students. Then in the summer I worked at the stables again."

"I thought you must have had some experience with

children, the way you help out with our lessons. Which do you like best—tending horses or teaching children?"

Without hesitation, Christina answered: "I like working with children, but I *love* tending horses."

"You know, Christina, I think talking about things that make you happy puts the bloom back in your cheeks. But I still think we should go and get you fixed up with one of the goat woman's tonics."

"All right," Christina agreed. "If you think it's important."

The next morning, Agatha and Christina rode a well-worn trail into rolling hills covered by yellow grass. Bert was in the lead, and the two women followed at a distance talking between themselves.

"How did you convince Ruth to let us go this morning?" Christina asked.

"I promised that we'd make breakfast tomorrow morning so she could go to town with John. They'll be gone most of the day so we'll have to make sure everything goes smoothly."

"Will they be picking up mail, do you think?"

"I'm sure they will, if there's anything waiting for them. Why?"

"I'm hoping that Charley sent a letter in care of Mr. Eiler."

"It might be a bit soon. Mail takes a long time out here, you know. Sounds like you're not mad at him anymore."

"I was never mad, Agatha. Not really."

Agatha looked at Christina, but said nothing.

"You know, the goat woman has all kinds of tonics. They're not just for restoring energy and building up the blood, but for helping a woman—bide her time."

"What do you mean?" Christina looked puzzled.

"When a woman doesn't want another baby for awhile, she's biding her time."

"They have something for *that*?" Christina said.

"I've been sneaking a special tonic since birthing the last child," Agatha admitted. "Sometimes when I know it's about time for John to share my bed, I take this tonic and it brings on my ladies time of the month a little early. He leaves me alone then."

"Is the tonic safe?"

"Seems to be. Hasn't hurt me yet. The old woman is part Indian, and she knows which herbs to gather to make the special tonic."

Christina took all this in, but didn't say much. She was surprised, but pleased that Agatha had taken her into her confidence. She no longer seemed like the docile young woman she first met.

"How did you come to be with John?" she asked.

The two women had fallen farther behind Bert who had crested the hill and was waiting for them to catch up.

"John knew my family back in Salt Lake City when I was growing up. We were all part of the Latter Day Saints—Mormons—and attended temple together.

When I turned seventeen, he asked my father for permission to marry me and make me his second wife." Agatha looked off in the distance as if reliving the moment. "That was before the church outlawed multiple marriages. John was rather good looking then and I could see no harm in it." She sighed loudly. "My only regret was in not finishing high school. But I knew that I was destined to be married off sooner or later. I came from a family of twelve children. Seven of us were girls."

"Twelve?" gasped Christina.

"Don't look so surprised. Large families are pretty common out here. Anyway," Agatha continued, "Ruth was—well—she was Ruth. Always a little stiff and formal—and bossy. That only got worse after I joined them. In those early days John was in my bed more than in Ruth's until I got pregnant." She lifted one shoulder in a shrug. "After the church banned multiple marriages, we were treated differently and so John moved us out here."

"You two gonna gab all day?" Bert shouted.

Christina prodded Buttercup forward and Agatha followed. When they were abreast of Bert, they looked down on the goat woman's spread. Smoke spiraled out of the chimney of a cabin that looked more like an old shack. It was constructed out of weathered wood that had never seen a coat of paint. There were no windows and the roof consisted of dry wooden shingles that had curled up.

The tinny sound of bells met their ears as goats of

various sizes and breeds roamed free on the hard-packed dirt surrounding the shack. Not a blade of grass was to be seen.

"Goats eat everything green down to the nub," Bert explained when Christina remarked about the starkness of the land. "They're just like sheep. Cattlemen don't like sheep *or* goats, because they eat up all the pasture. Leave nothing for cattle." It was clear that Bert was not fond of goats.

As they moved closer, the bleating sounds became louder. Billie goats with beards and yellow eyes strutted and bucked each other with their horns.

"Old woman!" Bert shouted before dismounting and helping Agatha down from Rosie, one of the tamer stable horses. Christina didn't need any help. She led Buttercup to Bert for tending.

A stooped woman dressed in dark clothes emerged from the cabin. She leaned on a walking stick and squinted into the bright sun.

"Who goes there?" Her high pitched voice cracked like a rifle shot. Christina wondered how old she was. She looked ancient. Her leathery brown skin and wild gray hair made her look like the scariest of witches in fairly tales. She turned her head and spit. A gob of snuff flew out of the old woman's craw, reaching an amazing distance. A young kid rushed forward and gobbled up the wad.

"It's Agatha from down a ways," Agatha said as she

moved toward the old woman. "Brought you some fig jam and bread, fresh baked this morning." The old woman looked up and grabbed at the packages Agatha offered.

"Thankee," she squealed.

"We've come for a tonic."

The woman nodded her head and motioned them to follow her inside. Bert remained behind, holding the reins of the horses while the two women followed.

Christina pulled back a bit when they entered the dark room that smelled of something rank. The goat lady lit a kerosene lantern hanging from a hook. One entire wall was lined with shelves loaded with jars. The colors of the liquids inside the jars varied from pale green to yellow ochre. Some were transparent and others revealed filaments floating through their contents. Christina peered closer and decided the floating matter was most likely from the herb's decaying pulp.

"What kind of tonic you looking to get?" the old woman said. She put the packages Agatha brought on a rough plank table in the middle of the room. Christina looked around and saw a sleeping mat in the corner covered with a quilt in some kind of Indian design. There were no other furnishings except for a rickety chair.

A goat had followed them inside and nudged Christina aside to get next to the old woman.

"You got some tonic for building energy?" Agatha lowered her voice. "And something for a woman's times?" The old woman looked up and gazed at Christina. Starting with her face and moving down her body, the old woman gave her the once over. She fixed her stare at Christina's middle and cackled. She poked at her breasts and belly.

Christina pulled away, offended by the old woman's scrutiny.

"Yep. She looks ripe. Needs something to keep the bees away."

The old woman reached for a jar smaller than the others and placed it in Christina's hand.

"This'll do."

The contents were devoid of color. Whatever was inside was disguised in a murky dark liquid. Christina reluctantly accepted it, but wondered if it was safe to consume. It was heavier than she expected and made sloshing sounds when moved—as if there were something alive inside. She was afraid to ask what was in it.

After a few more minutes in which Agatha accepted a larger jar, supposedly filled with the energy-building tonic, she negotiated a price on the two homegrown remedies and placed a couple of coins on the table. "Thank you," she said and turned to leave with Christina in tow.

The old woman hacked and Christina heard her spit again. The ping of the offending gob landed in the hollow container by the plank table. Christina shuddered as she remembered the tobacco-eating goat outside. She heard the goat by the woman's side and imagined it fishing the gob out of the container. She resisted the urge to turn around and check if she was right. Instead, she rushed through the door, anxious to leave the oppressive atmosphere.

CHAPTER TWENTY-FIVE

Christina

As the trio started on the return trip to the ranch, Christina hung back a little. She didn't feel like talking to either Bert or Agatha. She was still turning over in her mind the strange encounter with the goat woman. Although she didn't object to sampling the tonic that promised to make her stronger and healthier, she wondered whether she would ever have the nerve to unscrew the smaller jar of tonic meant to prevent another pregnancy.

The return was uneventful until Agatha's mount, Rosie, stopped short and shifted her weight—a warning before rearing up. Startled, Agatha nearly fell. Bert turned and pumped his rifle, taking aim at something near Rosie's right hoof while she struck her iron-shod hooves at a coiled snake. The echoing rifle shot spooked the mare, which spun and bolted. Agatha screamed and wrapped her arms around Rosie's neck as they raced toward the bottom of the hill. Christina stared at the rattlesnake Bert had killed. It was at least six feet long and, with the rocky terrain as the perfect camouflage, had blended in so well that it was almost impossible to see.

"Diamondback," he yelled as he took off after Agatha and her mare. Shaken, Christina gently squeezed Buttercup's sides with her knees and followed at a safe distance, not wanting her horse to become agitated as well.

Bert had reached Agatha. He rode along side, staying even with her horse for a few minutes until she slowed down. Talking calmly to Rosie, he reached over and grabbed the reins until she fell into a steady trot and finally obeyed his order to halt.

"You okay?" he asked Agatha.

She nodded, but looked shaken and pale.

That evening at supper, the discussion was lively as the children asked questions about the morning's near miss with the snake.

"Did it rattle?" Jasper asked.

"Was it as big as the one in the barn?" Chester said.

"I don't like snakes," Cecelia whined and leaned into her mother.

"They have their place," Bert said, wolfing down another one of Ruth's soda biscuits that were as big as cow pies. "Keeps the rodents under control." He looked at Cecelia. "They're more scared of you than you are of them."

"I doubt it," Agatha said under her breath.

"Well, ladies, think that's enough venturing off for a while?" John said, scraping his plate of beans. "What did you think of the goat lady, Christina?" He looked at her with a thinly disguised smile.

"She was—interesting."

"She gives me the willies," Bert added.

"What does she do with all those goats?" Christina asked.

"Raises them for meat and milk," Ruth interjected. "From time to time we get one of their kids. The meat is so tender."

"No need to buy the milk with our cows keeping us well supplied," John said. "With that and selling her tonics, I guess she makes out." He pushed himself away from the table. "You ladies went there for the tonics, right?"

Agatha looked down at her plate.

"Yes," said Christina. She wondered if he knew his wives were taking herbs to help control how often they became pregnant. Did he realize they were not that eager to bear all of his children?

That evening as the women were cleaning up after the meal, Brynn bumped into Christina, causing her to drop a large bowl that broke in half.

"Oh, I'm sorry," Brynn said. "My tummy keeps bumping into things." She stooped down to help Christina pick up the pieces. "You got more than one tonic today, didn't you?" She whispered. "The dark one?"

"Why yes. I did." Christina wondered where this conversation was headed.

"Just so you know, it doesn't work. I took it, but John's seed took root anyway."

"Didn't you want a child?" Christina looked around to

make sure they were not being overheard.

"Yes, but not just yet." Tears sprung to Brynn's eyes.

That settled it. Christina wasn't about to swallow something that looked that awful and probably stunk as well. She recalled the stench in the old woman's shanty. But now what would she do when Charley wanted to start a family?

CHAPTER TWENTY-SIX

Christina

A week passed before Christina felt like her old self. She helped more in the kitchen and assisted Agatha with the children's lessons just like she used to do with the younger students in Maggie's classes. With a common interest, it felt as if she and Agatha were becoming friends. In time, Christina thought that they might become *good* friends. Time, however, wasn't something she had to spare. As soon as she heard from Charley she would pack up and leave.

In the meantime, when Christina had finished her chores, she ventured into the barn to groom the horses— just to spend time in their company. She found comfort in the warm barn smell of manure. One afternoon she suggested that she was well enough to go in search of that "Spanish stallion that got away." Bert shot her down in short order.

"I'm not taking any more chances with that one, Christina. You might as well put that out of your mind right now."

Well, he doesn't have to be so rude about it.

By the end of the second week, she asked John Eiler when he was taking the hay to be shipped.

"I need to collect Charley's wages, Mr. Eiler. He's waiting for me and we need that money real bad."

"Oh? When did you hear from him? I didn't see a letter come through from Charley."

"Well, I haven't actually heard from him, but I want to be ready to go as soon as he lets me know where he's settled."

"I'll hold Charley's money until you hear for sure."

That seemed reasonable, although she would have liked it better if she were in charge of the money. Seemed odd that there was no letter from Charley yet— just to say he had arrived safely and where he was. There was no mail delivery to the ranch. When he went to Promontory, Mr. Eiler picked up mail for the family at the post office annex inside Myrna's café. If a letter *was* waiting for Christina right now, she wouldn't even know about it. She decided that if she hadn't heard anything by the end of the week, she would saddle up Buttercup and go into Promontory herself. Maybe there was something postmarked "General Delivery" with her name on it.

Eiler's eyes had been following Christina all week. It made her uneasy. At meal time he drew her into the conversation, hushing others who tried to speak. He followed her into the barn on several occasions, pretending to dig around in his tools looking for something or asking her a question he already knew the answer to, like the time he said, "How do you like tending the horses?" Even Bert shot him a puzzled look at that one.

A few days later in the middle of a late summer heat wave, while everyone was in a stupor, Christina finally faced the obvious: John Eiler was in hot pursuit of her.

After supper while the other women were cleaning up and getting the children ready for bed, Christina had begged off washing dishes.

"I'll give you a hand in a minute, Ruth. But first, I've just got to go outside and get some air." The sun hadn't set yet, and the blistering heat of the day had made everyone cranky.

"See to it, Christina." Ruth wiped sweat from her brow. "The greasy dishes will be right here waiting for you."

Christina headed for the shade, praying for a breeze. The few shade trees on the property were clumped together as if for mutual protection. They had been planted behind the house near a pond the children used for a swimming hole. The largest of the trees was a black oak with limbs strong enough to support a tree house. A thick rope hung from a lower branch. Chester liked to climb the oak, grab the rope, and swing out over the pond's middle before letting go. She lifted her skirts and dipped her toes in the cold water. Something had roiled up the water earlier and it was still murky. But at least it was wet.

"You going in for a dip?" Christina jumped and turned to see John Eiler watching her with a smile on his florid face.

"You startled me," she said. "I didn't hear you come up." Christina dropped her skirts and patted the material in place.

"Didn't mean to scare you, but I'm glad to find you alone, Christina. There's been something I've been aiming to talk to you about."

"Oh?" She shifted and moved closer to the tree.

"I've been watching you these past few weeks and you've settled in pretty well. Like you to stay with us instead of moving on when Charley contacts you. *If* he contacts you."

"He will. I'm certain of it."

"We'll see. Regardless, we can be more like your family and protect you."

"Never had a family protect me. Don't need it now," Christina blurted out.

Eiler ignored her outburst. "You seem to get on real well with the children and my wives. We could use a strong woman here to help bond our family. In time, you may be one of my wives." He moved closer.

"What!" she yelped. Christina blinked hard while staring into Eiler's greedy eyes. As he moved toward her, his breathing became more labored. With the back of his hand, Eiler stroked Christina's cheek, letting it drift down her neck and rest on her chest. Christina's skin crawled at his touch. *I would no more become one of your wives...* She left the thought unfinished. "Thanks for considering me worthy of your family, but I'm promised to Charley." She moved farther away from the old man.

"Well, people change and their needs change. Charley may need his independence right now while he searches for the perfect place to settle," Eiler said. "As a young man, he has more options open to him while he's single and can move around without a woman to protect." He took a step forward, blocking her escape.

Christina began to sweat more profusely. She hoped he hadn't noticed her sudden nervousness. *I wonder if he can detect the smell of fear like a cunning animal can?*

"I don't want to hear anymore, Mr. Eiler. You either give me what you owe Charley in back wages or—"

"No need to get upset, Christina. In due time, you'll get your money. Of course I'll have to deduct your keep."

"What?"

"That is unless you stay and become one of us. If you're family, then all of this is yours to share," he said waving his arm over the ranch.

Christina took a step backward. She turned and ran toward the house. The thought of becoming one of John Eiler's women made her sick. She had fought to be independent all these years and did not plan to have her plans upended by a man who collected wives and children like some men collected coins. She knew she was at risk out here in the middle of nowhere. There was no one who could come to her aid unless she could appeal to Bert. She thought that unlikely. He hadn't been sympathetic after she miscarried on the trail and had been cool toward her ever since.

It seemed she was surrounded by men who felt women were only good for two things: seeing to their comfort and bearing them children. She needed to leave the ranch—with or without Charley's wages. But how would she pay for a coach ticket on the train? Where exactly would she go?

CHAPTER TWENTY-SEVEN

Charley

Charley was dozing when he felt the train slow to a wheezing crawl. He had been riding for a full day through Utah and Nevada when the Central Pacific began climbing the steep Sierra Nevada range that divided California from Nevada. *I'll be in California soon!* He was too excited to remain still. Charley jumped up and began pacing. Immediately he was thrown off balance as the train engine strained at the rising grade. He laughed aloud as he veered backward and landed on a pile of sacks filled with onions being shipped west. Their outer skins made a crackling sound. Thankfully, there was no one else in the boxcar to observe his fall and tease him about his clumsiness. As always, other men hopped the train at various stops, but at the last junction Charley grabbed one of the last cars in line and was lucky to have the space to himself. However, he wished one particular person was with him to share his excitement of finally reaching California.

During the long ride Charley's thoughts often centered on Christina. With effort he pushed her out of his mind. There would be plenty of time to figure out how the two of them could repair the breach caused by Christina's deception. He had loved her for so long that it was difficult to acknowledge that she had flaws. He always knew she was unpredictable, but now he questioned what kind of wife she would be. Was it possible for her to change from the independent creature she was to a softer version of herself? But then he thought, h*ow docile do I want her to be? Wasn't it her fire and energy that attracted me in the first place?* These and other questions kept bombarding him as the miles of track flowed farther away from the woman he loved.

At one point the train passed through a long tunnel. Rays of light that slipped through cracks in the boxcars had disappeared. He was in total darkness. He could only imagine what the grueling work must have been like for the men who constructed tunnels through mountains made of granite. He had heard that Chinese laborers held the dangerous job of blasting rock and then moving the tons of debris in order for the tracks to be laid.

Hours later when Charley felt the train lumber to a stop, he slid open the boxcar doors to reveal a newly constructed depot nestled in a stand of evergreens. Next to it were the burned out remains of the old station. All that remained was a singed sign that read *Truckee.* He inhaled the fresh brisk scent of pine, a welcome change to the onion-laced air he had been breathing. Charley felt lighter, freer, as he hopped down from the boxcar and took his first step onto California soil. Stretching his stiff limbs, he executed a series of jumping jacks and let out a loud whoop in celebration.

When he sauntered into the Truckee station, the first thing he noticed was a large map on one wall. In bold print it identified towns in which Central Pacific had erected rail depots: *Emigrant Gap, Dutch Flats, Auburn, and Sacramento.* There were only three more stops before Sacramento. His goal to settle in California finally felt within reach. Satisfied, he left the station and scanned the surrounding terrain. Although he saw signs of established summer gardens dotting the hillsides, he doubted that, come winter, the rough, rocky terrain of Truckee would support a working farm. He reached down to pick up a handful of the red dirt and noticed that it was nothing like the dirt of Concordia. Too many rocks. Too porous for some crops. Charley knew from the altitude that this area probably received snow a good part of the year and that meant a shorter growing season. He wished Christina was by his side taking this all in. He had almost forgotten her deceit. *Almost.*

Other people had deceived him too. Charley wondered what it was about him that led others to so easily lie to him. Enoch Neamott had lied to him when he denied receiving payment from Mrs. Hunsinger in exchange for Jennie—thereby splitting the O'Brien family. Peter, who had been his business partner and the only friend Charley ever had, lied to him. When they had their falling out, it wasn't just a failed partnership that hurt him. It was also the loss of a friend. He felt he was a better judge of character because of these betrayals. Charley O'Brien promised himself he would weigh the words of men more carefully in the future.

It took another few hours of starts and stops before Charley ventured off the train again—just long enough to do his business in the bushes and to refill his canteen with fresh water. The train had stopped at Emigrant Gap, which was still in steep mountains, but was more forested land. The settlement appeared thriving with a post office, hotel, livery stable, saloon, and general store. Houses were scattered on the hills as well as off the main street.

Charley followed a tangle of blackberry vines that were still lush with berries. Having run out of the bread and cheese Ruth Eiler wrapped up for him, he was hungry. He picked as many as he could and stuffed them into his mouth. They reminded him of happier times on the Neamott farm when he and Sarah and Ruth stripped berries by the creek so that Emma could use them to make blackberry pies and jams. Funny how that seemed like weeks instead of years ago, while his last conversation with Myrna at the café days ago felt as if it had taken place in another lifetime.

"Had enough of the Eilers I see?" she had said when he had arrived pre-dawn.

"Got to move on, Myrna. Got to get settled in California before winter sets in."

"Where's Christina? She not going with you?"

"Not just yet," he said between compressed lips. He refused to be drawn into a discussion about Christina.

"That's not surprising, being in the family way and all."

"What? How did you know?" Charley felt the sting of disappointment all over again. Even Myrna had guessed at the truth of which he had been totally ignorant.

"It wasn't too hard to figure out. She was ailing when you two come through."

"She's just resting up a bit." He didn't want to share any more information than necessary about Christina—especially about losing their baby. "She'll join me as soon as I'm settled. I'll send word—write her a letter."

"Well then, guess I'll know you wrote to her before she does." She laughed. "That is, as the unofficial postmistress." She pointed to an area to the left of the counter near the kitchen door. A brass metal box hung on the wall with windowed doors and keyholes just like the one in Concordia's post office. "The post office annex is in the café," she reminded him. "You just address your letter to Christina in care of John Eiler and she'll get it. Or you can put her name on it and address it to General Delivery, Promontory, Utah." It was the last thing he heard Myrna say.

When Charley heard metal scraping metal he saw that the train engine was leaving Emigrant Gap. A couple of men and a few straggling boys were hopping the slow-moving freight ahead of him. One of the young boys struggled and didn't look as if he'd make it. Charley felt a sudden stab of fear for the kid and wondered what circumstances led him to become a rail rider. At the last minute the boy's friend reached down and gave him a hand. Relieved, Charley wiped his purple berry-stained hands on his pants and ran abreast of the last boxcar until he picked up enough speed to hop aboard. *So far, so good.* The next stop was Dutch Flats and then Auburn.

It was dusk as the train pulled into Auburn. The first thing Charley noticed was a large impressive building topped with a golden dome that looked over the town. The structure had to be something important. Auburn was bustling with lamplight glowing in most of the shops and businesses lining the mud-splattered boardwalks. Lively music and the sound of men laughing and arguing spilled out the doors into the street. Horses, as well as pack mules burdened with gold pans, picks, shovels, and other mining tools, were tied up in front of saloons.

After the isolation of the boxcar, Charley craved company. He was loathe to spend his money on food and drink, but was hungry for a hot meal where others took nourishment. He entered a cafe that turned out to be more saloon than cafe. Men leaned against a long curved bar facing an ornate mirror and a back bar lined with bottles of liquor.

"What can I get you?" the barkeep asked. He wiped

down the spot in front of Charley.

"Was hoping to grab some grub."

"We've got some venison stew and beans left over from lunch. If you want a beefsteak you'll have to come back tomorrow."

"Stew and beans will be fine." Charley pulled out some coins from his pocket.

"It's gonna cost you more than that," the man said.

"Okay. How much?" He reached in his pocket for more change.

"That'll be two dollars."

"What! That's highway robbery."

"Maybe. But food is scarce. Too many miners and drifters. Can't keep up with supply orders." The bartender leaned in. "Whiskey is cheaper."

"Okay," Charley said. "Whiskey then."

Charley was not much of a drinker. Ever since he tried whiskey in the Neamott's barn, he didn't like the taste. But at least it would keep him warm during the night.

The barkeep poured a generous serving of a rich, amber liquid and pushed the sloshing glass toward him. The first sip burned like the devil, but felt good going down. Charley knocked back the remainder of his drink in one gulp.

"Another?" The bottle was poised over Charley's glass.

"No. I'd better keep my wits about me." He tossed a

coin across the bar and headed for the door.

Charley felt better, more confident. He thought he might as well make good use of his time by trying to earn a little money before getting back on the train. The next freight wasn't coming through until late tonight. He was tempted to try his luck at cards in the gambling halls. He was pretty good at playing poker and blackjack and might get a good return on his money if he played a hand or two. Peter had taught him how to count cards to even his chances. Charley had a good memory and was good at numbers, so it was just a matter of concentrating and learning to keep a sober face. Maybe this would be a way for Peter to have done him some good—to repay him for what he had cheated him out of.

He approached the loudest of the saloons on the block. Stumbling out its door were men who were obviously drunk. If he played with someone in their condition, he might just win. Charley sidled past them into the bright lights and noise, circling the large room to look over tables of boisterous men. In the back, quiet gentlemen in waistcoats occupied one small table. *They look like serious gamblers. Maybe even professionals.* He weighed his chances. Would it be better to join in with a group of rowdies—who, if they lost to him, might turn violent—or sit in with calmer men who probably knew all the tricks of the trade and would be difficult to beat?

He opted to take his chances on the scraggliest group near the player piano. Although it was hard to hear over the tinny sounding melody, Charley grabbed an empty chair.

"Okay if I sit in?" he asked.

"Only if you got money to give away," said an oily-skinned man with a full black beard.

"What're you playing?"

"Five-card stud."

Charley sat down and put his ante in the pot. He watched as the dealer passed two cards to each of the four players—one card down and one face up. Charley had a five of hearts showing and a king of hearts in the hole. Before adding to his bet, he studied the cards of the other players. His third card was a ten of hearts dealt face up. Again, he noted that no one was showing hearts. By the time the fifth card had been dealt, he had added more coins to the pot and filled out his flush. A grizzly miner sitting across from Charley scowled, threw in a coin, and then plopped down a small goatskin bag in the middle of the table.

"Guess this oughta do," he said, slurring his words.

"Sure you want to do that?" the dealer said.

"On the hand I got? Hell yes!"

"Okay, then."

Charley turned over his hole card showing the flush. The miner's face fell. The other two players threw in their cards in disgust. Charley scooped up his winnings, including the bag of gold dust.

"Thank you, gentlemen." He started to rise.

"You ain't leaving yet!"one of the other players challenged.

"Got a train to catch." Charley sensed the mood of the
gamblers had soured. "Guess I had a bit of beginner's
luck."

"With your luck, you oughta stick around."

Charley looked at the men and assessed that they
weren't just rowdy. *They might be dangerous.*

"Well, guess I could sit in for a few more hands."
Charley decided the safest bet was to lose the next hand,
but he won with three of a kind. And in the next hand he
drew a full house. He couldn't seem to do anything
wrong. He was on a winning streak. The player piano
had stopped its noise, and gamblers at other tables had
turned their attention to him. The air was thick with
tension, all eyes trained on the pot.

Hours passed and Charley had lost track of time.
There were only two gamblers left playing at his table
and he seized the opportunity to finally withdraw.

"I'm calling it a night," he said firmly. He feared the
train might arrive early and move on without him. He
had to leave now or he would be stuck in Auburn overnight. Charley doffed his cap at the players and stuffed
his winnings, including the small bag of gold dust, into
his backpack.

Now that he had something to lose, he saw danger at
every corner as he walked down the main street of Auburn toward the train depot. He heard a whistle and saw

a freight barrel through without stopping. W*hat the heck!* Now he would have to search for shelter until the next train came through. It was late, but the town still rocked with noises of every type: pistol shots, braying mules, and the occasional scream of a woman. He wondered if Auburn was more civilized in the daytime.

He ended up in another saloon nearest the train stop. The barkeep was wiping down the plain plank bar, tending to the patrons leaning against it. There were only four tables in this narrow room, which also served as the lobby for a hotel.

"How much for a room?" he asked the bartender.

"Eight bits," he replied.

This time Charley was not surprised by the amount. Everything was overpriced in Auburn.

"Twelve bits if you want company." A woman in a body-clinging red dress stepped forward.

"No. No. Just the room."

The bartender passed him a brass key.

"Any chance of getting something to eat?" Charley asked as he put the key in his pocket. "I'd be happy with eggs and—"

"Eggs are three dollars—each."

"Must have been laid by a golden goose," Charley muttered under his breath.

"Hard getting goods in these parts. Ever heard of the gold rush?"

"Sure, but—"

"Well, the gold rush has passed, but the prices haven't. Take it or leave it, mister."

Charley didn't find the man's attitude friendly at all. He thought of all the eggs he had eaten fresh on the farm, and now to be charged this outrageous sum. The gnawing pain of hunger had returned, and since he did have some extra money, he agreed to order the food.

"That comes with bacon and coffee, right?"

"Sure, for another two bits." The bartender smiled.

When his food arrived, Charley wolfed down the eggs and chewed the tough fatty bacon in no more than three ravenous bites. He paid the bill, but decided against taking the room after all. He would find a place near the train depot and make his bedroll do.

"Thanks all the same, mister," Charley said. "Won't need the room." He pulled the key from his pocket and pushed it across the bar. He wanted to save his money for something more important than laying his head on a lumpy pillow for a few hours.

It was after midnight by the time Charley consulted the train schedule inside the depot. The next locomotive wouldn't be coming through until tomorrow evening. It was a lot of time to kill. He scouted for a safe place to sack out and finally found a vacant car among a string of boxcars on a railroad siding Before making the boxcar his for the night, he had one more thing to do—find a place to hide his winnings.

He climbed down an embankment near the tracks.

Next to a large boulder, Charley spotted some trash—probably left by one of the hobos who frequented the rail yards. A rusty tin can, perfect for hiding his silver dollars, jutted out from the mess. He quickly dug a hole with his bare hands, filled the can with the coins, and dropped it in the hole. For good measure he covered the raw dirt with dry weeds to ward off the curious. Anyone coming across it would think the old tin can had been there a while and wouldn't bother looking in it.

As he climbed back up the embankment, he studied the rowdy, wild town that the gold rush had produced—so different from the safe, calm Concordia he had grown accustomed to. Charley could never settle in a place like this.

CHAPTER TWENTY-EIGHT

Charley

The men jumped on him before he could wake up and defend himself. Charley's head was slammed against the side of the boxcar while the scraping shuffle of boots surrounded him.

"Grab his backpack," someone growled. He sounded like one of the men from the saloon.

"No!" Charley managed to yell.

"Take off his boots. See what's in 'em besides stinking feet," another said. Charley could smell his rank whiskey breath bearing down on him. The man attacking him shifted and began tugging at Charley's left boot.

With a burst of adrenaline Charley jerked his leg away, breaking the man's grip, and jumped into a crouching position. Using his head as a battering ram, he ran his skull into the man's stomach, knocking the wind out of him. He heard the others combing through the contents of his backpack which they had emptied on the boxcar floor.

"Here it is! The gold dust!" one of them hooted in triumph. They laughed at their friend lying on the floor, struggling for breath. Even though it was too dark to see them clearly, Charley was certain that his attackers were the gamblers he cleaned out earlier. Their voices were unmistakable.

"Hey, I earned that fair and square," Charley yelled. Before he could get his bearings, one of the thugs lunged at him. His bony fists were fast and the hard blows landed against an ear, an eye, and his nose, rendering Charley helpless. He fell to the floor with blood gushing from his nose. He tried to get up only making the man laugh. He kicked Charley in the ribs, causing him to double up next to the man he had gut-punched with his head.

"Give him one for me, Shorty!" the downed man moaned.

"Nah. He's had enough for one night. Ain't you, rube?" Shorty said. He yanked Charley's head up by the hair and thrust his face close to his. His foul breath was almost as offensive as his fists had been. He grunted as he dropped Charley's head, letting it slam to the floor. "That'll teach you to cheat at cards," he said, spitting on him. The men jumped down from the boxcar, laughing. The one Charley had winded was still gasping for air. "Slow down," he managed to wheeze. "Damn it, wait for me."

When Charley tried to move, pain shot through his side. He couldn't breathe through his nose and when he touched it, he heard a squishy sound like dry, brittle paper being wadded up. *Damn! It's broken.* He wiped the blood on his sleeve and assessed the rest of his injuries. It was no surprise that his head hurt and that there was a troublesome ringing in his ears too. His injured eye felt like it was swelling shut. When he was unable to focus on the open door, he figured the best he could expect was a swollen eye. He'd be lucky to see out a narrow slit.

Now what was he going to do? He had counted on that gold dust bringing in a fair amount of money. Come morning, he had planned to take it to the assayer to measure its worth—see if he could exchange it for bank-notes at the local bank. He should have hidden it with his other winnings.

True, the men had not succeeded in removing his boots where he had hidden money for the trip to California. He had scrimped to make it last, so all was not lost. And the gamblers hadn't found the silver dollars he had won from them and later hidden. But that was hardly worth the beating he had taken. His problem now was that he doubted he could retrieve the coins. He could hardly move, let alone walk. Climbing down and back up the embankment was out of the question.

He tried to pull himself up to a sitting position. *Damn!* It felt like getting kicked again. A sharp, sickening pain ran through his torso from ribs to neck. Charley flopped back down and braced himself with both hands, clutching the rough boards under him as dizziness overcame him. *What's happening to me?* A burst of bright light blinded him as his head exploded and he spun away.

He fell into a restless sleep for what seemed like only a few minutes, but must have been hours later because the dim light of dawn was filtering through the open boxcar. Charley heard voices outside and he cringed. *The gamblers?* Had they returned to finish the job they had started? Were they going to rob him of what he had squirreled away in his shoes? Charley moved stiffly, feeling worse than when he passed out last night.

A face appeared in the doorway.

"Look. Found another hobo. Get down from there, boy!" the man yelled.

Charley squinted out of his good eye and saw that the man was not one of the gamblers after all.

"Didn't you hear me?" The man leaned in. "Oh jeez, look at you." He climbed up and peered closely at Charley. "This guy is in a bad way. Give me a hand, here," he said to his friend. Another man climbed into the boxcar and gasped. Both men were wearing railroad caps with Central Pacific sewn across them.

"What are we going to do with him?'

"Don't know, but he can't stay in here. Let's get him to the hospital."

"Noo hos-pi-tal," Charley mumbled. He tried to protest further but couldn't make his lips move right. Only bits of words escaped, which were clearly unintelligible—even to his ears. "No hospital!" he tried again. With effort the words sounded clearer. An image of the dreaded orphanage infirmary with its sickening smells flooded his consciousness, sending a new pain across his skull. He felt the sensation of being lifted and must have passed out again, because when he awoke a third pair of eyes was staring at him.

"Why, he's just a young man," the newcomer said. "I guess I could take him to the hospital in my wagon."

"That would be mighty good of you, mister. But the idea of a hospital riled him," one of the Central Pacific switchmen said. "He at least needs a doctor."

"You're right, but this is the day Doc Moses is out making house calls. He could be anywhere in Placer County. Look," he said, "No sense in upsetting the young fellow. Until Doc returns, my daughter, Brigitte, can do pretty much what the hospital nurses do. From time to time, Doc sends her folks needing a little time to recuperate.

Charley felt himself being hoisted into a wagon. The men braced him against burlap bags filled with provisions so that he wouldn't roll around, but every bump felt like a spear piercing his side. The sun beat down on him and he was so thirsty, he couldn't produce any spit. Charley's lips felt swollen with the effort of breathing through his mouth. It was a blessing to fall asleep in spite of the bad dream.

Pap cried out as the train bore down on him. Mum cried too as she tugged on Pap's shoe trying to free him. The train whistle wailed in warning, but it was too late. "Stop! Stop!" Charley cried as a whoosh of air surrounded him when the train passed.

Charley awoke with a start. The wagon had stopped. Curious faces studied him. One face belonged to a pretty young woman who was directing the man with the wagon and his friend on the proper way to unload Charley without hurting him further.

"Put that board under him, now," she instructed. "We need to keep him still. Gently now, he's not another sack of beans."

He felt himself being lifted, and the weightlessness of injury gratefully suspended him. He felt a fire flash through him and then, blissfully, nothing.

CHAPTER TWENTY-NINE

Charley

When Charley awoke all he could see was the light of a kerosene lamp reflected in a window. He looked around as much as his stiff neck would allow and he saw that the cabin he was in was quite large. The single bed he lay in was tucked into one corner of a great room near a fireplace with a fire underway; pinewood popped and spit for company. A large kitchen table and a half dozen chairs stood near an old iron cook stove at the opposite end of the main room. A winding staircase wound itself to an upper floor, most likely leading to bedrooms.

Through his broken nose, he fought for air. Charley snuffled and called out for water. The woman he saw upon arrival materialized and leaned over him.

"You finally coming around?" she said. "Good. Now just take a few sips to begin with." She lifted his head and tipped a tin dipper of water to his lips. It felt shockingly cold as it trickled through his swollen lips and down his throat. The room began to spin and he waved the water away.

"That's okay, take your time. I'm not going anywhere," she said.

"Where am I?" Charley murmured.

"Oh, about three miles outside Auburn, where the North and Middle Forks of the American River join." She laid a cool hand on his forehead. "You don't feel like you have a fever. That's good, anyway." She smiled. "My father has a bar claim to go after gold in low-water riverbeds. But the diggings are pretty much played out by now. Still, he hopes for a big strike. All the men up here hope for a strike. It's in their nature, I'm afraid."

"Who are you?" Charley asked.

"My name is Brigitte. Brigitte Doyle. You should try to drink some more." She brought the dipper close to his lips again. Charley lifted his head and gratefully took in a bit more cold, sweet water before lying back down.

"And you're Charley O'Brien," she said. "Papa took the liberty of looking through your backpack to see who you might be."

Charley's eyes opened wide in alarm.

"Don't worry. Everything looked to be in order—a bit of a messy order I'd say." Brigitte laughed softly.

Charley shifted his legs under the cotton quilt covering him and discovered he was naked. His trousers and shirt had been removed as well as his shoes.

"My clothes. My shoes?" He started to sit up and thought better of it as soon as a pain shot through his side. He suddenly remembered the beating in vivid detail and flopped back down.

"I set them aside for washing tomorrow. Don't worry. The money we found in your shoes and sewn in your shirt are safe. The miners up here may be anxious to get rich, but they're no robbers."

"Didn't mean to accuse anyone."

"Papa said you had been robbed once already and once was enough."

Charley looked at Brigitte and saw light dancing in her eyes and a smile on her lips. He realized she was teasing him.

"What time is it?"

"Don't know. After nine o'clock I think."

"Got to get—night train—Sacramento," he faltered. His lips hurt when he talked.

"Well, you're in no shape to catch a train right now," Brigitte said. "What's your all fired hurry?"

"Need to get land—ready—for planting. Before winter," he said as if it weren't obvious. Brigitte dipped a cloth in the water and bathed his parched lips, following up with a minty tasting salve. She spread the balm carefully with the tip of one index finger.

"Don't worry. There are trains going to Sacramento every day. Doc needs to check on you first. At the very least he'll probably tell you to rest up while your ribs are healing. You're welcome to stay with us as long as it takes."

Brigitte's words were as soothing as the balm she had applied. Charley sighed and closed his eyes.

The next morning, Brigitte and her father, Brian Doyle, helped get Charley up. They got him dressed in one of Mr. Doyle's red flannel shirts and a pair of buckle-backed dungarees. The words, "Levi Strauss," were stamped on the leather patch sewn to the waistband. Charley was embarrassed about his dirt and bloodied nakedness in front of strangers, especially when one of the strangers was a woman. But he was in no position to protest. When he tried to cover up his lower body, Brigitte said, "Don't worry, Charley. You haven't got anything I haven't already seen."

"Brigitte, don't tease," her father said. "Brigitte learned doctoring from her mother—my wife—before she died. Being around miners all the time, she's not timid in her talk. Got to remind her to be more ladylike every once in a while." He winked at his daughter.

"Papa," she complained and blushed.

They helped him to the privy and fixed him food, although Charley couldn't eat much before he wanted to sleep again.

Doctor Moses finally made a house call several days later.

"Sorry to take so long in checking you out, young man," he said upon meeting Charley.

"Lots of folks to see spread out all over these hills. Now let's take a look." He pressed and probed Charley's torso, listened to his heart through a stethoscope, looked up his nose, and examined the black eye.

"Well, in spite of how you look, you're going to live. Nose will remain crooked, but that will make your face interesting. Give it character. Your black eye is progressing. It's a nice shade of purple about to turn green by now. Fortunately your eye, itself, appears okay. Ribs were broken, of course. Most doctors bind them, but I find it just makes my patients feel worse. Better if they heal by themselves. So, I'm going to recommend that we leave them be—as long as you remain inactive and rest." He adjusted his glasses and moved closer to Charley to check his face.

"Thanks to Brigitte and her salves, your cuts are healing nicely. Not much more I can do there. Now, young man, there's just one more thing to discuss." Dr. Moses returned his stethoscope to his black bag and snapped it shut. "Like my name implies, I'm wise like the biblical Moses. So when I suggest that you stay out of saloons and refrain from gambling, I hope you'll take my advice."

"No need to worry about that," Charley said. "I've learned my lesson."

A week passed and Charley was starting to get into the rhythm of the days. He was eating well, walking to build up his strength, and sleeping more than usual. He felt almost strong enough to leave and retrieve his tin can full of money buried at the bottom of the embankment. From there he would hop another train and continue on his journey to Sacramento. But then, Brian

Doyle explained what the diggings were all about.

"When gold from panning became less plentiful in the streams," he said, "men began to extract ore directly from the rocks. If a gold vein was visible, it was targeted for crushing or blasting. Underground mining followed. I prefer working a sluice box next to the American River, myself. My partners and I make a fair living at it. When you're up to it, we can always use an extra hand if you're interested."

"I don't know anything about prospecting," Charley responded.

"No one else did either when they first arrived in 1849. Some got rich and others just managed to eke enough from the ground to keep body and soul together. I never planned on staying this long myself, but when I decided to pull out, my wife got sick and we had no place else to go." Brian removed his hat and mopped his forehead with his bandana. "Brigitte and her man came to help care for the wife, but after my wife died I didn't have the heart to up and leave."

"And then..." He hesitated before going on. "Then, Brigitte's man left. Now it's just the two of us." His sober expression was replaced with a rueful smile. "We'll leave someday, but the life suits us—for now. Between the prospecting and selling supplies to the miners, we get by."

That explained a lot. But Charley couldn't see himself digging gravel and shoveling it inside the wooden sluice box all day. He preferred to work fertile land under his feet over inhaling dirt and dust. And still—maybe he owed it to himself to give prospecting a try.

A few days later he agreed to accompany Brian to the diggings. The river made soothing noises, drawing Charley to its side. Its swift, clear current burbled over rocks of many colors. Trout jumped and slid over the rocks unconcerned with the intruders at river's edge, who bent over their pans, swirling the contents with a circular motion. Charley edged closer and watched men scooping at the gravel. Some had their pants rolled up and were in the river near large boulders.

"Some of the biggest nuggets found were near or under big rocks like that," Brian pointed out. He handed him a blackened pan that had been seasoned by burning it. Brian had explained earlier that prospectors found out the hard way that if they used a metal pan that still had oil on its surface, fine gold dust could adhere to the oil and float clean out. "Want to try your luck?"

Charley accepted the shallow utensil and bent down, imitating the other prospectors. As he scooped and rolled the gravel in his pan, he noticed the separation of particles—heavier pieces of yellowish gravel landing on the bottom, lighter flakes floating to the top.

Brian looked over his shoulder. "Looks like a few little nuggets at the bottom, Charley."

"Really?" Charley took a closer look. He picked out one large shiny piece that sparkled and held it up to the sun.

"Not that one, Charley. You've got a piece of iron pyrite—fool's gold." He picked up a similar shaped nugget with a buttery yellow color. "Now this is real gold if I'm not mistaken."

Several men stopped what they were doing to come and look. Their indifference to Charley when he arrived earlier had now been replaced with keen interest.

"Beginners luck!" one shouted as he slapped Charley on the back in a friendly manner. The slap caused a twinge of discomfort—a reminder of Charley's healing injuries, but he laughed with the men and enjoyed the excitement of the moment.

That evening, with Brian's help, Charley safeguarded his diggings in an empty glass jar. He placed it on a shelf above the dry sink and gazed at it all night. Through the light of the kerosene lamps, the dull shine of the gold nuggets was spellbinding. He couldn't seem to keep his mind off of how easy it was to harvest the nuggets. No wonder men were lured to the gold fields. "How much do you think they're worth?" he asked Brian.

"Oh, I'd guess the assayer would weigh it at about half an ounce or so."

"Is that all!"

"Won't know for sure until you get it weighed and then to the bank. The price of gold changes. You might find that it's going at a pretty good exchange right now."

Charley hoped the nuggets were at least equal to the value of the gold dust he had won off the gamblers.

"When are you going to town, again, Brian?" he asked. "Was hoping to ride in with you and see for myself."

"Fair enough. I'm going in for supplies in a few days."

"Great. Maybe I'll go to the diggings with you tomorrow and try my luck again. See if I can add something more to it." Charley motioned to the jar.

"Sounds like you might have a touch of gold fever, Charley."

Charley laughed off the remark. But he did return to the river and tirelessly panned for several more days, growing exhausted in the hot sun. His hard labor was rewarded when he collected a few more nuggets and a finger of flakes in his pan by the end of each day. But the excitement over these findings were nothing like the first thrilling time. Nevertheless, he filled the small jar on the shelf and welcomed the opportunity to recoup some of what he lost in the boxcar.

Charley and Brian arrived in Auburn by late morning. The town appeared completely different in the daytime—calm, but bustling with folks going about the business of commerce and trade. It was nothing like the loud and rowdy night Charley had spent upon his arrival. As he looked around, he saw the mercantile store doing a brisk business as well as the other shops, the bank, the cafés lining the wooden boardwalk. Wagons creaked, donkeys brayed, and all manner of horseflesh crowded the dusty streets. There were plenty of ladies shopping with purpose as they peered in windows before entering the shops. Unshaven men that Charley guessed were miners because of their unkempt appearance led burdened mules from the assayer's office to the café or general store. Many more of them bypassed stores in favor of entering one of the saloons.

Brian stopped in front of the general store. "Coming, Charley?"

"In a little while, Brian. If you don't mind, think I'll go check the train schedule first." Be back in no time to help you load your supplies, though."

Charley jumped down from the wagon and headed for the train depot. He didn't really need to check the Central Pacific schedule. He knew it by heart. But he *did* need to check on the tin can stuffed with silver dollars that he buried below the railroad tracks. It was time to retrieve it. He walked the few short blocks to the station and crossed the tracks.

Charley looked around and, when he was certain no one was watching him, he slid down the embankment. He felt a stitch in his side and had to rest before continuing. He bent over and took some shallow breaths until he felt better. He had come this far and refused to turn back until he found his money. The big boulder was where he remembered it being, but he didn't see the spot where he buried the tin can. He walked around studying the ground for the thatch of dry grass he had yanked up to camouflage the raw dirt. He didn't see anything like it.

With the toe of his shoe he kicked at several promising mounds, but was disappointed. Below the boulder he spotted an irregularity in the ground's surface and slid a little lower to check it out. Something rusty protruded from the earth and appeared slightly damp. Maybe the rain from the other night softened the dirt, causing a small mud slide that carried the tin can with it.

Charley brushed the damp dirt from it and sure enough—it was the right can. By its weight, he figured his coins were safely inside. He shook it and the comforting sound of something hard hitting against its sides reassured him. But when he carefully removed the jagged-edged lid and peered into the container, all he saw were rocks. *Someone found it!* Charley poured out the rocks and threw the can to the bottom of the ravine.

When he finally made it back to the general store, Brian was busily hoisting gunny sacks into the wagon. "Find what you were looking for?" he asked.

"What? No." Charley answered. He bristled at the loss. After all he had gone through to get the gold dust and silver dollars, it was all gone. Charley grabbed one of the sacks and tossed it on top of the others. Lifting still hurt his ribs, but anger at his loss—and the accompanying discomfort—was like a balm.

They finished loading the supplies Brian purchased and then headed for the assayer's office. Charley plunked down his small jar of nuggets and the bag of gold dust he collected to be weighed.

"Used some of my diggings to trade for supplies today," Brian said. "Most businesses are willing to trade gold for goods." He withdrew a goatskin bag half full of ore from his pocket and placed it next to Charley's.

They watched as the assayer carefully examined the nuggets and weighed them. He then weighed their gold dust separately. Charley watched carefully to make sure that none of the dust remained behind on the scale. *Not that I don't trust the man....* After having the troy ounces converted and receiving written confirmation of the gold's worth, Charley and Brian headed for the bank, where they turned in their gold for bank notes.

As they left the bank, they passed by an apothecary shop. Along with medicinal items, the window display was filled with fancy glass vials of perfume, jars of creams, and boxes of lady's powders and other toiletries.

"I'll just be a minute, Brian." Charley turned and entered the shop, leaving Brian behind to puzzle the reason. Charley scanned the fancy goods and chose a round box with a colorful design on it. The clerk wrapped the package in brown paper and tied it with string. When he returned outside, Brian was smiling.

"An entirely successful trip, I'd say." Brian winked.

Not entirely, Charley thought. But then he smiled. No point in being ungrateful. He had more money than when he arrived in Auburn. It had allowed him to buy a treat just now, something he rarely had the money for. And he planned to safeguard the rest of his earnings to put toward the land he desired. *No more gambling.* He just wished that he hadn't lost his winnings. As if his thoughts conjured up the enemy, he saw two of the three gamblers who had beaten and robbed him. They were on the opposite side of the street, in front of the same saloon where Charley had met them. He turned aside so that the men wouldn't see him.

"What's the matter, Charley?" Brian asked.

"Nothing. I just saw two of the thieves who beat me. Can we hurry up and leave before they come our way."

"Sure. But don't you want to talk to the sheriff and make a report, now that you've seen them again. Get some justice."

"I just want to get out of here, Brian. Can we do that, please?"

"Of course, Charley. It's your choice."

CHAPTER THIRTY

Charley

Upon their return from Auburn, Charley sought out Brigitte. She was hanging laundry on a makeshift line strung between two pine trees.

"This is for all your kindness, Brigitte." He handed her the package from town.

She held it up to her face and sniffed it. "Charley, you didn't need to do that. But I'm glad you did," she said, smiling. When Brigitte lifted the lid from the box, a puff of perfumed talcum powder wafted toward her face.

"Oh, lilac. It's the perfect thing. Anything to get the dusty smell of the diggings out of my nose." She looked at her father. "Not that it's *all* bad."

"That's okay, Brigitte," Brian said. "Sometimes I forget how selfish I've been, subjecting you to the rough conditions here. You deserve better." He looked at Charley. "Good smelling things and time off to go dancing is what she needs."

"Oh, Papa. Listen to you." Brigitte flushed with pleasure.

Charley looked down at his shoes, embarrassed by the

genuine emotion he witnessed between the two. Brigitte suddenly looked younger and her father, wiser. The suggestion that she be entertained by Charley taking her dancing wasn't lost on him either.

He wasn't the only one she treated kindly. Brigitte didn't seem put off by long hours of work or serving spur-of-the-moment meals to miners down on their luck. Her father was right. She deserved to be treated with time off from the community of men and their uncouth ways.

Later that evening, Charley asked, "Do you ever get lonesome for the company of other women?"

"Sure, sometimes. But I've been far too busy to worry about the nice things of society." She looked off in the distance. "Someday, I'd like to settle down, get married, and have a slew of children."

"What happened to your man?" he asked at last. He wondered how anyone could leave Brigitte.

"We were going to get married and were leaving Montana to live in Idaho when Mama fell ill. Papa sent a telegram that he needed help. So Ned and I came and I tended to Mama until she died."

"I'm sorry," Charley said. "That must have been hard."

"It was." Brigitte paused a second before continuing. "Back when we were all still in Missoula, Mama taught me the ways of doctoring. She knew all about herbs and was in demand as a midwife. When I arrived in Auburn,

I had plenty of people to practice on besides her. Someone in the gold diggings was always getting cut or crushing fingers or getting fevers. Guess I did a fair job of keeping most of the men somewhat healthy. Of course they'd be better off if they gave up their whiskey, but there's only so much a woman can do." Brigitte sighed. "Sometimes Dr. Moses asks me to take in some poor suffering soul while he's getting his strength back."

"Like you did with me," Charley stated.

"Yes, exactly."

"What happened to Ned?"

"Oh, he got tired of the life and ran off. He said he'd send for me when he got settled..." Brigitte's voice trailed off. "But, he didn't."

"I'm going to send for my girl as soon as I get to Sacramento," Charley said. "Her name is Christina."

"I know what it is. Heard you saying her name in your sleep when you were feverish."

"Oh, I didn't know." Charley wondered what else he said in his sleep?

"Where is she?"

"Staying with some folks in Utah. She's waiting to hear from me. Thought I'd delay writing to her until I reach Sacramento. When I find a plot of land I'll send for her."

"Think she'll wait until then?"

"Sure, why not?" Charley's features screwed up at the question.

"It's just that folks get restless waiting. I think that that's what happened to Ned. I don't expect I'll ever hear from him again," Brigitte said. "It's been over a year. If we had gotten hitched, maybe. But, then again, it may not have made any difference." She dropped her head and shrugged her shoulders.

"So you're not bound to him?"

She shook her head. When Brigitte looked up and saw Charley's intense gaze, her cheeks turned a bright pink. *For all her brave talk, she's not so bold after all.*

He wished Christina felt the same way Brigitte did about marriage and children. There was something warm and life-affirming about her that was missing in Christina. Then, it was Charley's turn to blush. He'd have to keep his feelings in check. Although he was developing a soft spot for Brigitte and enjoyed being in her company, he reminded himself that he belonged to another. Maybe it was time to move on.

CHAPTER THIRTY-ONE

Lucy

Lucy had seen these instruments of torture before: metal devices soaking in alcohol. Some looked like bug pincers, others like the hinged jaws of dragons. Their mere appearance struck fear in her. The sight of metal pans that made pinging sounds when something was dropped into them looked cold and threatening. She began to tremble as Dr. Martin approached her.

"Open wide," he said as he placed a flat stick on her tongue to hold it down. "Say aaah."

It hurt Lucy to open her mouth. She concentrated on looking at Dr. Martin's face since he was so close. Maybe it would keep her mind off the discomfort of the exam. Light reflected off his glasses, the thick lenses magnifying his brown eyes. They were like the kind eyes of the stray dog she had been secretly feeding. The brown-eyed, long-haired shaggy dog with the bend in his tail came begging at the back kitchen door each morning after breakfast. She was forbidden to feed him, but she snuck food to him anyway, hiding it in the pocket of her pinafore while cook was distracted. She had decided to name the dog Brownie.

Dr. Martin's bushy eyebrows lifted as he backed away. "You can relax now," he said, giving Lucy's arm a little pat. He looked at Jennie and shook his head. "I've never seen tonsils so inflamed. You said Lucy has been sick a lot?"

"Yes. That's what she told us."

"Child, what did they do for you at the Children's Home when you fell ill?" he asked.

Lucy shrugged. She didn't know how to answer. During the times she was sick, life around her was a blur. She just remembered coughing hard and only sleeping between bouts of hacking. Her throat hurt so bad at times, she felt like there was something living in the back of her mouth—perched there like the gargoyles she had seen in books of fairy tales. She imagined them digging their talons into the red flesh they called her tonsils. When it was really bad, she couldn't swallow without crying.

"Needless to say, this child should be treated and watched closely to head off an infection," Dr. Martin said. "Maybe even have those tonsils removed."

"Oh my, what should I tell Violet, Dr. Martin? She's really in charge, you know."

"I never figured it any other way, Jennie. Of course she's in charge of any decisions. I'll recommend that Lucy be seen by someone at St. Mary's Hospital. They're in the best position to treat her."

"St. Mary's Hospital? I've heard of it, but where is it?"

"In Rochester, Minnesota. Pretty far from here, I know. But not so long by train." Dr. Martin grabbed a pad and pen. "I can write to the doctors there ahead of a visit. But first I need to discuss this with Violet. Please ask her to come and see me." He reached for a bottle inside his glass-fronted cabinet and turned to Lucy. "In the meantime, Lucy, I want you to gargle with this three times a day, avoid cold drinks and solid food, and drink *only* hot liquids like chicken soup and tea with honey."

"What about ice cream?" Lucy asked.

"No ice cream for now. But if your tonsils are removed you can have all the ice cream you want."

Her face brightened at the prospect. She looked at Jennie, who had just developed a deep furrow across her forehead.

"Okay," Lucy croaked, excitedly. "When can we do it? Get rid of my tonsils?"

Dr. Martin smiled. "Not so fast, young lady." He turned to Jennie. "If all goes well, Lucy's voice should sound a little softer as well."

As they left Dr. Martin's office, Lucy reached for Jennie's hand.

"Will you be with me when I get my tonsils out, Jennie?"

"Of course," she said with some hesitation in her voice. "But Lucy, let's not share all the new information with Violet just yet. I'll explain what Dr. Martin recommends to her this evening."

This time it was Lucy whose forehead furrowed. "Okay, but do you think she'll say 'No?' I mean, if you and the doctor think it's a good idea, won't Violet think so too?"

"One can never guess what Violet thinks is a good idea, Lucy. We'll just have to see."

They boarded the waiting buggy before Lucy said, "Aren't we going to see Peter today?"

"Not today, Lucy. I think we've had enough excitement for one day."

All Lucy could think of was that if they didn't meet Peter she wouldn't be getting ice cream. And if Violet said no to that place in Minnesota, she wouldn't get ice cream. This was a problem worth thinking about. Ever since she had been introduced to the frozen treat she just couldn't do without it!

CHAPTER THIRTY-TWO

Jennie

They did not go to the ice cream parlor that day, the following day, or any of the days that week. Jennie was too busy helping Violet prepare for a tea she would be hosting. It was not a good time to talk to her mother about Lucy's need for surgery or a convenient time to meet Peter. Jennie hoped he didn't think she was trying to avoid him. She really needed to send him a note of explanation. Lucy kept asking when they would be going for ice cream again with that "nice man."

"Hush, Lucy! Remember, that's just our little secret. You're not to mention Peter in this house unless we're alone in our bedroom. Understood?"

Lucy had nodded as her eyes blinked back tears. Jennie was immediately sorry that her words sounded so harsh. She had never scolded her before. Lucy was just a lively child full of enthusiasm and, like all children, had trouble keeping secrets.

Finally, Jennie wrote a note, sending it with Franklin, Violet's driver, who was going to town to pick up the mail. "You should be able to find Peter easily enough,

Franklin," she said, and began to describe Peter.

"I know what he looks like. Can't miss the likes of him in Concordia—dressed in gentleman's clothes."

Sounds as if Franklin disapproves of Peter. Oh well, men of success always have their detractors.

When Franklin returned from town, he carried a stack of mail that he left on the hall credenza—as was his habit.

"Anything addressed to me?" Jennie asked.

"No, miss. Nothing."

She had hoped that Charley had written to let her know where he and Christina settled. She worried about their safety riding the rails, but also envied them this adventure. She knew that she would likely be unable to withstand the difficulties of traveling in such a manner.

Funny, but Franklin didn't mention the errand I sent him on. Finally, she asked: "Did you deliver my message to Peter Stuyvesant?"

"Yes, miss, I did," he said, avoiding eye contact with her.

"Well, did he send a reply?"

"No, miss. He was kind of busy."

"Busy, how?" she pressed.

"Well, Miss Jennie. He was playing cards and in the company of one of those fancy girls at the saloon. Guess he didn't want to take time away from that. Sorry." He bowed and took his leave.

Jennie felt as if she had been struck. Her neck and

face instantly grew hot as humiliation washed over her. How foolish she had been to think that Peter—handsome Peter—years older than she, would be interested in her. He was sophisticated and probably accustomed to the company of women who were a little freer—and easier. And, truth be told, perhaps he *was* too old for her and maybe he *had* been secretly laughing at her naiveté and inexperience. If that was the truth, it stung, sharply. She would put it out of her mind until she was alone to figure out what went wrong. Maybe she was not as attractive as she thought she was. *All the things he said to me. Was he being insincere? Was he a liar and a cheat like Charley said?*

Well, she would just have to keep busy and forget about him. She had Violet to please, and Lucy's schooling and the child's possible surgery to prepare for. The first thing she needed to do was convince Violet to meet with Dr. Martin. Jennie hoped that his bedside manner would prune away any objections that her mother might raise at funding Lucy's medical needs.

The ladies were as noisy as a gaggle of geese, like the flock on the Neamott farm. Jennie saw this as a good sign and that the tea was a success. Violet was in her element. She liked nothing better than to entertain. There had been a note of envy in her voice when she talked about Cousin Mary Belle attending teas and soirees in New Orleans regularly.

"Even in the winter they have these little gatherings," Violet had explained. "Life is so much more civilized there."

That would explain why Mary Belle seemed as comfortable in this setting as the ladies Jennie met in the Paris salons. She smiled when she thought about the trip that she and Violet took touring Europe. It seemed so long ago—a time when Jennie was interested in art and aspiring to be a great artist one day. With this in mind, Violet exposed her to the finest works of art in Paris. She did enjoy much of the works, especially the pen and ink drawings and portraits, most of which were smaller in scale than the huge canvases depicting religious themes or violent scenes of battle.

She had not kept up with her art studies, but now that Lucy was here, she thought she would attempt to sketch her. She had such interesting features.

Jennie enjoyed the petit fours and artfully cut sandwiches that accompanied the tea, but the chatter about the most inane things got on her nerves. She kept thinking about the rebuff from Peter. Although she intended to call off all contact, there was a part of her that yearned to see him call on her one more time. She fantasized about seeing him beg her forgiveness for his lack of attention and his indiscretion with a common dance hall girl. It would give Jennie a great deal of satisfaction to withhold forgiveness and send Peter on his way.

CHAPTER THIRTY-THREE

Jennie

Time was growing short before the school term began. It was mid-August and Jennie had not informed Violet of Lucy's exam by Dr. Martin, nor his recommendations to consider surgery. She would need to do so if Lucy was to make the trip to St. Mary's Hospital and back before school started.

Luckily, she was relieved from that burden when Dr. Martin encountered Violet and Mary Belle in town on a shopping expedition. He asked when she was going to come and see him to discuss Lucy's condition.

"I was caught completely unaware, Jennie," Violet complained after returning home from town. "Why in the world didn't you come to me before now? Why did you take it upon yourself to take Lucy to see Dr. Martin in the first place?"

"I was afraid you wouldn't approve."

"Well, I'm not sure that I do. But now that it is common knowledge in town that Lucy is my responsibility, I'm compelled to address her health needs. Dr. Martin urged me to take her to St. Mary's Hospital."

"Isn't that a good thing, Violet? Taking her to experts for another opinion?" Jennie decided to press her advantage. "Doctors at St. Mary's Hospital can determine what should be done for Lucy."

"Yes, perhaps, but I'm more concerned about your growing attachment to Lucy to the neglect of your other responsibilities—to me and to your special interests." Violet looked at Jennie closely. "You seem to be preoccupied with Lucy's care." She took Jennie's hands loosely in her own. "I noticed you no longer want to join in social events we shared and enjoyed together. And I don't see you drawing any longer. I hate to see you ignore your talent."

"I know, Violet. But don't you see? Lucy has no one! At least when I was that age I had a brother. She needs all the affection and care she can get. And she is the nearest person to the sister I didn't have."

It was as if Jennie had let the air out of Violet. Her demeanor changed as her face sagged. She dropped Jennie's hands and turned to face the marble-flanked fireplace.

"I had hoped that what I provided you was enough," she said finally.

"It was more than enough, Violet," Jennie said as she went to her mother. "But, *together* we have so much to give Lucy. It can only strengthen our own relationship, don't you see?"

"I see that you are growing into a generous young

woman. Maybe too much so. I hope it doesn't cause you disappointment in the future." Violet stood taller, straightening her skirt. Very well, I'll talk to Dr. Martin about making arrangements with St. Mary's Hospital. When I take Lucy there, I assume you will accompany us to make sure she is cooperative. Frankly, her energy and grating voice tire me out."

"Of course, Violet. Thank you." Jennie threw her arms around Violet, who had regained her composure. She patted Jennie on the back with restrained enthusiasm.

The next morning while Violet sent Franklin to deliver a note to Dr. Martin and to pick up a train schedule to Rochester, Minnesota, Jennie unpacked her drawing supplies. She had convinced Lucy to sit for her. She arranged her on a stool by the parlor's bay window and tilted her head this way and that. She arranged her wild red curls in a manner that Lucy wouldn't have tolerated if anyone else had suggested it.

"Don't move, Lucy. You'll have to sit still just a bit longer while I get a rough sketch finished. Then you may have a break."

Lucy made a face, causing Jennie to laugh. After a few more minutes of Lucy's fidgeting, Jennie gave up.

"Maybe we can try this again later. I can see that sitting still is not your cup of tea."

"Can I go now?" Lucy said.

"Yes. Go." Jennie looked at a rough outline of Lucy's head and a suggestion of curls, but no details of her facial features.

"Oh goodie!" Lucy exclaimed. She slid the rest of the way off the stool and ran toward the kitchen. Jennie put her art supplies away and went to the back of the house where she happened to glance out a window. There on the kitchen steps sat Lucy feeding sausage links to a big brown dog. She laughed when she pictured little Lucy sneaking the string of sausages from the kitchen. There would be hell to pay if cook found out.

The animal wagged his tail so fast he looked like a wind-up toy about to take off. After he had gobbled down the treats, Lucy nuzzled his face in hers and giggled as his big wet tongue mopped her face.

CHAPTER THIRTY-FOUR

Charley

It was mid-September and Charley still toiled in the diggings, bending over the shallow water with a pan or shoveling gravel into the sluice box. Recalling the excitement of finding gold that first time, made up for the fatigue that overcame him by the end of the day. Charley knew the likelihood of "striking it rich" was a remote possibility, but he liked to daydream about it anyway.

"Those days may be over," Brian Doyle agreed with Charley. "But, a man can still make a living at it. It's no worse than a farmer digging in the dirt." Charley disagreed.

"It's different," he said, scooping up another shovel full of gravel. He dumped it in the long sloping trough used to separate gold from sand and rock. "A man gets to see his crops grow. He knows his hard labor will keep him from hunger."

"You've never met a farmer who went hungry?" Brian challenged.

Charley looked at the man who had literally saved his life after the beating and wondered if Brian had read his mind. The fact was that he *had* seen men who farmed go hungry. Enoch Neamott and his family were almost wiped out from windstorm damage and drought. But still, for a farmer, there was always the next year to look forward to.

"You farm at one time, Brian?" he asked.

"Yep. Most of the men in the diggings came from a farming or ranching life. Here, help me look over what's trapped in the riffle."

Charley laid his shovel down and began sorting rock from the heavier nuggets trapped in the grooves of the sluice box bottom. He had developed a keen eye and no longer was taken in by fool's gold.

"What happened?" he said. "Why'd you quit farming?"

"I stuck it out while my pa was still alive. He needed the help," Brian said. "But when he passed on and when we had bad blizzards two winters in a row, I decided it was time for something else." He stopped a moment to mop his brow with a blue bandana. "I was almost forty years old, Charley. I wasn't sure how many good working years I had left in me. Besides, my brother lived on the homeplace and decided to stay behind and see to things. He's still there, I reckon. For a long time I ignored tales about getting rich in California. But I finally figured, 'What the hell!' At least it wasn't as cold as Montana."

They worked in silence for a while before Charley asked, "When are you going to town again?"

"Thinking of tomorrow. Want to go along? Take in your diggings?"

"That, and I want to mail a letter to my girl. I'd like her to know where to reach me if..." He left his sentence unfinished.

"You worried about her?"

"A little. Christina is pretty hard headed and if I know her, she's plotting on how to capture a certain wild stallion."

Charley answered Brian's questioning look with the story about the attempted wild horse roundup, leaving out the part about her losing their baby.

"Sounds like she's a pretty tough woman, Charley. I'm sure she's getting on okay."

"I hope so," he said, worrying just the same.

Charley struggled with what words to put down as he composed a letter on the rustic table that evening after supper. Brigitte sat by the stove, darning her father's socks. She looked up occasionally, but remained silent as Charley hunched over the blank piece of paper.

Dear Christina, he began.

I am well after being sick a spell. Hope you are well.

No, that was too stiff and formal. He took another piece of paper and started over.

Dear Christina,

I hope you are well. I think of you every day, darling.

No. That wasn't quite true. Lately, there were days he hardly thought of her at all. He decided to continue the letter, however, as starting on another piece of paper would be wasteful. Paper was a commodity like everything else, and its cost was out of proportion to its value.

I've had a slight setback. My trip to Sacramento to search for farmland has been delayed. I'm in the town of Auburn at a gold mine camp with a couple who cared for me after I was injured. But don't worry. I'm healed up.

Charley didn't clarify that the couple caring for him were a father and his pretty daughter. He let it read as if the couple were man and wife.

You can reach me in care of Brian Doyle, General Delivery, Auburn, California. Please write and let me know you're okay. I will send for you as soon as my prospects improve.

Yours,

Charley

It wasn't the most informative letter—and a far reach from words a man missing his woman should write—but at least Christina would know how to contact him. Finally satisfied, he sealed the envelope. He said goodnight and slipped out of the cabin to his own tent-cabin that Brian had set up for him after Charley had healed. It was a regular tent anchored to a wooden platform laced together with leather strapping—much like a raft.

His own sleeping quarters gave him privacy, but he spent as much time in the house as possible. He had grown accustomed to the routine of sharing meals with Brian and Brigitte and enjoyed their company—maybe too much so. It was time to think about moving on. For now, he needed to get to sleep because Brian was planning to leave for Auburn at sunrise.

CHAPTER THIRTY-FIVE

Charley

Charley jumped down from Brian's buckboard in front of the assayer's office.

"Meet you back here later," he said. Brian nodded and headed in the direction of the general store.

Charley thought his bag of gold felt slightly heavier than the gold he had stored in a glass jar—impossible as that seemed. After all, adding the weight of the glass, the jar should have felt heavier. No matter—he felt certain that he had more gold this visit to the assayer's—or was that just wishful thinking? He entered the small office crowded with prospectors in worn dungarees and shirts with the tops of frayed union suits showing underneath. The stuffy space was fragrant with their unwashed bodies.

The clerk behind the counter examined the contents of Charley's bag made of smooth goatskin; he had chosen it because the bag didn't absorb gold dust like cloth or porous bags, which could reduce a miner's profit. After weighing the dust, the clerk sorted through the small nuggets and held one up to examine under a magnifying glass. He looked up sharply at Charley before discarding it.

"Fools gold," he announced. "Don't you know the difference by now?"

Charley heard the men behind him laugh and scrape their boots across the wood-planked floor.

"Are you sure?" Charley said. "It's the biggest one."

"That doesn't make it gold, son." The man pulled out a pen knife and ran it across the nugget's surface. "See how hard it is? Notice these striations running through the nugget? In addition, the color is too yellow. That's usually a telltale sign." The clerk threw the nugget in a box under the glass counter. "Don't feel bad," he added. "More experienced miners than you have been fooled."

Charley scowled. "Well, I was sure it was real gold." He scratched his head. "May I please have my rock back?"

"What for? I told you it wasn't real."

"I like the looks of it, is all."

The clerk reached under the counter and grudgingly handed over the rock.

"Much obliged," Charley said as he slipped it into his pocket. It wasn't that he thought the man was trying to cheat him, but he remembered the thrill of discovery and wanted it to remind him that not everything thrilling was genuine. He was given a chit verifying the value of his gold to take to the bank.

As he was leaving the office, the three gamblers who

beat him senseless walked down the wooden sidewalk heading in Charley's direction.

"Well, look who's here, gents. Auburn's newest card shark."

"The greatest card *cheat* you mean!" his friend said. The men laughed and jostled one another. "You still around? Thought we took care of you."

Charley tried to ignore their remarks and pass by, but they refused to move. The man who had broken his nose blocked his way and shoved a shoulder into him. "Looking for another drummin' are you?"

"Don't want any trouble, mister." Charley backed up.

"Should have thought of that 'afore you showed up in town again." The man pushed him, and the other two thugs moved in. Charley braced himself and took a defensive stance. *I won't be their victim again.* He raised his fists, prepared to fight.

The sound of a shotgun being pumped got their attention. Charley looked up and saw that Brian was standing in his wagon aiming a rifle at the men.

"Let up now or I'll blast you where you stand," he growled.

Charley had never seen Brian look so fierce. The men slowly backed away and moved down the sidewalk. One yelled back, "Wait until next time!"

Charley lowered his fists and climbed into the wagon.

"Thanks, but I had it covered."

"Yeah, I could see them getting ready to run."

"Didn't know you had a rifle."

"Most men out here have some kind of protection. If you're going to stay in gold country you should at least get a pistol. Ever been around guns?"

"We had a shotgun on the farm to keep coyotes away from the henhouse."

"Well, we've got our coyotes too—two legged ones."

"I don't much like firearms, Brian. They're a temptation to use if you've got one."

"True, some men like to hide their weaknesses behind a gun. Without one, you'd better be careful of men like those three. There's only so much that Brigitte can do if your face gets messed up again." He smiled and gave Charley's arm a playful punch to let him know he was joking. "Hey, it looks like you forgot to mail your letter." Brian indicated the tip of an envelope peeking out from Charley's shirt pocket.

Charley looked down and pulled out the envelope. "I was heading for the post office when I ran into those bastards."

"Well, let's take care of it before you run into more trouble." Brian laughed and gave a slight tug at Beulah's reins.

Inside the cool, dark Auburn Post Office, Charley nervously clutched the sweaty envelope. "How long before this letter gets to Utah?" he asked the postmaster.

"Utah, huh? Let me see." The postmaster consulted a dog-eared schedule and said, "Probably in about four or five days."

"That long?"

"Mebbe sooner. Mebbe longer."

"It's important," Charley said as if that made a difference.

"All mail is important, son." He looked at the addressee. "But since it's addressed to a lady, guess we'd better stop everything and get it going." The man pushed up his wire-rimmed glasses and smiled.

As he left the post office, Charley regretted mailing the letter. What if it wasn't strong enough? A lot was unsaid. When he boarded the train leaving Promontory, it was under unfavorable circumstances. If Christina was still upset with him, would his letter make clear his ongoing intentions toward her? Only to himself did he admit still feeling unsettled. Well, what was done was done. There was nothing to do now except wait for an answer. And while he waited, he might as well keep working at the diggings. He wasn't getting rich, but he was making a little money to add to what he had saved. And as a bonus, he enjoyed the good company he shared with Brian and Brigitte.

"Okay, let's go," he said as he climbed aboard the waiting wagon.

"Got your letter off to your ladylove?" Brian teased.

"Yep. Wonder how long before she answers."

"I wouldn't worry, Charley. She'd be a fool not to keep a tight rein on you. Bet you'll hear from her in no time."

CHAPTER THIRTY-SIX

Christina

Christina waited for her chance to leave. She had dodged John Eiler for weeks. It was the middle of October before she saw an opportunity to sneak into Promontory. Until now, she had tried to make sure she was never alone with John, for when they were in the same place she could feel his eyes follow her. His wives had to be aware of his interest, but no one said anything to Christina about the charged atmosphere in the home, not even Agatha.

Before sunup she crept into the barn to saddle up Buttercup. She was quiet, but not quiet enough. Horses began nickering as she led Buttercup out of her stall.

"Who goes there?" Bert growled from the tack room where he bedded down most nights.

"It's just me, Bert."

Bert emerged from around the corner wearing only his long johns, holding up a kerosene lantern. He set it down and turned up the wick. "What are you doing up this time of the morning?"

"I wanted to get an early start to town, Bert."

"To do what?" He rubbed his chin; the unshaven

whiskers sounded like sandpaper.

"Well, if you must know, I need to—to—"

"Too early to make up a good story?"

"Bert, I've got to get away from here," she blurted.

"Not exactly safe, you leaving on your own without a man to safeguard you."

"That's why I need to get away," she said. "The men around here haven't exactly safe-guarded me."

"Sounds like you're complaining."

"Bert, I appreciate what everyone has done, but I have to move on—and join Charley."

"You got his letter, then?"

"Letter? No. I haven't heard from him and I don't understand it." She took a deep breath before continuing. "It's been months since he left and there's been no word. Mr. Eiler said there's been no mail for me when he picks his up."

"That's what he said, huh?" Bert shook his head.

"Why? Do you know something that you're not telling me?"

"Let's just say that Myrna told me to remind John that there was still a letter for Christina and asked when he was going to pick it up. That's all I know."

"He's been holding out on me!" she yelled a little too loud. The horses grew more restless.

Christina threw the saddle blanket over Buttercup and struggled with seating the saddle. She lowered the cinches and raised the stirrups out of the way. "That does it. I'm leaving." She was so angry that her hands shook, making it difficult to finish saddling Buttercup.

"Wait, Christina," Bert said, moving closer to grab her hands. "Think this through. If you leave with Buttercup, you're as much as a horse thief."

"You don't understand."

"I understand. I know John has been working on you to become his next wife. I've seen the signs. We all know what he wants." Bert dropped his voice."I thought of taking a run at you myself when Charley left." He flashed Christina a rueful smile. "But, I decided I didn't want any trouble cuz John Eiler usually gets what he wants."

"Not this time, he doesn't," Christina declared. She jerked away from Bert and picked up the knapsack she had packed last night with all her belongings. In addition to lecherous John, she should be mad at Bert for thinking that she could be so easily won over.

"Okay, okay. If you're determined to do this, I'll go with you," Bert said, looking resigned. "Give me a minute to grab my pants and boots and get Lightning saddled up. We'd better move so we're back before the rest get up."

"I'm not coming back. But if you'd be so kind as to return Buttercup for me, I'd be obliged. I don't much like the idea of being hunted down as a thief," Christina said, the words clipped and angry. By the time Bert was ready to leave, she had mounted the mare, her knapsack wedged between saddle horn and body.

They rode in silence for a while. The sharp smells of mesquite and sage were strong in the wind. Christina inhaled deeply. She wanted to remember the scents native to this high desert region of Utah. Riding with Bert reminded her of the morning they went in search of wild horses. She would regret that she didn't get another chance at capturing the Spaniard and wondered if she would ever have dominion over a powerful beast.

Just before they reached town, Christina looked at Bert.

"Do you mind if I ask you a question?"

"Would it make a difference if I did?"

"Probably not." She smiled to herself. "Why do you stay with the Eilers? You don't seem to share the same beliefs and you could get work anywhere with your experience."

"A man can only start over so many times before he gets tired and wants to stay put. That's what happened to me. Started out in Missouri. Moved northwest to Nebraska, then south to Colorado and New Mexico, and back up north. Ended up in Utah. I don't have to agree with another man to get along with him," he said finally. "John Eiler's treated me okay over the years. I could do worse."

Christina could think of no response. It was clear that Bert might not approve of Mr. Eiler's ways, but he wasn't going to intervene in his employer's personal business.

When they arrived in Promontory, the café was already lit up with men walking toward it from the railroad station.

"Well, thank you for going with me, Bert." She dismounted and handed him Buttercup's reins.

"Why don't I wait for you? Maybe after reading Charley's letter you'll want to head back to the ranch after all."

"Why? Do you know what's in the letter?" She had a sense of foreboding.

"Nope. It's just that quick decisions are often followed by regrets. I'll have a cup of coffee before I leave. If you want to go back, I'll be out front."

Myrna was busy with customers when Christina stepped into the steamy café. Christina hovered at the end of the counter near the postal boxes lining the adjacent wall, waiting to get Myrna's attention.

"Be with you in a minute, Christina," she shouted, flashing her a warm smile. She poured coffee for Bert and refilled cups for the rail workers before greeting Christina with a welcoming embrace. "How you doing? Wondered when you'd show up again," she said.

"I've come for my letter, Myrna."

"Of course you have. I wondered how long it would take before you showed up to claim it. Tried to send the letter with John, but he refused to take it." She shook her head. "What the heck's going on out there?"

"It's too long a story, Myrna. Maybe someday, we can talk. But for now, I'd like to read my letter."

Myrna took a key from her apron pocket and unlocked post office box #39, which had the name John Eiler printed under it. She reached in and withdrew an envelope covered with heavy block letters, Charley's unique style of penmanship.

Christina took the letter from Myrna and headed for the stairs. She sat on the bottom step and tore open the envelope. A single sheet of thin buff-colored paper slipped out. She smelled a faint scent of violets. Sure enough, when Christina lifted the page to her nose, she detected the unmistakable fragrance. She sat looking at the sheet of paper a moment, wondering if it had come from a lady's stationery.

When Christina had finished reading the letter, she felt confused and scared. Charley had been injured. He had not gone into detail about how or where he had been hurt, just that he was better and had been under the care of a couple who had taken him in. She could only imagine the worst. And then, there was the general tone of the letter. He had never called her "darling" in person, but now was addressing her as such. It sounded false, not like Charley at all. It was as if he was trying too hard to sound like her lover without ever declaring his love. Not once did he use the word "love" in his note. What was she to think? The letter was three weeks old. Could he still be in this place called Auburn? For all she knew, he might have moved on.

The only thing Christina was sure of was that she

couldn't return to the Eiler ranch. She had never been given Charley's back wages and had little money of her own. He had been the one to hold their savings, including the money from the sale of her mother's ring. What could she do? Should she remain here in town until she heard from Charley again or hop a train, resume dressing as a man in order to disguise her sex, and ride the train to California? Christina would have to take a chance on finding him when she wasn't even sure that he wanted her anymore.

She felt truly alone and, although she had always made her decisions independent of anyone else's influence, she now wished for wise counsel or, at the least, a warm shoulder to cry on. She looked up to see Myrna watching her from behind the counter.

CHAPTER THIRTY-SEVEN

Jennie

The month of August, almost over, held a hint of fall in the air. Just as Jennie had feared, plans for entering Lucy in school had to be postponed because the trip to Rochester, Minnesota, had been scheduled. After Violet had consulted with Dr. Martin, it took no time at all for him to contact a colleague at St. Mary's Hospital and arrange for a consultation. To her credit, Violet put everything in motion by reserving three train tickets to whisk them northeast to Minnesota.

During the days-long journey Lucy prattled nonstop about all she saw out the window. Her exuberance wore on Violet, and Jenny saw that she would have to act as a buffer between the two. That was a wearisome task in itself.

"Shh, talk softer," she'd whisper in Lucy's ear. To Violet she said, "She's just excited at seeing so many new things. How nice that you're making this possible for Lucy."

When they arrived in Rochester, Violet and Jennie, with Lucy in tow, disembarked from the train to board a streetcar heading directly for the hospital. For once, Lucy was quiet.

The streets of Rochester were busier, the buildings larger, and the people dressed more fashionably than those in Concordia. In front of a public building, Jenny noticed a tight line of women dressed in long skirts, fancy hats, and gloves, carrying signs. One read: WOMEN BRING ALL VOTERS INTO THE WORLD—LET WOMEN VOTE.

"What's that?" Lucy asked. "Why are those ladies carrying signs?"

"They're suffragettes, Lucy," Jennie said. "They're marching to bring attention to the fact that women do not have a right to vote. They're hoping to change that." Jennie had read all about the suffrage movement and its fight for equality at the ballot box.

"Why do they want to vote?" Lucy asked.

"Why, indeed," Violet harrumphed. "They should be attending to more important matters if you ask me."

"Oh, I don't know, Violet. I think choosing our leaders and considering matters that affect our welfare are just as important as anything else we do. Someday women might not only vote, but also run for office and win— if we only have the vote."

Violet sent a sharp look in Jennie's direction.

"If not me or someone from my generation, girls Lucy's age might be elected."

"Don't be ridiculous," Violet muttered.

Although she couldn't see herself as a professional in the world of commerce, Jennie thought she might like to help write new laws in the legislature or govern a city. It seemed to her that women were just as capable as men to do so. Seeing the young and a few not-so-young women march for a common goal made Jennie feel hopeful and proud. Like so many scarecrows protecting a wheat field, the straight-backed marchers waved their signs in front of males passing by.

She noticed one lady in particular who made eye contact with her. Jennie flashed a tentative smile her way and was rewarded with a small wave from the marcher. There was something in the manner in which she was acknowledged which stirred Jennie. She wished to remain feminine and, at the same time, be strong like the suffragettes.

CHAPTER THIRTY-EIGHT

Lucy

Lucy fidgeted while Violet consulted the ink-faded form that accompanied her from the Boston Home for Children. It was sparse and didn't cover much of her history. Nothing in her medical records described how the orphanage assigned her to work in the cotton mills where cotton spooling created dust in the airless warehouses. It made her cough something fierce at night. And, mercifully, Lucy's records did not reveal that she was placed with a couple who wanted her as a companion for their youngest child, but then rejected her after she suffered bouts of illness. They reported back that they didn't want her or "her nasty germs" and sent her back to the Home.

Lucy had not shared these stories with Jennie. She didn't want Jennie to learn she had been unwanted, that she was a failure as a child. Instead, Lucy made up stories about a pretend family. The only true thing she mentioned was that she was left at the orphanage when she was only three or four years old—like someone's wet laundry. She did not have a firm picture in her mind of a family except for her red-haired mother. A blur of other faces might be brothers and sisters, but she couldn't be sure. She had no recollection of her father at all. Lucy withheld this information because she had learned that folks don't really want to hear sad tales. They already had too many of their own to bear listening to the suffering of others.

Upon reaching St. Mary's Hospital with Jennie and Violet, Lucy sat on the examining table while a nurse asked questions and filled out a form. The doctor had just completed his exam of her as Dr. Martin had done. Finally, after consulting with Violet, it was concluded that Lucy was a good candidate for a tonsillectomy.

"When can this be done?" Violet asked.

"Considering the distance you've come, Mrs. Hunsinger, we could do the surgery in a day or two."

Lucy looked from Violet to the doctor and back.

"No sense in sending you home and scheduling surgery for a later date. Winter travel conditions are likely to be more difficult the longer we wait."

Lucy's shoulders slumped as they talked over her. They acted as if she wasn't even in the room.

"Besides, Lucy is probably as stable as she can be right now. There's no sign of infection or fever," the doctor said. "These are the right conditions under which to operate."

"It's settled then." Violet gave one firm nod of her head as if she were concluding a business deal.

Lucy changed her mind. She didn't want to be here in the hospital with doctors and nurses hovering over her, pushing and prodding, asking her to "open wide" all the time. She didn't mind the way her voice sounded. No one ever had to tell her to "Speak up child," the way they did with the timid kids in the orphanage.

The doctor planned on taking her into a large place he called an operating theater where he would cut out her tonsils. She wondered why they called it a theater. *Isn't a theater for play acting?* As if that were not bad enough, nuns kept appearing by Lucy's side, frightening her with their stiff, white wimples. They hung over her like birds of prey spreading their wide wings.

She lay on a gurney being wheeled down a long green hall with high ceilings that echoed sounds of the busy hospital. The wheels squeaked as they rounded corners and came to an abrupt halt before going through the double-wide doors marked "surgery." Jennie's face appeared above hers.

"You're going to do just fine, Lucy. We'll say a prayer for you."

Oh no, not prayers. That's what they said when they thought I might die.

She was taken into a large room and placed under a blinding light. She scanned the faces surrounding her, but they were all a blur. Lucy heard the unmistakable sound of metal hitting metal. That sound always meant trouble.

"Are you comfortable, Lucy?" someone asked.

"Yes," she croaked. But she wasn't.

"Good. Now, can you count backwards from ten?" A white cone dropped toward her face.

That's a silly question, she thought. Of course I can count—backwards? "Ten, nine, eight..."

"Just relax and breathe deep," the voice said.

"...sev—en."

When Lucy woke up she was in a long, narrow room with other children. Beds lined both sides of the room, just like at the orphanage.

Her throat felt aflame and she couldn't talk. Didn't even *want* to talk.

"She's awake, Violet. Look, Lucy's awake," Jennie said. She sat on a white metal chair beside the bed and held Lucy's hand, her smile tinged with relief.

Violet stood at the foot of the bed. Even she was smiling. "That's good to see," she said. "How are you feeling, Lucy?"

Lucy attempted to speak, but the words were marbles in her mouth and wouldn't roll out. Her tongue took up too much space. All she could manage was a smile. Lucy's heavy eyes drooped as sleep reclaimed her.

When she awoke a second time, it was to witness Jennie holding a cup of something pink. This time curiosity won out. Lucy struggled to sit up and looked at the cup more closely.

"It's strawberry. Your favorite," Jennie said.

Lucy reached for the spoon and sunk a big crater in the ice cream. The cool richness filled her mouth. At first it hurt when she swallowed, but then she found that the coldness numbed the pain just as ice on an insect bite helped dull the sting.

"Like Dr. Martin promised, Lucy—you can have all the ice cream you want."

CHAPTER THIRTY-NINE

Christina

Christina felt overcome by the stew of feelings roiling inside her. On one hand, she was afraid that Charley no longer loved her. His letter did nothing to ease her fear. On the other hand, she regretted the rash actions that had put them both at risk and farther apart than they had ever been. She sat in the Promontory Café with Charley's crumpled letter in her lap and seethed at the unfairness fate had forced upon her—the unwanted aspects of being a female in a male-dominated world. She felt scared of being on her own for the first time since her mother died, forcing her to take to the streets of Pittsburgh. But she was determined not to let doubt cripple her. She could write Charley a letter, but then she would have to wait for an answer that may or may not be to her liking. A response might not come at all. No—she must leave Promontory before she changed her mind or someone tried to change it for her.

She folded Charley's letter and stuffed it into the bottom of her knapsack where it wouldn't be a reminder of her dilemma every time she opened the bag. She waited until the last of the rail men left the café before approaching Myrna.

"Just wanted to say goodbye, Myrna. Thank you for everything you've done for me."

"Where you goin' honey? Not leaving for good, are you?"

"Charley's sent for me at last," she lied. She figured it was a reasonable lie. Myrna continued wiping down the counter.

"Where you two settling?" she asked.

Christina shrugged. "I just know he's in a place called Auburn in California."

Myrna came out from behind the counter to give Christina a hug. "I can't see Charley letting you travel on your own, but he knows you better than me, so I guess it's okay. You be careful just the same. Do you need anything?"

"I'm a little short on money, but I'll make do."

"Wish I could help you out there, but I'm barely getting by as it is." Myrna began wrapping up biscuits.

Christina didn't have the nerve to tell Myrna how she'd been cheated out of Charley's wages, admit how she had been fooled and taken advantage of by John Eiler. It wouldn't do to tarnish the reputation of a man who was known in these parts. After all, Eiler was one of them.

"I can at least send you on your way with something to nibble on during the ride." Myna handed over a brown paper bundle of buttermilk biscuits still warm from the oven.

When Christina left the café, she noted that Bert was no longer waiting. He had left with Buttercup. *Good. One less thing to worry about.* She made her way to the railway station just as the Central Pacific engine was discharging black smoke from its stack. *Is it getting ready to leave?* She ran inside the depot and rushed to the ticket window.

"Do I have time to catch the next train?" she asked.

The ticket agent consulted his schedule. "Leaving in five minutes. Want a ticket, miss?"

"Yes please, and hurry."

"Where to, miss?"

"Auburn, California." Christina glanced over her shoulder to keep an eye on the train.

"First class, second class, or a third class ticket?"

"First class, I guess." Christina reached into her pocket and pulled out a one-dollar bill and some change, pushing it toward the agent. He looked up from under his visor and frowned. He began counting in an unhurried manner and consulted a rate sheet taped to the wall.

"I'm afraid you don't have enough money for a first class ticket to Auburn."

"Okay, second class." The agent dropped his chin and looked at her over the rim of his glasses.

"Third class, then," she said impatiently.

"Miss, I'm afraid you don't have enough here. The closest I can get you to Auburn is—let's see." He ran his

finger down a well-worn schedule. The man was painfully slow, making Christina's stomach do flip flops.

"For eighty-five cents you can go third class as far as
Winnemucca, Nevada. And I hope you're not in a hurry
because this is a mixed train. Hauls both passengers and
freight so there will be frequent stops—to unload the
freight, dontcha' know."

Christina heard the train whistle. "I'll take it," she
said. The agent marked a ticket and opened his cash
drawer to make change from the dollar.

Can't he see I'm in a hurry? She grabbed the ticket,
scooped up her change, and ran out the door. All she
could think of in her frustration was that she now had
less than a dollar to last her until she reached Charley.
She hoped she had no need to spend it on anything other
than food. Once she boarded the train, she would have
time to try to figure out how she was going to scratch up
enough money for the next leg of the journey to California. Something would turn up. It had to.

"Wait! Wait!" Christina shouted as she sprinted down
the platform. The porter had just picked up the portable
step used for passenger boarding. He obliged by returning the step in front of the coach door She boarded just
as a large burst of steam hissed out from under the
wheels.

Once underway, Christina was so tired that the
rhythm of the train rocked her to sleep. She awoke hours
later to discover she had slept most of the day away. She

looked out the grimy window and saw she was in desert country. The flat horizon extended as far as she could see. A distant mountain range barely registered as mountains, appearing instead as a thin blue line. The setting sun sucked the last of the light from the sky, leaving behind a panorama awash in pinks, reds, and a band of yellowish gray.

"Where are we?" Christina asked the porter when he came down the aisle to punch her ticket. "We're about to enter Winnemucca." He looked at her ticket closely. "Your destination, I see."

"But it looks like it's almost nightfall."

"Yes, ma'am," he said. "Looks like this every night about this time." He smiled at his little joke. "Didn't the agent master tell you the estimated arrival time when you bought the ticket?"

Christina shook her head.

"Well, I'm sure your folks will be here to meet you." He returned her ticket and moved further down the aisle. "Next stop—Winnemucca," he shouted.

Now what would she do? Spending the night in a strange train depot all by herself didn't appeal to Christina. She had only minutes to make a decision. She stood up and grabbed her knapsack, moving to the end of the car where the water closet was located. She opened the door to a musty-smelling area with a disgusting looking toilet. It was such a small space, Christina could barely turn around. She gingerly stepped out of the skirt and

removed the soft white ruffled blouse she had been wearing when she boarded the train. She regretted not returning the items to their rightful owner—Agatha—
from whom she had borrowed the outfit.

Fishing through the knapsack for her men's dungarees and chambray shirt, she dressed quickly before any
passengers needing to use the accommodations knocked
on the door. Christina retrieved the cap she had worn at
the beginning of her journey and stuffed her thick black
curls up and into it. She tugged at the cap's bill to help
shield her eyes and long eyelashes, wondering if she
could pull off her disguise as a man this time. It had
worked until she had encountered Gus, the boxcar thug
who'd jumped Charley. Gus had not been fooled. Neither
had Clay, the Indian who had come to Charley's rescue.

Christina felt the train slow down. Before they arrived at the stop, she sought out the porter.

"Do you have scissors I can borrow?" she asked. "A
grooming scissors. I need to trim some loose threads."

"I have some grooming implements, young man," he
said. "A cloth for shining shoes, a shoe horn, combs, but
no scissors." He looked at her suspiciously. "Don't see
any loose threads."

'Never mind."

"You might check in the dining car. Besides chopping
vegetables, the chef cuts up a lot of meat—especially
poultry and their bones. He must have a pair of shears
you can borrow."

"Thanks," she yelled over her shoulder as she moved down the corridor. In the dining car, nicely dressed couples sat at linen-covered tables dining on meat and potatoes and sipping steaming cups of coffee. Large servings of pie waited to be consumed for dessert. Her stomach growled as she passed by them.

Christina stopped one of the dining attendants to ask if he could procure scissors for her. He looked at her strangely and she realized he was sizing her up, trying to decide if she belonged in the formal dining car. With her disheveled appearance, she no longer looked like a lady *or* a gentleman. She dropped her voice to a lower register.

"If the cook will loan me the use of his cutting shears for a few minutes, I would be obliged."

"Chef's busy now. Doesn't like to be disturbed when he's cooking."

"Just ask him for me," she begged. The attendant dropped his large serving tray to his side and cocked his head.

"Okay, but if he yells you'd better hightail it, fast."

The red-faced chef craned his neck around the corner of his cooking station and glowered at Christina. "You the one who wants to use my shears?" Christina was about to retreat when he threw up his hands. "Take it! Take it!" he yelled at the attendant. "Just get the hell out of my kitchen!"

The attendant removed the shears from a hook and

handed them to Christina. "Be quick and get this back here before cook has our hides for interrupting him." The shears looked like the ones that Maggie used to cut roses, but they weren't as large or heavy. The thought of the red roses twining around Maggie's front porch pillars left Christina nostalgic for her friend.

After she returned to the water closet, Christina stood before a small mirror mounted on the door. She began hacking at her curls, cutting them as best she could with the shears. She managed to chop her hair short above her ears—the result was shaggy and uneven. But, it was the best she could do. It was only necessary to cast doubt on whether she was a woman. Christina wasn't about to be vulnerable to harassment again by a man who figured out she was female. She pulled the cap down over her sheared head. Without her thick curls taking up space, it fit better and rested lower on her forehead.

She felt the train coast to a stop and heard the porter cry out "Win-ne-muc-ca!" Christina started to leave the shears behind, but then changed her mind. She stuffed them in her knapsack. A girl never knew when she might need protection. She headed for the nearest exit and stepped down from the passenger coach to the platform crowded with people getting on and off the train. With her knapsack thrown over one shoulder, she headed for the back of the train where freight cars were coupled to the passenger coaches. She hoped she would be able to board a boxcar on her own. In the past, Charley always helped pull her up if she had difficulty.

Before she was ready, the steaming locomotive began to chug forward. She raced alongside and managed to grab a boxcar ladder with one hand and swing a foot onto the bottom rung. The heavy knapsack made it difficult to shift her other arm in position to lift up and grasp the next rung. She dangled precariously—half on, half off. The locomotive picked up speed and all she could do was flatten her body against the car.

Christina could feel her bag slipping away. She swore she would not be left with only the clothes on her back. She grunted and jerked against the momentum until— with one final burst of energy—she swung her other foot onto the bottom rung and pulled her arm bearing the knapsack close to her body. It ached something awful. She waited a moment and then climbed the remainder of the rungs. When she reached the top of the boxcar, she lay down on her back, exhausted, and gazed at the emerging stars overhead. Cool air washed over her. Christina let go one full-throated scream of relief. Only then did she allow herself to cry until the wet tears grew cold on her cheeks.

CHAPTER FORTY

Christina

Several hours later, Christina still sat atop the boxcar, shivering from the cold. She hugged herself, but relief was slow in coming. Her teeth didn't stop chattering until the train pulled alongside a water tower. She stood up on stiff, shaking legs and squinted at a horizon too dark to see. *Better find an empty car in a hurry.* The train wouldn't stop for long. She clambered down the ladder and raced along the tracks searching for a boxcar in which to take refuge. After trying several, whose doors wouldn't slide open, Christina saw one at the very end that looked promising. Its door stood slightly ajar. She approached cautiously and pulled it open further for a look inside. She saw only darkness, but didn't hesitate to throw her bag aboard.

Christina had one leg inside the boxcar when she felt the train begin to move again. She quickly scrambled inside, shutting the door as far as it would go, which wasn't far. It was stuck. She sat catching her breath a moment when she heard a stirring noise in the corner. Startled, she shot to her feet.

"Who's there?" Her voice came out weak and squeaky, an octave too high. She reached into her bag and yanked out the chef's kitchen shears she had borrowed. She held the makeshift weapon in front of her like a knife.

The noise persisted. *Probably just a rodent.* But a moment later, the sounds she heard definitely came from a human—a loud cough followed by a string of curses.

"Show yourself," Christina demanded, although she would have preferred not putting a face to the voice. It clearly belonged to a man—a man who was sure to be hard-featured and threatening. "Keep your distance!" she yelled.

"Make up your mind. Do you want to see me or should I keep my distance?"

"Just come out of the corner so I can see you."

What had been total darkness was slowly broken by a looming figure inching toward Christina. The air around them was disturbed like water that gives way with the passing of a boat.

"It's not polite to interrupt a man's nap."

"That's far enough," she said as she strained to make out the man's features.

The striking of a match and the smell of sulfur was followed by a small burst of flame.

"What are you going to do, snip me to death with that thing?" He indicated the shears Christina had been opening and closing and now thrust toward him. He backed up and lifted the matchstick higher. He laughed. "I wondered what was making that clipping sound."

Christina held the kitchen shears steady, trying to look sinister.

"Hey, I know you," he said.

"What? How? I don't know you."

"Sure you do. We rode together a while back when you and your friend was on your way to California. We threw that no-good man off the train who was bothering you. Remember?"

"Clay!" she shouted, lowering the shears. "Is that you?"

"Was the last time I looked. Christina, ain't it?"

"You saved Charley and me." Christina plopped down and pulled off her cap.

Clay blew out the match and lit another. "Say, you don't look much like the last time I saw you. What happened to your hair?"

"I wanted to disguise myself better this time." She reached up and ran her fingers through choppy cowlicks.

"Like I 'tole you a'fore. It's gonna be hard passing yourself off as a man—no matter what you do."

"Thanks, I guess."

The second match burned out, but not before Clay dropped it with a curse. "You mind if we talk in the dark a spell? Finger's getting burnt."

"That's fine now that I know who you are."

"Where's your man—Charley?"

"He went on ahead to California. To a place called Auburn."

"I heard of Auburn. Used to be a lot of gold in those hills. Why didn't you go with him?"

"It's a long story."

"Well, you know it ain't safe for you to be riding these rails alone."

"I was riding the train up front with other folks, proper-like, Clay. But, I ran out of money."

"Charley knows you're coming, then?"

"Not exactly." Christina was glad that it was dark, for she knew her expression would give away the truth more than any words she might say."

"Hmm," Clay said. "Well, now that you're here, you might as well get some shuteye. Morning's coming soon enough and trouble with it. Central Pacific guards most likely will be checking boxcars at the next station." Clay coughed and spat. "We might have to hop off the train a stretch. Catch it on the run if we want back on."

Christina was too tired to ask Clay any questions. She trusted he'd know what to do when the time came. She headed for the opposite side of the boxcar and lay down, curling up on her side with her lumpy knapsack serving as a pillow.

Shivering herself into a restless sleep, Christina hoped she was up to whatever the next day's challenges turned out to be.

CHAPTER FORTY-ONE

Jennie

The rhythm of the days felt different since the three had returned to Concordia. Violet threw herself back into the role of being the perfect hostess to Cousin Mary Belle's needs. Jennie, who had turned a quiet seventeen while they were gone, no longer was satisfied with the quiet, predictable days in Concordia after observing the confident, independent women in Rochester. She discovered a desire to explore new interests outside her sheltered home and began to frequent the public library more often. And Lucy, with her softer, tonsil-unencumbered voice, began attending school. She had missed almost a month of classes. And although she was a struggling student, she made several friends among the children, which made up for the difficulty of her lessons. She seemed to blossom under not only Miss Maggie's attention, but also that of Jennie, who was willing to help her with homework.

Jennie was relieved that Violet had finally softened toward Lucy; she felt certain that the orphan from Boston would have a permanent place in their home. After learning about Lucy's attachment to the stray dog, Brownie, Jennie took up the cause. She not only prepared a sheltered place for the animal in the carriage barn, but also began feeding the hapless creature on the sneak without telling Lucy.

Although fall temperatures had gradually been dropping since their return to Concordia, it was a beautiful, sunny Saturday and Jennie was determined to take advantage of it.

"I'd like to take Lucy to town and outfit her for winter, Violet."

"As long as you two are back for tea." Violet had resumed the English custom of serving tea in the afternoons before dinner.

"Of course." Jennie pecked Violet on the cheek and went in search of Lucy.

Lucy had been given much more freedom in the house lately and could be just about anywhere. She was known to poke around the empty spare rooms as well as explore the formal quarters and had been seen touching Violet's expensive art glass collection. Jennie held her breath that her mother's collection didn't end up broken.

Among other changes, Lucy had graduated from the kitchen to the dining room to dine with the adults. It was apparent from the beginning that she needed instruction in table manners; Violet visibly blanched when she observed Lucy reach across the table to fill her plate to the brim without waiting to be served.

"She acts as if she were starving," she complained. "Jennie, you must take on the responsibility of training Lucy if she is to continue joining us. Her manners are deplorable."

"I know, Violet. It's the way children survive in an orphanage. Manners become secondary to getting enough food."

Jennie remembered her days in the Pittsburgh Children's Home and how Charley would supplement what she received with food from his plate. Thoughts of Charley jolted her memory. She still had not received word of where her brother and Christina had settled and how they were faring. It had been many months without word and she was worried. Would they have written Maggie and Carl or the Neamotts before her? She made a note to herself to check with them.

After Jennie and Lucy had spent over an hour in the stuffy air of the mercantile store with its musty smells—everything from onions to leather boots to the inky newsprint on which *The Concordia Blade-Empire* was printed—Lucy became restless. She pestered Jennie mercilessly to leave. Jennie finally agreed after purchasing her a new coat and muffler as well as sturdy boots to hold up against the cold, wet winter.

"Could we get some ice cream now?" Lucy asked. Her eyes lifted like Brownie's when he begged on the back steps. Although she had been promised all the ice cream she wanted, now that she was healed and healthy, ice cream had been replaced with custards, flans, and other soft desserts. Jennie had not treated Lucy at the soda shop in weeks.

Of course Jennie agreed and they ended up at their favorite table, Jennie with a single dip of vanilla ice cream in a cut-glass bowl, and Lucy with a cone filled with two scoops of strawberry. She prattled on about the antics of some of the more undisciplined boys at school while she licked at the ice cream drips before they melted and ran down the side. Jennie was preoccupied, and except for a quick "uh huh" or "hmm," her mind was miles away. Replaying in her mind were scenes she had seen in Rochester: the woman who looked at her without flinching, another who waved a handwritten sign, and a young girl who was too young to vote handing out tracts to any passerby who would accept one. Jennie could imagine what it must be like to feel the heft of a sign in one's hands while marching, putting one tired foot in front of the other until all the marchers squeezed together into a tighter and tighter circle.

"Look Jennie, there's Peter." Lucy pointed with her spoon. Peter Stuyvesant was walking by the soda shop window in the company of an elegantly dressed woman. The thick makeup she wore on her face did nothing to disguise her age—she was no longer young. But the woman was shapely and noticeable in a flashy way with her thick black hair secured with multiple jewel-encrusted combs.

"Yes, I see," Jennie said, turning away.

"Look, he sees us." Lucy stood up and waved.

"Lucy, don't do that," Jennie hissed. She hoped Peter had not seen her stare at him and the woman he was with.

Lucy looked stunned at the rebuke and sat down. "But Jennie, he's coming inside," she whispered.

Jennie straightened her skirts and patted her hair on one side. When she gazed up, Peter was smiling down at her. He acted as familiar as if they saw each other daily.

"Good afternoon, Jennie. Lucy," he said, bowing slightly. "It's so good to see you both looking so well." His eyes crinkled with amusement. "May I present my friend, Mrs. Marie Lucia Rossi. Marie, this is Miss Jennie Hunsinger and Lucy McCleery."

"Happy to meet you," Marie said. She didn't *look* happy to meet them. Her smile lifted and disappeared so fast, it was as if it had never happened.

Manners dictated that Jennie ask Peter and his lady friend to join them. She grudgingly said, "Would you care to have a seat?"

"Thank you, no. We have another engagement to attend," Marie said before Peter could respond. His face registered surprise, but it was quickly replaced with a sardonic smile.

"I see you still like ice cream, Lucy," he said.

"Oh, yes. But I don't get as much as when you used to meet us," she blurted.

"Lucy!" Jennie said. "That's rude."

Peter threw his head back and laughed. "Guess we'll have to see about that in the future. Now if you will excuse us."

Jennie could barely wait until they left the shop. "Lucy, it was not nice to say that in front of Peter's new friend."

"I'm sorry, Jennie. But it's true. You said to always tell the truth." Her big eyes began to tear up.

"It's okay, Lucy. Just don't let it happen again."

Flustered, Jennie felt bad for snapping at Lucy. It wasn't the child's fault. She was angry at Peter for assuming he could flaunt this woman in front of her after not responding to the note she sent him months ago. If he had, she might understand. But, by not responding it was as if she had never meant a thing to him—that she was not even worthy of a farewell.

After dinner that evening as dishes were being cleared away and dessert was announced, Lucy piped up. "Oh, goodie! That's two desserts in one day, right Jennie? First the ice cream cone and now this." She dug into a piece of chocolate pie topped with whipped cream. "I'll bet if Peter had stayed with us, he would have bought me a big sundae like he used to."

Violet's head popped up. "What do you mean by that, child?"

Sensing that she had said something wrong, Lucy looked at Jennie in confusion and then stared down at the table. "I—I—don't know," she stuttered.

"Jennie?" Violet waited for an explanation.

Jennie sighed. She was surprised that Lucy had kept their little secret this long. "From time to time, we ran into Peter Stuyvesant at the soda shop and he treated Lucy. That's all, Violet." Jennie looked at her mother, feigning innocence.

"He's not the kind of man you should be running into, Jennie. I thought you knew Mr. Stuyvesant's reputation."

"I've heard."

"If it's male companionship you want, there are ways in which it can be arranged in a more proper way than meeting someone in such a manner."

"Oh, yes," Mary Belle interjected. "In New Orleans we have a coming-out party for young ladies and always there are cotillions and other socials during the holidays." She looked off dreamily before continuing. "We have so many suitable men in the city. And Jennie—you're such a beautiful young woman that you would be swimming in potential suitors."

"I wish we had more civilized opportunities here," Violet said. "But Concordia is so provincial." She picked up her dessert spoon.

"I have an idea," Mary Belle said with sudden enthusiasm. "Violet, wouldn't it be lovely if you and Jennie returned with me to New Orleans for the holidays? Then, you could see for yourself, Jennie. Would you like that?"

Violet looked up with interest. "It would be a lovely experience to be exposed to culture again. It might be like our trip abroad. Remember Paris, Jennie?"

Jennie *did* remember Paris: the museums, the art, the quaint cafés with music. Even the salons. The experiences had taken her outside herself and reinforced her appreciation of art—especially drawing. There were so many subjects to draw there.

She had heard of New Orleans and some of their quaint customs that survived the Civil War: parades featuring gaudily dressed marchers; food—both continental dishes and regional dishes primitively seasoned with hot spices; riverboats that lazily traversed the Mississippi River into the Port of New Orleans; and ladies in hooped skirts carrying parasols, who still resided over colonnaded mansions.

"Yes, it was lovely," she said. "But we have just got Lucy enrolled in school. I'd hesitate to pull her out for a trip when she's doing so well."

"I quite agree," Violet chimed in. "Lucy should remain in Concordia to attend class.

That doesn't mean, however, that we can't make the trip," she added. "We should only be gone for a few weeks or a month at the most. With all the household help, I'm certain that Lucy can get on without us for that length of time."

"But it's going to be the heart of winter soon."

"You're right, Jennie. All the more reason to be

somewhere without freezing temperatures and snow."

Lucy's head turned from one woman to the other, eyes big, lips slightly parted.

Jennie bowed her head, cheeks burning. "Perhaps we can talk more after dinner, Violet. May I be excused?" She placed her napkin on her plate.

Violet nodded and flashed a victorious smile. "Of course, dear." She turned to Mary Belle. "There are so many plans to make," she chirped.

"Come, Lucy," Jennie said, standing up so fast that she bumped her plate into her glass, almost overturning it.

"Did I do something wrong, Jennie?" Lucy also stood up, her napkin still tucked into the top of her dress.

"No, Lucy. You were just being you." Jennie had the feeling that Violet and Mary Belle had planned this trip all along. She doubted that it was a spur-of-the-moment idea that suddenly occurred to them when Lucy spoke Peter's name and his possible interest in Jennie. They had probably been plotting for weeks—maybe even before the trip to Rochester for Lucy's surgery. Jennie should have seen it coming. She thought Lucy's position here was secure, but the idea of leaving her for any length of time was very disturbing. She felt helpless. There didn't appear to be anything she could do to derail this runaway train of an idea the two women had cooked up.

CHAPTER FORTY-TWO

Charley

It had been a month and still there was no letter from Christina. Was she still upset with him? Was that why she hadn't responded to his letter?

"It seems like you're getting more restless, Charley," Brian said on the way back from town.

"Is it that noticeable?"

"To me it is. I'm used to seeing restless men in the gold fields. That's what brought them here in the first place—a restlessness that only adventure and discovery could calm. But I'm guessing you're uneasy for a different reason."

"All my plans have gone to hell," Charley said, glowering. "By now I was supposed to be settled somewhere in the Sacramento Valley tending my land and sending for Christina. But, I have neither."

"Maybe if you explore Sacramento and its surroundings, you'll see what can be had for the money you've saved. Might make you feel better." Brian let this set in a moment before continuing. "As I see it, you'll find out one way or another whether you're ready to get settled there. If not, Auburn may be more to your liking. It's not a bad life." He looked intently at Charley. "Just ask Brigitte."

"Brigitte does seem pretty settled," Charley said. "She ever talk about marrying up?" He already knew the answer to the question. Brigitte had said as much to him.

Brian looked at Charley before answering.

"Not to me she hasn't. She was pretty upset about her fiancé leaving, you know. If Ned came back tomorrow asking forgiveness and a second chance, I'd knock him flat."

Charley noticed an edge in Brian's voice he had heard only once before—the day he aimed his rifle at the gambler thugs threatening him.

"You'd never treat a woman like that, would you?"

"No, never!" But a part of Charley questioned whether his leaving Christina behind with the Eilers was the same thing. Maybe Brigitte's man planned on coming back or sending for her later and it just didn't work out.

That night, out of the corner of his eye, Charley watched Brigitte as she served supper. She had been quieter lately. He caught her looking at him when he was busy at some task, but the minute he looked up her eyes shifted.

"Thought about what you said today, Brian. A trip to check land values in Sacramento is the perfect thing to get my mind thinking straight again. Mind if I borrow Beulah and the buckboard?" Charley asked.

"W-e-l-l," Brian said. His fork stopped halfway to his mouth. "It's about a day's ride by mule. Maybe a little more if you take the buckboard. It's the only rig I've got and it gets used pretty regular."

"I'd take good care of Beulah and the wagon."

"I know you would, Charley. The point is I could only spare them for a couple, three days at most."

"That should be enough. I'd be mighty grateful."

The next day Charley hitched up the buckboard to Beulah and set out at dawn. Heading due west, he left the evergreen-covered foothills to descend into the distant valley filled with early autumn foliage. Oaks and deciduous trees were already turning colors; their leaves shone in yellows and russet. Large swaths of land appeared to be moving as wind rippled through the wild grasses anchored there. Streams wound west through fields to empty into the Sacramento River and flocks of birds flew overhead. Red-tailed blackbirds and hawks were plentiful as well as egrets hiding among the cattails and reeds in the marshy swales. Geese lined up into a V-formation, heading south, a sign of an early winter to come. There had been just enough rain to turn the dry ground a kind of winter green—not quite the emerald of spring and early summer, but more a moss-green underneath the ruff of dry, spent summer grasses.

Charley filled his lungs with fresh, clear air—a welcome change from breathing the dust-filled clouds of gravel shoveled into sluice boxes.

When he arrived in Sacramento late afternoon, the activity was overwhelming. Flanked by the river on two sides, the busy docks teemed with stevedores loading ships with supplies to be delivered to San Francisco and towns developing on the river's banks. Saloons, mercantile stores, and hotels of questionable repute added to the bedlam. From what Charley saw, the fancy ladies lounging about the hotels outnumbered the patrons.

A settlement of Chinese occupied a central portion of the river town; the pungent smells of exotic spices and cooked meats hanging in windows wafted from their shops. All Charley knew of the Chinese is what he had heard—that they did most of the hard labor of building the railroads.

Charley tied Beulah to a hitching post in front of a stone building. The words CHEAP LAND painted on the window enticed him. He stood before the door and hesitated a moment before entering. Inside, a man sat behind a large, cluttered desk with his feet propped on top. When he saw Charley, the man planted his feet on the floor and stood up.

"Good day, young man," he said, pumping Charley's hand. "Name's Gil Parker. What can I do for you?"

Charley accepted the man's hand, which was smooth like a woman's.

"What kind of land you got for sale?" He came right to the point.

"Depends. What do you want the land for?"

That's an odd question. "Well, for planting crops of course."

"Land is used for many things in Sacramento besides crops, lad. Men buy land on which to establish their businesses or to build houses for their families. Sacramento is growing fast." Mr. Parker winked. "You know," he continued, warming to the subject, "rancheros begun with Mexican land grants have been subdivided and changed hands many times over the years. It's 1900 after all. We're no longer just a ranch town."

"I don't need a plot close to town. It can be further out. Needs to be near water though."

"That's good planning, son." Parker placed his hand on Charley's shoulder. "However, water from the rivers can be a problem during flooding season. Have you thought of that?"

Is he trying to scare me off? "No. Can't say that I have," Charley said.

"What kind of cash are we talking about? Do you have enough for a downpayment?"

Charley was becoming uncomfortable with the questions and the gloomy projections of the salesman. *Does he want to make a sale or not?*

"The reason I asked about your financial situation is because you might do better checking out land southwest of here—in the direction of Rio Vista. The Sacramento River runs through the islands, which are cheap by our standards."

"Islands? What kind of islands are you talking about?"

"Acreage between here and Rio Vista is low, but fertile, and surrounded by water."

Charley scratched his head. He had trouble visualizing a farm surrounded by water. In his mind an island consisted of palm trees and sand surrounded by tropical seas.

"How far away are these—islands?"

"Rio Vista is about thirty miles as the crow flies. But you'll get an idea of the terrain as you make your way over roads and bridges."

"I don't have much time to explore. I borrowed the rig." Charley nodded toward Beulah tethered outside the office. "If I was to take a look-see, how much an acre?"

"Depends on many factors. The man to talk to is Dutch Hansen. He owns much of the land out there. He started out just like you, young man, and now they call him the Delta King."

Parker flashed a smile, which Charley noticed included a gold-covered tooth. He couldn't help but try to estimate how much money the man's tooth would bring in at the assayer's office.

"Dutch might even have a piece of land he's willing to part with," Parker said. He pulled a piece of paper from his pocket and scratched something on it.

"Now, if you change your mind and want something closer to Sacramento, come see me." He handed Charley the paper on which he had drawn a rough map and the name, Dutch Hansen.

Although the day was almost over, there would be a few more hours of daylight. Charley decided to follow the map and see where it took him. He rolled out of Sacramento and urged Beulah to go faster as he passed other travelers on horseback and in wagons full of supplies from town. He had only so much time to explore if he was to keep his promise to Brian about returning in three days.

The wide, dusty trail was deeply rutted, but yielded to the wagon wheels, throwing swirls of dirt behind them. He came upon a narrow road marked by a wooden signpost with a stick drawing of a bridge etched into it. He turned onto it and threaded through spots where branches hung over the roadway, obscuring his vision. Charley finally located the bridge without too much trouble. He consulted Parker's crude map and decided he was going in the general direction toward Rio Vista. Energized by this minor success, he ventured on and yielded to the sun, eventually removing his jacket and then shirt. The heat felt good on his bare back at first, but soon turned searing hot. He slipped his shirt back on in defense.

After crossing the bridge over the channel crudely marked on the map, Charley faced a fork in the road and wondered which of the ever-narrowing paths to take. He took the one pointing south that had the word Isleton chiseled into it. Writing that looked like Chinese characters appeared below the name, raising the question of who lived there.

Surrendering to darkness, Charley finally pulled under a tree to camp for the night. He hoped to run into civilization by early morning because the landscape spread before him stretched on forever without sign of human life. Could he have gotten lost?

CHAPTER FORTY-THREE

Charley

Eucalyptus trees lining the levee road above the Sacramento River towered over Charley and his rig. He scanned the fields below being tended by stooped workers wearing bandanas over their heads on which pointed straw hats sat; they weeded young plants in orderly rows. A bucket detail followed and irrigated the fragile seedlings with care, pouring water in furrows surrounding them. Charley didn't recognize what kind of crops had been planted. They didn't look anything like the corn and wheat he and Enoch had sown in Concordia.

He clicked his tongue and tugged lightly on Beulah's reins. She refused to move until Charley yelled "Hie!" and gave the reins a more forceful pull. Without warning, the wagon rolled down the levee toward the fields at an alarming speed. "Whoa! Whoa there!" he hollered, trying to correct the trajectory before they crashed. Once on level ground, the mule stopped short and twitched her ears. Slow progress was okay with Charley as long as it was steady, but old Beulah hadn't figured it that way. She had been as cooperative as a mule could be through most of their journey, but must have decided that she'd had enough when she was forced to leave the cool breeze coming off the river to land in the warm shallows of land below.

Charley clicked his tongue again and Beulah obeyed, moving toward a field of late tomatoes.

"Hello there," Charley said as the wagon pulled abreast of a group of young, brown-skinned men. They looked up out of curiosity, but no one spoke. "Wonder if I could get some directions. Do any of you know a Mr. Hansen?"

One man stood and moved away from the group of workers. Charley could see that his face was delicately featured with almond-shaped eyes. "Dutch Hansen?" he asked.

Charley withdrew the piece of paper with directions on it from his shirt pocket. "Yes," he said after studying it. "It says Dutch Hansen."

"He live that way." The man pointed to a large white house in the distance. "Not home. He look over..." His broken English stumped him as he pointed to the surrounding fields. Thumping his chest several times, he said, "You wait. He come soon."

"Much obliged. By the way, my name is Charley O'Brien." He tipped his cap.

The young man bowed in acknowledgement. "Tao Chin." He pointed to himself. Tao turned and picked up a short-handled hoe and resumed weeding, loosening the dark black soil.

Charley jumped down from the wagon and followed Tao Chin, stooping to pick up a handful of the dirt.

"Say, what kind of soil is this? I've never seen any this dark." He made a fist of it and was surprised to see that it didn't compact into a hard clod like the clay in Concordia. It also differed from the red, rocky dirt in Auburn. He opened his fist and the breeze stirred the soil, lifting it from Charley's open palm to send it flying away in a plume of dust.

Tao looked at Charley without comprehension and lifted his shoulders.

"The answer is peat dirt, mister." A large man on horseback was approaching. He eyed Charley and finally dismounted to face him. He didn't look quite as tall as he had in the saddle, but he made up for it in girth. "Strangers don't usually ask my laborers questions. They come to me directly." He nodded toward the house on the hill. Charley noticed that Tao Chin had moved farther down the row, as if to distance himself from this man whom Charley guessed was his boss. The man did not introduce himself. He remained standing on higher ground while Charley balanced himself in one of the furrows.

"Mr. Hansen? Mr. Parker in Sacramento said I should talk to you." Charley walked toward him extending his hand. "My name is Charley O'Brien."

The man ignored Charley's hand. "Well, Mr. O'Brien.

You're on private property and interfering with my workers."

He's not very friendly. Charley tried a different approach.

"I sure didn't mean to do that. I'm here looking for some land. Might be interested in buying some acreage in the near future." Charley dropped his hand and stepped back. "Just wanted to get a closer look to see if it's any good for farming. I can see it's just fine."

"It's more than just fine, Mr. O'Brien. This soil comes from ancient volcanic activity and then was flooded and became marsh land for a long time. But all of that was reclaimed." He waved his hand to take in the vast territory. "Took the Chinese years to build all the levees and bring the land back to usable shape. And as you can see we have easy access to water."

"Yes, I see. So, do you know of any land hereabouts for sale?"

"Can't say that I do. I own most of Brannan Island. The only way you can get access to real estate hereabouts is to lease it or be a tenant farmer like the Chinese. Law says they aren't allowed to own land."

Charley thought Mr. Hansen pompous and too prideful in his speech.

"Some Chinese remained behind to farm after the reclamation project had been completed," he explained. "But you don't look Chinese to me." He laughed.

"No, sir. I'm Irish."

"Well, I wouldn't count on the Irish to know much about farming. Didn't they leave Ireland because they couldn't make a go of it? Everyone knows about the potato famine." He laughed again.

"The famine had nothing to do with their ability to run a farm," Charley said, defending his ancestors. "A blight killed off the plants underground. Wasn't any fault of their own." Charley's neck felt hot as his hands twitched, itching to close into fists.

"Well, I guess you were too young to be responsible. You're not just off the boat are you?"

Charley took a deep breath, deciding to ignore the slur against his people. "I don't see myself leasing the land, sir. Or becoming a tenant farmer. I no longer want to work for someone else." He lifted his chin. "Mr. Parker said there were some smaller plots of land available. Who would I see about that?"

Dutch Hansen's bushy eyebrows scrunched up over beady eyes. They looked like two caterpillars crawling across his forehead. "Guess you'll have to ask *him*. I'm not in the business of selling land. I just *buy* it. Now, if you'll excuse me, I have work to do." With that, he remounted his horse. Looking down on Charley, he said, "There *is* a small section next to the levee northwest of here. For the right price I might consider selling. If you leave information with Parker on how I can reach you, I'll let him know if I'm interested."

Dutch Hansen headed toward a field filled with

mounds of strawberry plants. Charley saw a young woman, who was placing berries into her basket, startle as Hansen neared her, barking orders.

Tao Chin had worked his way back to Charley. "You leave soon?" he asked.

"Guess so. Seen everything I'm likely to see today. Got to get back to Sacramento before dark, or Beulah and me will have to bed down somewhere out here." He looked up at the sky as if it would darken into nighttime momentarily. The blank look on Tao's face reminded Charley of his language limitations. He was surprised when Tao responded.

"I show you. You wait please. I get grandfather."

"But Tao, I really should leave now. This rig is borrowed."

"Not take long." Tao gave him a pitiful look. "Please."

Charley was about to say no, but Tao's face said what words couldn't convey; his eyes darted from the retreating landowner—now at a comfortable distance—back to Charley.

"You bring to Walnut Grove. To *jiating*. Family. Grandfather be with family." Tao laced his fingers into a prayer-like gesture. Before Charley could respond, the Chinaman ran past him toward ramshackle housing adjacent to the owner's big house on the hill.

CHAPTER FORTY-FOUR

Christina

When she awoke, Christina was covered with Clay's blanket. He sat on the opposite side of the boxcar rolling a cigarette.

"You slept a long time," he said.

"Did I?" Christina sat up and stretched. "What time is it?" She could see light filtering through the slats.

"A little past sunup."

Her hips and back ached from sleeping on the hard floor. But at least she had warmed up some.

"Where are we?" she asked.

"'Spect we're somewhere in the middle of Nevada by now." Clay pulled himself up and shuffled to the door, sliding it back a few inches to peek out. A blast of cold air whooshed in filling the car. "Yep, looks like Nevada, all right."

"You been this way before?" Christina pulled the blanket closer and struggled to a standing position. She joined Clay at the door.

"A few times. But there's not much here to my liking. Just sagebrush and rattlers."

"What about horses? I heard there are herds of wild horses in Nevada."

"Yep. That was true last time I was through here."

"I almost captured a wild stallion back in Utah," she boasted, "but he got away."

Clay raised an eyebrow. "That's hard work for an experienced wrangler. How'd you make out?"

Christina described the morning of the roundup, embellishing a few details as she went along.

"What were you going to do with the stallion if you captured him?"

He's asking the same question Charley asked, Christina thought.

"I was going to try and break him and then train him," she said. "I did most of Gabriel's training."

"Who's Gabriel?"

Christina resurrected the story of how she worked with Gabriel until Carl sold him. "So you see why it's important for me to have another horse like him."

Clay ran his hand over the stubble covering his chin. "If you was to stay in Nevada a spell, we might find a crew who runs wild horse roundups regular-like." He took a last drag on his cigarette and flicked it out the boxcar door. "Last time I was in these parts I heard Fort Ruby and Fort McDermit bought their horses from outfits like that. 'Course I doubt if a horse crew would hire a woman for the job."

"We don't have to tell them, do we, Clay?"

"I don't know. Let me think on it. I don't plan on staying in the desert for long. It depends on how fast we can find a group of bronco riders." Clay left the door and fell silent while Christina mulled over what he had just told her. She let her imagination spin freely as she pictured another attempt at capturing a beautiful, wild mustang. She forgot all about her journey to California to search for Charley.

Later that morning, the train slowed and lurched to a gradual stop. Except for the train depot, there was no town to speak of. A post office, a general store, and a few wooden structures in the distance were the only signs of civilization. Christina welcomed the break from the stuffy boxcar and found a privy behind the train station. She was gone only a few moments. When she came out the train was pulling away. *Oh my God!* She looked around in panic. *Clay went on without me.* She rushed into the station and found Clay at the ticket window talking with the agent. She let out a sigh of relief.

"We're in luck," he said when she joined him. "There's a crew a ways yonder that captures horses. We might sign up with them to get that horse you're hankering after."

"They train them?"

"Break 'em *and* 'train 'em."

"What about my plans to keep moving west? And your dislike of the desert?"

"There's always another train. Do you want to check

it out or not?"

She hesitated only a second. "I do!" She had never been more certain of a notion.

"Let's get going then. From the directions it looks like a long hike, but I figure we can make it in a couple of hours." Clay picked up his gear. "Let's see if we can get there before the worst heat of the afternoon."

Although it was officially fall, they were suffering through a period of Indian summer with plenty of hot afternoons. Christina knew enough not to get stuck in the desert when it was scorching. She picked up her backpack and followed Clay outside, searching for a café near the station like there had been in Promontory. Seeing none, she honed in on the only other establishment with food.

"Think we can pick up something to eat at the general store first?" Christina said. She didn't want to complain about being hungry, but she couldn't make that hike on an empty stomach. Clay gave her a disparaging look, as much as a stoic Indian could muster.

"Should have gotten back on the train," he muttered as he tramped ahead of her toward the store.

After purchasing beef jerky, Christina spied a barrel filled with apples. The thought of biting into a piece of fresh fruit made her mouth water. She couldn't resist buying a couple with what little change she had left. She passed one to Clay and bit into the other, letting the juice run down her chin. When she reached the core, she ate it too, including the seeds. Clay watched her and handed her his apple.

"Here, I think you need this more than I do."

"Thanks. I'll save it for later."

They filled their canteens from the well behind the store, pumping the handle with a few vigorous jerks until the water ran clear.

"I could sure use a bath," Christina said as she splashed the ice cold water on her face and neck.

Clay made a guttural noise in agreement. "We best get going," he said.

They headed north, navigating through the desert toward the ranch house they could barely see in the distance.

Yucca plants and mesquite bushes, as well as sagebrush and sedges filled the desert. Their chartreuse foliage came in variations of grayish-greens, creating a colorful palette. Desert plants had their own kind of beauty, Christina decided. Small lizards sunning themselves on rocks and skittering under them at the least provocation amused her. There were other critters she couldn't see but knew were abundant in the arid land. Christina had read about them when she assisted the younger students with their lessons in Miss Maggie's class. She remembered seeing pictures of scorpions, tarantulas, and other insects with pincers whose bites were said to be stinging, and in some cases, lethal. And then there were the snakes. Her greatest fear was one sneaking up on her. She thought of the rattler who spooked Agatha's horse. She had had enough of the indigenous rattlesnakes of the West and was especially vigilant anytime they passed rocks.

They stopped to rest near an outcrop of quartz to get out of the sun. But, only after Clay had checked the area completely did she agree to sit down and settle against it. She drank from her canteen, heeding Clay's warning not to drink too much too fast or she would get stomach cramps.

They had been walking for over two hours and it didn't look as if they were any closer to the ranch. "How much farther?" she asked.

"Couple miles. Better let me do the talking when we get there," he said. "Your voice rises when you're excited. Better pretend to be a man like before."

"Okay," she said. "If you think that's best." She tucked her already short hair under her cap the way she had at the beginning of her journey with Charley. She also loosened her shirt, letting it hang over her pants to disguise her female curves. "How's this?"

Clay looked her over and frowned. "Better," he said. "Cutting your hair helped, but you have to move more like a man. Slow your walk some. Get a little roll and hitch into your hips like a bow-legged cowboy who's been on his horse too long."

"Like this?" Christina lengthened her stride with her legs farther apart.

"Jeee-sus! Now you look like you're trying to step over a mess someone left behind." Clay shook his head. "Just slow down some, that's all."

"How about this?" Christina rolled her shoulders and advanced with a flat-footed step forward.

"It's an improvement. Just be mindful not to be lady-like," Clay said. "If that's the best you can do, it'll have to do."

Christina smiled and fell in beside Clay. "Don't worry. I'll let you talk for both of us. I'll just tell them the experience I've had working with horses, and that's all."

Clay's face was expressionless. "Good," he said. "The less said the better."

They picked up their gear and headed out once again toward the ranch. Waves of heat shimmered across the sand, leaving Christina to wish they had rested a while longer. But she didn't complain and kept putting one foot in front of the other.

When she heard horses whinny, Christina perked up. As they approached the ranch's corral, she scanned the horses confined there. The majority were mustangs of various sizes and colors with a few American paints and an Appaloosa or two moving about restlessly. One horse, which looked like Gabriel, made her stop short. A second later she saw that this stallion, with the same coloring, had something Gabriel did not have: a distinctive white blaze on its muzzle.

A lean man with an uneasy gait and a sharp-angled

face emerged from the barn behind the corral.

"Looking for someone?" he said in a short, unfriendly burst.

"The outfit's boss." Clay responded in an equally abrupt manner.

"He's up at the house." The ranch hand looked them over suspiciously. "You got business with him?"

"Hope to."

"We're looking to get a horse," Christina blurted.

Clay shot her a look of warning.

"Don't sell horses, mister. This is a working ranch, not a stable."

"Mind if we go on up and see your boss?" Clay said.

"Sure. Ain't none of my doing."

Christina lowered her voice. "You weren't very friendly," she said to Clay as they approached the house.

"Not my business to act friendly. You want to get a horse, don't you?"

"Yes, but—"

One look from Clay and Christina nodded her head. "Okay," she said, resigned.

The crew boss was sunburned and leathery. A scar ran down his neck and disappeared below the collar of his shirt. He stared out with hooded eyes and shifted his body with a minimum of movement, like a man who had been thrown by horses one too many times. Christina had seen this same thing in half-crippled men when they came to Carl's stable to have their horses shod. She'd overheard them tell of being thrown and of other accidents involving their horses. It was a warning of what could befall the best of horse handlers. But of course she just knew it would never happen to her.

"You men looking for work?" the man asked, his eyes coming to rest on Clay. "Had any experience with horses before?"

Clay explained how he helped capture horses for his tribe when he lived on the reservation.

"What about you?" he asked Christina. "You strong enough for this kind of job?"

Remembering to lower her voice, Christina told the man about working with Carl at the stable and how she helped train Gabriel, describing him as fierce and a more difficult horse than he actually had been. By the time she took over, Carl had taken some of the starch out of him.

"Well, we can always use a couple of hands on the roundup. Where are your mounts?"

"Had to sell them along the way," Clay piped up. "Needed some cash."

"Guess you can use a couple of our stable horses. Better get used to them before we go out, though."

"When's your next roundup?" Clay asked.

"We're getting ready to go out next week," he said. "If you want the job, stick around. Bunk house is out back. Breakfast is at sunup and supper at five. By the way, name is Buck." He extended his paw of a hand.

"Clay. This is Christin—" He caught himself in time

before saying Christina's full name. "Chris. This here is Chris."

They stowed their gear in the bunk house and washed up in a horse trough for supper.

"Why didn't you say something about us wanting to capture horses for ourselves during the roundup?" Christina said.

"You're the only one wanting to get a horse. The outfit keeps the horses they capture."

"But I thought that if I helped in the chase, I'd have first choice," Christina protested.

"They'll probably charge you about the same they get from the army unless you work it off or haggle with them for a special deal."

"What about you, Clay?"

"I'm only in this for the capture. I ain't gonna plant my ass in a saddle for long. That train will be calling me soon, Christina—I mean Chris. I'd better get used to calling you that."

That night in the bunk house with a dozen snoring men surrounding her, Christina wondered what she had gotten herself into. She had wanted the adventure of getting and owning a horse for the first time. She had no doubt that she was capable of capturing and breaking a stallion. But how was that going to work if she had to spend time working off the price of a horse? She hadn't realized that the time it would take to earn her horse would also keep her from her search for Charley.

She remembered then that the people who cared about her in Concordia thought she and Charley were safely together. Friends and family were supposed to keep track of these things, and she considered Carl and Maggie her family. However, they didn't know where she was or anything about her predicament. *How did things get so far off course?* Christina tossed and turned and finally fell into a fitful sleep.

CHAPTER FORTY-FIVE

Christina

It had been a hard couple of weeks. Christina had toiled alongside Clay and the unfriendly cowhand who had greeted them their first day on the ranch. She had trouble remembering the names of the other ranch hands except for those who had odd nicknames like "Sly" and "Duke" and "Four Fingers Frank," who earned his moniker after an accident that cost him a pinky finger. They all looked alike too. They were sinewy thin, but strong. Most sported beards of one type or another. Their weathered skin was leather-brown except in places their shirts covered. Flesh not exposed to the elements was white like the underbelly of a lizard. They drank whiskey, played cards, and chewed tobacco, which they spit into old tin cans.

The stench of their sweaty bodies made Christina nauseous. Their proximity to her and the fear that they would find out that she was really a woman robbed her of sleep. In her nightmares, she kept seeing John Eiler's lecherous smile superimposed on their faces as they moved inevitably toward her. When she startled awake, she asked herself what she would do if one of them tried to assault her.

In spite of using work gloves, Christina developed calluses on her hands. She became bruised and sore from moving bales of hay and mucking out the stables of a dozen horses—all the things she had enjoyed when she was doing them for Gabriel and Buttercup, but not for the wild horses in the corral. No one told her which ones had actually been broken when she approached a fine-looking red roan. She flattened out her left hand, balancing an apple on it, and reached through the corral's split-rail fence. A searing jolt of pain shot through her hand and up her arm. The horse had bitten her.

"Damn!" she screamed as she ran to the nearest horse trough and dunked her hand into cold water. It throbbed just the same.

"Here." Buck grabbed her hand out of the water and, after examining the broken skin, slapped a foul-smelling salve on the wound and wrapped his bandana around it. "Keep it covered," he said and walked away. A couple of cowhands who had witnessed the bite hung back, laughing. One of them slapped his knee and called her lefty.

Finally, one morning Buck said it was time. He heard rumors of a herd heading their way. They saddled up and rode toward hills west of the ranch and waited on a bluff. They didn't have to wait long before horses thundered through the pass, kicking up dust. Several stallions were in the lead. A smoky black caught Christina's eye and she followed his movements, mesmerized. Many of the other horses were mares and yearlings with a few colts ambling alongside. Lagging behind were the older, thinner of the herd, just trying to keep up but failing with every stride. Christina recognized signs that they were malnourished; their hooves were dry and their coats of coarse, dull hair were lackluster.

"What about these stragglers?" she shouted to the cowhand next to her.

"We don't pay any attention to them," he yelled. "They won't last through the winter, so it's a waste of time feeding them."

"What happens if they're sick?"

"They die of course."

"What?" Christina cried.

"We ain't in the business of capturing horses just to sell 'em off to the glue factory," he shouted over his shoulder as he pulled ahead of Christina.

That's so cruel. She was sure that some of them could be nursed back to health.

Christina watched as Buck and two of his wranglers headed downhill toward the herd, singling out the smoky black stallion. Each man took a position alongside the mustang, swinging his lariat at its neck. Buck was successful on the first throw, but the other two cowhands landed short. They rode past and turned back to take careful aim a second time. When the ropes of all three wranglers had reached their mark, the stallion writhed in panic. He reared back and stomped his front hooves against the hard-packed earth, twisting against the ropes. A high-pitched scream rang out from his throat, piercing Christina's ears. His massive chest heaved and his eyes rolled, showing the whites.

Buck and his men worked as a team, circling and pulling at the ropes until the horse fell to his front knees. Buck slid from his mount and secured his rope around the stallion's two front legs, hobbling them to a hind leg. The horse struggled and stumbled until exhaustion overtook him. As he gasped for air, his ribs moved up and down under his taut skin like the keys of a player piano. Forced to lie on his side, the stallion's massive head and neck followed and lay flat against the ground. Air from his flaring nostrils blew little plumes of dust away from his muzzle.

Although it was thrilling to witness the capture, Christina was sorry to see the stallion defeated. He had fought so hard to remain free. She knew the feeling. She pulled herself away to join Clay and the other men, who had cut a half-dozen horses from the herd. Ropes circled overhead made a singing sound.

Christina's rope landed on a bay-colored mustang on her first try; the bay spun and retreated, taking the slack out of the rope. She quickly dallied the rope around the saddle horn, letting her horse take the weight of the retreating bay that swung sideways and shook his mane like a rag mop. She feared she would be yanked out of her saddle. Her gloved hands burned where the taut rope had dug in, rubbing against the calluses she had already acquired. She sat heavy and solid in the saddle and clamped her strong knees harder against her mount until she felt her thighs quiver with the effort.

Clay and Duke were out of their saddles and hobbling the mustang before Christina remembered to release the rope from around the saddle horn and allow it to be pulled from her hands. In all the confusion—the dust, the cries of the horses, the yells of the men telling her to "let go"—she forgot to pay attention to details. Afterwards, Christina tried thinking of a way to save face after her poor performance. She concentrated on calming the horse she was riding. Thankfully, no one said a critical word to her or she may have cried.

The crew captured seven horses in all, one of them a young mare. They herded the exhausted, roped horses like cattle back toward the ranch. Christina and Clay brought up the rear when rifle shots rang out behind them. Christina turned to see Duke shooting the thin, sick horses. As they fell and stopped moving, so did Christina.

"Why?" she shouted. "Why kill them?"

"They was going to starve to death anyway," Duke said. "I'm just saving them from a more painful death."

"You don't know that!" she protested.

"Leave it alone," Clay said to her. "Just keep moving."

The excitement of going on the capture was quelled.

If it was cruel to abandon the weaker horses instead of rehabilitating them, she considered it downright criminal to kill them for no good reason. "They deserved a chance to survive, didn't they?" she said. Clay did not answer her.

Christina was so upset she didn't join the others for supper that night. She was saddle-sore, her arms and shoulders ached, and the calluses on her hands had blistered over and felt raw. But most of all, she despaired over the cruelty she witnessed to a point of being heartsick.

After supper, Clay returned to the bunk house carrying a plate of cornbread.

"Here," he said. "Figured you needed some vittles. You're always hungry."

"Thanks." Christina choked down a couple bites of dry cornbread and coughed. "I could sure use some water to go with this. Come with me to the well, Clay?"

"Sure," he said. They were silent until Christina had her fill of the ice cold well water and was wiping her mouth.

"Feel better?" he asked.

Christina nodded. "A little."

Clay looked around to make sure no one was within earshot of them.

"You finally got to go on a roundup," he said. "How did it feel?"

She looked up and feared that he might judge her.

"I didn't know it would be like this, Clay. It seems like a waste to have killed those sick horses. Why couldn't we have tried to help them instead?"

"Nature can be cruel," he said. "Not all living things are meant to survive."

"I didn't know Indians felt that way."

"We don't waste life. We either capture it for food or for a purpose."

"What purpose did killing them serve?"

Clay was quiet for a minute and looked down at his boots.

"I guess for no good reason except to supply food for other critters."

Christina blanched at the remark.

"Look, it don't sit well with me, either, Christina. But some white men are like that. They take what they want and leave the rest to waste."

"I'm sorry." She knew that her being white had a stigma attached to it that she didn't deserve. But she understood how Clay felt.

She labored on the ranch another month before reaching the conclusion that she needed to leave. Christina didn't want to go on another roundup. She saw the process of capturing wild horses as tainted by cruelty and greed. She also knew she wouldn't last long enough to earn the money to buy a horse from Buck.

She turned to Clay on the night before payday. "When you're ready to leave, take me with you, Clay. I don't want this life after all."

"You giving up on getting a horse?"

"For now. I don't want to get one this way."

"Okay." Clay shook his head. "Let's collect our wages and head out in the morning." His face twisted into something approaching a grin.

Buck didn't look surprised when Clay and Christina asked for their wages the next morning after breakfast.

"You couldn't hack the work, huh?" he said. "Well, not many can."

Christina cast a last look at the smoky black stallion in the corral. He was pacing and snorting, his nostrils open to a scent coming from the hills. She couldn't bear to watch the men try to break him and thought, *He's going to give them a hard time.* For the first time Christina realized the process of breaking wild horses took someone stronger than her. The niggling thought that she wasn't as strong or as capable as a man occurred to her, but she vowed to never say those words aloud.

Having money in her pocket felt good to Christina as she walked alongside Clay. It didn't take nearly as long to reach the train station as it had been to reach the ranch. That was because she was stronger now and the weather was nearing winter so they didn't have the desert heat to contend with. As soon as they were out of sight of the horse ranch, she pulled off her hat and let her hair fall loose. It had grown out a little from the hack job she gave it on the train and should be presentable by the time she found Charley—that is, *if* she found him.

    She decided to press on to California, with or without Clay.

CHAPTER FORTY-SIX

Jennie

"It's unbearable for Mary Belle," Violet said. "My cousin isn't accustomed to snow and the harsh winters of Concordia."

It was December and as cold a winter as the Plains of Kansas could deliver.

"But Violet, I hate the idea of being away from Lucy over the holidays," Jennie complained. "It's her first Christmas with us."

"There will be other Christmases for Lucy in Concordia, but perhaps only one Christmas for you in New Orleans."

All Jennie had to hear was the possibility that Lucy would remain with them to ease her fears about Lucy's place in the household. After all, her six month trial period had almost passed and she was still with them. It would be prudent of her not to press Violet. She would sacrifice her time away from Lucy *now* to guarantee they had time together in the future. If that meant her agreement to accompany Mary Belle and Violet to New Orleans for the Christmas holidays, so be it.

Lily promised to keep a careful watch over Lucy while they were gone, and Maggie said she would do the same. Jennie was satisfied that she had done all she could to insure that Lucy's physical needs would be seen to. She just hoped she wouldn't be too lonesome.

Jennie stared out the train window as it edged toward the city of New Orleans. They had passed through the countryside of Louisiana with both its grandeur and poverty on display. She saw vast plantations and stately mansions, behind which stood unpainted shacks with sagging porches and barefooted black children. It offended her sensibilities to realize there were two different realities in this genteel society. Just as the suffragettes laid bare the political inequities between the sexes, Jennie thought that economics in the south may not have improved to a degree that enabled freed slaves to advance. Otherwise, why would they still live like this?

One white-pillared mansion, larger than the others she had observed, was set farther back from the rail line. Rows of giant oak trees lined both sides of the narrow road to the manor, obscuring sight of the front door. She imagined the entrance to be grand and ostentatious like the mansion itself. The oaks, with strands of moss hanging from their branches, reminded Jennie of old men with long beards.

She was rudely pulled from her reverie when the train lurched, throwing Jennie forward.

"We're here at last," an excited Mary Belle said. She stood and issued orders to the porter on how to carry hat boxes and valises from their compartment.

"Yes, ma'am. No, ma'am," he uttered while trying to balance the load. *Poor man,* Jennie thought. *Thankfully, he won't have to manage our entire luggage.* Mary Belle's steamer trunks, as well as suitcases that Viola and Jennie brought with them, were stowed away in the luggage car.

"Oh, look. My driver, Henry, is here to fetch us," Mary Belle cried as she looked out the sooty window. Jennie took a quick peek at the man Mary Belle was pointing to. It was dusk and the lights from the gas street-lanterns cast shadows against the sides of buildings, creating an aura of mystery and making it difficult to make out the man's features. All she could see was that Henry was tall and thin and leaned heavily on a cane. He hardly looked the part of an able servant.

"Come along now Jennie," Mary Belle said with enthusiasm. "You are going to just love our city."

It had rained earlier. Puddles remained standing in the streets. Jennie lifted her skirts to avoid soiling the hem, but her fashionable buttondown boots were already getting wet. Once seated and covered by the carriage blanket, she enjoyed the carriage ride as their horse sloshed through dirty puddles, splashing mud on other hacks.

The coach made its way through the garden district,

turning south on Magazine Street until it reached a narrow magnolia-tree-lined lane. The large, waxy leaves of
the southern magnolias dripped water from the earlier
rain, but Jennie thought them beautiful as they framed
the large colonial at the end of the road. The mansion's
front porch railing was festooned with boughs of evergreens, holly, and red bows. Through a bay window a
large fir tree could be seen lit with candles. It shone like
a beacon.

Inside, a maid and butler attended to their luggage
and led them to their rooms on the second floor. Jennie
was pleased with her large, comfortable room and the
French doors opening onto a balcony. She could see herself throwing open the doors in the mornings and gazing
at stars from it late at night.

She joined the others in the front parlor where the
ten-foot Christmas tree stood with a fire crackling nearby in the huge fireplace. She was served a beverage
called a hot toddy. There was a sharpness to it, although
the toddy was also sugared and contained a hint of lem-
on. Jennie thought it interesting that no matter what
friendly name they assigned the drink— a toddy sounded
like a big, friendly teddy bear—it was most likely laced
with alcohol. These Southerners might be prissy about
some things, but apparently young ladies getting acquainted with strong drink was not one of them. She
rather liked that as she enjoyed the light feeling in her
head after consuming the toddy.

The next morning while eating breakfast in the glass conservatory, Mary Belle told Jennie about the cotillion they would all be attending the following evening.

"It's a holiday celebration at which New Orleans debutantes will be introduced. All of the better young people in society should be there," she explained. Mary Belle spooned a generous serving of orange marmalade onto her croissant. "Your escort will be Mr. Covington."

Jennie stopped mid-bite of her pastry. "Escort?" she said.

"Kyle Covington is the son of one of my oldest and dearest friends," Cousin Mary Belle went on. "I hear he's a marvelous dancer. You *do* dance, don't you, Jennie?"

"Well, I—" Jennie looked at Violet.

"We don't have much in the way of cotillions or coming-out parties in Concordia, Mary Belle. But Jennie did learn the basic two-step and the waltz from her tutor," Violet said. "And she had ample opportunity to practice when we were in Europe, didn't you Jennie?"

Jennie smiled and nodded her head. Violet always knew how to make her appear more polished than she actually was. The fact was that she was *not* a good dancer. She never felt confident in herself as a dancer or in her gracefulness as she attempted to follow her partners on the dance floor. She itched to lead, not follow. This cotillion Mary Belle spoke of—it could only spell disaster. She hoped she would not bring shame on herself and embarrass Violet.

CHAPTER FORTY-SEVEN

Lucy

When Jennie and Violet left her behind, Lucy was up-set—but only for a little while. She knew that Jennie didn't really have a choice. She began eating in the kitchen again with the help, which was okay with her. It was warmer there and, besides, Lily gave her seconds and extra dessert. Attending school was more fun now that the class was getting ready for the holidays; they were making tree ornaments and learning Christmas carols. She was happy and surprised that when she sang, the sounds coming out of her were no longer croaky and off tune.

As for the ornaments, one of hers was voted the most original. It was a ball of yarn she covered with glue made of flour and water. When it hardened, she painted it with Jennie's water colors and stuck whole cloves in it. Besides looking fancy, it smelled good too.

Just as she suspected, the classroom was slow to warm up in winter. But after she returned from St. Mary's hospital, Lucy had been moved closer to the pot-bellied stove. "We don't want you catching any colds,"

Miss Maggie had said. It was turning out that school was becoming one of her favorite places to be—second only to the ice cream parlor.

"Carl and I want you to join us for Christmas." Miss Maggie said as classes were being dismissed for the holiday break. "Would you like that?"

Lucy nodded and felt very special. She bet that none of the other students were invited to the teacher's house. *Too bad.* If there were other youngsters, Miss Maggie would be less likely to notice if she did something wrong. She knew her table manners were still a little off.

Lucy had not been without company her own age. Jennie had been inviting Lucy's school friends, who lived in town, to be her guests from time to time. While they were in the Hunsinger house, Lily always made sure to serve fresh cookies and hot cocoa.

The only time Lucy felt lonesome was at night when she got into the big featherbed alone. It was too big for just one person. She missed the warmth of Jennie's body next to hers and the lilac-scented toilet water she wore. Splashing a little of the perfume behind her ears, as she had seen Jennie do, gave Lucy the illusion of Jennie being nearby.

Lucy no longer dreaded winter with its inevitable rounds of colds. Before she had her tonsils removed, she'd had a bout of the dreaded croup that kept everyone in the house awake. Dr. Martin had made several midnight calls to minister to her when she couldn't catch her breath. In her fevered state she saw that Jennie's eyes were opened wide and her face looked pale. *She thinks I'm going to die.* This scared Lucy more than anything. Violet and Mary Belle were only good at wringing their hands and waving their handkerchiefs in the hallway, uttering "Oh my."

"The lass is turning blue," Lily had said, almost as distressed as Mary Belle when she brought kettle after kettle of hot steaming water to the room. After pouring the steaming liquid into a large bowl, Jennie held Lucy as she leaned over it with a towel over her head. The steam eventually helped, but so did a secret elixir that Violet produced. Through the fog enveloping Lucy's head, she heard Jennie say to Lily, "I think there's some alcohol in here or something else that calms her cough. What do you think, Lily?"

"Don't know, ma'am, but at least its bringing blessed sleep to the child."

It was after she recovered that arrangements to have her tonsils removed were put into high gear. Before Lucy knew what happened they were on their way to Minnesota. That was all behind her now. She felt like just another kid looking forward to winter pastimes like ice skating and building snowmen.

At first snowfall, Lucy ran outdoors with Lily in tow.

"You need to put on your hat, lass!" Lily shouted. She waved a tasseled knit cap, while being hatless herself.

"Don't need it, Lily!" Lucy shouted back. *After all,*

the sun's shining. Lucy didn't want to be so overdressed that she felt bogged down.

Brownie came lumbering out of the carriage house and high-stepped through the drifts as if he were in a marching band. Lucy called him and he ran in crazy circles and rolled in the snow, making doggie snow angels. She laughed until her sides hurt.

Lucy had begun feeding Brownie more openly now, ignoring the protests of cook, who was just going to throw out the scraps anyway. One particularly cold afternoon when cook was done for the day, Lucy brought Brownie inside the house—something that was forbidden by not only cook, but Lily, and she suspected Jennie, too. The dog acted hesitant at first, as if testing his good luck. When his confidence kicked in, he ran amok across the smooth wooden floors in the long entry hallway, sliding the entire distance until he was stopped by the front door. He then followed Lucy up the grand staircase, running at full lope and then turning and running back down. The downward momentum made him look awkward. Lucy followed him down, running faster than she ever had before to see what it felt like. It was delicious. However, her fun was short-lived.

Uh oh. Lucy had forgotten to check Brownie's paws. She looked in horror at wet muddy paw prints covering the surfaces he had crossed. Before she could clean up after him, Lily rounded the corner.

"What's all the racket in here? Oh my lord, child,

what have you done? Look at this mess!"

"I'm sorry Lily. I didn't know__"

"Well, I hope you know now. It's going to take us all afternoon to clean this up. Out Brownie!" she cried. "No more, bringing that wild thing in the house, do you hear?"

It was the first time Lily had been stern with her. She was just glad it wasn't cook or Violet who discovered the mess. She led Brownie to the back door and after giving him a hug, shooed him outside. He stood looking at her with his tail between his legs before heading back to his place in the carriage house. Lucy would just have to figure out a better way to sneak Brownie into the house without leaving evidence behind.

CHAPTER FORTY-EIGHT

Jennie

Jennie sat gazing in wonder at all she saw from Mary Belle's carriage on their way to the cotillion. They passed buildings with black wrought iron balconies decked out with yuletide decorations, and lampposts twined in ropes of holly. Jennie hadn't seen anything as bright and exciting since her time in Paris. She heard music that was new to her ear floating from open doorways and longed to ask the carriage driver to stop so she could hear more.

When they arrived, the large ballroom bustled with activity. A full orchestra was already playing a Vienna waltz and couples were spinning elegantly around the floor. A tall, trim man approached Mary Belle. He kissed a gloved hand and stepped back.

"Oh, Kyle. I'd like to present Mrs. Violet Hunsinger and Miss Jennie Hunsinger," Mary Belle said formally. "Violet and Jennie, meet Mr. Kyle Covington, the son of my dear friend I told you about."

"Madam," he said, bowing to Violet and then to Jennie, who offered him her hand. "Miss Hunsinger, charmed." His green eyes looked her over. He waited a beat before addressing her.

"You are much more beautiful than described," he said. "I see that living in the Prairie has only made you mysterious."

"Oh? Mysterious in what way?" Jennie asked.

"Mysterious in that you have apparently survived— no, thrived— in a hostile land devoid of culture."

"I'm not so sure we're totally deprived of the finer things." *I'm going to dance his feet off for that remark.* "Perhaps I'd better show you," Jennie said, batting her eyes, coquettishly. She never behaved like this, but his smug attitude made her want to shock him. Violet expelled a nervous little cough and opened her fan with a snap.

"Shall we, then?" Kyle offered the crook of his arm and led her onto the dance floor. He placed a hand possessively on her waist, dipping Jennie to the side as they began circling the room.

"You're a very fine dancer, Mr. Covington," she murmured when the music stopped. He smiled as if receiving praise was his due.

"I think they're going to play the New Orleans version of the Virginia Reel next. Then you'll see what true dancing is all about."

Oh no. I don't know that one. Jennie tried to think of a reason to excuse herself, but she was spared the humiliation when the orchestra failed to play the reel and segued into another waltz. She managed to keep up through three more numbers and then begged off.

"Oh, you're much too good for me, Mr. Covington. I think I'll sit out the next one to catch my breath." She opened the fan that was secured to her wrist by a ribbon and began fanning herself.

"As you wish, Miss Hunsinger," he said, bowing. He walked her back to the other ladies and then took his leave. Jennie watched him move across the room to a beautiful dark-haired debutante. The duo expertly whirled away and out of sight. Minutes passed and two more dances were played, but Kyle did not return.

"Would you care to dance?"

Jennie turned to see a young man with wideset blue eyes and a wispy blond mustache. He was half a head shorter than she. About to decline, she saw earnestness in his face. When she nodded he broke into a wide grin and twirled her in an unambitious circle onto the dance floor. Jennie found him much easier to follow and finally relaxed.

After polite chitchat she learned that his name was Patrick O'Hearn and that he was a friend of Kyle's.

"Kyle and I are roommates," he said. "We go to the same prep school. I knew he was being set up with someone tonight and I thought, 'Poor Kyle.'"

Jennie pulled back. She glared at Patrick.

"Not that he wouldn't have noticed you on his own, Miss Hunsinger," he said. "Kyle always finds the prettiest girls in the room."

"Did Mr. Covington ask you to distract me so he could spend more time with the girl he's with?" Jennie asked.

"Not exactly." Patrick blushed. "He just pointed out that you were visiting New Orleans and didn't know anyone your own age and—"

"Well, I don't need to be pawned off," Jennie retorted. She turned and hurried from the dance floor, leaving Patrick alone, looking flustered. Trembling with anger, she rushed through doors to the balcony where a welcome wave of fresh air washed over her.

"Please, Miss Hunsinger," he said. "Don't be upset." Patrick had followed her.

He removed his jacket and placed it around Jennie's shoulders. "Here, you're shaking with cold."

"I'm not cold!" She shrugged off the jacket and handed it back to Patrick.

"Oh," he said, slipping back into his coat. "Miss Hunsinger, you are truly a beautiful young woman and deserve better than Kyle. Better than me, for that matter."

"Why better than you?" She turned and looked at him with renewed interest.

"Well, for one thing I'm not as good a dancer. But I do appreciate music. I would love to show you what *real* music sounds like."

"What do you mean?"

"Let's get out of here and I'll show you," he said, grabbing her hand and pulling her after him.

"I...don't...know." Jennie hesitated only a moment as she considered the daring of such behavior. But, for some reason she trusted Patrick. He seemed to have been honest with her where other men had not been. And it would be a relief to escape from having to return to the heavily perfumed room full of swishing ball gowns and the stiff shirt she had been foisted off on by Cousin Mary Belle.

Patrick and Jennie made their way down the back stairs of the building that led out onto a sidewalk full of noisy revelers. In just a few minutes they were surrounded by loud, raucous music like Mary Belle's carriage had passed on the way to the cotillion. She looked up at a sign that read Canal Street. She and Patrick meandered down several more blocks, stopping at times to hear snatches of songs. Some were vocals, others instrumentals.

"What *is* this music?" she shouted over the noise. They had stopped by one club to listen by the open door. She heard piano, trumpet, and the high, sad notes of a clarinet being played against the syncopated rhythm of the drums. The musicians were all dark skinned.

"It's called New Jazz or Hot Jazz," Patrick said. "Take your pick. Each year during the Mardi Gras parade you can hear different versions of the same style of music. Some call it—" Patrick stopped and snapped his fingers, trying to remember the name. "Dixieland!" he finally shouted. "That's it—Dixieland."

Jennie moved to the music, swaying her hips like other women around her were doing. They wore short, slinky dresses that clung to their curvy bodies. On them the swaying looked seductive. She wondered if they were the "ladies of the night" she heard Mary Belle and Violet whisper about. She felt Patrick's eyes on her and when Jennie gave him a sideways glance, pleasure was written across his face. He stomped his feet in time to the music and clapped his hands in encouragement.

"You dance very well, Miss Hunsinger. It's as if you were made for this music."

"You may address me as Jennie," she said. "Under the circumstances I think we may call each other by our first names, don't you?"

"By all means, and you should call me Patrick," he said, grabbing her around the waist. As he guided her around the small dance floor, Jennie felt happier and freer than she had for days. *Peter should see me now,* she thought. She doubted that Peter Stuyvesant could move like this.

Jennie felt at ease dancing with Patrick. He had a compact build and was not so tall that she had to crane her neck to look into his face. As he pulled her closer, she found joy and surprise in the fact that they seemed to fit together without any effort. Her body had grown loose-jointed and had settled into a sensual torpor. She felt quite unladylike as perspiration trickled between her breasts and down her sides.

"You smell so—" Patrick whispered in her ear. It was

if he had been reading her mind.

"—good," he finished.

Jennie threw her head back and laughed.

They left the club and stopped to watch a young Negro boy tap dancing on the corner for money. She found herself clapping, urging him on. When he finished with a flourish, bowing to the nice-sized crowd, people threw coins into his waiting hat. An older white boy, twice his size, broke from the crowd and scooped up the hat, emptying the change into his own cap. He turned to escape and ran into Jennie, sending her reeling. Just as she was about to fall to the ground, Patrick's strong arms caught her.

"Are you okay, Jennie? Someone, grab that boy!" he yelled.

She was none the worse for wear, but the hem of her gown had suffered from the assault. It had picked up a coat of dirt. Together they tried to brush it off, to no avail.

"We'd better return to the cotillion," she said in a panic. "Violet will be worried." Jennie lifted her skirts and began running. Patrick ran after her and grabbed her by the elbow.

"Jennie, slow down. I don't want you slipping. You'll only look more disheveled, and really alarm your mother."

"Disheveled?" she cried. "Do I really look that bad?" Jennie said, patting at her hair. Curls had fallen down around her neck.

"Just a little," he said smiling. He tried to work her loose curls back into the bouffant style in which they had been arranged. "But you look lovely to me."

By the time they returned to the cotillion, Jennie was breathless with her cheeks in a full flush. The room seemed especially stifling now that she had been out in the fresh air. The scene before her was boring compared to what she had just witnessed—people engaged in dance moves that were totally unpredictable. And to think that she had been one in the strange brew of folks mingling together, unabashed by their mixed heritage.

Violet descended on her. "Jennie, where have you been?"

"I was just taking a little night air," she replied. "It grew too warm in here."

Violet eyed her suspiciously. "And your gown. Look at the hem. It's all dirty."

"I—uh," she stammered.

Patrick bowed and introduced himself. "Jennie was safe with me," he said. "But I'm afraid that when she tripped on the veranda, she soiled her dress."

"Yes," Jennie said. "But everything turned out okay because Mr. O'Hearn was by my side."

Mary Belle and Kyle walked toward them and stood by Violet's side.

"Patrick, when I asked you to look out for Miss Hunsinger, I didn't mean for you to steal her away," Kyle said. He looked on with amusement. Jennie felt a surge of something hateful rise up at his condescending manner.

"Well, the cotillion is pretty much over," Mary Belle said, sounding disappointed. "I'll have Henry bring the carriage around. I think we should leave."

"I agree," Violet said. "Thank you young man for looking out for Jennie."

"Ma'am, I hope you will allow me to call on Miss Hunsinger while you're visiting our city."

"I would like that very much, Mr. O'Hearn." Jennie smiled and looked at Violet for approval.

"Well—" Violet said and then nodded.

Once inside the carriage, Violet turned to Mary Belle.

"Does Mr. O'Hearn come from a good family?"

"I assume so if he was invited to the cotillion," she replied. Mary Belle sounded exhausted. "I really expected Kyle to stay by your side, Jennie. I'm disappointed that he behaved badly."

"That's okay, Mary Belle. To tell you the truth, I like Patrick, I mean Mr. O'Hearn, much better than Mr. Covington."

Violet and Mary Belle looked at each other with raised eyebrows and then lapsed into silence.

Jennie couldn't help but think of all she had seen that piqued her interest much more than the cotillion. She hoped that Patrick would call and that he would show her more of this fascinating city.

CHAPTER FORTY-NINE

Charley

Charley wondered how he had been tricked into taking on passengers when his sole mission had been simple: explore the Delta for suitable acreage. Tao Chin, the young Chinaman he had just met, and an old man who must be Tao's grandfather, stumbled over the fields toward the wagon. The older man's bones looked as fragile as a bird's. Although he appeared light enough for one man to pick up, it took both Tao and Charley to lift him into the buckboard because his knees kept buckling. Tao settled him against the gear in the back and then climbed into the front next to Charley.

"Grandfather need more help. Gets lost," Tao said. He tapped his head and rolled his eyes to indicate confusion. "Forgets to eat."

Charley heard that old people sometimes lost their faculties. However, he hadn't been around anyone who looked as old as Tao's grandfather.

"Looks like it's starting to get dark," he said. Worry was beginning to creep into his thoughts. He assumed they didn't call this tract of land "the islands" for nothing. There was no safe way to travel through this terrain surrounded by water in the dark.

"You know a place we can bed down for the night, Tao?" A sheltered spot?" Charley wasn't sure how much English Tao understood. He made a rounded gesture to indicate what he meant by the word "shelter."

Tao nodded and pointed east. "A cove. Not far."

Good, at least we can communicate. He let out a sigh of relief.

They traveled along the dirt road on which Charley had arrived until Tao pointed to a trail that was little more than grass tamped down by the weight of horses and other wagons. He never would have spotted it if he had been alone. They covered a short distance until they dropped down a slope to a stretch of hard-packed dirt. Water lapped against the shore, and the sounds of croaking frogs and chirping crickets filled the air.

Tao jumped from the wagon, heading for the rear.

"Good. Grandfather still asleep." He pulled out a couple of grass mats from a canvas bag and laid them on the shore. Charley gathered what food he had brought with him and flung his canteen on one of the mats.

"Don't have much food, but you're welcome to it," Charley offered.

Tao looked at the slim pickings of biscuits and beef jerky and shook his head. He got busy rolling up his loose pants legs and slipped off his sandals. Searching the shore until he spotted a broken tree limb, Tao snapped off a sturdy branch. With a pocket knife, he sharpened one end of the branch into a sharp spear and waded into the water. He eased himself toward the tules, where he stood still, listening.

Charley wondered what Tao planned to do among the reeds filled with croaking noises. He didn't have to wonder long as Tao raised his arm high and thrust the pointed stick in the water. When he lifted it, a large gigged frog struggled to break free. He repeated this process until there was a small pile of frogs.

Charley gathered kindling and started a fire. Although he was reluctant to eat something as ugly as a bullfrog, he welcomed the idea of hot grilled meat for supper instead of cold jerky.

Tao proceeded to prepare the amphibians for cooking by cutting their long legs from their bodies. He threaded the legs on the branch he had used for gigging, after first pulling the outer skin back.

Charley thought it very efficient. He watched as Tao held the stick over the fire, turning it constantly. Soon, the glistening legs sizzled, dripping fat. He grew hungrier by the minute, his mouth watering with anticipation, as he stared at the charred meat.

"Never had frog legs before," he said. He bit into the flesh. Juice ran down his chin.

Tao nodded. "Many frogs and fish here. I show you how to catch."

After they ate their fill, Tao brought one of the legs

to give to his grandfather, but returned with it still in his hand. "Grandfather sleeps a lot." He offered the leg to Charley.

"Much obliged," he said, accepting the food.

Although they didn't talk much, Charley enjoyed Tao's company. He was aware that agreeing to take Tao and his grandfather to Walnut Grove was going to slow him down, but he still favored being friendly. They had surpassed the awkwardness of not sharing a common language, and Charley wanted to know more about him.

"How long have you worked for Dutch Hansen?" he asked over the dying embers of the fire.

"Long time. Grandfather, longer."

"But he's so old."

"Yes, but when young—like me." He pointed to himself. "Helped build islands. Work in water up to—" Tao touched his waist. "He dug dirt. Laid rocks."

"He must have been pretty tough."

"Yes, tough." Tao paused and looked across the water. "He good farmer. Come from Pearl River Valley."

"In China?"

"Yes. Very good farmers in Pearl River."

"Were you born in China too?" Charley asked. Tao shook his head.

"No. I born here. Can't send me back." He thumped his chest and gave a single nod of his head that encouraged no further discussion on the matter. Charley changed the subject.

"What do you think about me leasing land from Dutch Hansen? Be a tenant farmer like you?"

Tao looked down. "Not good. I give money. Not enough. He give land by levee with small hole. Muskrat make bigger. Water floods crops. Not good."

"But that doesn't make sense. If it leaked, wouldn't the water flood other land as well?"

"I fix fast. Fill hole with more rocks and clay. Watch over it. When muskrat return, I kill." Tao demonstrated by lifting a rock and slamming it hard against the ground. There was no doubt in Charley's mind that Tao saw an imaginary critter.

"Eat muskrat for supper." Tao flashed a self-satisfied grin and Charley laughed out loud and slapped him on the back.

"What happened then?" he said.

"Have to work off ..." Tao searched for the right word, looking frustrated.

"Debt? You have to work off the debt?"

"Yes. Debt. I bring dishonor to family. Must work long time to be free."

"Why don't you leave if it's so bad? You said you had family in Walnut Grove."

Tao shrugged. "Must pay off debt first. Earn family honor."

Charley was speechless. He had no reason to doubt what Tao was telling him. But if that was the case, Tao was no better than an indentured servant. He wondered if Gil Parker, the land agent in Sacramento, was in on Dutch Hansen's scheme.

After checking on his grandfather one more time, making sure to cover him against the damp night air, Tao kicked dirt on the fire to extinguish it. He moved his mat to higher ground near the wagon and lay down without another word.

Charley also decided to call it a night. He grabbed a blanket from his gear and laid his mat on the other side of the wagon. He had better sleep fast because morning always came too early and he needed to cover as many miles as possible tomorrow. He wanted to honor his commitment to Brian by returning his outfit as promised. But first he had to deliver Tao and his grandfather to Walnut Grove. God only knew how long that would take.

In a way, this change in plans turned out to be to Charley's benefit. He would always be grateful to Tao for the warning he gave about the true character of Dutch Hansen. He had seen for himself that Dutch came across as loud and rude. And it appeared he could be cruel and dishonest as well. Too bad, because this land, covered by the rich black peat he had held in his hand, looked perfect for the crops Charley hoped to plant. He bet that seeds dropped in this soil practically grew themselves.

He tossed and turned as he listened to the night sounds of the delta—the lapping water against the shore, a chorus of crickets—and loudest of all—croaking bullfrogs. They made scolding sounds as they lamented the loss of their mates. It reminded Charley that he may have lost *his* mate, *Christina*. *Why hasn't she written?* Morning couldn't come soon enough to suit him.

CHAPTER FIFTY

Charley

Red-winged blackbirds were making a ruckus, waking Charley.

"It's not even daylight yet," he grumbled. He burrowed deeper under his blanket but surrendered to morning when cawing crows joined the chorus. Stiff from sleeping on the ground all night, he sat up and looked around. He couldn't see anything except a dense white fog that had enveloped the campsite.

"Tao!" he called out.

"Over here!" came the reply. Charley turned toward the sound of Tao's voice, but still couldn't make out his new friend. He could have been an arm's length away and not be seen in the murky conditions.

Charley got up and relieved himself a short distance away from their camp and gathered kindling to make a fire. The least he could do was make some coffee to ward off the damp cold of the fog. *Coffee? Would Tao want coffee?* He heard Chinese drank mostly tea. He stumbled to the back of the wagon to fetch a small pan in which to boil the chicory and nearly bumped into Tao.

"Everything okay here?"

"Yes," Tao said over his shoulder. He was busy trying to hoist up his grandfather's pants. The old Chinaman's bare bottom hung out and he was wriggling about like a young child who refuses to wear clothing once he's tasted the freedom of not wearing it.

Charley decided to leave Tao to his task, rather than offering to help. He had handled nappies for little Rose and later for Willie Neamott, but this was different. He had heard that the Chinese were private people. Tao might be too proud to accept help with a personal task like this.

They had a quick breakfast of the stale biscuits and thick bitter chicory; it turned out that Tao drank coffee after all. And then they got the wagon reloaded. Tao's grandfather sat up front with Charley and Tao and seemed much more animated than last evening. To Charley's amusement, he babbled nonstop in his native tongue. Tao nodded and answered him in Chinese sometimes, but ignored him for the most part.

"What's he saying, Tao?"

"He talks of the old country. Of people long dead. Today, he thinks I'm his brother. He very confused."

"Tao, is it safe traveling in this weather?" Charley squinted and waved his hand around. "I never saw fog like this except on the Monongahela River when I was a boy." He could see less than ten feet ahead.

"It's tule fog. You go slow—be okay."

"Well, I sure hope you know where we're going 'cause I can barely see a darn thing."

"Sun come out. Fog leave. Go! Go!" he urged Charley on.

They backtracked on the grass-trampled pathway and proceeded slowly until they had reached the main crossroad with the wooden sign. By this time the fog had lifted enough for Charley to see a fair distance. They headed due east to Walnut Grove instead of northeast to Sacramento, the direction from which Charley had come yesterday. *Was it only yesterday?* Charley felt like yesterday's events had happened days ago.

They would arrive in Walnut Grove as soon as they reached the northern fork of the Sacramento River, Tao explained. This would be a part of the river Charley had not seen. Along the way, Tao pointed out fields reduced to stubble.

"That one—corn," he said. A little later, "This one—wheat."

Whoever farmed these plots would need to plow the spent crops under before spring, Charley thought.

"What time of year do farmers plant out here?" he asked.

"End of March or April. Ground must dry from rains first. Asparagus grow early. Ready to trim and eat in March.

"As-par-a-gus?" Charley asked. "What's that?"

" Green stalks. About this long." Tao held his hands

about eight inches apart to indicate size. "Taste good."

"California sure grows a variety of crops compared to Concordia." Charley went on to explain to Tao about the tractors he and Peter had tried to sell in Kansas and how it shortened the work of farmers. He didn't know if Tao understood a word he said, but Charley couldn't help thinking about the possibilities of introducing machinery to California farmers. He could see Dutch Hansen using a tractor on all the land he owned. Of course, if he did, would that eliminate the need for all his workers who depended on him for their livelihoods? *It's something to think about.*

Thoughts of tractors brought Peter to mind. He wondered what his old partner was doing right now—this very minute. He laughed out loud. It was a sure thing that he wasn't out in the middle of nowhere like him.

Tao looked startled when Charley laughed.

"I was just thinking of something from back home," he explained. "What will you do when I leave you, Tao? Are you staying in Walnut Grove or going back to the ranch on Brannan Island?"

"Go back. Need money. Have to pay off debt."

"Oh yes, your debt. But won't Dutch be hard on you for leaving without a word?"

Tao shrugged his shoulders.

From what Tao had told him about Dutch, he expected the man to be harsh with his workers. He wished there were something he could do to help.

"Since it's getting on toward winter, there will be less field work to do. Why don't you come with me to the diggings in Auburn for a spell? They can always use more men in the mines."

Tao shook his head. "No mines. Bad air."

He couldn't fault Tao there. Air in the mines was *not* good. You could tell a man who had spent years like an underground mole by the pallor of his skin and the ground-in dirt under his fingernails, not to mention his chronic cough. He'd heard some men practically cough their guts out. Stooped shoulders were also common among miners. Charley guessed that came from the constant bending as they navigated through the tunnels. The same was true of coalminers back home in Pennsylvania.

He had been underground only twice, and the oppressive feeling of being under a mountain capable of collapsing on him overcame Charley. He panicked and refused to enter another hole in the ground. He would take his chances working the sluice box and panning in the river.

His thoughts were interrupted by Tao, who pointed to a wooden bridge in the distance.

"Turn there," he said.

Charley could see that the bridge was the only entry point leading to a teeming community built on the waterway. When they reached it, the narrow bridge proved

barely wide enough for the wagon and it creaked something terrible. But Charley succeeded in getting them
into the village where small shacks along the river were
supported on stilts. Smoke came out of crooked stove
pipes thrust through rusted metal roofs. Docks below
bustled with activity as boats arrived with goods and left
with fishermen. He saw dense walnut orchards sitting
back from the river, their trees bereft of leaves. The sun
had finally come out, dissipating the fog, and filtered
through tree branches in bands of multi-colored rays. It
was almost like looking through a prism, Charley
thought.

They stopped at a small house set back from the river. Clothes hung from a line and fishing poles leaned
against the side of the clapboard structure. An Asian
woman emerged and bowed when she saw Charley.

"Auntie," Tao said, also bowing before climbing
down from the wagon. Several children emerged from
the house and stared at Charley. They examined the
wagon and surrounded Beulah, who twitched her ears
and accepted their attention tolerably well. Charley
helped Tao lift the old man from the wagon. From there,
Auntie and Tao saw him into the house. Charley unloaded his passengers' sleeping mats and other meager belongings, assigning them to the children. They accepted
the gear Charley handed them, struggling with the heavier items, and traipsed after their elders.

Charley waited but Tao did not return. He didn't

want to leave without saying goodbye, but he needed to get going. He clicked his tongue at Beulah and she moved slowly forward. He turned her toward the bridge and as they crossed it, he saw Tao emerge and bow in his direction. He took his hat off and waved. He would miss Tao, even though they didn't talk much. There was something steadying about how the Chinaman had faced hard times. It made Charley think that he, too, could handle whatever hardships came his way. If Tao could survive, so could he.

He arrived late afternoon in Sacramento. There was one last thing Charley needed to attend to before he began the long trek back to Auburn and the ravines. Heading directly to the land agent's office, he girded himself for what he intended to say.

"Saw the land you sent me to look at and talked with Dutch Hansen, all right," he said after he entered the small office. "How about you give me some real honest leads without a crook attached. Think you can do that, mister?"

Gil Parker's eyebrows lifted in surprise.

"I don't know what you're talking about," he said. "You liked the land didn't you? Saw that it was prime growing soil?"

"I did and I liked what I saw. But I also learned some of Dutch's little tricks and how he keeps his buyers beholden to him—stuck in servitude. Men don't do that kind of business where I come from."

Parker backed up and cleared his throat.

"I think you have this all wrong."

"I can't prove it, but I think you get something back from Dutch when those kinds of deals go through."

Parker puffed himself up, protesting. "I resent what you're suggesting, sir. Why, anyone in Sacramento can vouch for my honesty."

"I'm not *suggesting* anything. I'm saying it outright." Charley figured he knew the signs of being cheated by now and he wasn't about to let it happen a second time. "Before I go to one of the other land offices," he said, pointing out the window, "I'll give you one last chance to make good. Is there anything on one of those islands available for sale? I have the gold to buy it outright if it's the right price."

"Well, well, let's see here." Parker thumbed through the messy stack of papers on his desk. "There's..." He held up one and then shuffled it beneath some others, shaking his head. "Or how about..."

"That's what I thought. I'll take my business elsewhere." Charley could hardly believe the words came out of his mouth. They were strong and he meant them, but he never thought he could call a man a crook to his face. Once he left the office, he felt like a different man—one his pap would have been proud of.

On a hunch, he decided to wander around the neighborhood to see what other land offices existed. After several blocks he decided they all pretty much looked the same. Since nothing had piqued his interest, Charley was about to turn back when he saw a hand bill posted on a fence. It read: Public Auction. He squinted at the fine print and read that the auction was for the purpose of selling foreclosed properties on which taxes were delinquent. It was to be held a week from today. The circular went on to spell out the terms: "Cash only, payable at time of purchase."

The land and acreage listed was accompanied by a rough map. There were several plots by water, and one of them looked to be near where he had camped last night. He remembered seeing the name Tyler Island along with Walnut Grove etched into the wooden sign they passed. From what he had observed, all the land in that area looked good. He tore the handbill off the fence and stuffed it into his pocket. This might be the stroke of luck he needed. He was so excited that he slapped both knees hard to make sure he wasn't dreaming. Startled birds in a nearby tree took flight."Whoo hoo!" Charley yelled as he ran back to the waiting wagon and Beulah.

CHAPTER FIFTY-ONE

Charley

It was nearly sunup by the time Charley arrived back in Auburn. The last couple of miles were harrowing because it was so dark that he couldn't get his bearings. He had almost gotten lost—twice. There was only a quarter moon to guide him until he neared the town of Auburn where the bright lights of early morning risers were a welcome sight. He had made it. He kept his promise.

"We just about gave up on you," Brian said, greeting Charley. He was seated at the table with a cup of coffee. Brigitte, with her back to him, stirred something on the stove.

"I know. I'm sorry I didn't get back sooner." Charley grabbed a coffee mug and poured himself a cup of the strong brew. "Good morning, Brigitte." He sat down and took a careful sip of the coffee and then a big swallow. "I needed this," he said, beaming.

"From the looks of you, the trip must have been a success?" Brian said. Brigitte studied Charley and then abruptly turned back to the stove. She dropped eggs in the sizzling fry pan.

"I'll tell you, Brian. You wouldn't believe the richness of the land in the Sacramento Valley. There's water everywhere you look: The Sacramento River, American River, Mokelumne River, and creeks running between them. And it's good clean water too." He looked up as Brigitte placed full breakfast plates in front of her father and then him. "They have all this soil raised up creating islands—all with different names. And the soil..." Charley stopped to guide a forkful of eggs to his mouth. "...it's black as midnight. They call it peat dirt. Why, a seed dropped in that dirt would throw down roots out of gratitude."

"That good, huh?" Brian cocked his head to one side.

"From what I saw, with luck, a farmer could get three growing seasons from those fields. With a mild winter, maybe four."

Brian grinned. "Slow down, Charley. We get it. But did you *actually* see any land for sale?"

Charley's expression changed. He chose his words carefully. "Well, there's land there, but a lot of it is in the hands of this sort of land baron. They call him Dutch. Not a very friendly fellow and from what I've heard, he's not an entirely honest man to deal with." He reached into his back pocket and pulled out the handbill announcing the auction a week away.

"But this looks promising." He handed it to Brian.

Brian scanned it and then looked at Charley. "An auction? Do you have the ready cash to bid on land?"

"I got to do some figuring on that. I've got most of my gold converted to cash, and I have a little set aside. I might be able to swing it."

"Ever been to an auction, Charley?"

"I've seen livestock auctions."

"Okay. So you know that you have to keep a cool head and not get caught up in the frenzy of bidding. It can be like gambling, and you don't always know what you've got until you get it."

"Sounds like you've been to one or two."

"I have, Charley. Even if you get the land, will you have enough money left for farm equipment? Will you be able to buy seed, a plow, and a mule to pull it?"

Charley shrugged. "Depends on what I get the land for, I guess."

"Don't mean to discourage you," Brian said. "But farming is like any other business. You have to look at all the conditions and have enough to live on while you're waiting to plant and then wait some more for the harvest."

"I know you're right. But, I'd like to give it a go, anyway. Might not get an opportunity like this again."

Silence fell over the table while Charley considered what Brian had said.

"Guess the first thing I should do," he said finally, "is buy my own mule for the trip to the auction. Like you said, I'm gonna need a good work mule."

"Charley, wait until you see if you actually get some

land before you invest in a mule. You can borrow Beulah again. Say," Brian said brightly, "If you want I can go with you. I haven't been out of Auburn for a spell. Might even pick up a few things from suppliers in Sacramento instead of waiting for them to be shipped to Auburn. Prices should be lower if I buy direct. What do you say? Want some company?"

"I'd like that a lot," Charley said. "I'll appreciate your advice, Brian. You've been a good friend." He turned to Brigitte who had remained quiet. "You too, Brigitte." He grabbed her hand and squeezed it. "Maybe you'd like to come along too."

"I don't think so, Charley," she said, withdrawing her hand from his. She stood up abruptly. Too much to do around here. I'm happy for you, Charley, but wish you weren't leaving us."

"Well, I haven't left yet." He laughed and looked at Brian, who was having trouble suppressing a smile on his face. *Does he know something I don't know? What did I miss?*

The next day Charley penned another letter to Christina to let her know of his prospects. He hoped she would answer this one. He had not heard back from her since his first letter was mailed weeks ago. He wondered why and hoped nothing was wrong. He also sent a brief note to his sister, Jennie, to let her know that he was okay and where he could be reached. Up to now he didn't want to tell her where to write because he didn't think he would remain in any one place for long. He wanted her to think he had been successful.

He accompanied Brian to the diggings each day, more eager than ever to get as much gold out of the creek as possible before the auction took place. Gold meant money and money meant land—even small amounts of gold dust added up and increased his odds of realizing his dream.

The night before he and Brian were to leave for Sacramento, Brigitte was buzzing around doing odd chores instead of sitting by the fire, reading or sewing, which was her habit. Her restless activity suggested she was agitated about something. Charley wondered what. When he spoke to her, she answered in one-syllable words and wouldn't meet his eyes.

"Brigitte," he said. "Is something wrong?"

Brian looked up and headed for the door. "Got to check on Beulah," he said. "I'll be a few minutes."

Neither Charley or Brigitte acknowledged him. Brigitte turned slowly toward Charley.

"Guess I'll never learn," she said. "I kind of hoped you were going to be different than other men."

"What do you mean?" He felt a rush of heat rising up the back of his neck.

"We were getting on okay," she said. "Don't you think?"

"Well, sure."

"Didn't figure you for someone who would lead a girl on."

"Brigitte, I sure didn't mean to do that." Charley was astonished to be accused of insincerity. "You're a delight to the eye and steadfast and..."

"Sounds like you're describing a horse, not a woman."

Firelight shone in her eyes, but there was something else too. Charley saw puzzlement, which was what he was feeling himself. He was baffled why she regarded him romantically.

"I thought you knew that I was waiting for Christina," he said.

"Well, where is she then? This mysterious girl named Christina who hasn't even answered your letters. Maybe she doesn't care about you any more, Charley. Maybe you're just too—"

"Dumb to know it? Is that what you're trying to say?" Now Charley was the one whose hackles were up. "You may be right, Brigitte. But I don't know that. And until I do, I can't consider another, even if I wanted to."

"Does that mean you would *want* to consider another...then?" Brigitte moved closer.

Charley could smell the scent of lilacs on her—the lilac talcum powder he had given her.

"Oh, Brigitte," he said, placing both hands on her shoulders to stop her from coming closer. "You make my heart beat faster. But, don't do this just now. I'm a man in a complete state of confusion."

She raised herself up on tiptoes and leaned in to look Charley in the eye. His hands dropped from her shoulders to her waist, drawing her close. She kissed him fully on the lips.

"Take that and think about it, 'man in a complete state of confusion.'"

CHAPTER FIFTY-TWO

Christina

It was mid-afternoon, but it looked later. The sky had turned a steely gray by the time Christina and Clay were in sight of the Central Pacific Rail Station. A wind had picked up and sagebrush blew alongside them; some rolls of the sage-smelling shrub racing past were half as big as Christina. A streak of lightening lit up the sky followed by rolling thunder and the pungent smell of something burning. It felt as if the heavens had split open as the rain began sheeting down, soaking them before they were able to run for cover. She had never seen such a display before, and it frightened and thrilled her at the same time.

"When will the next train come through?" Christina asked, shivering. She and Clay stood on the train platform under the station roof.

"Hard to say, but I 'spect it will be along before dark." Clay pulled his tobacco pouch from a shirt pocket. But seeing the bag was soaked through, he cursed under his breath. "Can't smoke wet tobacco."

"Sure could use something hot to drink," Christina

complained.

They both looked in the direction of the general store where a dim light inside beckoned to them. As if they had read each other's minds, they hoisted their backpacks over their shoulders and ran for it. They couldn't get any wetter than they already were, but by the time they covered the short distance through the muddy street they were mired up to their ankles.

Once they stepped inside, Christina headed immediately to the potbellied stove to warm herself. A couple of locals, gathered around it, sat on wooden kegs. They looked over the two and scowled, appearing to resent the intrusion and having to make room for strangers. The store proprietor looked none too happy with the mess they brought in. He grabbed a mop and began scrubbing the floor they had soiled.

"How much for a cup of coffee?" Clay asked.

"No charge if you buy something," he said without looking up.

Clay reached into his pocket and slapped coins on the counter, where a stack of cups lay.

He reached for two and proceeded to fill them from the pot steaming on the stove.

"Thanks, Clay," Christina said through chattering teeth. She held her cup with both hands in an effort to warm them and lowered her face over the vapor rising from the cup. The strong coffee, though bitter, felt good going down. One of the men finally stood and offered her his keg to sit on.

"Might want to get them boots off and dry them by the heat, some," he told her.

"Obliged," she replied. But when she handed her cup to Clay and reached down to pull her boots off, they wouldn't budge. Finally, with a whoosh, she yanked off the first and tipped it, emptying a pool of water on the floor. "Sorry," she said to the storekeep." She proceeded to the other with the same results. Her muddy socks were soaked through too. They were like a second skin and she had to peel them off. Christina laid them on the hot stove where they made a sizzling sound. One of the socks had worn through making a big hole on the heel. Clay handed back her coffee.

"Anyone know when the next train comes through?" he asked.

The man who gave up his seat said, "If the rain don't wash out any of the track, should be coming in 'bout five o'clock or so."

"That's less than an hour," Christina said.

"Time enough." Clay reached in his pocket again and, as he approached the counter, he pointed to items he wanted to purchase: tobacco, beef jerky, apples from a barrel. "Better throw in a block of that cheese," he said pointing to a generous slab of yellowish cheese placed next to some cured meats. "Be sure and scrape off that mold first." The proprietor stacked the items on the counter.

"That bread fresh?" he asked. "Give me a loaf of that too. This oughta do for awhile," he said, looking back at Christina. "Oh, and we need some dry socks. Thick ones. You got any?" The storekeeper nodded and produced pairs of heavy gray men's wool socks from beneath the counter.

"Will that be all, mister?"

"Might want a couple of your licorice sticks. You like licorice, Christina?"

She nodded.

"Two licorice sticks then. What do I owe you?"

The storeowner pulled out a pencil stub and tallied up the items on a piece of brown paper he had just torn off a roll. "That will be a dollar and two bits," he said.

"Want to check those figures again," Clay said, scowling.

"The man bent over the row of numbers and began adding on his fingers. "Guess a dollar even will do it." He flashed a weak smile in Christina's direction and began wrapping the merchandise in the brown paper, when Clay reached out a hand to stop him.

"Leave out the tobacco and licorice and a pair of them socks. You can wrap up the rest." While the bundle was being tied with string, Clay handed the licorice sticks and the socks to Christina. She promptly began working on the anise flavored candy while wrestling on a pair of the new socks. "Oh, that feels good," she said, wiggling her toes in them like a young child. Between the coffee and licorice she began feeling her energy return.

Clay rolled a fresh cigarette and lit it, smiling with the first draw. "Guess we'd better go if we're going to catch that train," he said.

"But it's so pleasant here," she said. Clay didn't reply, but the look he gave her said plenty. Christina sighed and pulled her boots back on. They were still wet, but somewhat warm from the fire. She picked up her backpack to follow Clay, who stood by the door waiting for her.

The rain had let up, but the air had turned colder. Clay looked up. "Might snow by morning," he said.

They returned to the station just as a train was heard in the distance making its way toward them. The engineer must not be stoking the locomotive with much coal, for the volume of smoke coming from its stack was barely a wisp and the engine sounded as if it were exhausted.

"Think you can go on by yourself?" Clay said.

"What? What do you mean, Clay? Aren't you coming with me?"

"Well, Missy. You know I never intended to go all the way to California. I tole you that."

"I know, but—" Christina felt a veil of disappointment about to descend once again. "I thought you would see me through for a little while longer."

"I'll make sure you get on an empty boxcar with no bums inside it or train guards to kick you off, but then I got to go."

"I thought you liked riding the rails."

"Trouble with riding the rails is that a body gets used to staying on longer than it should—just riding along with the clickety-clack ringing in your ears all day long. Soon enough you lose your gumption and you're just riding to be riding. Where you been and where you're headed feels the same."

"But where *will* you go? It might begin storming again. And snow—you said it might snow."

"I'm not afraid of a little rain or snow. I'll get by. Clay thrust the brown-wrapped package into her arms. "Take these extra socks and the food until you can find more to your liking along the way. Good luck to you, Christina. May the spirits guide you and protect you."

Christina felt like crying, but there wasn't time to let her emotions have their way. The train was in the station, and Clay was already opening and shutting the doors of boxcars, checking them for other riders, keeping a lookout for the guards. He finally motioned to her and helped her board an empty car. He lit a match so she could see inside and get oriented. From the smell of it, the car must have carried animals at one time. There was straw in one corner that would come in handy for bedding down and, as bone weary as she felt, she knew it wouldn't be long before she fell asleep.

Before Christina could thank Clay, he was already closing the door. She put her hand out to stop it. She peered out a last time at her Indian companion—a man whom she never would have guessed could become her friend.

"You saved my life more than once, Clay. I'll never forget you." She let go of the door and Clay finished closing it, giving it a good slam. She heard him respond, his voice very faint: "Me too, gal."

CHAPTER FIFTY-THREE

Christina

As soon as the train was underway, Christina relaxed. Certain that she would not be discovered, she stripped off all her wet clothes, spreading them on the boxcar floor. She hoped they would dry by the next stop or before anyone checked out this particular car. All she had on was the second new pair of dry wool socks Clay had given her. Heading for the straw, she scooped out a hollow like a small burrowing animal might do, and crawled in. The straw scratched her bare skin, but provided warmth. A moment later Christina felt something crawling on her. She was so tired that she just slapped it and burrowed deeper.

She awoke, needing to relieve herself in the worst way. *How long before the next stop?* She needed to get off and find a place to take care of her business. But maybe that was too risky since she was riding alone. She didn't want to miss getting back on the train. Always when she had been desperate, either Charley or Clay acted as her lookouts and helped her reboard.

Christina decided to pee in the boxcar and headed for

the corner opposite the straw bed. She didn't like violating this space, but who knew what critter—animal or man—had occupied it before her and had done the same thing without reservation. That made her feel better. As she stood up from the crouch she was in, her legs buckled. The car began to spin and she stumbled toward her straw bed on wobbly legs.

When she came to, Christina sensed the train slowing. She checked her clothing and most of it was dry, though icy cold as she slipped back into her shirt and pants. Her boots were definitely still wet. She hated putting her new dry socks inside them, but she had no choice.

"Anyone in there?" a voice bellowed. A sharp rapping on the side of the boxcar followed. Christina scrambled to hide in the farthest corner. The ratcheting sound of the door sliding and the sight of bright light assaulted her senses, forcing her to remain still and hold her breath. A burly man in striped coveralls wearing a thick mackinaw peered in. He started to close the door, but then stopped. He grunted as he climbed into the car and looked in her direction.

"Hey Max, looks like someone slept here." He was looking at the nest she had made in the straw. "And it smells like someone took a piss too." He held up a lantern and looked around. "Might as well come out, lad," he said, looking directly at Christina.

She moved slightly, afraid to say anything and give

herself away as a woman.

"Come on out, I said!"

On shaking legs, Christina moved toward the guard.

"Let me stay on just a little bit longer." She was careful to lower her voice. "Please, mister. Got to get to Auburn."

"Auburn! You're a ways from Auburn. Can't let you stay on the train, kid. Gotta get off here." He took her by the arm toward the door where he gave a little shove. Forced to jump down, she made a clumsy landing in the snow and cried out.

"Hey!" she said. "Where are we?" She squinted, seeing that she was in the mountains.

"Truckee, California."

Christina had never heard of Truckee. "How far to Auburn from here?"

"Depends on how you go. By train, it's about a day—depending on how many stops in between. A day and a half at most. Now, if it's by horse and wagon, probably three, four days unless you've got an old horse." He laughed. "If you're on foot, who knows? Wouldn't consider going by foot though, not this late in the year and after what happened to the Donner party."

"Donner Party?"

"Yep. Whole group of folks got lost when they tried to take a shortcut through these mountains. Got snowed in for months. Ended up having to eat each other or starve," he said.

"Oh, how terrible!" Christina shuddered at the thought.

"You got any people waiting on you?"

"Yes, my aunt," she lied. "She sent for me. Needs a man's help around the property." Christina hitched up her breeches and tried to look taller. She almost said fiancé, but that would have been a mistake. It sounded more desperate to have an old, needy aunt awaiting her arrival.

"An auntie, huh? Well, she should have warned you against riding the rails, especially this time of year. Looks like winter is hitting early. I hear that another storm is coming through."

Christina figured out later that her face must have registered alarm, because the guard let her go.

"All right, kid. I'll let you pass through this one time, but don't let me ever see you on one of our trains again, you hear?"

"Yes, sir," Christina answered, her voice squeaking unnaturally. *Oops!* If he noticed the sudden change in her voice, the guard let it pass. He even gave her a boost to climb back inside the boxcar.

"Remember what I told you, now," he said as he slid the boxcar door shut. "No more free rides!"

"Whew!" Christina said aloud as soon as the train started lurching forward. "That was a close one." She would have to be more careful in the future—a future she hoped would come soon because she wasn't cut out to be cooped up this long. When she shared the ride with Charley and Clay, their company kept her mind off the hardships. Now that she was on her own, she noticed every little discomfort. She returned to her pile of straw and flopped down, exhausted. The confrontation with the guard left her so unnerved that she doubted she could pull off her male impersonation a second time and get away with it. Actually, she didn't know if she got away with it this time or whether the guard just took pity on her and let her slip through.

She heard the wind howl and felt it aggressively force its way through the slats of the boxcar. There was just no warming up. At one point she got up and walked the perimeter of the car, speeding up and then running to keep warm. All she got for her effort was perspiration that chilled her, making her feel colder. It also rendered her helpless with a tightness in her chest and a cough. She lay down and fell into an exhausted sleep.

When she awoke it was because her insides had cramped up. *The cheese.* The cheese was bad. Christina had finished the last of it earlier and it was playing havoc with her stomach and bowels. *Have to get off the train!* She paced trying to keep her mind off the fact that she was sick, was going to be sick. Once more she ran for the corner away from her bed and threw up. It made her more ill to smell her sickness and she heaved again, and then fell to the floor. Christina felt clammy, too weak to get up. She lay there a few minutes, moaning and gasping. The taste in her mouth was vile. What she wouldn't give for a drink of water. She finally managed to crawl across the floor to her bed and collapse.

Some time later the train stopped. Christina had lost all sense of time between bouts of drowsing off so that she didn't know if it was night or day. She worked her way over to the door and listened closely before trying to slide it open. Because of the wind howling against it and her weakened state, it took a monumental effort to move the door even a few inches. But finally, she was able to wedge her body through a narrow opening and jump down. Her landing was a hard one that threw her forward away from the boxcar. The train was lined up on an embankment. It wasn't steep, but Christina couldn't get her balance and rolled a few yards downhill from the railroad tracks. Patches of snow covered the ground in some places, but where she landed it wasn't enough to cover the sharp rocks hidden underneath, nor the dormant juniper bushes that grabbed at and scratched her cheeks. She crawled back up a few inches without getting any traction.

Christina needed to find water and clean herself up a bit before getting back on the train. She looked for, but saw no station at this stop. In fact, she wasn't certain why the train had halted. She paused long enough in her struggle to grab hands full of dirty snow. She crunched the crystals between her teeth, letting them melt in her mouth and trickle down her throat. Hoping the snow would refresh and energize her, Christina rubbed some on her face. But it only served to chill her.

She felt the pressure in her bowels start up. "Oh no," she cried. "Not again!" With little warning, she relieved herself, ashamed to be sick out here in the open like some helpless, dumb, farm animal.

As she tried to again ascend the incline, the train began belching smoke and crept by her. She scrambled as quickly as she could, hoping she was strong enough to run alongside the train and reach one of the metal ladders. She wasn't certain she remembered how to do it, though Clay demonstrated the correct way to jump onto a train without falling beneath it.

Christina needn't have worried about hopping the train because she couldn't even get up the incline. She lay there crying as the train picked up speed and passed her, its whistle blowing, the sound fading into the distance. Everything she owned remained in the boxcar. Her clothes, a little food, and her wages from working on the horse ranch. Now what would she do?

Well, she couldn't just lie there! Christina used her fingernails like talons and dug the tips of her boots into the snow-covered soil until she could get a foothold. She inched her way up the incline until she arrived at the top of the levee on which the railroad tracks lay. When she stood up she saw a ranch below. The snow looked a little deeper there, but at least it was on level ground. It should be more manageable.

She calculated her chances of making her way across the field to the barn situated southwest of the ranch house. Could she make it to the barn without being seen? Without making too much noise? The whistling wind should cover any sounds she made, including the crunching of snow underfoot. All the while she studied the ranch she didn't see a single living soul emerge from the house or the barn. She heard animals, but didn't see any. What were her chances of appealing to the people in the house for help or hiding out in the barn until she felt able to continue her journey?

It appeared that she had passed through the highest part of the mountains because due west flattened out into foothills. And beyond those foothills she guessed was a valley. Auburn was her destination. *Was it in the foothills she saw before her or in the valley beyond?*

Christina considered approaching the ranch house, but worried the people who lived in it might be like the Eilers—nice and proper on the surface but underneath their friendliness, a darker side. She opted for the barn. She would rest up there and study the place while recovering from whatever illness had gripped her before deciding her next move. She was so close to her goal. She just couldn't give up now.

CHAPTER FIFTY-FOUR

Christina

Christina ran across the wide expanse of snow-covered ground to the barn, hoping she hadn't been seen. All anyone need do to discover that someone had been trespassing was to follow the footprints she left. However, if snow fell overnight, the footprints would be filled with no one the wiser.

The comforting, familiar smell of animals and manure greeted her when she slipped into the drafty old barn. It wasn't as warm as she had hoped, but it was an improvement over the bitter north wind, which had cut through her since she left the train. This farmer must be doing okay, she thought, based on the number of livestock she counted: a dozen cows and four horses. She grabbed a horse blanket draped over a stall and made her way up the ladder to the loft. Piles of hay were a welcome sight. Her body ached to lie down and sleep, but first she checked the hay, disturbing a couple of nests. She didn't much want to share her sleeping quarters with mice.

It was almost dark when she heard voices coming toward the barn. She hunkered down in the straw and willed herself not to make noise. The voices belonged to two young boys who she figured had been sent to do the evening milking. Christina chanced a peek at them and saw that they were around ten or eleven years old, with fair hair peeking out from under their caps and facial features that were almost identical. *Brothers*, she decided. With them was a humpback yellow dog. The boys grabbed a bucket apiece and jostled into each another, using the buckets as battering rams, with their dog running between them, barking. They shouted back and forth in the echoing structure and at one point squirted milk at each other, aiming cow teats like pistols. Laughing at their cleverness, one of them reminded her of Chester Eiler. She couldn't help but smile as she witnessed their innocent fun. How she wanted to call out and ask for help. They looked nice enough, but she was still reluctant. It wasn't the children she needed to be wary of, but the adults. Christina had had her fill when she let her guard down with John Eiler.

Soon the boys had finished milking and poured their buckets of milk into a large metal can with a handle on the side. It looked like a cream separator. Christina guessed that someone older in the family would see to the actual task of separating the milk from the cream— which would slide into a separate bucket. A farmer would not chance the milk being spilled or wasted.

After the boys pulled the barn doors closed, she could still hear their fading laughter as they made their way back to the ranch house. When she was sure they were out of earshot, she climbed down the ladder and ducked into an empty stall. She squatted in the stall corner and finally relieved her full bladder—which was in agony during the milking. The sound of the milk hitting the sides of the buckets made her feel as if she would burst.

Weak from hunger, Christina searched the buckets for any leftover milk. She was lucky that the boys had been lax in their pouring duties—she was able to tip both buckets and drink from them. The milk was still warm. Sated, she returned to the loft and added extra hay to her makeshift bed. The blanket was barely on top of her before she fell into a hard, fast sleep.

It wasn't even daylight when she awoke to the sounds of the boys returning. They repeated their milking routine, but were quieter than the night before. The cold had apparently put a damper on their high jinks. In no time, they were done and left. This time, Christina peeked out the loft's hay door and watched as they made their way through new snowdrifts to the ranch house, where warm light shone through windows and smoke spiraled from the chimney.

Christina imagined the scene inside the kitchen: bacon and eggs cooking, coffee boiling on the cook stove, maybe biscuits hot from the oven served with butter and homemade jam. Her mouth watered, her stomach rumbled and complained. But this time it was from hunger, not from being sick. What she wouldn't give for a bite of fresh biscuits, or even stale ones. She longed for the comfort that the farmhouse promised, but she feared how the guise of kindness might turn into something else.

Instead, Christina climbed down from the loft again. She located a bag of feed for the horses and, reaching in, scooped up a handful of raw oats. She chewed on the grain kernel, greedily. Hulls in the unprocessed oats made the mixture so dry that she almost choked. She spit them out and ran for the separator, scooping up milk infused with cream, lapping it from cupped hands like a thirsty dog. The rich mixture filled her up and made the oats slide down her gullet a bit easier.

When she heard another set of crunching footsteps approach the barn, louder than those of the boys, Christina ran for cover in the nearest horse stall. The horse occupying the space made a nickering sound, but allowed Christina to squeeze in behind her. The mare was a big draft horse—maybe a Belgian from what Christina could see of her sorrel and white coloring. Christina's view was limited as she crouched uncomfortably in the corner. The Belgian shifted slightly, lifted her tail, and released an impressive pile of droppings near Christina's feet. *Oh great!* She kicked straw toward the manure and tried to make herself smaller. Minutes later, she was thankful that the horse was so mellow—especially now that she had done her business.

A man entered the barn, passing the stall in which Christina was hiding. He stopped at the next stall and in a rich baritone said, "Hello, Beauty. Didn't think I forgot you, did you? You'll get your exercise soon, when I'm done with my chores." A horse neighed in response to the soothing voice, and the farmer laughed. Christina heard grain being scooped into bags and the sound of the man's footsteps as he moved down the line to feed his horses. As he reached the Belgian draft, she held her breath.

"I'll come back for you in a little while, Cinnamon. At your age you don't need much exercise. You deserve to take it easy." He patted the horse on the neck and moved on. She could hear him opening up the other horse stalls. The clopping of hooves was loud as he led his horses outside, probably to the open corral she had seen behind the barn. Before she could scoot around Cinnamon and open the stall, the farmer had returned. The sound of a handle being turned told her that he was using the cream separator. The faster it turned, the more clanging and whining the machine made as centrifugal force separated the cream from the milk. Over the noise came his whistling. There was enough noise to cover Christina climbing back up to the loft, but she decided to stay put until he left. It was a calculated risk. If he returned to let Cinnamon out for exercise, she would be discovered like a ship stowaway.

Luck was with her. The farmer didn't return. Christina's legs ached something terrible from crouching so long. As soon as she heard the barn door close, she beat a hasty retreat from Cinnamon's stall and climbed the stairs to the loft. She remained there until after he returned the horses to their stalls several hours later.

Christina thought long and hard about what to do. She couldn't stay here indefinitely, and she was still afraid to ask for help. She feared being lulled into a false sense of security. She didn't want to end up like unwanted kittens lowered into warm water only to be drowned. Finally, Christina weighed two possibilities: hop a freight train again and ride through to Auburn or leave the hard way—by horseback, in hopes of reaching the nearest town.

She doubted she would be able to hop the train where she got off because of the terrain. The narrow shoulder on both sides of the tracks wasn't wide enough to run alongside without slipping down the embankment. Although she felt better, she didn't feel strong enough to pull herself up a ladder. She should have paid closer attention when Clay demonstrated the best way to hop a boxcar. Christina hadn't really concentrated on what he was trying to teach her. After all, she had him or Charley ready to pull her up if she faltered.

The only sensible plan was to travel by horseback. She would be homeless and living on the streets again like when she was in Pittsburgh. Only then, Sean had looked out for her. Christina had stayed alive because of thievery, and here she was faced with having to resort to it again in order to survive.

Nighttime will be best. It was risky, but she had no other choice. After the evening milking, she would leave. She hoped that by then the yellow dog would be sheltered for the night in one of the outbuildings she saw near the house and be unable to hear her and give warning. From what she could see looking out the hay door, there was a decent trail between the barn and house that undoubtedly led to a main road. If she kept the railroad tracks in her sights, she knew it headed for Auburn. Therefore, she would travel parallel to them.

Her nerves taut, Christina fidgeted until the boys finished their milking chores that evening. She had already fashioned the horse blanket into something she could wrap around her body like a poncho to fend off the night chill. She gave it an hour and then led Cinnamon out of her stall. Christina took a good look at the mare. She was broader and heavier in stature and shorter than other horses, measuring fifteen hands instead of seventeen. *She's a draft horse, all right.* Christina saddled her and grabbed one of the feed bags from the bins. She filled it with oats for her mount and herself if need be. She led the Belgian out of the barn and up the trail to a dirt road that appeared to head in the right direction. With effort, she pulled herself up into the saddle and clucked her tongue against her teeth to get Cinnamon moving.

They had gone only a short way when she heard the howling of a dog. Whether it was the yellow dog or a neighbor's mongrel, Christina couldn't afford to travel at a modest pace. She put her heels to the Belgian. They needed to put some distance between themselves and the ranch. Finally, when she could no longer hear the dog, she leaned forward. "Whoa, Cinnamon. Easy, girl," she said, until they had slowed to a more measured gait.

As they clopped along, Christina admitted to herself that she had just committed a serious crime. She never imagined she would stoop so low as to steal a horse. She heard the owner describe Cinnamon as "old." Maybe the farmer wouldn't mind as much as he would have if Christina had stolen one of his younger, finer horses. She might even be doing him a favor by taking Cinnamon. Save him the difficult job of putting her down later.

Traveling by horseback in winter made her think about the fate of the Donner Party. She couldn't allow herself to get lost. Still, she needed to remain on secondary roads and remote trails where she would more likely go unnoticed. It was certain the farmer would report his horse missing, and she didn't need to be identified as the person who took her. Christina had been warned that horse thieves shared a low expectation for a long life.

CHAPTER FIFTY-FIVE

Jennie

The pace in Mary Belle's household was hectic as servants prepared for the holidays. The aroma of Southern favorites like bourbon-laced fruitcake, ginger cookies, and pralines permeated the downstairs rooms. Thoughts of Lucy and how she loved to hang about the kitchen when Lily helped bake made Jennie miss her all the more. She could picture Lucy sampling goodies that Lily somehow had slipped into her pinafore pockets.

Jennie was surprised to discover that she was homesick. She wrote letters to Lucy and Maggie, begging them for return letters to keep her spirits up. There wasn't much time for brooding, however. When she tried mingling with the kitchen and wait staff the way she had in Concordia, she was encouraged to participate in the social life of New Orleans instead.

"We're guests here, Jennie," Violet reminded her. "You must not socialize with the servants. It's not seemly."

Jennie knew Violet's attitude didn't allow for befriending those who served her, but it bothered Jennie just the same. Her mother pressed her to join in the afternoon teas and to attend concerts in the evenings, where ladies practiced beautiful manners and wore elegant gowns, some ordered directly from Paris. Violet was ecstatic about the social whirl surrounding Cousin Mary Belle, whereas, Jennie yearned for a diversion other than that of sitting around for hours balancing a tea cup and saucer on her lap. She wanted the excitement of seeing more of the sights and hearing the sounds of New Orleans, which Patrick had introduced her to when they fled the cotillion. She enjoyed the slow, measured approach to time, which matched the languid, musical inflection of the Creole French and Cajun dialects spoken in the city.

Why observe from the isolation of a carriage when she could walk among men and women mingling together on city boardwalks? She would rather be part of the crowd.

She thought back on the night she and Patrick danced freely to the "new jazz" being played by Negro musicians in saloons and open-air clubs. Now that she had been exposed to a different kind of life, Jennie yearned to experience the thrill of the unknown by the side of someone who appreciated the differences in people. Someone like Patrick.

Instead, she was again paired off with Kyle Covington whom Mary Belle invited to a dinner party that she was hosting. Though disappointed, Jennie was determined to make the best of it.

When Mr. Covington arrived that evening, he acted as if they were the best of friends. He *was* handsome and his drawing room manners were impeccable, but Jennie still found it difficult to forgive him for abandoning her on the cotillion dance floor. She wished it were Patrick sitting by her side, not Kyle.

"How is Mr. O'Hearn?" she finally asked. "I had hoped to see him again." She pierced her fork into a piece of roast beef, dipping it into the port wine sauce.

"How amusing of you to ask," he said. "Patrick said the same thing about you."

"He did?" Jennie's fork stopped midway to her mouth. "What did he say?"

Kyle smirked. "Something about you being adventurous and fun to be with."

"Oh." Jennie felt her cheeks grow warm.

"So, I thought I would see for myself." He picked up his wine glass and raised it in a toast. "Here's to getting reacquainted."

Jennie peevishly ignored his gesture. She declined to pick up her wine glass and acknowledge his toast.

"I thought you had given up the idea of getting acquainted when you handed me off to your friend." She resumed taking a bite of the roast beef, and chewed it longer than necessary. She then turned to the guest on her other side, snubbing Kyle. She hoped to discourage him from further conversation.

At evening's end, Kyle bowed and kissed her hand. "I

can see that I have a rival for your attention, Miss Hunsinger. I'm not a man to stand in the way of true love, so I will bow out of the race and wish you and Patrick well."

"Race? There's no race, Mr. Covington. I'm not a prize to be given away to the first man who crosses the finish line." Jennie couldn't help but try to puncture the man's ego a bit. It was clear that Jennie meant nothing to him but a social obligation. She could have stopped there, but went on. "I think you misunderstand. Mr. O'Hearn and I have genuine affection for the same things, that's all." She took a deep breath and with all the determination she could muster, she looked Kyle in the eye and said, "Whereas, you and I have totally different interests."

Kyle's eyebrows shot up, but he quickly regained control, presenting a blank face with little emotion.

"As you wish. I will communicate your desire." As he was leaving, he winked at Violet who was standing within hearing distance.

"That was rather unnecessary, Jennie," Violet said after he was gone. "Where are your manners?"

"I'm sorry. He had it coming."

"Well, I know he acted inappropriately, but really!"

"Goodnight, Violet." Jennie lifted her hand to her forehead. "I've suddenly got a headache. Will you excuse me?" Jennie headed for the stairs and her room. *She knows I never get headaches.* She felt remorse for the frosty words she had spoken to Kyle. After all, he was

Mary Belle's guest. *But that man makes me so mad!*

The next morning when Jennie entered the dining room she was surprised to see Patrick deep in conversation with Mary Belle and Violet. Coffee had been poured and they were waiting for breakfast to be served.

"Ah, here she is," said Patrick rising at her entrance. "Good morning, Miss Hunsinger."

"Good morning." Jennie had had no doubt that Kyle would report back to Patrick about the night before, but she didn't expect to see him so soon. "Are you joining us for breakfast?"

"Actually, no. I've been given permission to take *you* to breakfast and on a tour of New Orleans for the day."

Mary Belle and Violet looked as if they had been caught napping by the announcement. But they had the good grace to agree to the arrangement rather than look powerless.

As Patrick and Jennie descended the steps of the mansion, a compact buggy harnessed to a gray dappled mare awaited them. The horse looked out from under long eyelashes and peered at Jennie while Patrick helped her aboard. The buggy was small and unadorned. It pleased her to see it was as unpretentious as Patrick himself.

The driver delivered them to Café du Monde in the French Quarter where Jennie was introduced to strong coffee with chocolate and cream that they called café au lait. Accompanying the brew was a basket of beignets, deep fried pastry covered in powdered sugar. Jennie couldn't get enough of the puffed dough that reminded her of the fritters popular in the Midwest. Jennie had abandoned the ladylike habit of moderation Violet had drummed into her. She was still licking the sugar from her lips when Patrick dismissed the driver, saying the rest of their tour could better be seen on foot.

It had rained the night before, so Jennie was concerned about soiling the hem of her dress as she had the night of the cotillion. Ominous clouds hovered with more rain being predicted later in the day. But to show her faith in Patrick, she agreed that a little rain would not slow them down. They first walked to Jackson Square where they viewed the famous St. Louis Cathedral and then to the wharf overlooking the Mississippi River where stevedores loaded bales of cotton and tobacco onto steamer ships. Colorful paddlewheel riverboats dotted the bay as well.

"Many of our riverboats are little more than floating gambling casinos," Patrick said.

As they meandered among the shops, Jennie stopped before one that displayed unusual items in its window. Chicken feet and hanks of hair tied with ribbons, as well as jars, whose contents looked mysterious and unidentifiable, caught her eye. "What kind of shop is this?" Jennie asked.

"Nothing you need know about," Patrick said. He took her arm and tried to steer her away from the window.

"May we go inside and look around?"

"I'm not sure your aunt would approve, Jennie. This is a botánica that serves those who practice voodoo."

"Voodoo?"

"Yes, you know, black magic," he replied.

Jennie had heard of black magic, but thought of it as she did fairy tales and ancient myths, something to contemplate late at night in a story book. *Pure fiction and fantasy.* She didn't think it existed, let alone practiced by civilized people.

"It's a folk religion brought over by the slaves from places like the West Indies," Patrick said. "Marie Laveau was a famous voodoo priestess with many followers. In fact, she was so generally recognized and accepted that she's buried in the St. Louis Cemetery."

"Fascinating." Jennie brushed past Patrick and entered the dimly lit shop, made more cramped with its narrow aisles and high ceiling. She smelled something strong and cloying, but couldn't determine its source. Rows of dark opaque bottles lined crude shelves behind a counter. Dried herbs bound with string hung upside down from the rafters. There were other objects that looked as if they had come from animals—things like beaks, parts of wings—but none of them appeared to be the source of the odor.

Patrick followed a few paces behind.

"What is that strange aroma?" she asked the attractive mulatto woman standing behind the counter. She wore a colorful silk scarf wrapped around her head like a turban. She smiled and selected a vial she withdrew from under the counter. She pulled out the glass stopper.

"It's a love potion," the woman said as she thrust the bottle toward Jennie. "Very strong magic. You need one for your young man?" She nodded toward Patrick.

Jennie laughed. "I don't know. Do I need a love potion, Patrick?"

"It's not necessary," he said, smiling. "I've already been smitten."

Jennie thrilled to his teasing manner. "So soon? See," she said to the woman, "I don't need a potion." She moved deeper into the shop where she saw a wall of masks adorned with feathers in bright turquoise, red, and gold. "Ooh, they're beautiful. I wonder how it would look to wear one at another cotillion, or better yet, at a costume party?"

Patrick lifted one of the masks from the wall and held it up to Jennie's face. She looked into a looking glass on the counter and saw an exotic person of mystery looking back at her.

"It's for Mardi Gras," Patrick explained.

"Oh, I must have it!" she said. "Not for me, of course, but for Lucy." Jennie had told Patrick all about her attachment to the young orphan girl Violet had agreed to foster. "Lucy is all the more important to me because I was once an orphan," she had explained, "before Violet took me in and later adopted me." Patrick showed interest in hearing about her background and had encouraged her to expand on her life story until Jennie felt the pull of her first Concordia home with the Neamotts overwhelm her. She still felt shame in admitting how she hadn't been able to adapt to the life of privation compared to her brother, Charley. Some day she might expand on the stories that had dimmed over the years. She had been so young.

"For Lucy?" Patrick said. "You must have one too, Jennie. The Mardi Gras season will be here soon and you'll look so fetching in a mask. I know you and Violet will love our lavish celebration with parades and parties."

"I'm sure you're right. When is Mardi Gras?"

"The carnival season starts on January 6th and continues through Fat Tuesday, which can be anytime between February and March."

"Oh, that's too bad. I know we're destined to leave long before that."

Patrick removed the mask from Jennie and handed it to the woman behind the counter.

"Would you wrap this please?" He turned to Jennie. "Allow me to purchase this for Lucy then."

They left the botánica and window shopped until Patrick said that they were to have lunch in the oldest restaurant in the quarter: Antoine's.

"They've been in business since 1840," he said after they were seated in the formal dining room. They enjoyed a leisurely meal of shrimp Creole and crusty bread, followed by pecan pie for dessert.

"I thought I had dined in the best restaurants in the world when Violet took me to Europe. But I was too young to appreciate fine food then." Jennie wiped her mouth with a corner of the linen napkin. "So, this is very special, Patrick. It's not that we don't eat well in Concordia, but Violet's cook is Irish and you know..." She stopped herself from saying more lest she sound critical. To her own ears, Jennie was beginning to sound a bit snobbish.

"Ready for more touring?" Patrick asked as they left the restaurant.

"I'm not sure I can walk after all that rich food." The waist of her dress felt a bit tighter than when they had arrived.

"It's a common problem after dining in the quarter. Come on!" Patrick grabbed Jennie's hand and ran to catch a streetcar coming down the avenue. "We'll ride instead."

Jennie was out of breath by the time they boarded. She plopped down on a wooden seat and fanned herself before looking at the passing scenery. Patrick explained they were approaching the famous garden district. Victorian homes with lavish gardens lined the streets. Even in December there were shrubs beginning to bud: camellias and azaleas and the white waxy plant with the overpowering scent—gardenias. Massive magnolia trees, with piles of brown leathery leaves lying below their canopies, stood sentry in yards surrounded by wrought iron fences. They rode in silence for a while, Jennie being lulled by the motion of the streetcar until she felt revived.

"I think I can manage to walk now, Patrick. My lunch has settled," Jennie said.

"Good. Like I said, the best way to explore New Orleans is on foot." Patrick offered his hand, but Jennie decided she could manage on her own. However, when she stepped down the steps, it was into a low spot that had filled with water. Her shoes sank into the puddle with a whooshing sound; they were totally submerged. Patrick helped Jennie extricate herself from the muddy water onto dryer ground, but it was too late. The leather shoes were ruined.

"Oh, no. What'll I do now?" She cried. "I can't seem to avoid getting wet."

Patrick pulled off her shoes and stuck them into his jacket pockets.

"No, Patrick. You're just going to get dirty too," she protested.

"Hush. A little dirt and water never hurt anyone." In one fell swoop, he picked her up and carried her through a gate leading to a bench inside a rose garden. He settled her on the bench.

"May I?" he said as he bent to remove her stockings.

"Oh no, you don't need to do that," she said, embarrassed.

"It's okay, Jennie. Don't want you catching your

death of cold." He reached into his breast pocket and withdrew a handkerchief, which he used to wipe each foot with care and, then, rubbed them briskly between his hands.

"Are your feet getting warmer?"

"Yes."

"Good. Then, I'll continue." He flashed a smile.

"Now what do we do? There's no buggy and the streetcar left. Patrick, I'm not sure I can walk home like this."

"No need to. I'll carry you."

You can't possibly carry me all the way home."

"I think I can. I'm very strong, you know."

He didn't need to tell her that. Jennie had guessed at his strength when he picked her up and she threw her arms around his thick neck. The jostling caused her to fall against his muscular shoulder. He might be short, but he was compact and strong.

"Besides, we're only a short distance away from Mary Belle's."

"What? How is that possible?"

"Guess you didn't notice that the streetcar was headed in the general direction of her neighborhood. She's not officially in the Garden District, but very close by."

He scooped her up again and began walking down the street. Several streets later Jennie saw Mary Belle's mansion on the hill just as it began raining again. She pulled the wrapped package containing the mask closer to her breast. She couldn't allow it to get wet.

"Patrick, please put me down before you slip and we both fall." He complied, setting Jennie on her feet. They held hands as they ran up the driveway leading to the wide veranda. They were out of breath as they reached the steps. Patrick lifted the door knocker.

"At least you can't say you had a dull time with me," he said.

"No, I can't say that."Jennie reached up and kissed him on the cheek just as a maid opened the door.

Patrick touched the spot her lips had grazed and grinned. He turned to leave, but pivoted back, facing her. "May I call again?"

"Of course. I insist!"

"I'm at your command," he said, bowing. Jennie laughed as he turned once again and then skipped down the steps, heading into the rain.

"Miss Jennie!" the maid cried. "What did that man do to you?"

"He thoroughly entertained me," she replied, "like I've never been entertained before." She lifted her wet, soiled dress and raced barefooted up the stairs before Violet caught sight of her disarray.

It was then that she realized Patrick still had her muddy shoes and stockings stuffed into his pockets.

CHAPTER FIFTY-SIX

Jennie

The South wove its spell on Jennie in no time. Patrick acted as her personal guide to New Orleans and introduced her to sights she couldn't have pictured in her wildest imagination. She realized after seeing both the privileged as well as the impoverished people of the city that here was a richness of character and history unparalleled by any other region or country she had visited. Much of this was Patrick's doing as he approached everyone they encountered with the same degree of respect.

He joked with street musicians, joining in their jam sessions by pulling a harmonica from his jacket and sliding it across his mouth. She recognized the sounds the instrument made as the "new jazz" she heard the night of the cotillion. As they made their way around the promenade of Jackson Park, he stopped to speak with artists, revealing his knowledge of drawing. This was an area in which Jennie felt competent to add her observations. She still liked to sketch whenever the mood struck her. Patrick insisted that she sit for a portrait. After the artist completed the sketch in oil pastels, he whispered in Jennie's ear, "It doesn't do you half justice. You're more beautiful than that." She blushed with joy at the compliment.

When they dined out, Patrick lavished praise on the cooks, whether they were chefs in fancy French restaurants or fry cooks in six-stool fish shacks skirting the bayou. "Love your fried catfish, mama," he'd say as he licked his fingers clean. He took her on tours of antebellum mansions, some of which had been nearly destroyed during the Civil War and later restored.

One day he chose the famous St. Louis Cemetery on Basin Street for their outing. "They call our cemeteries 'Cities of the Dead,'" Patrick explained, "because there are so many stone crypts and mausoleums here that they resemble villages. You see, New Orleans was built on a swamp so our dead have to be buried aboveground."

Jennie shivered. "It seems so—I don't know—so ancient, so primitive. Don't you ever feel uneasy walking among the dead?"

"On the contrary, I take comfort in the fact that I'm among family. There's something peaceful, and at the same time, reassuring when I look around at the stone crypts. They're like fortifications against outside invaders." Jennie looked at him and scrunched up her face. He laughed.

"I guess that sounds a bit fanciful," Patrick said. "But seriously, with our frequent rainfall and tropical storms, aboveground burial is the most practical way to hold on to the bones of ancestors." Patrick went on to explain: "Even with earthen levees built to hold back water from the lowlands, flooding has always been a threat. The floods of 1849 and 1882 were devastating." He shook his head. "The little bit of rain we've been experiencing since you arrived is nothing by comparison." They walked farther into the cemetery without further conversation.

"See that crypt over there?" Patrick pointed to an elaborately carved tomb with fresh bouquets of flowers laid at its base. "That's where Marie Laveau, the voodoo queen I mentioned, is buried. You never know whom you're going to meet here."

By now Jennie was getting used to Patrick's sense of humor. She grabbed his arm. "You know so much about so many subjects, Patrick. I guess that's what college does for a person."

"Even though it's hard work, I enjoy my studies. But I'm glad to be on break so that I can spend more time with you," he said. Jennie smiled and held his arm tighter.

They had spent as much time together as possible. With Christmas Day nearing, they would be separated by family obligations.

"I would like to further my education too," Jennie confided. "I've begun to realize that there are so many things to learn." She told him about seeing the suffragettes picketing in Rochester, Minnesota, and how their dedication intrigued her.

"I think you would do well in the classroom, Jennie. You have a natural curiosity that makes for the perfect student." He looked closely at her. "And I hear that more women are being accepted into colleges than ever before."

Jennie basked in the warmth of Patrick's approval, which was something she desired more than flattery. "My mother would differ with you," she said. "When the subject comes up, she says a year of finishing school is all I need." She let out a big sigh. *To think, there's a whole life outside of Concordia.*

Later that afternoon they walked through one of the old neighborhoods. By chance, they witnessed an elderly black woman struggling to carry an overstuffed shopping bag with one hand and hang on to a young child with the other. The woman, whose hair was as white as the angel hair draped over Mary Belle's Christmas tree, walked with a slight limp. She was ill-equipped to keep up with the boy who was trying to wrestle free of her grip. Her shopping bag flipped open sending fruits and vegetables onto the cobbled street.

"Ooh," she cried as she fell. At the same time, the boy, seeing his opportunity for freedom, ran down the street. Patrick ran after him while Jennie rushed to assist the fallen woman.

"What! What you want!" she cried as Jennie crouched down beside her.

"Grab my arm, grandma," she said. The woman pulled back and turned away. "Please let me help you." Jennie edged closer. But the woman shook her head and with great effort raised herself to her knees. In the meantime, Jennie began picking up the woman's belongings.

Patrick appeared with the squirming child. "You mind your grandmama now, or the bogeyman's going to get you," he said. The child's eyes grew bigger as he considered this new development.

"Yes suh." He nodded his head.

Patrick set him down and placed a hand under the woman's elbow, pulling her upright before she could protest further. She glanced warily at Patrick and then, with a defiant expression, accepted the shopping bag that Jennie had refilled. She grabbed the hand of the boy and limped away without saying a word.

"I don't understand," Jennie said. "Did I do anything wrong to offend that woman? She acted as if she resented my offer to help."

"Some black people her age have suffered greatly at the hands of white men—and white women for that matter. They often shy away from interacting with us. Some never let their guard down," Patrick said. "Unlike many towns in the South, there's more intermingling of the races in New Orleans. And still there's mistrust of white man and his motives. You didn't do anything wrong, Jennie. If anything, through your kindness, you showed your humanity."

"I feel funny having the black servants wait on me at Mary Belle's," Jennie said. "Even though she seems to treat them well, I wonder—"

"I think you'll find that Mary Belle and Violet have not allowed themselves to catch up with the times. Some ideas are too new and threatening for them to embrace." Patrick's brow wrinkled as he hesitated a moment before continuing. "It doesn't make them bad people—just a little behind." He turned to Jennie. "We're the generation who will need to make big changes for the better."

Jennie heard the passion rising from Patrick as he expanded on his views and plans for the future. "I hope to foster those changes when I graduate from college and finish law school." He turned to her and said in a lighter tone, "Who knows? Maybe someday I'll even run for political office. Mayor of New Orleans or—"

"Governor of Louisiana," Jennie chimed in. "Or President of the United States."

"Oh, Jennie," Patrick said. "One day you'll make some lucky man feel like a king. I only wish to be in the running." He pulled her into his arms and brushed her lips with his, gently at first and then with more urgency.

Jennie matched his passion with her own until she realized they were in a public place making a spectacle of themselves. She pulled back and straightened her dress.

Looking into his eyes, she saw that he was quite serious. It thrilled and frightened her at the same time.

There was no denying that her friendship with Patrick had developed into something more. She wasn't certain she was able to understand or manage these strong emotions, especially since they wouldn't have the time to see where their relationship led. Jennie would be leaving within days after Christmas—or at the latest, by the New Year.

"We should get back," she said.

"Yes, of course, Jennie. I'm sorry if I took advantage."

She shook her head. "No, you didn't take advantage of me, Patrick. But you must think me brazen for letting you kiss me in broad daylight in public." Shocked at her forwardness, Jennie began to cry, surprising them both.

Patrick produced a handkerchief and handed it to her. She noisily blew her nose and turned her face away.

"Come," he said. "Let's get you home. We can talk about this later." Patrick whistled for a public carriage. A livery driver appeared out of nowhere as if awaiting them all the while. Patrick helped Jennie into the hack and hoisted himself up beside her. When he pulled the lap robe over them both, he found her hands clenched into fists, resting on her knees. He reached over and loosened them a finger at a time and then held one of her hands in his, stroking it gently.

They were silent during the ride back to Mary Belle's. Jennie felt humiliated, certain that Patrick found her unsuitable and ill mannered—a silly prairie girl just like Kyle thought. She had turned seventeen, but had acted much younger.

When they arrived, Patrick walked her to the door and bent to kiss her hand instead of her lips. It was a noticeable omission.

"I must see you again soon," he said. "May I call on you after Christmas Day?"

"As you wish, Patrick."

"I wish to very much."

Jennie knew she would remember this Christmas Eve for a lifetime. The rooms were filled with evergreen garlands that were placed everywhere: one draped the mantle, several were woven between the staircase rails, and the others framed doorways. Food had been artfully arranged, as pretty as some floral displays, and a string quartet played chamber music. Guests were New Orleans' finest, most distinguished, and brightest; their light chatter distracted her for a time, until the end of the evening when she thought about home in Concordia— Lucy without her—and Charley as far away west as he could get. Probably in California by now.

Thoughts of her brother Charley reminded her of Christina, the girl who should be his wife, but preferred to remain his lover until such time as all her conditions for marriage had been met. Jennie wished she were more like Christina, who had always acted sure of herself. Jennie couldn't imagine that Christina would ever find herself in a situation she couldn't manage, or allow anyone to take advantage of her.

She tried to erase Patrick from her mind, but he kept creeping back into her thoughts. She didn't question the strong feelings she had for him; they were genuine. This was no schoolgirl crush. But she knew the circumstances were impossible for them to build a lasting relationship, if for no other reason than distance. If only she were older than her seventeen years and independent, Jennie could see herself surrender to a man like Patrick. He was nothing like Peter Stuyvesant, whom she now saw as the shallow, shady character everyone had warned her about. And Patrick was not manipulative and condescending like Kyle who had passed her off as an unwanted social obligation.

No, Patrick was a man of substance who made her feel important and worthy, a woman his equal. Jennie looked around at all the people engaged in conversation, including Mary Belle and Violet. They wouldn't miss her if she turned in early. She had had enough of partying and forced gaiety for one night.

CHAPTER FIFTY-SEVEN

Lucy

Christmas was supposed to be a happy time, but Lucy felt that Santa had forgotten her again, just as he had all those years at the orphanage. She should be happier having a beautiful Christmas tree and gaily wrapped packages to gaze upon. But underneath the glitter and hominess, she had only one thought: *I wish Jennie were here.* Miss Maggie and Carl had done everything they could to make the season meaningful to her, including an invitation for children her own age from school to visit. Together they baked cookies and strung a popcorn garland they wound around the tree. Carl had even gone to town and picked up Brownie from Violet's carriage house and brought him back for her to play with.

The mutt was delirious when he was reunited with Lucy. He followed her through every room of the house, in spite of Miss Maggie's stern rule that he be kept outdoors. "An animal's place is in the barn, Lucy," she said. If only she had known that Lucy was not trustworthy in complying with certain rules. While Violet and Jennie were gone, and before coming to stay with Miss Maggie and Carl, Lucy had snuck Brownie up the stairs to her room where the two snuggled in Jennie's big feather bed.

Miss Maggie finally relented and placed a warm, braided rug next to Lucy's bed on which Brownie could curl up. During the night Lucy resorted to her old tricks; she urged him to jump up beside her to be hugged and nuzzled. But by the next morning, there he was on the rug again, looking all innocent.

It would only be a short time until Violet and Jennie returned to Concordia. Lucy had received a letter each week from Jennie and, recently, a package with written instructions on top: *Do Not Open until Christmas.* Lucy wrote back to Jennie once. She still had trouble with her penmanship, but Maggie helped her with the capital letters. Why did a capital "*J*" look so different from a small "*j*" she wondered.

On Christmas Eve Lucy and Brownie curled up before the fireplace while Miss Maggie put the finishing touches on a baked goose. The smell of roasting meat was tantalizing, although Lucy didn't much like looking at the bird, whose head and long neck were still attached. When Lucy objected to the goose's glazed eyes looking at her, Miss Maggie wrapped a piece of cheesecloth around its head and tied it behind. "There, now you won't have to look at Mr. Gander," she said, smiling. But now, Lucy thought, it looked like the poor bird was blindfolded and about to face a firing squad.

After they had dined on the goose, the grownups enjoyed a drink called a "hot toddy," which made Miss Maggie's cheeks turn a deep pink and Carl's laughter sound louder. She had never seen grownups have so much fun before. Finally, Lucy was allowed to open her Christmas gifts. From Miss Maggie she received a hand-knitted sweater in a soft, red wool.

"The next one is from me," Carl said, handing Lucy an oddly shaped package. "It's for both you *and* Brownie." She ripped the paper off and discovered a collar and leash made from the finest of leathers. She held it up to her nose. "Mmm," she murmured. "I like the smell." She started to drop the collar over Brownie's head, but he backed away. "Look Brownie. You're going to look so smart when I walk you from now on." He whined and ran behind the horsehair sofa, which made them all laugh.

"Thought if you got your dog to mind better and see to his training, you might have an easier time getting Violet to ease up on—"

"Hush, Carl," Miss Maggie said.

"I'll help Lucy train Brownie. I haven't forgotten how to train animals, you know." Carl frowned as if he had been insulted.

"Thank you, Miss Maggie. Thank you, Carl," Lucy said, anxious to get to her last present—the mystery package that had arrived all the way from New Orleans. When she opened it, they all oohed and aahed at the feathered Mardi Gras mask.

"Well, will you look at that," Carl said.

"Try it on," said Miss Maggie, who ran to get a looking glass.

Lucy put it up to her face and Carl pretended to be frightened by the sight of her. She laughed and pranced around the room imagining she was all powerful. Brownie barked ceaselessly at the sight until Lucy reluctantly put the mask away.

"I can't wait to show this to Sarah the next time I see her," she said. "I bet no one in Concordia has ever seen a mask like this before."

"Maybe for next Halloween we can make a cape to go with it," Miss Maggie said. Jennie had told Lucy that Miss Maggie was an expert seamstress.

Lucy went to bed tired, but happy that night. She knew after New Year's Day Jennie and Violet would begin their return trip to Concordia and she could resume her normal life with them.

"It won't be long now, Brownie," she said, giving him an extra hug. Brownie responded with a lick across Lucy's face before he burrowed deeper under the covers.

CHAPTER FIFTY-EIGHT

Jennie

January 3, 1901

Jennie gazed out the train window as the locomotive pulled away from the New Orleans station. *A new year.* She wondered what the year 1901 would bring. Patrick was unable to see her off as his classes had resumed the previous day. They met one more time, however, on New Year's Eve in the same ballroom where the cotillion was held. It had been transformed into a mad, frantic scene of revelers who waited to celebrate the countdown to midnight with champagne, balloons, and all the transient glamour associated with the holiday.

Patrick had arrived just before midnight and pulled Jennie out to the veranda where they had originally forged their friendship. In the crowded space it was difficult for Jennie to hear Patrick speak over the loud music coming from inside. The streets below were also filled with merrymakers dancing and mingling in unruly clusters, some wearing costumes and masks.

"You should see the streets during Mardi Gras," Patrick said. He leaned into Jennie. "I know we said our goodbyes the other night, but I had to see you one last time." He pulled Jennie out of the way of a lurching lout in a party hat. Sparkling wine sloshed from his champagne flute, leaving a wet trail wherever he walked. Jennie fell clumsily against Patrick, but then regained her balance and composure.

"I'm surprised you're still in New Orleans, Patrick. I thought classes begin tomorrow?"

"They do. I'm leaving within the hour, but I couldn't leave without telling you what I've learned. I've been checking into the possibilities of you entering college. Are you still interested?"

"Well, yes, of course. But—"

"It turns out that Tulane University, right here in New Orleans, is a fine school and accepts women in some fields. There was a time when they considered higher education too progressive for genteel women of the South because it trained them for the practical life." Patrick raised his voice to be heard over a ruckus in the street below. "Up North, colleges have been accepting women for a long time, training them to become lawyers and doctors and—" Patrick took a deep breath and moved them farther away from the noise. "The point is that young women can receive training more easily now."

"Oh, Patrick, go to school in the South? I'm sure Violet would never approve. She will say I'm too young or that it's too far away or—"

"But don't you see, if the school you attend is in New

Orleans you might stay with Mary Belle. What do you think?"

"I think you are very clever." Jennie smiled. "Not only smart, but clever. And self-serving also, I may add." Patrick smiled slyly and put a finger to her lips.

"Shh. Don't tell anyone."

"Well, I *am* seventeen and by this time next year, I'll be eighteen. Perhaps, then, Violet can be convinced that if I'm with her family, attending school will be permissible. I truly want to get a formal education, earn a degree."

"That's what I thought." Patrick urged her on.

"I would love to be like the suffragettes or answer a call to service in nursing. If I could help heal or comfort the ill, I would feel like mine was a life well served." Jennie felt her eyes tearing up. "Oh, listen to me making little speeches," she said, embarrassed.

"I love that you're so passionate about the subject."

"It's because of my pap. I barely remember him, Patrick. But I do recall the suffering he went through when he injured his leg and what it would have meant for him to have better medical care. And little Lucy. I so admired the nurses who tended her during her hospital stay." Jennie bowed her head. "But then, sometimes the doubts crowd in. What if I'm not smart enough to attend college?"

Patrick lifted Jennie's chin. "Knowledge begins with the desire to learn, and I can see that you have that in abundance. Besides that, you have a good heart."

"Oh, this is all so new." Jennie shook her head and tried to move away. Patrick took hold of her hand.

"Jennie, I won't try to fool you. I want these things for *you*, but also for me. I can't imagine being apart from you."

The music stopped abruptly and partygoers began to filter out to the veranda. They crowded closer together in anticipation of midnight. "Ten, nine, eight..." The countdown had begun. Balloons inside the ballroom could be seen floating down from the ceiling. Tinny horns bleated below in the street. "...three, two...one... Happy New Year!"

Patrick grabbed Jennie and kissed her for so long that she thought she might faint if she didn't get some air. Finally, they parted, only to be bumped into and jostled closer together again by the boisterous crowd. They made their way to the side of the veranda, clinging to the railing for protection until the crush of merrymakers moved on. They looked at each other for a split second and then broke out laughing.

"Are you okay?" Patrick yelled. By now the throng was in the middle of singing "Auld Lang Syne," which drowned out any hope of conversation. Jennie had to read Patrick's lips. She cupped her hands around her mouth to shout: "Yes. Okay!"

The train picked up speed and Jennie leaned back,

trying to get more comfortable for the long journey. She touched the pendant Patrick had given her and dared to believe it would bring her good luck. Jennie smiled as she recalled the night he gave it to her a few days after Christmas. The weather had cleared after further rain, and stars shone in the black, moonless night.

They had been more formal with each other since Jennie allowed Patrick to kiss her publicly, and then rebuffed him for having done so. She feared she had been too forward in allowing him these advances and so ended up acting more aloof when they were together.

As soon as they were alone in the parlor, Patrick produced a wrapped package from inside his jacket. It was in silver paper topped with a red velvet bow.

"Oh, Patrick, what's this?" she said, fingering the bow.

"Something to remember me by," he said.

"I could never forget you, Patrick." She opened the box and lifted a necklace consisting of a chain with a silver carved medallion hanging from it.

"I got it at the botánica," he confessed. "The madam said it's a good luck charm."

"It's beautiful. I'll treasure it always, Patrick."

He took the necklace from her hand. "May I?" he asked.

Jennie turned and lifted the hair from her shoulders. Patrick slipped the necklace around her neck and secured it with the clasp. "May I write to you, Jennie?"

"Oh yes. And I promise to do the same." She turned to face him. "There is so much I want to say, but time is too short." She rushed into his arms where he encircled her tightly and kissed the side of her head and cheek. She had vowed not to cry this time and ruin the last image he would have of her. Instead, she inhaled deeply, capturing his clean masculine smell. She allowed her lips to brush his neck where a vein stood out, visibly beating.

The view from the grimy train window dulled the diminishing lights of New Orleans until they were barely a memory. Now that Jennie was leaving the glamour of the city and its influence on her, she'd have time to think over what she and Patrick had talked about on New Year's Eve: college. The question of whether she met the requirements to enter an institution of higher learning seemed more daunting. Her desire for change had not diminished, but doubts about the feasibility of executing such a bold plan took hold.

Violet would not be easy to convince, and then there was the subject of young Lucy. Jennie had manipulated Violet into accepting the responsibility of taking Lucy into their home, of caring for the child. So she couldn't very well just abandon her. Even the specter of Charley and Christina crossed her mind. If she remained in Concordia, she might be in a position to help her brother if he needed financial help. Violet had turned him down in the past, but it was always possible that under the right circumstances, she might reconsider helping Charley in the future. Only time would tell whether Jennie could make these hard decisions that affected the lives of the people she loved.

She soon succumbed to the rhythm of the moving train as it picked up speed, its wheels click-clacking on the tracks. She rubbed her finger across the carved medallion and began to doze. Her dreams were filled with confusing images. In one, the old, limping black woman by the trolley turned into one of the dancing girls who lifted her skirts while moving to the "new jazz." It was in the same club Jennie and Patrick had visited. That dream faded into a new dream where Jennie saw herself soaking wet in Patrick's arms while he carried her down the street in the rain. The two of them laughed when they saw Jennie's shoes left behind, mired in the mud.

Jennie woke with a start, still touching the good luck charm. She felt flushed as she tried to reorient herself. She saw that the train was far from the city, steaming past a bayou where moss-covered trees loomed darkly.

CHAPTER FIFTY-NINE

Charley

The day of the auction, Charley was ready to leave before dawn. He and Brian had hours to travel before reaching Sacramento in time for the auction scheduled to begin in the late afternoon. He'd had difficulty sleeping since Brigitte revealed her feelings for him. He had to admit that she ignited emotions that had been dead since parting from Christina. Brigitte was a strong woman like Christina, but unlike her in many ways. *Could I be happy with her?* Most certainly he could—if he knew for sure that he would never see Christina again.

It was crisp outside as he fed Beulah, harnessed her to the wagon, and waited for Brian. He stamped his feet and rubbed his hands together for warmth. When he saw smoke coming from the chimney, Charley knew Brian would soon appear with steaming mugs of coffee. He gathered his meager belongings and loaded them into the wagon. There wasn't much: a few articles of clothing, an extra pair of boots, a bag of gold dust, and the hidden cash he had hoarded since the beginning of this journey from Concordia. He had counted it as many times as

there were days between his discovery of the auction notice and this morning. He hoped it would be enough.

"Charley, you *did* inspect the land up for auction,
didn't you?" Brian asked. They had made their way from
the Auburn hills in record time and were now overlooking the Sacramento Valley.

"I saw it on a plat map posted next to the auction notice. I know where the general location is, but no, I didn't
get a chance to actually step foot on it. Why?" Charley
thought the question niggling, at this point.

"Just wondering. Good to know how much of the land
is usable."

"It's all good land, I tell you." But Brian's comment
did raise questions in Charley's mind.

They found the auction site just as the bidding was
about to begin. A small cluster of men gathered around
the auctioneer and a man in a dark business suit, who
held notes on the properties to be auctioned. The two
men stood atop the steps of the Sacramento County
Courthouse. At the outset, Charley wondered if he was
too late. Did he miss out on important instructions?
When he spied Dutch Hansen at the fringe of the group,
he feared that the trip was going to be a wasted one. The
delta land baron had boasted that he owned much of the
land in the area and had the money to buy more.

As the various properties were presented—some containing houses in the city, but most consisting of land in
the area—it was clear that Hansen was there to expand

his empire. Of the nine parcels offered, he won the bid on five of them. The plat Charley was interested in was the last one to be auctioned. Charley felt fear creeping up his spine. *I'm in over my head. What made me think I could compete with the likes of Dutch Hansen?* He felt Brian's eyes on him; he was probably wondering the same thing.

"And now, for our final offering today, gentlemen!" the auctioneer yelled, waving a piece of paper over his head. "A fine piece of property near the Georgiana Slough. It's twenty acres on Tyler Island, good for growing alfalfa." What do I hear as a starting bid?"

"Fifty dollars!" yelled a man standing in front of Charley.

Charley raised his hand. "Fifty-five," he said.

"Sixty," came a voice from the rear.

"Sixty-two," the first man said, less loudly this time.

"Seventy," Charley yelled. Brian looked sharply at him. "Go easy," he murmured.

"Seventy dollars," the auctioneer repeated. "Do I hear seventy-five?"

A hush fell over the gathering. "Seventy dollars for this fine piece of land, folks?" He looked at the man to his side who nodded. "Seventy dollars, then. Going, goin—"

"Seventy-five!" Hansen's voice rang out.

Charley's throat constricted, his pulse raced, as he tried to make a decision. He lifted his arm high over his head and stared with determination at the auctioneer. Brian poked him.

"What are you doing, Charley?"

"Seventy-six!" Charley said, his voice barely audible.

"The man says seventy-six. That's less than half its value, folks. Do I hear more?" The auctioneer shifted his glance toward Hansen, who shook his head and laughed.

"Very well. Last call. The man scanned the crowd and then settled his eyes on Charley.

"Going, going, gone—to the gentleman for seventy-six dollars."

Charley looked at Brian, stunned. "Did I get it?"

"You got it, Charley." Brian slapped him on the back. "Congratulations!"

As Charley made his way toward the auctioneer, the realization of what he had done struck him. He had just spent almost all his money on a piece of land he hadn't even seen. Sweat broke out on his forehead. He removed his cap and, through a haze, counted out his money and handed over the bag of gold to the man in the black suit, who signed off the property, making the transfer of the deed official.

Charley folded the deed and slipped it inside his jacket pocket. Who would have thought such a light piece of paper would feel so heavy in importance. He looked up to see Hansen approach him.

"Well, we meet again, Mr. O'Brien. Ready to become a landowner?"

"Yes, I'm more than ready," Charley replied. He tried to project an air of confidence he didn't feel.

"I figured if you wanted that land that bad, I'd let you have it. I have plenty. Hope it didn't take your last dime. It's never smart to put all your money in one enterprise."

"I'll get by just fine." Charley knew Hansen's comments were meant to be insulting. He stood his ground and returned the hard stare directed at him. There was no sense in letting him think he was desperate—which he was, of course. He had little money left to buy equipment with which to cultivate his land. But Charley refused to let reality ruin the excitement of the moment.

After a night of little sleep and the sudden realization of his new responsibilities, Charley was in a state of bewilderment. In an effort to bolster his spirits, Brian treated him to a fine dinner in one of the hotel dining rooms. Tomorrow they would go and see the land for themselves and then decide what to do from there.

The next morning Brian bought supplies he needed for the Auburn diggings, which left little room in the wagon for things Charley would require to get settled in his new home, which would be a tent for the time being. He purchased basic farm implements, the tent, and some provisions to last a month or so. At the last minute he bought an old mule from a fellow off the street. He opened the mule's mouth to inspect her teeth and also noted the abundance of gray hairs around her muzzle.

"She's a little long in the teeth, mister," he said. "She still strong enough to pull a plow?"

"Reckon so. Mayzie's been a pack mule a long time.

She was strong enough to haul tons of gold from the hills."

"Hmmm." Charley knew the old man was exaggerating, but he saw that the mule's eyes were clear, not rheumy like some, and he liked the way her ears perked up when her name was spoken.

"Mayzie is good company," the man said. "She likes to be scratched behind the ears."

"Sounds reasonable," Charley said. He gave the mule a few good pats on her flank and a bit of vigorous scratching behind her ears.

With Mayzie in tow, tied to the back of the wagon, Charley and Brian went in search of Charley's land.

"Not that Mayzie won't be a fine, hard-working mule, but I wish I had one of those gas tractors." Charley had explained to Brian about his time running the gas tractors in Concordia and how great an invention it was. "It will surely improve over time. If it hadn't been for being swindled by Peter, I would have stayed in Concordia and bought my land there." Charley laughed and purposely bumped against Brian's shoulder. "But then I wouldn't have had the adventure of moving west and the pleasure of meeting you and Brigitte."

"You know, you don't have to settle on your land immediately," Brian said. "With winter coming on, you can't do much farm work yet. Come on back to Auburn with me and return in the spring."

Charley shook his head. "I want to get the feel of

things as soon as possible. You know how it is."

"Sure, I know how it is. Well, I've got to shove off as soon as we inspect your place. If you change your mind, I'd be happy to take you back with me."

Since he had brought his belongings with him, there was no need to return with Brian except to say his good-byes to Brigitte. He hadn't really wanted to say goodbye to her, so he had put it off.

"Tell Brigitte as soon as I set up housekeeping—that sounds funny, doesn't it? Soon as I'm settled, I'll come back and pay a visit. And if you come to Sacramento for supplies again, maybe she can come with you and—"

"Charley, you don't know Brigitte. She's not one to give a man a second chance once she's been passed over."

"I didn't mean to—"

"If it's all the same to you, I don't want to hear your side of things right now. She *is* my daughter and that's where my loyalties lie. But if you were to ask me, I think the two of you would make a handsome couple. You'll just have to figure that out for yourself, though."

Charley said no more. This kind of talk took the shine off his victory. He didn't want anything to dampen the excitement he was feeling.

According to the map, they were nearing a turnoff heading west. Charley thought he recognized some of the landmarks he saw on the way to transport Tao Chin and his grandfather to Walnut Grove. But he couldn't be certain. All the islands looked alike. What differentiated them was the location of water surrounding them. Some islands were flanked by wide channels, while others had narrow inlets or sloughs running through them. There was only one way on and one way off the island. It was necessary to cross Tyler Slough over an earthen dam near Walnut Grove.

As they rode around, identifying boundaries as best they could from the map, including the Georgiana Slough, Charley smelled the aroma of licorice permeating the air. Anise and fennel, as well as wild dill and Queen Anne's lace, dotted the landscape. Ducks and other water fowl, congregating on the Mokelumne River, gracefully threaded their way through the reeds. Was it his imagination or was his land sitting substantially lower than the road? *An illusion.* Doubts could not quell his excitement. "This is it!" he shouted.

Charley jumped down from the wagon and scooped up a handful of loose dirt, smelling it, urging Brian to do the same. Brian smiled and indulged him. He eased himself out of the buckboard and toed a few clods with his boot. Charley threw dirt into the air and let it rain down on him. "At last!" he shouted, coughing from the shower of fine soil sifting upon his head and shoulders. "At last, my own farm!"

CHAPTER SIXTY

Charley

The harsh reality of the wild land he now occupied hit Charley like a hammer the next morning. Water had seeped into his tent during the night. He bolted from his sodden bedroll to throw open the tent flap. Water covered what he remembered as the bank.

"What the hell!" he shouted. It was disorienting to see the slough appear wider. He had not planned for the rising tide. The Georgiana Slough, which was fed by the Sacramento River and abutted his land, had swollen overnight. As he sloshed from tent to his tools, the water appeared to be receding.

Charley felt like a fool. *I didn't think about the tides.* And when he and Brian saw the slough cut through the land, he never thought about low spots flooding. He hadn't looked for telltale signs of water damage: tamped-down grass of a different color or sandy spots where the native plants had been uprooted or worn away by wind and water. He hadn't thought to place his supplies on higher ground out of danger. *Just plopped them down any old place.* He was relieved that Brian left last night instead of staying until morning to witness his incompetence.

Charley searched through burlap bags of supplies he had purchased. *Damn! They're wet too.* The flour was a goner—all gummed together like a paste. The dry beans were soaked, their skins puckered, ready to cook. *Maybe they'll be okay.* The coffee beans he had the storekeeper grind for him would make a weak brew at best. The bacon was all but gone; only a streak of fat remained to testify of its earlier existence. It and the beef jerky had been gnawed—he saw the teeth marks clearly. *Rats.* River rats must have found the meat and feasted while he slept.

He was so stunned he didn't know whether to laugh or cry. Here he was, just as green as a man could be who had never worked the land before. He realized now that Dutch Hansen probably knew the exact layout and conditions of this plot and never intended to buy it. His only interest was to up the bid so Charley paid more than it was worth. *Son of a bitch!* He remembered Tao's tales about how his grandfather helped build dikes around the islands to hold back water from inundating the land. It appeared that he needed to take the same or similar measures. Charley could sure use Tao's advice and know-how.

He spent the remainder of the morning cleaning up the mess. He hung his clothes and the canvas tent and bedroll over some bushes to dry. He wiped down his hoe, shovel, and the small hand plow in which he had invested. Couldn't let rust set in.

Since most of the food was ruined, he decided to try his luck at fishing. He rigged up a pole by cutting a branch from a nearby tree, and he twisted twine down the length of the pole before tying knots at each end. Charley fashioned a hook out of some wire he had in his supplies. There was no shortage of live bait to attract the fish: red worms had actually arisen from the saturated soil voluntarily when the water receded. He dropped his line into the slough. The murky water concealed any activity below, but occasional bubbles floating to the top looked promising.

Charley didn't have time to sit around and fish. He had real work to do. He thought of river fishing as a leisurely activity, a pastime for old men and young boys. He pictured Tom Sawyer sitting on the bank, not him. However, from other tales he had heard, fishing was not easy work. He reluctantly gave credit to those men who fished for a living on the high seas. He believed they might live a rougher life than a farmer.

After only a short time, Charley was surprised that he caught a big fish that fought like the dickens to get away. The devil almost escaped until Charley backed up the bank and literally dragged it out of the water. It was an ugly gray thing, with tight, slick skin like an eel. Stiff spines stuck out on both sides of its mouth, reminding him of whiskers on a cat. He knew that catfish were the scavengers of the delta. They were said to be plentiful, but not as desirable to eat because they were full of bones. He was so hungry he didn't care. He got a good fire going and, after gutting it, pan-cooked the catfish and ate his fill.

Charley did not want to spend another morning wading in his bedroll, so he went to work building a wooden platform. He lashed the tree branches together with rope and when it was finished, he imagined it looked like the wooden raft on which Huckleberry Finn and Jim the slave navigated down the Mississippi River. *Enough about made-up characters and stories.* He needed his raft-like platform for survival, not for moseying down the river. He took the precaution of dragging it to higher ground and finally pitched his tent on top as the evening tide was coming in.

For weeks he ate fish and more frogs than he could count. He craved food he was more accustomed to—a beef steak, potatoes, and coffee with cream and sugar. He needed to replace his lost staples in order to remain civilized. Charley decided to dip into funds he had been saving for a rainy day. *Hah!* He had already seen rainy days and then some.

His hope was that he could experiment by planting early. He had already tried Mayzie out by hitching the hand plow behind her and tilling a small section of land on a rise above the campsite. Time would tell if she had the stamina to work long hours at the job. For that matter, Charley wondered at his own strength. He was anxious to test them both by preparing more acreage for seeding. A stretch of Indian summer that materialized the end of October had been perfect for field work. He heard that in a good year, a first planting could be managed by the end of February or the first of March. But first, the land needed to dry out.

He wondered if Tao was still in Walnut Grove with family. *Doubtful.* He was probably back working for Dutch Hansen. But a thought came to mind as Charley shoveled dirt to create a berm against the high tide. He saw where rocks set into the soil would reinforce his manmade earthen dam, but it would take a long time to find and drag big rocks for that purpose. What was it Tao had told him about his grandfather helping to build levees? If only he were here, they would work together and Charley could learn the ancient Chinaman's skills.

Charley stopped to mop his brow and lean on his shovel. He had worked up a big sweat in spite of the cool air around him. He suspected that as the air began warming there would be insects to deal with. In Concordia it was grasshoppers and cicadas and black horseflies as big as the tip of his thumb. And he remembered gnats and sweat bees zooming in on a man's wet brow—usually when both hands were occupied and he was unable to swat them away. Anywhere there was water there were sure to be mosquitoes. He dreaded that time because it wasn't just the bites, but the constant droning. He had been told that while the pesky buggers torpedoed a man, the sounds could drive him crazy.

Before he knew it, more weeks had passed. Occasional warm days came with humid nights when Charley dragged his bedroll outdoors and slept under the sky— that is when the crickets and frogs eased up. Most nights they joined voices in a cacophonous chorus to keep him awake. Eventually, he became used to the racket. He'd lie back with his arms folded under his head and gaze at the explosion of stars. The loamy smell of the wet earth made Charley feel primeval—as if he had just emerged from the ooze along with the first invertebrates. He hadn't had much schooling, but he remembered seeing a book once that described Charles Darwin's theory of evolution. When he mentioned it at home—how man developed from more primitive animals over time, his mum became angry. "That's against church teachings. Blasphemous is what that is! Don't mention that man's name in this house again."

Charley had managed to erect a more durable structure than the tent. He scavenged driftwood and any solid material he ran across along the slough. An old marooned boat along the shore provided most of the wood he used to construct his shack. He covered the top with boards lapped over each other. It was the closest thing to a roof that he could manage. He knew his new home was nothing more than a shanty like those he and Christina had seen from the train. Whole settlements made up of these kinds of shacks were named "shanty towns."

One afternoon while Charley was working near the water's edge, a rider emerged on the horizon, heading his way. He squinted into the sun and didn't recognize him right away until he spoke. It was Dutch Hansen wearing a grin on his whiskered face.

"So, this is your prized land, eh Charley?"

"Hello Dutch. What brings you this way?"

"On my way to town and decided I'd be neighborly and see how you're doing?"

"Doing fine, thank you."

"Well, I don't know about that. Looks like you might have bought yourself a piece of bottom land, here." He laughed.

Charley felt his blood turn cold at the snide remark.

"Something I can do for you, Dutch?"

"Not sure you can do anything for anyone, including yourself. I'd light out if I were you."

"If the only reason you came by was to insult me, you can be on your way." Charley turned and scooped a shovel full of mud filled with small rocks. He threw it toward Hansen's horse. The horse shied and reared up. When Hansen regained control of his mount, he jumped down and stood chin to chin with Charley. "If you ever try a trick like that again, I'll level you. Understand?"

"Like you have all the other growers in the islands!" Charley growled, refusing to back down.

"You'll regret not taking my advice."

"From where I'm standing it doesn't sound like advice. Sounds more like a threat."

"Pshaw!" Hansen exclaimed. He slapped his hat against his thigh and remounted his horse. As he turned to leave, Charley threw his shovel after him. He was so mad he was shaking.

Early the next morning, Charley decided to make a trip to Sacramento to replenish his supplies and see if any new seeds were available. After yesterday's confrontation with Dutch Hansen, he was more determined than ever to make this land suitable for planting. Although he had plenty of alfalfa, which was good for Mayzie for feed, he didn't know what kind of price he'd get for it at market. He needed to diversify with something with which he was familiar.

He planned on buying corn and other vegetable seeds to start with. He might even check into planting asparagus, that strange sounding vegetable Tao told him about. Maybe later, he'd buy or barter for animals to make it a self-sustaining farm. He could start with chickens to provide eggs and meat. Of course, they would have to be securely sheltered against wild animals in the area. He had seen a fox and her pups once and heard the howls and yips of coyotes. Charley remembered the night that Enoch Neamott woke to the sound of slaughter. A wolf had destroyed almost his entire flock of chickens.

There were other animals he could raise for food. Pigs came to mind. But he had no experience in the necessary process of butchering them. It was a time-honored practice, but one that never set well with him. Cows he knew about. But raising cows would have to wait. He didn't need the milk and he had his fill of milking them for a lifetime.

It would be a different matter if he had a wife and family. Babies and children needed milk. Thoughts of children raised the sharp memory of loss. He had lost his baby before it had even rooted in its mother's belly. Hell, there was no sense in worrying about providing milk for a family when he hadn't even heard from Christina.

For some reason his mind jumped from Christina to Brigitte. He missed her too. He thought of how she made a room warmer with her quiet presence, but how she could also work up a surprising passion. Their kiss was most satisfying.

"Mayzie," he said, "there's no sense in wishing for what might have been or supposing what could be. I've just got to get on with making a decent farm here and hope that some woman, some day, will join me to make it a home." Mayzie's ears twitched and she gave out a sound that was half whinny, half bray as if she understood what Charley had said and agreed with him.

CHAPTER SIXTY-ONE

Charley

It was slow going to Sacramento. Tule fog hugged the ground, obscuring the road and landmarks Charley needed for navigating. He had decided he would first venture through Walnut Grove to see if he could locate Tao Chin—strangely, he missed his company. He guessed he had grown used to the raucous ways of the miners and the fatherly advice Brian gave him from time to time and was lonesome for someone to talk to. Although there was a language barrier between them, he thought Tao to be a halfway friendly sort who also possessed intelligence not always apparent because of his quiet manner.

He hoped to find the house at which he dropped Tao and convince him to return with him to Tyler Island. Charley needed advice on the best way to protect his crops from flooding. He almost gave up finding Walnut Grove in the thick blanket of fog when he heard the unmistakable sounds of activity on the river: heavy wooden crates being dropped, chains clanging, the lapping of waves against a dock, and the low guttural language of men toiling at work.

When he encountered the old wooden bridge, Char-ley felt certain that he was near the spot where he dropped off Tao. Mayzie clopped over the rough planks and, once on the other side, Charley recognized the large walnut trees for which the town was named. He made his way to the Chin family house. A small bent woman an-swered the door. She bowed, reducing herself to an even more diminutive figure. Charley removed his cap and returned the bow.

"Is Tao here, please?" he asked.

"Tao?" She turned to someone in the dark, deep part of the house and spoke in Chinese.

"No Tao." she answered. "Maybe later." She smiled, revealing the loss of her front teeth.

"You speak English?"

"No English. No Tao." She gently closed the door.

Charley turned to leave when he saw a young boy feeding Mayzie a piece of fruit that looked like an apple. Upon closer inspection, it was a mottled golden color and oddly misshapen. *Another piece of produce foreign to me—just like asparagus.*

"What are you feeding my mule?" he asked the boy.

"This quince." He reached in his pocket and with-drew another of the strange looking fruit, offering it to Charley. "You look for Tao?"

"Yes. Do you know him?"

"He's my uncle."

"Do you know where he is? I need to speak to him."

"Come back later. He's on boat."

"Will you let him know that Charley came by? I'll stop tomorrow on my way home from Sacramento."

The boy nodded and gave Mayzie a last pat on her muzzle.

"Don't forget now." Charley reached inside his pocket where he had stuffed the quince and withdrew a coin. He flipped the coin toward the boy. *A little insurance that he doesn't forget*, Charley thought, as he took a bite of the strange-looking fruit. His mouth immediately puckered. *Too tart. Not as good as an apple*, he thought.

Charley sat in a café on the Sacramento waterfront elbow to elbow with big muscled stevedores and day laborers. He was enjoying his first hot meal in weeks. Like a starving man, Charley ate fast and with serious intent. He shoveled in beans, a thick gravied stew, and bread called sourdough he had never tasted before. He sopped up every last drop of gravy with the bread and then asked for more. He topped it all off with a slab of apple pie and drank at least a quart of milk all by himself. Coffee. He couldn't get enough of the strong brew that he missed after his coffee got ruined by the incoming tide. He drank several mugs full and finally asked the waitress if she would just leave the pot.

"Don't want to wear out your arm pouring for me," he joked.

Charley purchased his provisions and talked to men at the grain exchange to learn of commodity prices in the area and finally carefully chose the seeds he wanted for small crops of corn and barley. He knew barley was in demand for making beer after being malted. Many Germans in Concordia brewed their own ale. He would start small and put only half of his land into production this first season.

He decided to treat himself by getting a room for the night at the hotel and having his first bath in a month. Upon leaving Sacramento, he felt refreshed and mentally energized for the first time in weeks. As he spun out plans in his mind on the long drive back, Charley spied a broken-down wagon lying on its side among the tules. He stopped to check it out, thinking he could sure use a wagon during harvest time to bring his crops to town. *A man has to plan ahead*. It looked beyond repair, and still—it might be salvageable by someone with fix-it know-how and a good set of hands. He wasn't experienced at woodworking, although he had helped build a coffin in which to bury one of the Neamotts. He could learn to fix things if he was shown how. He wondered if Tao and he might repair it—that is, if Tao agreed to join him. They would need the right tools to make repairs. *Can't do much without tools.*

He arrived in Walnut Grove late afternoon and found Tao almost immediately. The young boy had come through, passed word that Charley had been to see him.

"Hello good friend," Charley said, shaking Tao's hand.

"We meet again," Tao said.

Charley was surprised. Sounds like his English has improved.

"Yes. Much has happened since our last meeting." He explained about the farmland he bought and the problems with it. Tao nodded that he understood.

"Yes, much of land gets wet." They discussed what could be done and how long it might take to build a levee.

"Oh. I was hoping it wouldn't take too long. Sure like it in place before spring when I hope to plant my first crops."

Tao shrugged his shoulders. "Need many hands to do it fast."

"Are your hands available, Tao? If you help me, I couldn't pay you much, but you could have some of my profits when I sell my crops."

Tao bowed again. "I will help. No pay." He shook his head solemnly. "You helped with grandfather."

"I don't expect to take you away from your job without paying for your time. Do you still work for Dutch Hansen?"

"No. No more. He cheat me again. I live here now."

Although Charley was sorry to hear Tao had been cheated, he wasn't surprised. He tried to show his concern while a part of him felt relief that Tao was ready and willing to work with him.

An hour later before sunset, the two men started out with a few of Tao's belongings. They had to double up on Mayzie, sharing the mule, riding her bareback. Charley told Tao about the broken wagon he saw on the way.

"Think you and me could fix it?"

"We fix. But first, we build levee."

Charley nodded as they headed for the hard job of shoring up Charley's land.

CHAPTER SIXTY-TWO

Charley

Charley and Tao had been working side by side for over a month. It felt much longer.

The work was grueling and gave Charley a big appetite. But there never seemed to be enough food to satisfy his hunger. Those few times when there was, he and Tao were almost too exhausted to eat. Charley would get a good fire going while Tao gigged frogs or caught a fish or two, but the time it took for the food to cook felt agonizingly long. One night after Tao had scaled a salmon and skewered it, he lowered it over the coals and waited. Before it had finished cooking, he withdrew it from the fire. With a few deft slices of his knife, he filleted the salmon and laced it onto a couple of willow stakes.

"You eat." He handed one of the stakes to Charley.

"What? Eat it raw?"

"Yes. Is good, raw. Chinese eat raw fish long time." Tao leaned his head to one side to bite off a strip of the pink flesh.

Charley watched curiously. He felt overcome with revulsion, but took a tentative bite. He found the texture different—tough, but also yielding. It actually wasn't bad, he thought. Not fishy-tasting at all.

Tao wiped oily residue from around his mouth. "Oily fish, taste better," he explained.

The levee was taking shape with rocks in place and dirt packed in the gaps. Charley hoped that plants would take seed there, and when mature, help hold the soil in place. They had pulled rocks from the edge of the slough as well as dug out sizable specimens in the fields. The abandoned wagon Charley had spotted on his return trip from Sacramento, and which Tao repaired, came in handy. They used a ramp and pulley system to hoist heavier boulders into the buckboard and move them into place.

Most of the fields had been cleared for the alfalfa crop that already existed when Charley bought the land. The rocks cleared from it were stacked a ways off on the perimeter. He wondered if the previous owner intended to build a rock wall with them.

As if he had read Charley's mind, Tao said, "Chinese make good rock walls. Build walls on many farms and dig out caves too."

"Caves? Why caves? Couldn't the bears find their own caves?" Charley laughed at his little joke.

"To store wine." Tao never missed a beat. "In Napa Valley," he said.

Charley was disappointed that Tao didn't get his joke. *He's always so serious.*

"My friend, you're like a book. All I have to do is ask about something, and you know the answers," he told him.

"Know many things. Especially about Chinese labor."

They worked companionably side by side and eventually developed a rhythm in which one of them would anticipate what the other needed, and either a rock or a tool was handed over to get the job done. In this way, the work went smoothly and Charley learned a great deal just by observing his new friend.

In spite of the biting cold some days and rain on others, the levee was almost done. Charley could barely wait until the days grew longer and the ground warmed up. He had decided to experiment by planting seeds early as long as the danger of heavy frosts was over. It all depended on what the Farmer's Almanac predicted.

Charley was at the farthest end of his property when a large rock in the slough caught his eye. He thought the levee in this area needed a few more rocks to shore it up. He rolled up his pants, but didn't bother to remove his old boots. The water was icy cold and he didn't much want to subject his tender feet to anything sharp and unseen on the bottom.

The rock wasn't heavy, but it was awkwardly shaped. When he tried to pick it up, it wouldn't budge. He lowered his body and braced his legs and pulled harder until it suddenly loosened. The momentum of Charley's tugging threw him backward with the rock riding on top of him like a frog hitching a ride on a lily pad. He tried to right himself, but when he did, he stepped into a sudden drop-off. He felt himself being pulled under by his heavy boots, which acted as anchors. Charley thrashed about in surprise and sank even lower into the soft mud. *What the hell!* He gasped and gulped some water and began choking, all the while kicking his legs and flailing his arms.

He finally broke air and yelled for help, but promptly sunk again, taking on more of the muddy water.

So this is it. He felt the weight of water pressing down on him, his lungs about to burst. *I'm going to drown!* Muffled sounds from above echoed, comically. They reminded him of old drunken men singing. *Pap and his cronies the night before they went out on strike.*

His arms were so heavy, they dropped. And then he was moving upright through the water. Something strong had wrapped around him and was lifting, pulling his limp body upward. Disoriented and in a panic, Charley resisted and swung at the air. Tao jerked him harder until they both slammed into shore. Charley threw up, spitting out muddy water. They lay there a few minutes unable to speak. Finally, Charley pulled in enough air to utter a few words.

"You saved my life, Tao."

Tao nodded and smiled. It was the first time Charley had seen him do so. "I'm in your debt forever," he said.

"Shouldn't it be the other way around?"

Tao shook his head. "In my culture, if a man saves

another, must watch over him always.

"Well, I could sure use a savior," Charley said between chattering teeth.

They pulled themselves up and jogged in the direction of their camp, slapping their arms for warmth.

"Why you don't know how to swim?" Tao asked.

"Never had a need to." Charley stopped. "Let's just walk fast. Running makes me colder." Tao nodded in agreement.

"Didn't learn to swim in Homestead where I was born, even though we lived by the Monongahela River. Mum wouldn't allow me to go *near* water. She told me she had been afraid of it since crossing the Atlantic Ocean from Ireland. Made me afraid of it too." Charley stopped and bent over, putting both hands on his knees. "Just a minute, Tao. Got a stitch in my side." He stood up and took a few deep breaths before resuming walking.

"Once I got to Concordia, Kansas, there wasn't much opportunity to frequent the Republic River and learn to swim. Old man Neamott had me working all the time. I settled for a nearby creek to cool off in during the summer, but it was only waist high. Hard to drown in."

"You need to learn to swim," Tao said, his brow furrowed.

"Oh, I don't see how."

"I teach you." Tao churned his arms in the air in imitation of a breaststroke. "I teach you—when the water not so cold." They both laughed.

"We'll see, Tao. We'll just wait and see."

Charley's brush with death made him reflect on important things left undone—like contacting his sister and Brian and Brigitte. They might like to know how things were progressing and that he was okay. No need to tell them about almost drowning. He would let them know how to reach him if they were so inclined. He had been concentrating only on his needs and goals. *How were they faring? Were they okay?*

Now Christina was another matter. She had not responded to either of his letters, but regardless of her rebuff, he wanted to make sure she was all right. He should write her one more time. He'd send it in care of the Eilers as he had done before.

A week later Charley delivered Tao to Walnut Grove and then went on to Sacramento. He noticed that Christmas decorations were up in store windows and wrapped around gaslight poles on each corner. The shabbiest of places looked improved with fresh fir trees and wisps of red ribbon on their boughs. He had forgotten about Christmas.

It jolted him to realize he had lost all track of time while living away from civilization. He wondered what his loved ones were doing without him to help celebrate the holidays. It made it all the more important that he communicate with them, and he headed directly to the post office where he established a post office box. He then wrote brief notes to Jennie, Brigitte, and finally to Christina.

Charley thought about these three women who were important to him, two of whom had rejected him at one time or another. Jennie, when she willingly left the Neamott farm, choosing to be with Violet Hunsinger, and again when she declined joining him after he finished his foster child obligation. Charley didn't consider himself a bitter man. He and Jennie had gotten on better as she grew older. He still hoped they could be together one day.

Christina, now, was like a burr under his saddle. Even when she was not with him, a part of her remained—like the nettle, reminding him of her need for attention. If you scratched at the nettle's irritation you were rewarded with relief—at least for a little while. She made life interesting.

Brigitte was the only one who accepted him for who he was. He felt safe and strong in her presence. He missed her, but still hesitated to make any kind of commitment until he heard from—or never heard from—Christina. It was the fair thing to do. Sometimes being fair felt burdensome, he thought.

He dropped the three letters into the mail slot, hoping that by the next time he came to Sacramento, he would have replies waiting for him—and answers.

CHAPTER SIXTY-THREE

Christina

Christina realized the folly of her decision soon after she left the safety of the barn. Traveling at night was difficult enough when you *knew* the terrain. Setting out in darkness when you had no idea where you were was downright foolish. She thought that by following the railroad tracks she would head directly into Sacramento. She had forgotten that trunk and spur lines veered off the main line into more remote areas. By the time she realized that she had been following a branch line that took her north instead of due west, she and Cinnamon were completely off course. They had been gradually climbing into steeper terrain with no landmarks to guide her and were now in a clearing. A sharp wind had come up and whistled around them.

"Sorry, old girl," she said. "Think I got us into a bit of trouble." Christina refused to acknowledge that she was lost. She couldn't be lost. Come daylight, all would be fine. After `Cinnamon trudged a while longer, the horse stumbled on loose gravel and abruptly stopped.

"What's wrong, Cinnamon?" She patted the old

horse's thick neck.

That's all I need. Have the horse die on me. Not only would she truly be isolated, but she would be a horse thief turned horse murderer. Christina tried to make out her surroundings, but the light of the quarter moon provided little help. She could see that she and Cinnamon were in a precarious situation. The trail had narrowed and the inky blackness beyond suggested there was a drop off. She didn't want to venture further only to fall into a deep chasm. Christina dismounted and tried to turn the horse, but Cinnamon literally put her foot down. She refused to budge. There's no sense in spooking her, Christina decided. The only thing to do was wait out the night and get her bearings in the morning. After she heard owls hooting and the chittering noises of other nocturnal birds, Christina's senses were on high alert. She could tell that the chatter made the otherwise calm and unflappable Cinnamon nervous too. Tricks of sound assaulted them so that Christina thought they were nearby one minute, only to hear the same sounds in the distance seconds later. Finally, when the screeching cry of a mountain lion rang out, there was no hope of sleeping. Instead, she leaned forward and rested her head against Cinnamon's neck for warmth and comfort.

By dawn she saw that they were indeed lost. *We could both die out here!* If she couldn't figure out a plan for retreating, the threat might be imminent. They were high enough in the mountains for Christina to see that the valley floor looked farther away than it had when the train left her behind. She saw no sign of civilization—no ranches, barns, or grazing livestock in sight. From the sound of rushing water she figured there was a river not far off. Maybe even a waterfall. But Christina resisted the impulse to head toward it, as sound could be deceptive. It might actually be farther away than she thought. She had no intention of climbing higher and risking injury to Cinnamon. As current circumstances dictated, she would have needed a stronger, more reliable mount to consider that. If she were riding a horse like Gabriel, she wouldn't be worried.

As it grew lighter, she was relieved to see that she and Cinnamon might descend the mountain safely after all. She would back up Cinnamon a few feet toward a widening curve in the path. From there, Christina could easily turn the horse around to head in the right direction. She grabbed its reins and picked her way down the mountain, hopefully heading in the same direction from which they had come. If she were right, she should be able to spot the main train line soon.

The feed bag was empty; she and Cinnamon had shared the last of the oats this morning with melted snow to wash it down. But they would need more food for the remaining journey of who knew how many more miles? After having been sick, Christina was cautious about what she filled her stomach with. However, there wasn't much to pick from and she couldn't afford to be too particular. Clay talked about a variety of wild edibles that Indian squaws in South Dakota gathered for food: things like berries, acorns, and certain roots. The goat doctor in Utah also used natural herbs for her tonics. The only thing was that Christina couldn't be certain that the ones growing in California were the same as the ones in Utah or South Dakota and were safe to eat. She also had Cinnamon to consider.

As soon as she spotted any tufts of grass emerging from the snow, Christina stopped and yanked them out. She remembered to be careful what and how much she fed Cinnamon because horses could get their guts in an uproar if they ate too much forage at one time. There was no time for colic on this trip.

After hours of walking, Christina finally spotted the railroad line again.

"Oh, thank God!" she cried. In her excitement she rushed downhill too quickly. Her right ankle twisted inward, bringing her to her knees. The pain jolted Christina into crying out.

"Now, what have I done?" She straightened up, but couldn't bear full weight on her right foot. She limped to Cinnamon's side and laid her head against the old horse's flank. The sobs started and didn't stop until her body shook from the effort. Cinnamon shifted uneasily, but stayed put. Her emotions spent, Christina wiped her eyes and nose and stood as straight as she was able. She had to make it down to the rail line or perish where she stood for that mountain lion to feast on and for the buzzards to finish off. "You'll just have to get us out of here, Cinnamon," she said. "I'll be damned if I'm going to be stuck like those folks in the Donner Party."

Christina struggled to mount Cinnamon. Using a tree branch for a crutch, she could get her left foot into the stirrup. But lifting her right leg with its useless, twisted ankle and swinging it over the horse was impossible. She looked around and saw a spot that was next to a rise that she might use to her advantage. By standing on the hillock, she would be level with the horse's back and could more easily transfer. It still took three tries before she could get saddled up. She slipped her left foot into the left stirrup, but the injured ankle lay helplessly against Cinnamon's right side instead of in its stirrup. Christina felt unbalanced without both feet being secured, but trusted the horse to carry her gently through the rough landscape. By now she was sweating profusely and in excruciating pain. Luckily, the throbbing ankle kept her awake and focused, which is what she required to get off the damn mountain! *Lucky me,* she thought.

CHAPTER SIXTY-FOUR

Christina

Christina's face lay to one side of Cinnamon's broad, muscular neck. The only thing keeping her awake were the flyaway strands of hair from the horse's mane tickling her nose. She dared not fall asleep; if she slid off Cinnamon with this swollen ankle she might never be able to remount. Her tongue felt too big for her mouth. It kept darting out like a lizard's in search of moisture. *Thirsty. I'm so thirsty.* She had not eaten or drunk anything for almost three days. At least Christina thought it was three days. She had lost track of time. If she ever got out of this, she would drink a gallon of water straight off, she promised herself.

"Hey there! Miss, are you okay?"

Christina started. She had dozed after all. She looked up to see an old man in worn breeches and dirty work-boots. Beyond him in the distance was the welcome sight of a town. *Civilization at last.* She rubbed her crusted matted eyes and tried to speak, but couldn't get the words past her cracked, bloated lips. It hurt to even take in air.

"You look like you've had a rough ride." The man dismounted from his mule and unscrewed the lid to his canteen. "Here, you better take a swig of this."

Christina touched the canteen to her mouth, savoring the metallic taste. Water trickled over her lips. She tried again and sipped at the cold liquid, swallowing painfully.

"Gotta say your horse here doesn't look much better than you." He took the reins of both Cinnamon and his mule and began walking toward town. "Let's have Doc take a look at you. Someone at the stable can check over your horse," he said. "She don't sound so good. Her lungs are rattling a little."

Christina felt tears of relief rising up ready to spill over, but no moisture came forth. She was too parched to even cry.

"You're lucky I happened along and found you before the buzzards did."

The old man's words, harsh as they sounded, were a comfort to her. She and Cinnamon would be safe.

"Where am I?" she managed to rasp.

"Just outside of Auburn."

Auburn. I made it, she thought. The old man's words didn't fully register as Christina nodded off again.

Through an exhausted haze, she became aware of being helped off Cinnamon and supported as she stepped up to a wooden sidewalk and into a building. She was led to a quiet room where she was told to lie down on a cot until Doc returned.

She slipped into a restless sleep. When she awoke, Christina felt a presence. A man, who must be Doc, sat by her side with a stethoscope around his neck.

"Try to lay quietly, miss." He held her arm loosely and was taking her pulse; two fingers pressed lightly on the inside of her wrist. Doc placed the stethoscope to her chest and leaned over to listen before turning her on her side. He moved the instrument around to her back. Christina noticed that the room was occupied with a rolltop desk and a glass-fronted cabinet filled with vials and bottles and no-nonsense-looking metal utensils.

"Cough," he said. He listened to Christina's lungs and declared, "You're clear. No pneumonia. But at the very least you need to get rehydrated and rested up while that ankle heals." He proceeded to wrap her bad ankle tightly with bandages. He was quiet while he attended to the task, giving Christina time to study him. Doc was thin with somewhat stooped shoulders. His face consisted of angular features softened by a silvery gray mustache. Christina made him out to be on the far side of fifty.

"I'm Dr. Moses. Your name, miss?"

"Christina—Batachi."

"Miss Batachi, do you have any kin here in Auburn?"

Christina began to shake her head, but thought better of it when a sharp pain shot through her neck.

"No," she said. *Unless Charley is still here.* She and Charley were almost related—or would be once they got married.

"Well, that *is* a problem. We don't have any beds in our hospital right now." Dr. Moses opened his rolltop desk to reveal stacks of books and a messy pile of papers inside. He reached into one of the cubbies and withdrew a dogeared piece of paper and studied it. "There are a couple of local ladies who help out folks. Take them into their homes while they convalesce. They're like practical nurses by now." He screwed up his face in concentration. "I'll see who I can rustle up."

"Cinnamon?" Christina asked. "Where's Cinnamon?"

"Pardon, Miss Batachi?"

"Cinnamon, my horse."

"Oh yes, your horse. Don't worry," he said. "The man who found you took your horse to the town stable."

But Christina *did* worry, because Cinnamon was as frail, or maybe more so, than she. She asked for a piece of paper and pen and managed to scribble a brief note. "Would you see to it that this is delivered to the stable, Dr. Moses? It's real important."

He looked over the note.

Please take care of Cinnamon. She came from a ranch off the Central Pacific Train line past Truckee. I had to borrow her. Sorry.

Dr. Moses looked at the note a long time and finally raised his eyebrows. "You sure you want to send this?"

"Yes," she whispered. Christina just wanted to sleep. She would explain further after she could think straight.

When she awoke, a different man was in the room

with her—a man who took up more space and smelled of tobacco.

"Good. You're awake," he said in a gravelly voice. "I'm Sheriff Piper." He was holding Christina's note. "Kid working at the stable sent this over." He waved the paper. "Miss, am I to understand that you took this horse without permission?"

Christina tried to clear her mind, search for the right answer. She finally sighed and sat up, but she was too weak. She flopped back down. "Yes, I took her. I was desperate, you see."

Sheriff Piper shook his head. "You know that's a crime—stealing another man's horse?"

"Yes, sheriff, I know. But, I—"

"We'll track down the owner. Although it may take some time from your vague directions. Have him come and get the horse—that is if it survives." He took a few steps toward the door and stopped. "We're not really set up to house a woman in our jail, but that *is* the law. Horse thieves go to jail like any other thief."

Tears sprung from Christina's eyes.

"But seeing as you aren't in any shape to run, I'll go along with Doc. He wants you to be cared for by one of our local charitable ladies. But this isn't over. You *will* have to answer for this, Miss Batachi."

Christina turned toward the wall as she heard the sheriff open the door and leave.

Hours later, Dr. Moses returned with a woman.

"Christina, this is Miss Doyle. She'll take you into her home and care for you until you're well. I'll come out in a day or two and check on you."

Managing to pull herself to a sitting position, Christina looked carefully at the woman. She was young and pretty, though her hands looked older, worn—probably from hard work. Tall and slim, but muscular like Christina had once been, she could see the woman was probably physically capable of caring for her and any number of ill patients. The only thing that seemed odd was the somewhat pained expression on the woman's face.

"It's nice to meet you at last, Christina," she said. She stepped forward, offering her hand.

"My name is Brigitte."

CHAPTER SIXTY-FIVE

Christina

"So, you're the famous Christina Batachi," Brigitte said.

"What? You've heard of me?" Christina noticed that Brigitte had been studying her ever since she brought her home to convalesce.

"You're all Charley talked about." Brigitte's smile disappeared.

"Charley? You know Charley O'Brien?" Christina felt a charge of energy pass through her.

"Yes, I know him. Like you, he arrived in Auburn in terrible shape. He was beaten by a couple of sore losers over a card game. I nursed him back to health."

"He was here?"

"Lying in the very bed you're in."

Christina didn't like Brigitte's possessive air when talking about Charley. Just how well did she know him?

"Where is he?" she asked.

"He wrote to you, but you never answered."

"I never got his letter."

"Well, he didn't know that. Thought maybe you'd given up on him. He's gone now."

"Where? Is he okay?"

"Don't know if he's okay." Brigitte turned away and began tidying up the kitchen. "He was when he left here."

"But where did he go? I must see him." Christina tried to get up, but became dizzy and fell back against the pillows.

"You had better rest."

A while later Christina overheard Brigitte and her father arguing outside the cabin. "You have to tell her everything, Brigitte. It's not fair to hold back information."

"Fair? But, father, what's fair to me?"

"It's not up to you to decide. Do you want to win by default? That would be a hollow victory, don't you think?"

She heard Brigitte cry and consoling sounds follow.

That evening at dinner, while Christina sat in her cot with a bowl of soup, Brigitte and Brian ate at the table without talking. They looked over at Christina from time to time.

"You doing okay over there, Christina?" Brian asked.

"Yes, thank you. The soup is very good, Brigitte."

"Heard about your troubles on that broken down horse," Brian said. "I checked when I was in town and was told the old mare is going to make it. Guess she's tougher than she looks." He cleared his throat and glanced Brigitte's way. "Don't worry. They'll find the owner eventually."

"The sheriff said I still would have to answer for my crime," Christina said.

"Well, I suppose that's true. A lot depends on what the horse's owner wants and what the sheriff decides. Let's wait and see." Brian got up from the table and pulled a chair next to Christina's cot. "Guess you have questions needing answers," he said. He looked over his shoulder at Brigitte. "Charley was okay the last time I saw him. Took him to Sacramento where he bid on a piece of property at auction. He got it too!" Brian shook his head and smiled. "He was so excited. I suspect he's been working hard trying to get it ready for planting."

"He finally got his farm?" Christina said. "I'm glad. He's wanted his own place for so long."

"Charley was real concerned, Christina, since he never got answers to his letters. But I don't think he's given up on you."

Brigitte stood up from the table and began clearing dishes, pumping water at the dry sink, and generally making enough noise to drown out what Christina was saying.

"I never meant to worry him. The man we were staying with was dishonest. Never picked up any mail addressed to me. I never saw Charley's letter until I was leaving Promontory City. Later, I was on a train and then at a horse ranch and then..." She ran out of breath and began coughing.

"That's okay. You don't need to go into all the details

if you don't want to. Save your breath and concentrate on getting stronger for when you see Charley."

Christina perked up. "When can I see him?"

"Well—we did get a letter not too long ago from Sacramento. Guess you could write him there in care of General Delivery. Who knows how long it'll take for him to get it, though. Suspect he only goes into town once a month or so."

Brigitte slammed down the cast iron skillet.

"But I know the way to his parcel. Maybe after things get settled here with the sheriff, we can take you there."

Brigitte turned sharply toward her father and shot him a look. "We?"

Brigitte's hostility was not lost on Christina. She realized that she had feelings for Charley and was, in all likelihood, a rival for his affection. Her best defense was to will herself back to health as soon as possible.

CHAPTER SIXTY-SIX

Christina

A week later Christina was strong enough to move about using a walking stick while her ankle continued to heal. She was still a little unsteady, but wanted to make herself useful. She offered to set the table and to wash dishes, but Brigitte declined her help. It turned out that Brigitte was a good nurse, but her cool attitude toward Christina felt uncomfortable. Though they were in close quarters, she spoke little. Clearly, Christina thought, the situation was awkward because they both had feelings for Charley. *Oh, well, it won't be long before I'm well enough to leave,* she thought. *That is if I'm free to leave.* Dr. Moses had visited and pronounced her on the way to recovery.

Sheriff Piper also arrived one day to explain that Cinnamon's owner had been located and would soon pick up his mare from Auburn.

"From the general location you described, it sounded like the rancher lived northeast of here. I sent word to Sheriff Nelson in Nevada County and sure enough, he got a report of a stolen horse."

"I'm glad. But, what's going to happen to me,

Sheriff?" she asked.

Sheriff Piper removed his hat and looked directly at Christina.

"I'll be honest with you Miss Batachi. In some states, they still hang horse thieves."

Christina felt a stab of fear and flinched as if she had been struck.

"Sheriff Nelson talked with the horse owner, who was mighty upset. Cinnamon was the first work horse he owned. At one time he was dependent on her for his livelihood." The sheriff shifted his stance and continued. "But now the horse is in retirement while his other horses do the hard work. He keeps her around for old time's sake."

"I knew he favored her," Christina said. "I heard him talk to Cinnamon in the barn. He took real good care of her too."

Sheriff Piper nodded. "He said he would have helped you if he had known your predicament. And when he heard of the rough trip to Auburn and that Cinnamon recovered, he was more inclined to ask mercy for you. Especially since it's nigh onto Christmas."

Christmas? I forgot all about Christmas. Christina nodded, feeling the threat of hot tears forming.

"Course that doesn't mean you're going to go without punishment. We just can't have people going around stealing horses!"

"I know," Christina said through quivering lips. She

grabbed the back of the chair for support. She hated to look weak. *Quit acting like a girl.* "I understand, Sheriff," she said.

"I'll talk to the judge. See how he wants to handle this." Sheriff Piper put his hat back on, adjusting it a quarter turn. "In the meantime, stay put." He shook hands with Brian and nodded to Brigitte.

Christina couldn't believe it. Cinnamon's owner sounded like a decent person after all. If only she had trusted him and spoken up in the barn, all this misery might have been avoided.

"I just know that the judge is going to send me to jail," Christina cried when Sheriff Piper left.

"You don't know that," Brian said, but he didn't sound very convincing. "Do you want me to take you to Charley before this goes before the judge?"

"But the sheriff said to 'stay put.'"

"I doubt the sheriff will pursue you out of his jurisdiction once you're gone."

"You would do that? I don't know, Brian. I don't want to get you in trouble."

"Well, you could go and see Charley and come back for your day in court."

"What if Charley doesn't even want to see me anymore?"

"Well, I guess you won't find that out until you see him."

Brigitte, who had been listening, chimed in. "He gave

up a lot to wait for you, Christina. If you didn't want to be a wife to him, you should have said so. There were others who would have gladly stood by his side."

The manner in which Brigitte spoke confirmed Christina's suspicion. She loved Charley too.

"But he remained loyal to you," Brigitte said. "He waited all this time to see you or at least hear from you."

"I didn't know what to say!" Christina whined. It was true, but it sounded like a flimsy excuse. "I'm surprised that Charley didn't snatch *you* up," she said. "You're the kind of woman he's always wanted—one who will tend to his needs, keep his house, bear him children."

"I would, too," Brigitte declared. She raised her chin and looked directly at Christina. "I gladly would have done all those things and more."

"Ladies, stop before you say something you'll regret," Brian interjected. The two women ignored him as if he weren't in the room.

"Well, I—uh—I always wanted more out of life," Christina said. "Never wanted to be kept in place drudging over household chores and having baby after baby. What's the adventure in that!" *This woman tried to take my Charley.*

"All those things are adventurous if you do them for the person you love." High color had crept into Brigitte's cheeks.

Christina didn't know whether to explain herself further or stop before she said too much as Brian had warned. She sighed.

"Well, maybe you'll get your chance at Charley yet, Brigitte. I may give up on him. Move on until I find a place where I'm free to become the horsewoman I know I'm meant to be."

"You can't!" Brigitte cried. "Not until you talk to Charley. See whether you two were destined to be together or not. Otherwise, he's always going to carry on about you and forget that I'm waiting for him."

"So I'm supposed to do this for *your* sake?"

"For Charley's. For both our sakes."

Christina regarded Brigitte, acknowledging the power of her love for Charley. Had her own love been as strong and as unselfish? The answer hit her like a lightning bolt. *No, I was more selfish.*

She had acted without thinking, set events in motion without first considering Charley's feelings. But in the next instant she thought, *I didn't follow him this far to leave things unfinished. Am I really that afraid of being tied down?* She was aching to make a decision—any decision—just not yet.

CHAPTER SIXTY-SEVEN

Jennie

When Jennie and Violet returned to Concordia, it was to a snow-covered landscape.

"It's good to be home, but I'm going to miss the milder temperatures of the South," Violet complained. She stepped from the train, shrugging tighter inside her heavy wool coat. Jennie followed Violet doggedly, too tired to comment. The sleepy town of Concordia on a winter day couldn't have been more of a contrast to the vibrant rush of activity in New Orleans.

Franklin was waiting with the carriage. After loading their mountain of luggage into the vehicle, he helped the ladies get settled with a lap robe to keep them warm during the ride. Light from the weak winter sun reflected off the white expanse of snow, blinding them. Violet's carriage made slow progress as it plowed through snowdrifts turning to slush.

When at last they arrived home, Jennie saw a curtain move in the parlor, followed by Lucy running down the steps to greet them. She wore only a blouse and jumper. No coat or warm wrap in which to take refuge.

"Jennie! Jennie!" she shouted, jumping up and down.

As soon as Jennie stepped out of the carriage, Lucy threw herself against her. "I missed you so much," she said.

"We missed you too." Jennie gathered her in a big bear hug.

As if Lucy suddenly remembered her manners, she turned to Violet and hugged her also.

"Yes, yes." Violet patted Lucy on the back. "Child, get inside this instant before you catch your death! Imagine running out here without a coat." She shook her head.

"She's just excited to see us, Violet." Jennie had hoped her mother would respond more warmly toward Lucy after all this time away.

That evening in front of the fire, Lucy asked a million questions, and Jennie tried to answer each one patiently. Violet had retired early, exhausted from the days-long train ride. But there was no talking Lucy into going to bed until she had answers to all her queries.

As Jennie and Lucy were slipping into their nightclothes, Lily warmed their bed sheets with a warming pan filled with hot coals. She moved closer to Jennie, lowering her voice.

"Just so you know, miss, that young man you were seeing—Mr. Stuyvesant."

"Peter? Yes, what about him?"

"It's been all over town."

"What has, Lily?"

"Gossip. A Pinkerton detective tracked him to Concordia. He was a *wanted* man." She stopped to appraise what effect this had on Jennie. "Something about a financial scandal he was involved in."

"Are you sure, Lily?" Jennie could hardly believe her ears. *Peter really was a crook—just as Charley said.*

"Yes, ma'am. The agent arrested him and took him back to New York to stand trial. And, there's a rumor that he's married too," she whispered. "Just up and left his wife and children."

"Wife? Children? How can that be?" Jennie could feel herself flushing. "Well, that's just terrible!" She regained her composure long enough to dismiss Lily. "Thank you for sharing the news with me first. It might be best if I inform Violet of this scandal instead of you. You know how she can be."

"You needn't worry about that, ma'am." Lily shook her head. "I don't want to be the one to tell her." Lily was still shaking her head when she left the bedroom.

How could I have been so blind? Jennie thought. She was embarrassed at how naive she had been, swayed by a good-looking man with a smooth line. If her judgment had been so flawed about Peter, she wondered if she could be wrong about Patrick's character too? How much did she really know about him?

"Nonsense!" she said aloud.

"What?" Lucy said, startled.

"Nothing. How about you scrambling into bed before the sheets turn cold again." She patted the bed.

Jennie rejected the idea of Patrick being in the same league as Peter. Patrick had been fun-loving, but forthright, a gentleman in all ways, and had chosen the profession of law as his vocation. She had faith in him, believing him to be honest.

Lucy finally climbed into the big feather bed, reclaiming her rightful spot. While she was in New Orleans, Jennie had been accustomed to sleeping alone. It was going to take a little getting used to having the wiggling child snuggling next to her again and throwing a leg over her in the middle of the night. Jennie no longer worried about the occasional snuffling noises coming from Lucy since her tonsils had been removed. She was relieved that the child's general health had greatly improved. She looked fit, a testament to the good care she received while they were gone.

Jennie was especially grateful that Maggie and Carl had provided for Lucy during Christmas. Next year, for sure, she and Lucy and Violet would be together for the holidays—unless Violet took it in her head to return to New Orleans. If they did, Jennie could spend more time with Patrick. I *musn't think of that.* She felt guilty for wanting to be back in the adventurous city with the man with whom she had fallen in love. Her first consideration should be for Lucy. She didn't want the child to ever feel abandoned again. But, if for some reason they did go to

New Orleans for Christmas, she would make sure that Lucy was included.

During the long train ride from New Orleans to Concordia, Jennie had plenty of time to think. On the one hand, she daydreamed of going to college in New Orleans and spending more time with Patrick. On the other hand, she wondered how this would affect Lucy. She worried that without her presence, Violet might discontinue being Lucy's foster parent.

And Charley. What about Charley? A letter from him was waiting for her when they arrived home. He mentioned that he had been in a town called Auburn, California, but recently had acquired some property outside of Sacramento, a place called Tyler Island on which he had settled. *Oh good, now I can add where Charley lives in the little black booklet Mum left us.* She refocused on the last two lines of the letter, slowing down to savor them.

"I know farm life is not for you, Jennie. But I wish you could see how lush things grow in California. Maybe someday you'll come and visit.

It sounded as if Charley had finally recognized that she did not have the same physical endurance for the hardships of farming life that he and Christina possessed. *Funny that he didn't mention Christina.* Wasn't she in California with him?

Jennie acknowledged that her decision to stay with Violet instead of returning to the Neamott farm and

Charley had been selfish. Her timidity and her need for safety at that young age had cost her. Her sheltered, pampered existence had led her away from a life with a full range of experiences. Oh, she was lucky to have had the best of everything, but it was a life devoid of passion and purpose until Lucy entered her world. She shivered when she remembered how tender her brother's feelings were and how she trampled them mercilessly. She would make it up to him someday.

Jennie was eager for Charley to see that his love for her was not ill spent. She was now fostering and maybe even mentoring a child just as he had done with the Neamott children. They had so much to talk about. So much to share. She would reply to Charley's letter first thing in the morning, suggesting that she and Lucy visit him by train in the summer. She wanted the child to discover trains other than those that transported orphans to an uncertain future. She wished to introduce her to trains designed for leisure and adventure.

Still feeling restless, Jennie slipped out of bed and put on her robe and slippers. She hugged herself against the cold as she looked out the window at the vast white landscape lit by a full moon. This must be her place for now. But she knew she had a different destiny—another place waiting for her where women pursued bigger goals and emerged as leaders in their own right. She was determined to be one of them when she completed the education she desired, just as she knew she would be by

Patrick's side. If he truly loved her, he would wait. He could ask no more and no less of her, just as she could accept no less of herself. And Lucy would always remain part of that life. Of that she was certain.

She turned to look at the sprawling form in the bed that was Lucy and smiled.

CHAPTER SIXTY-EIGHT

Charley

February 1901

Charley *did* learn to swim. His strokes were not as fluid, nor as graceful as Tao's, but they were serviceable; with head barely above water, his strong arms cut through the still frigid water, his kicking legs propelled him, churning up the slough. Tao had insisted on teaching him to swim before he had another accident. "Dog paddle!" Tao had yelled from shore. "You not swim, Charley. You paddle like dog."

Tao had arrived from Walnut Grove to help Charley plant the first crop of corn and then had returned again to family who needed his support. But, he promised to come back to Tyler Island as soon as it was time to sow bean seeds and to construct a support system of lath and string on which the vines could climb. Charley still considered it a miracle that a week of spring-like weather had come early. It was incentive enough for him to begin planting.

Charley felt good as he hitched up Mayzie. He had been looking forward to time off from the back-breaking work of plowing and planting. It had been almost two months since he had been in the port city of Sacramento and established a post office box there. He hoped to find letters waiting for him, especially from Christina and his sister, Jennie.

While he was in town Charley planned on treating himself to a shave and a hot bath at the hotel and replenish his stores of food, especially coffee. The day was warm and promising.

"Gonna get you a companion, soon, Mayzie," he said. "A horse to help you with the work. Not that you're not a passable ride, but pulling a wagon and carrying me has to be a bit much for a lady of your years." He had been without company for so long, that Charley had resorted to talking to his mule.

Tao had not been a big talker, but he was a good listener. And the memory of his normally reserved friend laughing at Charley's pitiful attempt at swimming was a powerful one. Regardless, when Tao wasn't available to listen to him, Charley got so lonesome he could talk to a fence post.

"Hie!" Charley urged Mayzie to go faster.

When it came to talking, Charley missed the chatter of children and a woman's enthusiasm for conversation the most. He had heard enough from both over the years beginning with the Neamott children to the Eiler brood and from two strong women. Neither Christina nor Brigitte were afraid to express their opinions. Although their words were mainly soothing, sometimes they were irritating. Always a challenge, the women he knew and had loved had filled him with a sense of purpose.

Once reaching town, Charley saw to his business and then went to the post office. There was a note from Brian inquiring about the progress of his farm and a line at the bottom from Brigitte in which she asked after his health. "Hope to hear from you soon," she wrote. He smiled and remembered their kiss. There also was a letter from Jennie, which he would save to read at supper. But there was nothing from Christina. Guess that's it, he thought. It's been seven months with no word. *She's given up on me. Maybe I should do the same.*

When he finally opened the letter from his sister, Charley immediately felt nostalgic. Jennie's penmanship was still in the same loopy style as when she was a girl practicing her letters.

Dear Charley,

I hope this letter finds you safe and healthy. I'm happy that you have found what you have been searching for—a place of your own. I have finally discovered what is important in life—which you have known all along: treasuring people over things. I regret our being separated all these years. Can you ever forgive me?

Much has happened since you left Concordia. I have fallen in love with a good man from New Or-

leans and with Lucy, a young girl off of the orphan train. I protect her the way you protected me all those years. The idea of you and I being so far apart is painful. I would like to bring Lucy with me to visit you and Christina this summer. Maybe we can be a family again, if you'll still welcome me.

Love,
Jennie

Charley felt his face crumple with emotion. At long last he would be reunited with his sister. His prayers had been answered. His family would be whole again. The only sad note was the reference to Christina. It appeared there would be no Christina by his side when he saw his sister. He wrote back to Jennie that very night and mailed it before he left town the next morning.

On his return from Sacramento, thunderheads appeared in the west and a good wind was working itself up. A rainstorm on Tyler Island was the last thing Charley's new plants needed. He urged Mayzie to go faster, although he didn't know what good that would do. He had done all he could to protect the young seedlings. *Maybe I should have listened to Tao. He warned me about planting too early.* When he and Tao had finished the levee, they were banking on its strength to hold back waves. But, it hadn't been put to the test yet.

That afternoon and night Charley paced the shoreline a dozen times checking for possible weak spots before retiring to his shanty to look on helplessly. He had covered a few rows of the tender plants, but the heavy rains pelted hard and, in the end, they were inundated. The levee was breached in one area, but most of it held. Where it had weakened, strong winds forced waves ashore, creating a swamp.

It would take time to drain the water from the low spots and reinforce the levee. That is, if more rain held off. The fragile corn stalks were ruined. Even the plants that hadn't been uprooted in water would likely be blighted with mildew. *Useless! I'll have to start over and replant. Lucky I didn't plant the beans yet.* Luck? What was he thinking? Lady luck had *not* been kind to him. Neither in the saloon, where his winnings earned him a beating, or in the fields where weather had become an unrelenting adversary.

In anger, Charley railed against the elements. He raised his fist toward the heavens and cursed. *What made me think I could succeed as a farmer?* His cheating partner, Peter Stuyvesant, had said as much.

"Don't know why you want to work the land, Charley. You want to be like all these other failed sod busters we see?"

"You don't understand, Peter. When you own something, it's yours forever," he had answered. "It's like a family member, really. When your land is productive, you're relieved and proud. And when it fails, you need to support it until it improves."

"You're quite the philosopher, Charley." Peter mocked him with his sardonic smile. "Do you really believe all that hokum?"

"Yes, I do. Most men around here are proud of their dirt farms."

"But that's the point, don't you see? All that their dirt farms grow is more dirt."

Tears of anger streamed down Charley's face as he thought about Peter's words.

The next morning the sun was out. Blue skies prevailed. It was as if there had never been a storm. Birds and small animals sprang up from nowhere, inspecting what was left of his crop.

"Go ahead!" he yelled. "At least you critters will get use out of it."

Exhausted, Charley stood over the damaged section of the levee and thought about how to best reinforce it. He and Tao could use a more sandy soil—or sand itself—if it could be found. There was no extra money for buying sand, but Tao was resourceful. He might know if and where they could barter for it. Charley was tired of thinking of "what if's" and even more tired of digging drainage ditches, but there was nothing to do but get to it. He lifted his shovel and plunged it into the saturated soil. He threw the heavy water-sodden dirt over his shoulder and thrust the spade in for another shovel full and then another—his arms and shoulders ached with the burden of it. But he kept at it for hours, taking only small breaks for water.

It was late afternoon and the sun was dropping lower on the horizon. A wagon carrying two people approached from the trail; they were too far away to make out their features. He rarely received visitors and so was curious. Charley stopped what he was doing, took off his hat, and leaned on his shovel.

"Hello there," he called out.

CHAPTER SIXTY-NINE

Christina

After the brouhaha between the two, Christina tried to make up for the trouble she had caused Brigitte.

"You've done enough for me and I'm grateful, but I think things would be better if I left here, Brigitte. I'll try to find work and a place to stay in town."

"Oh no, you don't," Brigitte replied. "I'll not have Doc thinking I neglected my duty by kicking out one of his patients before she's well."

"I'm getting on better. The least I can do is help out at the stable after they boarded and cared for Cinnamon. I can probably grab a cot there."

"How can you even consider that?"

"Well, I slept many a night in less than ideal lodgings," she said, thinking of the various barns she'd slept in starting with the one in Carl Schmitz's stable. And it was nearing spring, so some nights were not so cold.

Brigitte remained quiet a moment as if she were mulling over the idea.

"No!" She shook her head. "I can't have you sleeping there. If you think you're up to doing some light work in the stable and it makes you feel better, okay. But you must return and sleep here at night. I insist."

The stable owner was happy to accept free labor to work off Cinnamon's board. Of course, the draft horse was long gone, having returned to the mountain ranch from which she was taken. Christina showered her affection on the remaining occupants, feeding and watering them and with every brush stroke across their hides, feeling her guilt lift a little.

It wasn't long after Christina began helping out at the stable that men passed by just to gawk at her. She overheard them say things among themselves like, "The horse thief must be checking out her next victim," or "Isn't she like a fox in a henhouse?" Christina tried to ignore their coarse remarks as best she could. After all, Sheriff Piper told her recently that it looked as if the judge would not likely hand down a stiff jail sentence since the horse was restored to health and had been recovered by the owner. He added, "Maybe the judge will credit you with the work you're doing here. I know I wouldn't mind you grooming my horse." She knew she wasn't completely out of the woods. She still had to wait until her case was formally heard in court before knowing her fate. Until then, her plans to go to Charley were stymied.

Brian heard about the remarks and more. One evening over supper he told Christina and Brigitte that there was talk of lynching. "At first I didn't pay much attention," he said, "because it was common barroom talk and everyone knew that there wasn't a-one of the men aiming for the spittoon who had the gumption to tie a decent knot in a rope."

"I don't think you need to worry, Christina, but maybe you ought to skip going to town for a few days."

"But my job. They expect me at the stable now."

"Well, I'd give that some thought."

She didn't get much time to ponder the problem because one of the men from the diggings arrived, looking harried. He asked to talk to Brian privately. Brian stepped outside where he and the man huddled on the front steps. Their conversation sounded urgent and only lasted a few minutes before Brian burst through the door with disturbing news.

"Christina, I think I'd better get you to Sacramento after all, no matter what the consequences." They hadn't talked about her going to Sacramento to meet Charley since right before Christmas. "My man was in town and heard a bunch of thugs spout off about how horse thieves should be hanged. I'd think it was just more of the same kind of talk, except one of the men was the lowlife who attacked and beat Charley." Brian reached for a rifle hanging on the wall. "You never know what angry, drunken men will do. They had all come from the saloon and were yelling things like, 'If the judge don't order it, there's always lynching.'"

"But the sheriff wouldn't let that happen, would he?"

"Let's not wait to find out. Do you want me to take you to Sacramento or not?"

Brigitte stood by quietly, looking stunned as Christina gathered up her few belongings.

"Better hurry, Christina." Brian grabbed her parcel and his rifle and headed for the door.

Christina turned to Brigitte. "I'm sorry for saying things before..." She was at a loss for words. "Thank you for everything."

"No need to thank me." Brigitte stood straight and stiff, but her face had softened. "Better get going," she said. "And say hello to Charley for me."

Christina climbed aboard the wagon where Brian already held Beulah's reins in hand. They took a back road out of Auburn to avoid drawing attention. She trembled at the thought of her dangerous escape from frontier justice and the unknown awaiting her in Sacramento.

Although it was a pleasant enough evening when she and Brian started out, as the hours passed, it grew cold like thick molasses on a frigid morning. They had to travel slowly with only the light of a quarter moon to guide them.

"I think we'd better stop, Christina," Brian said a few minutes later. "I can't see a damn thing. You bundle up in the back of the wagon and I'll stretch out on the buckboard. At dawn we'll start out again."

"Whatever you say, Brian." She just wanted this night to end. She curled up on some old blankets in the back. Before sleep overtook her, unsettling thoughts edged their way into her consciousness. By fleeing the law, she was bringing trouble with her. If not now, later. Was it fair to expose Charley to her problems?

She wondered how her life had gotten off course? Christina had been defiant for so long that she didn't recognize a good thing when she saw it. She didn't know how to bend, to yield; she was always afraid that if she let her guard down that she would be overpowered and lose herself. She hadn't wanted to become just another docile, unnoticed woman in the rural landscape.

Christina wondered if she had made one mistake too many? When she lost their child, whom she hadn't even acknowledged carrying, Christina wasn't surprised that it hit Charley so hard. After all, he had always been almost slavish in his devotion to family.

Brigitte had been brutally honest with Christina. Should she fight for Charley or let him go? For all she knew, he had given up on her and was only waiting for final confirmation of her unworthiness before turning to Brigitte.

She was so tired of trying to do the right thing, only to make things worse. Her ankle ached in the cold. Her heart ached even more.

CHAPTER SEVENTY

Christina

The well-muscled man who greeted them had been examining a withered plant. When he looked up the figure was a facsimile of Charley. This man looked sunburned and older.

"Hello, Charley," Brian said.

"Brian!" the man shouted. He shaded his eyes with his hand and squinted. "Is that you?"

"It's me, all right." Brian hopped down from the wagon and offered his hand.

"What a welcome surprise!" He looked past Brian. "Is that you, Brigitte?"

"No, Charley." Brian spoke before Christina could respond. "Brigitte didn't come with me."

Charley took a step closer to the wagon and stopped. "Then, who is…"

Christina gazed down at him, trying to find her voice. Now that she saw Charley in the flesh, her knotted heart loosened, any reluctance she had felt before, dissolved.

"It's me, Charley," Christina said, her voice faltering.

"Christina!" Charley closed the gap and reached up

for her hand. "I had given up hope."

Christina accepted his rough, calloused hand covering hers a moment before allowing herself to be lifted from the wagon. She threw her arms around Charley, burying her face in his neck, and inhaled his male scent as if it were as essential for life as oxygen. She could not find the words to speak. The only sound coming from Charley was a rumble vibrating through his chest that could have been a laugh—or a cry.

Brian coughed and looked away.

"Well, I guess my work is done here," he said.

"Oh, Brian, Excuse my manners." Charley set Christina down. "It's just that Christina and I have some catching up to do."

"I can see that." He smiled and reached inside the wagon to fetch Christina's belongings. She reached up to accept the tied bundle and hobbled a step toward more level ground.

"Why are you limping?" Charley asked.

"I'm not, usually. It's a long story, Charley."

"Well, maybe you had better start, then." A furrowed line on his forehead deepened.

"There's so much to tell," she began. "First, Mr. Eiler never brought me your letter. I didn't see it until I left. I ran because he wanted to marry me, but I hopped a train leaving Promontory to get away and then I ran into Clay. You remember Clay?" She rushed on without waiting for an answer. "We rode boxcars for a while and took work on a ranch helping to capture wild mustangs. Just like the ones we saw from the train. Remember? But then they shot the weak ones to lie there and rot. That did it for me." She shook her head. "I hopped back on a boxcar and traveled alone, but then got sick. *Real sick*, Charley and missed getting back on the train where all my stuff was stowed."

Charley placed a finger on her lips. "Shh. Slow down, Christina."

"You don't understand," she gulped. "I finally holed up in some farmer's barn and had to take his horse so I could get to Auburn where your letter said you'd be and—"

"You stole a horse. *You?*"

"I'll fill you in, Charley," Brian said.

"I didn't want to," Christina said, growing ever more breathless while trying to finish her tale. "You see, I broke my ankle, got lost, and..." To her dismay, Christina burst into tears.

Charley reached to pull her into his arms, but she put a hand out to stop him.

"I'm okay. I need to finish telling you what happened next. Her speech grew thicker as she said, barely above a whisper, "Brian and Brigitte took me in. Got me back to health. But the sheriff was going to put me in jail and these men in town were going to...to...string me up."

Brian cut in. "We thought it best for Christina to leave Auburn."

"Oh, Christina." Charley hugged her to him in spite of her reluctance. "You can tell me all about it later."

"But Charley, you must have so many questions."

"I do, but we'll have plenty of time together to sort things out."

Christina felt weak after purging her tale in its entirety. Even she was amazed at the sad string of events she just recited. The difficulty of the long ride from Auburn to Sacramento only added to her fatigue. Yesterday at dawn, she and Brian saw the clouds in the west moving east. They were forced to take shelter from the storm until it passed, using up valuable time. It took another night of sleeping in the wagon and all of today to reach Charley's farm.

After the excitement of seeing him again, and his willingness to forgive her, she ached to sleep. And would as soon as Charley finished helping Brian set up camp for the night. In the meantime, she checked out Mayzie, calculating the mule's age by the gray hair peppering the darker ones around her muzzle and by curling back her lips to check her teeth.

"Guess you're a senior by now." She stroked Mayzie behind the ears and patted her side.

"You missing a horse, Christina?" Charley asked as he led her to his shanty. "Guess Mayzie is a poor substitute."

"Shh, she might hear you." Christina smiled, but then her mood darkened. "I don't know that I'm worthy of having another horse, Charley."

"Of course you are."

"But I actually *stole* a horse."

"Don't worry, you're with me now. I won't let anything happen to you."

"I'm awfully tired, Charley. Do you think I could get some rest before we talk more?"

"Of course."

They entered the shanty, which she thought looked as neat as possible considering that it was surrounded by dirt. At least it was warm and dry.

"Gee, Charley, You didn't have to make it so fancy," she remarked, feeling and sounding more like her old self.

"They don't call these huts 'shanties' for nothing," he said in his defense. "We'll have better. You just wait and see."

"It looks beautiful to me." She reached up and kissed him. Charley embraced her, but she pulled away. "Just let me sleep a bit, Charley, and then you'll get all the loving you want."

Christina headed for Charley's sleeping cot and lay down. She felt her shoes being removed and a blanket placed over her and then—nothing. She was so tired she didn't even dream.

When she awoke, Charley was sleeping facing her with one arm casually thrown over a hip. Christina studied him. He was the same person, but calmer, steadier.

Even in sleep, his face told her a lot. Added to the worry lines were creases he probably earned by working in the sun all day. His face had settled into the man he would become.

She wasn't so certain that he could be changed or influenced by her as he once was. She didn't even know if she wanted to change him. *Well—maybe just a little bit.*

Being close to Charley in this wild, godforsaken place suddenly felt right. A fool could see that they had each survived without the other and grew stronger in their own way. She thought of how strong they would be if they stayed together. Their lives might be comfortably ordinary, but as Brigitte pointed out, ordinary things could be fulfilling if you were with the one you loved.

Christina vowed that for Charley's sake, as well as her own, she would make the ordinary, extraordinary.

CHAPTER SEVENTY-ONE

Months later, mild weather turned to brow-wiping heat. Wildlife of the Delta chirped, croaked, and tweeted, and the water teemed with activity. When the beans and corn showed evidence of growing well, Charley finally took a deep breath of relief. He possessed the farmer's cautious temperament regarding the subject of luck. He didn't want to jinx any luck coming his way by taking it for granted.

He guessed that he felt the same way about Christina. She was with him, but who knew for how long? The good news was that the Placer County judge rendered his decision on the horse-theft charges. He had imposed a sentence of one year, but then reduced it because of her volunteer work at the stable. Apparently Cinnamon's owner wrote a letter of support and Sheriff Piper spoke on her behalf. She was reprimanded sternly by the judge who then set her free.

Brian had sent a detailed letter in which he also described how the drunken mob that had set their sights on lynching Christina had been dispersed. A number of the men were in jail for a variety of charges that had them focusing on their own problems and not on Christina.

Charley caught himself studying her face when she wasn't looking, mainly in the early hours of morning before she awakened. She had changed. Her dark hair had grown in thick and long again. But it remained wild and unruly like her spirit. If her face was lined around the eyes and a bit ruddier from the elements, she was still beautiful to him. Charley predicted that Christina would grow into a handsome woman as she grew older, all sharp angles and muscle, instead of turning to fat.

Maybe it was time to put the question of marriage to her once again. And this time he expected an answer that included setting a date.

It was getting on toward evening. Christina was feeding Mayzie before cooking their dinner when Charley decided to put his plan into motion. He approached the two and patted Mayzie on the flank.

"You're still good with animals, Christina. Mayzie responds to you and seems to be more energetic since you arrived."

"Well, all animals respond to kindness. She knows we appreciate her and she just wants to please us."

"I know this isn't what you expected." Charley cleared his throat before continuing. "I guess you still want a horse and a chance at a life that doesn't deliver such harsh conditions. I wouldn't blame you a bit if you wanted to hop on another train in search of a good horse and the adventure you crave." His eyes shifted elsewhere while waiting for a response.

"I've had enough of trains for a lifetime, Charley." Christina reached up and touched his face. "Someone once told me that a man without plans might as well be riding on a train to nowhere. Well, I'm *somewhere* and I intend to stay."

"Well, then," Charley said, his chest puffing out. He picked up Christina's hand and kissed the tips of her fingers. "I have an important question to ask you."

Acknowledgements

My heartfelt thanks to critique group members, Barbara Toboni, Amber Starfire, Sarita Lopez, and the late Patsy Ann Taylor for their thoughtful and knowledgeable suggestions for improving my continuing story of orphan train survivors. I treasured their loyal support through the novel's various drafts. I also owe a debt of gratitude to Wendee Walker who educated me on the behaviors of horses and pointed out more colorful phrases with which to describe their activities when she said, "horses do more than trot."

I'm indebted to Esther Koopman of the Sacramento River Delta Historical Society for her assistance in researching the topography of the Sacramento Delta in which much of the novel occurs during the turn of the twentieth century, and to Bryanna M. Ryan, Curator of Archives for the Placer County Archives & Research Center for Placer County Museums. Her answers to questions relating to the gold mining practices and the justice system in 1900 Placer County were especially helpful.

Thank you to the following for their professional services: Arlene Miller, The Grammar Diva and author of *The Best Little Grammar Collection Ever!* for copy editing and Amber Starfire, author of *Accidental Jesus Freak: One Woman's Journey from Fundamentalism to Freedom* for book formatting and cover design.

I would be remiss in not acknowledging the influence trains had on me as a child. My memory is dotted with stories my father told me about riding the rails as a young man. It is also filled with my mother's voice for she also desired adventure, but instead kept the home fires burning.

And finally, a special thanks goes to my husband, Michael, who had confidence in my ability to continue the story begun in *Trains to Concordia* by encouraging me to write this sequel.

About the Author

Marilyn Campbell revisits the subject of the orphan train and its survivors in her sequel, *A Train to Nowhere*. A keen observer of the human condition, she applies the knowledge she gained working as a social worker for a public agency to the development of her characters as they enter adulthood. Marilyn published *A Train to Concordia* in 2015 and continues to compose short stories and poetry for anthologies and small journals. She lives in Northern California with husband, Michael.

Study Questions

1. What impression did you have of Charley and Christina as rail riders in the first chapters? Do you think they took reasonable precautions for their safety?

2. When Charley and Christina stay with the Eiler family in Promentory, Utah, what did you think of their different reactions to their delayed plans?

3. Christina's miscarriage is a major setback to Christina and Charley's relationship. How did you assess her honesty at this point in the story?

4. Do you empathize with Christina's desire to have another horse like Gabriel, even if it means hardships and delays to her and Charley's plans? Have you ever wanted something so much that it affected your relationships?

5. The subject of birth control is discussed between Christina and Ruth. The followers of The Descendants, a Mormon offshoot, have very strict rules about procreation. How does this compare with current views of birth control? What would you have done if you had been Christina?

6. Jennie is faced with some simple truths about her

past as an orphan and her choices to move out of poverty. Why do you think she responded so strongly to Lucy at the train station?

7. What effect did Lucy's surgery have on her and how did it change the relationship she had with Jennie and Violet?

8. What did you think when Jennie left with Patrick at the ball in New Orleans? And later, how did he influence her to explore new options for furthering her education? Has there ever been a person in your life who influenced you?

9. When Christina and Charley disagreed about continuing on to California and it caused them to part ways, what did you think would happen to their relationship?

10. Christina's predicament with Mr. Eiler who wants to make her one of his wives is uncertain. What choices did she have other than staying on the Utah ranch or traveling on her own to find Charley?

11. Describe your feelings about the wild mustang roundup in Nevada?

12. Do you agree with Christina's choice to move on and give up on getting a horse of her own?

13. When Christina becomes ill and is left behind by the train, what were her options?

14. What were your feelings about Christina stealing a horse? Is it ever okay to break the law?

15. Charley forges a relationship with Tao Chin, a Chinese laborer in the Sacramento Delta. How did their friendship change Charley's perception about foreigners and fairness?

16. Brigitte Doyle was a significant figure in both Charley and Christina's lives. In what ways did she influence each of them? Who has had influence over you?

17. Charley worked hard to farm in a rugged, unpredictable environment. Have you ever been faced with natural disasters or dealt with harsh physical elements in order to survive?

18. How had Christina and Charley changed by the end of the book?